The Distant Cousin

Another James Goodfellow Investigation

Clive F Sorrell

authorHOUSE

AuthorHouse™ UK
1663 Liberty Drive
Bloomington, IN 47403 USA
www.authorhouse.co.uk
Phone: 0800.197.4150

© *2017 Clive F Sorrell. All rights reserved.*

No part of this book may be reproduced, stored in a retrieval system, or transmitted by any means without the written permission of the author.

Clive Frederick Sorrell has asserted his right under the Copyright, Design and Patents Act, 1988 to be identified as the author of this work.

This novel is a work of fiction. Names and characters are the product of the author's imagination and any resemblance to actual persons, living or dead, is entirely coincidental.

Published by AuthorHouse 04/12/2017

ISBN: 978-1-5246-7996-5 (sc)
ISBN: 978-1-5246-7998-9 (hc)
ISBN: 978-1-5246-7997-2 (e)

Print information available on the last page.

Any people depicted in stock imagery provided by Thinkstock are models, and such images are being used for illustrative purposes only. Certain stock imagery © Thinkstock.

This book is printed on acid-free paper.

Because of the dynamic nature of the Internet, any web addresses or links contained in this book may have changed since publication and may no longer be valid. The views expressed in this work are solely those of the author and do not necessarily reflect the views of the publisher, and the publisher hereby disclaims any responsibility for them.

In
Memory
of
Sophia

BOOKS BY THIS AUTHOR – PUBLISHED BY AUTHORHOUSE

Stories For Dark And Stormy Nights
Siddiqui
Kawthar
Jumana
Duress - the Life and Death of a Ton-Up
Ingrid's Children
The Distant Cousin

PROLOGUE

SHANGCAI - 1026BC

SHU DU THREW HIMSELF over the wall and quickly rolled down the grassy slope to stay ahead of his brothers who were right behind him. Guan and Huo jumped over the wall together and were soon lying beside him, the warm breath of the three brothers staining the night air with wisps of white. Beyond the wall they could hear the rhythmic pounding of leather soles as scores of soldiers ran past their hiding place.

'Ours or theirs?' Huo whispered as he half drew his sword.

'It doesn't matter which,' Shu Du replied. 'Both sides want to separate our heads from our bodies.'

Guan just grunted.

Ten years earlier King Wu had given regency of the Cai region to Shu Du who relied on the loyalty of Huo and Guan to administer the State of Henan that was within his control. The manner in which the three brothers respected and protected people earned them a reputation for being just and fair to all, whether nobleman or peasant, and they rightfully earned the title of The Three Guards.

On King Wu's death one of Shu Du's eight other brothers, Dan, the Duke of Zhou, snatched his chance and took over the supervision of the government for the new and very young King Cheng. Within a matter of weeks he had decided that the Shang forces to the east might rise up against the weak rule of the young king and he wrested complete control of the State of Cai from Shu Du. Any questions by any of the minor administrators about the duke's action were harshly answered by the executioner's sword.

Subjugating Shu Du caused great loss of face for King Cheng's uncle and Shu Du called upon the loyalty of Guan and Huo to protest strongly and, if they were ignored, to join him in rebelling against the new regime. With the sworn allegiance of his brothers' two thousand vassals who held feudal tenure of land and his own six thousand men-at-arms a vicious war began to lay the land to waste.

After three years of constant campaigning, in the final battle for a town called Chonglixiang, the duke's latest war machine proved to be too much for Cai's opposing force. Hundreds of Zhou chariots had been brought to the battlefield in great secrecy and these took advantage of the level terrain to slice through the assembled ranks like a butter knife. Each chariot carried a nobleman who was a skilled archer and a swordsman and while he wreaked havoc another handled the powerful, leather-caparisoned horses. The rainstorm of arrows and flailing bronze jian *(double-edged sword)* decimated Shu Du's forces in the central troop formation.

Huo encouraged his captains to charge in on the right while Guan tried to rally his soldiers on the left flank but the chariots countered by splitting into two forces and attacking both brothers head-on.

The orderly battlefield disintegrated into a turbulent sea of hand-to-hand fighting that was clearly going against The Three Guards and soon the first groups of Cai soldiers changed their allegiance and began cutting down and slaughtering their comrades and those loyal to the brothers.

Shu Du hacked his way through the mass of screaming men to a rise where Guan, a razor-sharp bronze jian in each hand was whirling the blades non-stop, causing a bloody river to flow where once lush grass swayed passively in past summer breezes.

'We are done, Guan,' he shouted as he fended off a spear by removing the attacking arm with one sweep of his heavy sword. 'We must make for Shangcai and see to the protection of our families before the Duke decides to take them as hostages.'

Guan nodded without looking at his brother. 'Where is Huo?'

'Here,' a strong voice cried and the two brothers glanced into the mêlée of hacking and stabbing on their left: their brother, his rhino-skin body armour covered in enemy blood, pushed and stabbed his way through the crowd of battle-crazed warriors.

'Then let's go before our men turn on us,' Shu Du shouted and the three brothers fought their way shoulder to shoulder to where a large stand of bamboo offered some form of cover. They slipped between the mighty grass stalks killing all who hindered their progress, whether Cai or Zhou soldier, until the high, dense canopy darkened the interior as though night had fallen.

It took the brothers three days to travel the 70 li to the main city of Shangcai, constantly checking and hiding from any eyes that might betray them. They killed those who saw them for fear that the Duke of Zhou would learn of their whereabouts and race ahead to wreak revenge on their children and womenfolk even though it was customary to let one male heir survive to carry on the family name.

The sun had long set and the moon was bright when the brothers separated on the outskirts of the sleeping city and went to their respective palaces. Shu Du slipped silently through the main gate that was standing wide open and paused to study the large earthen courtyard for any signs of an ambush. Nothing stirred and he trotted to the elaborately carved door and entered his audience chamber. It was obvious that it had been ransacked for everything of value had been taken or violently stripped from the walls and tables.

Moving from one vandalized room to another he found the palace bereft of people until he heard a whimpering sound from within one of the many storerooms. He silently slipped the jian from its sheath and slowly pushed against the heavy door. Oil lamps lit the interior and he immediately saw that the storeroom had been stripped of all food and household goods. Cowering in one corner were three servants grouped around a shrouded figure lying on the earthen floor.

There was a gasp when the trio became aware of his presence and they instinctively pulled away until they recognized the intruder and all grief was briefly forgotten.

'My Lord,' the oldest man cried out. 'You live!'

'That I do but who is that you mourn?'

The younger servants moved to one side with heads bowed and held up oil lamps so that Shu Du could see clearer. As the old servant drew the white cloth away Shu Du gasped for he saw that it was not one but two figures, Yi and Fa, two of his eldest brothers. The cloth continued to be pulled down and the ghastly marks around the necks made it obvious that they had been hung.

'The duke's men came yesterday and brutally took all the ladies, servants and children. Lords Yi and Fa tried to stop them. They were immediately hung from the arch of the gate as a warning to us and anyone else who dared to challenge their right to appropriate your palace and everyone in it.'

Shu Du felt a surge of rage in his breast and he was on the point of killing the three servants with his bared blade for not defending the women and children and their lords when the door flew open and Guan rushed in.

'They've killed my wife, my children – my whole family.' His sobbing caught in his throat when he glimpsed the corpses of Shu Du's kin. 'They've been here, too,' he whispered unnecessarily.

Huo quietly entered behind Guan. 'My whole family was reduced to commoner status two years ago whilst we were campaigning in the south and the few remaining servants told me that they all fled east for fear of reprisals by the peasants.'

Shu Du knew how the peasants hated the noble classes. They called all aristocrats 'rats' for the way they lived in luxury and took food from the families who toiled on the land.

'You may also have been made a commoner and I would suggest that you leave the region and follow your family before you fall into the hands of the duke's men,' Guan murmured as he wiped the back of his hand across his eyes to clear the moisture gathering there.

'I must stay and try to find out what has happened to my family,' Shu Du said sheathing his blade. His eyes blazed with hatred for the men who had desecrated his home. 'Huo, with your agreement, there is something I would like you to do for me.' The older man turned to face him. 'It concerns many important items that I put aside for our ancestors and those who have served us well. I know the raiding troops couldn't have found them as they were hidden in a large bronze vessel. The ritual *ding* (cauldron) has many sacrificial *bi* (jade discs) to carry our messages to the heavenly court of *T'ien*. As you know, these attest to the good character of our ancestors and many of our deceased subjects and are their only chance of attaining a higher place in heaven.'

Shu Du placed a hand on his brother's shoulder. 'I charge you to keep them safe until such time as I can follow you with my family. Then we can place them in the family tombs together. They must never fall into the hands of an enemy who would undoubtedly revel in the eternal purgatory our ancestors would suffer.'

Huo knew what a great weight of responsibility had been placed on his shoulders yet he still nodded his agreement and followed Shu Du from the storeroom and down a long corridor until they entered a much smaller chamber that appeared to be that of a senior servant.

'This was my astrologer's office. I knew it would be the last place the duke's men would have bothered to look. Even my diviners were unaware that I had hidden something here for I had sent them to an eastern province to heat the shells of tortoises for any ancestral messages; one of my administrators was seeking some guidance.

The outbreak of war and knowing who I was opposing has obviously prevented that cowardly lot from returning to my service,' Shu Du added between thin lips. He started scraping the floor in the corner of the room with the tip of his sword.

It was not a regular soldier's bronze weapon but a work of art that had been made by repeatedly folding and beating different hot metals until a blade had been created that was capable of holding a sharpness never known before. In battle it was incredibly strong, capable of slicing through thin leather armour and Shu Du had named the new metal blade Dragon's Breath.

Huo crouched and watched his brother work until a small wooden panel was uncovered. He rose to his feet expectantly as Shu Du lifted the crudely made cover to reveal a deep hole in which was concealed a bronze bowl that was the length of a man's forearm in diameter and the same in height. Using all his strength Shu Du heaved it out and stood it on the floor before shuffling back on his knees and standing up to join his brother who was staring reverently at the large ancestral vessel.

Huo took a step closer to marvel at the sculpted designs on the casting that stood on three ornate legs. A line of unrecognizable characters ran around the top of the vessel. A piece of fine leather covered the top and when Shu Du flipped it back Huo cried out in amazement for it was filled to the brim with scores of bi. The small jade *Ears of Heaven* filled the vessel to the brim. Huo had never seen so many pure white discs of ancestral communication in one place before.

'It seems too heavy for one man to carry any distance,' Huo managed to stutter as he gazed at the bowl in wonder.

'Those servants are now yours,' Shu Du said as he turned to point at the men who had followed them into the astrologer's room. He then addressed them, looking at each man in turn. 'You are released from all fealty to me and you will now swear to serve Lord Huo. You will go wherever he goes and you will guard this vessel with your lives. Now fetch wood and make a crude box that disguises the heavenly messenger.' The servants looked puzzled at first but then nodded, bowed deeply to Huo and hurried from the room to do his bidding.

The moon had moved into the next quarter of the sky when the three deposed lords finished sealing the seven orifices of each executed brother with jade plugs and buried them behind the palace. They set out, followed by the servants who had fashioned a cradle for the ding that now hung from a stout bamboo pole, and headed north. They had only travelled a short distance when they heard the approaching sound of many feet.

The moon briefly slipped behind a cloud and Shu Du could see nothing; being cautious he signalled to the servants and pointed to a narrow alley between two peasant workshops. The three men struggled beneath the weight of the heavy wooden box hanging from the bamboo pole as they disappeared into the shadows. Shu Du listened until he was sure the soldiers were marching directly towards them before striding across the road to the roughly hewn stonewall lining the road. He leapt over the parapet and disappeared, swiftly followed by his brothers.

The column of soldiers dressed in *wei gia*, sleeveless coats made from boiled rhinoceros hide overlaid with turtle-shell breast plates, were marching at the double with spears held upright. Flaming torchlight glittered on the many elaborately decorated helmets and spearheads as they passed where the lords were hiding.

When the last of the soldiers faded into the night and the dust had settled Shu Du climbed back up the slope wall and cautiously raised his head above the wall to check the road. The cloud had begun to drift on and once more the pale beaten earth of the road was visible. He looked both ways before beckoning to his brothers as he scrambled over the meticulously arranged blocks of stone.

'Where next?' Guan asked when he joined Shu Du in the middle of the road. 'We certainly cannot follow this road.'

'We head for Zhoucou and then cross the Jialu River where we'll be able to arrange a meeting with our cousins. With their help we should be able to raise an army of at least five thousand archers and a good number of swordsmen which will be more than sufficient to take the war back to the Duke of Zhou and gain his head.'

'That means travelling deep into the duke's home territory. Every person we meet whether man, woman or child will be our mortal enemy,' Huo protested.

'Precisely, he will not be expecting us to escape by crossing his own lands which is why I believe he chose to take my family that way.' Shu Du's bared teeth gleamed white in the dark.

'If I was the duke I'd be sending scouts to seek us in the west and the south,' Guan added with a confident smile.

'Exactly,' Shu Du grinned. 'So let's add the sound of our feet to those who have just passed.'

'Forgive me but in order to take proper care of the vessel I must travel east,' Huo said as they arrived at the village crossroads. 'My wife and her brother's family live by the Hung-Tse Lake which is sufficiently far from Zhoucou and the duke's men to provide a safe sanctuary. I am sure I will find her there. When you are done with the Duke of Zhou you can send me a message, possibly with his head, and I will return with the ding.'

Shu Du nodded his agreement and the brothers embraced and parted. Huo led the way eastward and the servants followed, the long pole digging into the brawny shoulders of the two younger men as the old man shuffled alongside, occasionally steadying the swaying box with his hand.

Shu Du and Guan broke into a military trot and went north, swiftly covering the ground until they suddenly spotted the column's rearguard ahead of them. Guan thought he saw one of the men look over his shoulder as though hearing their approach but the man made no sign that he had seen them. Guan glanced at Shu Du who pointed to the bamboo forest on their left.

'We can pass them without being seen if we go that way,' he said softly.

Guan grinned and they both left the road and ran across the small meadow to enter the forest of towering grass. Perspiring heavily beneath their heavy cuirasses they soon vanished from sight amidst stems that were as thick as a man's thigh. The constant clacking of the swaying bamboo stems could be heard throughout the forest as they turned sharply to the left and trotted parallel with the road that was only one *li,* five hundred long strides distant, from them. Occasionally they caught sight of the soldiers by the flickering tips of their spearheads in the moonlight.

They had dodged between the closely packed bamboo for a good ten li before dawn's first light began filtering down through the lofty stems.

Guan looked to his left but was unable to see the column and assumed that they had long passed them. 'We must have left them behind already,' he gasped with spittle flecking the corner of his mouth.

'Then it's time for us to rest until we catch sight of them again,' Shu Du said, coming to a standstill. 'We still have 50 li to go and we cannot afford to tire ourselves too much. We may still be faced by more awkward obstacles than bamboo.'

Guan nodded and the two men thankfully sank down to lie upon the soft, moss-covered forest floor and immediately fell into a deep sleep.

The sun was directly above the bamboo canopy when Shu Du first stirred, his sleep disturbed by a laughing thrush and he rolled onto his back to stretch his arms. Without any warning his wrists were swiftly grabbed and bound together by two heavily armed soldiers. He cried out to warn Guan while struggling to free himself from their grips but two more soldiers leapt upon his body, driving all wind from his lungs and pinning him to the ground. He was soon trussed as tightly as a pig being readied for market. As he was dragged to his feet and roughly turned he saw that the same fate had befallen his brother who had, in addition, been gagged to prevent him from alerting Shu Du.

They were surrounded by a large number of soldiers whom Shu Du recognized by the markings on their cuirasses and pennants as the column they had been avoiding.

'Do you know who I am,' Shu Du said with great indignation. 'I am the –'

'I know who you are,' a deep voice shouted and a tall, burly man swaggered through the jeering throng of soldiers to stand before the two captives. 'I am Shen, a captain loyal to King Cheng and you are Shu Du of

Cai, a lowly vassal of King Cheng and brother to Dan, the Duke of Zhou.' The soldiers cheered his words.

'Then untie us immediately you fool,' Shu Du shouted.

'I cannot do that my Lord as I am under instruction to take you, and only you, to my master the Duke of Zhou.'

'How did you know where we were?'

'I have a very eagle-eyed rearguard soldier who saw your cowardly run into the forest. I sent two of my best scouts to follow you and the rest was easy when you elected to fall asleep.'

'If I'm the only one to be taken before Dan what is to become of my brother?' Shu Du nodded his head to indicate Guan.

'Guan, who was known to be one of The Three Guards, was formally judged in his absence by the royal court and found guilty of high treason. He has been sentenced to death which is to be carried out by any officer of the Duke of Zhou's forces who is fortunate enough to capture him.'

Guan struggled when he heard he fate and one of the soldiers hit him with the flat of his sword blade.

'You do not have the authority to execute a lord,' Shu Du protested, his eyes flicking from the captain to his brother who had stumbled from the unexpected blow and was now kneeling.

'Tell that to the duke when you see him.' Shen laughed drily as he drew Shu Du's blade from its ornately decorated scabbard and strode to stand beside the stunned man. He handed Dragon's Breath to a burly soldier and stood back.

'You have a miraculous weapon,' Shen said as the soldiers pulled on ropes to stretch Guan's arms back while another grasped a handful of hishair and pulled forward. The strike was swift and Guan's head was cleanly separated from his body to be held aloft and shown to the cheering group of men. Shen stepped away from the fountain of blood jetting from the neck and on taking the weapon proceeded to clean the blade with a piece of silk cloth.

Far above their heads the laughing thrush fell silent as though showing respect for the fallen warrior.

'I will present your brother's head to his brother, the duke, as he does not need the whole man as proof of death.'

'When I am freed from these bonds by the duke you must be sure to be on your guard night and day Shen, for I will seek reparation for what has been done this day.' Shu Du stared into the man's face before seeking out the heavy-set executioner with the same threatening look.

Shen laughed and then instructed the man who had wielded the sword to put Guan's head in an empty rice bag and bury the body. 'Thinking that you will ever be a free man is the dream of a fool. I would not be at all surprised if the duke, your own flesh and blood, doesn't wish to kill you himself.'

The captain took the scabbard of Dragon's Breath from Shu Du's waist and fixed it to his own belt. He sheathed the blade and strode back to where a soldier had been instructed to hold his horse and mounted without a single look in Shu Du's direction. The column returned to the road and marched north with Shu Du stumbling along in the dust thrown up by many feet. His arms were roped painfully to a length of bamboo that rested across his shoulders. When he fell he was dragged until he managed to find his feet again.

As Shu Du was taken north on the road to Zhoucou his surviving brother and three servants were making steady progress eastward. They had travelled 150 li through the bamboo forest on the road to Hung-Tse Lake when the steady rhythm of their feet was broken. They were at a crossroads near a small village called Taihe and were facing a further trek of 450 li when the two younger men at the ends of the bamboo pole began to complain about the weight of the box. Despite the constant urging of the older man, Huo knew he would have to let them rest.

'We will leave the road and rest behind that thicket,' Huo said as he pointed to three shrubs that could hide them from any travellers on the same road. The servants thankfully sank down on their haunches with the box lying on the soft lichen bed between them. Huo remained on the road to check and when satisfied that they could be seen he went to join them.

He was about to squat down when he spotted two mounted men cresting the brow of a small hill and clearly silhouetted against the cloudless sky. Huo judged them to be about 5 li away and he warned the three servants to remain silent. The old man began to wail and beat his breast.

'We all be killed because of this madness. This warring between the nobles will shame us all,' one of the young servants said as he stood up and backed away. 'I suggest we run deeper into the forest and hide before they can find us.'

'You cannot leave the ding and the *Ears of Heaven* here,' Huo snarled drawing his sword. 'You must take them with you.'

The second servant also backed away from the box. 'We cannot escape carrying such a heavy load.' He turned to leave and Huo roared and rushed towards him with his weapon raised. The servant screamed and ran onto the road in the direction of the approaching men and was instantly followed by his friend.

The older man looked at the offending box and then at Huo as he beseechingly held his hands out with a look of total helplessness. 'I am too old and feeble to take any responsibility for the ding.' He too walked out onto the road and began to shuffle after the young men.

Huo heard a distant scream and saw that one of the riders had dismounted and was standing by the body of one of the younger men. The second young man had fallen to his knees and was still pleading when the soldier swung his sword to remove his head. The old man had turned around and was hurrying towards Huo's hiding place. The second rider spurred his horse and soon caught up with the terrified servant who turned and pointed towards Huo's hiding place. Without a word he spurred his horse into the man, killing him, and galloped towards the shrubbery.

'Come out and give us your name,' the soldier shouted and Huo unsheathed his sword before stepping out from behind the shrubbery and onto the road.

'You know my name.' Huo recognized the man as one of Dan's scouts. 'Now state your business and why you killed my servants.'

The reined in his horse and stared at Huo with the eyes of a stalking wild cat.

'Huo Shu of Cai, you have officially been exiled by my lord the Duke of Zhou but unofficially he charged us to put an end to The Three Guards.' The soldier dismounted and was immediately struck down by Huo's swinging sword before he could unsheathe his own weapon. The second rider leapt from his saddle and rushed at Huo with a spear but the deadly tip was easily sidestepped and the sheer impetus of the man's charge helped thrust Huo's blade through his throat to partially decapitate him.

As a matter of habit Huo took the silk cloth that was tucked in the armhole of his cuirass and wiped the blade clean before returning it to its sheath. The stench of freshly spilt blood upset the two horses; they reared away from the corpses, turned and galloped back along the road.

Huo cursed as his only means of carrying the box galloped westward. With straining muscles he dragged the two heavily armoured men through the shrubs and into the bamboo forest until they could no longer be seen from the road. He returned to the box and sat upon it as he pondered his next move.

He eventually decided to leave the bronze ding where it was and travel to Hung-Tse Lake empty-handed. Then he would be able to fight unencumbered should the need arise and return to recover the ding when the war was won.

Huo planned to hide the sacred vessel and then mark the spot so that he or his brothers could recover it at a later date. He swiftly levered the wooden box apart and with weakening arms he lifted the bronze vessel and carried it to the base of a young oak sapling. There he carefully removed a square of the springy moss and dug a deep hole with his sword. Taking three of the amber bi he reverently used the tip of his dagger to mark the location of the sapling on each one before tucking one beneath his cuirass and slipping two in his boot. Huo resealed the ding and filled in the hole. Earth was rammed down hard to prevent settlement before the square of moss was relaid. After randomly scattering a little leaf litter all signs of a burial having taken place were eradicated. The bamboo pole, ropes and remnants of the wooden box were taken three li further on down the road before Huo entered the forest and hid them beneath bushes.

After eight tortuous days of walking and lodging in small villages populated by surly, suspicious field workers Huo breasted a rise and was confronted by a glittering expanse of water. It was Hung-Tse Lake and his heart expanded joyfully, in anticipation of being reunited with his family.

1

HONG KONG – 2015AD

THE BRITISH AIRWAYS A380 took off on time to rise above the island's glittering towers and swiftly reach maximum cruising height before passing over Macau.

The last passenger to board had groaned softly as he leant back against the soft leather of the first-class seat and waited for the orange light above his head to switch off. As soon as it chimed he unfastened the seat belt and after fractionally easing his discomfort he began browsing on his smart phone. He searched for any news about Hong Kong and with fingers beginning to go numb he thumbed the keys as fast as possible. Just when the aircraft was fast approaching the extreme range of the phone a TVB iNewsflash caught his attention.

Gunfight At The Airport the bold caption screamed and he scrolled down to read that two limousines had collided on the main North Lantau highway, a quarter mile from the airport, and that the occupants of both vehicles had exchanged gunfire. The police discovered a total of four bodies in and around the cars but none had survived the car crash or the subsequent shooting.

Eyewitnesses had claimed that the driver of the Land Cruiser had deliberately rammed into the back of a BMW making both vehicles spin into other cars before leaving the road and rolling down to the Cheung Tung Road that ran parallel to the airport highway.

One woman insisted that she had seen a man run from the scene before suddenly falling down as though hit in the back. Then she added that he appeared to be unharmed for he had picked himself up and ran in the direction of the airport.

The connection was lost and Huang lowered the dead phone to his lap in frustration. The excruciating pain internally had dimmed to a cruel numbing sensation yet he could still feel blood trickling down his back despite pressing hard against the soft upholstery.

Huang Xiao Shi had covered the last half-mile to the airport on foot and when he reached the departure concourse he removed his ticket and passport and stuffed the linen jacket he was wearing into a litterbin. Then, when nobody was looking, he took a lightweight raincoat from an unattended luggage trolley while the owner was paying his taxi driver.

A row of telephone booths beckoned but he resisted the urge. He could no longer trust any of his colleagues and he dare not put any of his friends in jeopardy.

Trying hard to prevent the pain from showing on his face he walked into the airport terminal and hurried to a cubicle in the public restrooms. He folded lengths of toilet paper to make thick pads that could be pressed against the lightly leaking bullet hole in his back. These pads were then firmly held in place with his tie before he slipped on his shirt and the stolen coat and left the blood-stained cubicle to wash his hands at one of the many sinks. A passenger already engaged at the next sink glanced briefly at the whirlpool of blood disappearing down the plughole and hurriedly left.

As Huang passed through the security arch the customs officials glanced up at the bright sky showing through the glazed roof and then at the tightly belted raincoat with some curiosity. Seeing nothing untoward on their electronic screens they shrugged at the man's eccentricity and waved him on.

Huang's face was ashen when he arrived at the plane's entrance and a concerned flight attendant led him to his First Class couchette. He shook his head when she offered to take his coat and he thankfully lowered himself into the seat. Waiting until the flight attendant had retreated to the galley area he switched on his phone to check for any news.

He looked at the useless phone on his lap for a few seconds before deciding on his next course of action. With shaking hands and blurring vision he laboriously began tapping in a text message and then keyed it to be sent as soon as the signal reached sufficient strength again.

Huang placed it on the drinks shelf, covered it with the menu card and slid the complimentary *Do Not Disturb* sleeping mask over his head. The pain had seemed to fade completely although he was beginning to feel a chill. He used the complimentary blanket, closed his eyes and soon drifted into a cold sleep.

Thirty-two minutes later while the autopilot was banking the plane to compensate for a course deviation death claimed Superintendent 1st Class Xiao Shi Huang of the Hong Kong police.

They were seven and a half miles above Mandalay and the Irrawady River when a concerned flight attendant lightly touched Huang on the shoulder; when he didn't stir she shook him harder. The body fell to one side revealing the blood-soaked seat and her stifled cry alerted a colleague who, after taking one brief look, quickly slid the passenger's privacy shield shut. As they hurried to report their finding to the captain the faint chime from Huang's smart phone was unheard. The text message had been sent.

KENT – ENGLAND

Mr Feng Choi had spent a fruitful morning in East Steading market and was full of high spirits when he returned to his restaurant the Forbidden City. Just as he stepped from the van outside the premises his phone giggled like a naughty child in his pocket, signalling an incoming text from his brother in London. The ringtone app had been a birthday present from his little daughter.

'MST TLK!' The text read and Feng frowned for it was very unlike Han to be so cryptic. He unloaded the van and stowed the fresh vegetables in the kitchen larder before speed-dialling his brother. The ringtone was answered almost instantaneously. It was as if Han was holding his mobile in readiness for Feng's reply.

'I'm in big trouble, Brother,' Han said in Mandarin. 'I think someone has been stalking me ever since I received a small packet in the post from home.'

Home for the two brothers always meant China and like Han Feng replied in Mandarin, 'I don't understand, Han. Who's following you, what's in the packet and why the hell didn't you telephone?'

'Our second cousin sent me a beautiful jade bi.'

'A bit of jade doesn't sound like bad news to me.'

'It's a funerary jade from three thousand years ago that was placed on the chest of the deceased to ensure Shang Ti the Supreme Ancestor knew of the owner's good character and would reward him with a place in heaven.

'I only know that accepting a decorative bee is the sure way to get stung for a lot of money but I know nothing about your bee character witness. Valuable is it?'

'This is not the time for any of your Western jokes, Feng. It's spelt B-I, and it's a jade disc,' Han whispered. 'I also received a weird text from the same cousin who I trust implicitly.'

'What did it say.'

'It didn't say anything I could understand. It was simply a series of letters and numbers that I can't make any sense of.'

'You think it's something to do with the bi?'

'It could be because I checked and found the damned thing is worth two thousand pounds in auction and the note that accompanied it is written in old characters that I can't understand or even begin to translate. I also think the note and the disc are being followed by persons who would do someone great harm to get their hands on it.'

'Bloody hell!' Feng exclaimed in English. 'It seems this bi could really sting you. How can I help?'

'Simple. I've posted it to you along with my cousin's note and I want you to hide them in a safe place until I think it's safe enough to come down to East Steading to retrieve them.'

Feng heard a distant bell ringing on the line. 'What's that?'

'There's someone at the door, I'll call you later tonight about what we should do with the disc when I arrive but until then just keep it well hidden.'

'I will and make sure you keep yourself safe too.'

'That I promise to do brother – ' the line went dead.

Feng listened to the electronic white noise for a moment before slipping the mobile into his pocket with a puzzled expression on his normally jolly features.

'Who was that,' Jiao asked as she swept through the kitchen swing doors into the restaurant and planted a kiss on her husband's round cheek.

'It was a rather strange call from Han,' Feng said as they both returned to the kitchen to get ready for the lunchtime trade. While he was prepping the Kung Pao spicy chicken dish he related what his brother had told him and what they were to expect in the post.

Pausing in her vigorous vegetable chopping for the Lion's Head soup Jiao gave her husband a worried look. 'Will this jade disc present any threat to us and Lin-Lin?'

'Not at all,' Feng said all too quickly. 'Being stalked by strangers is just the result of Han's creative imagination. After all, he does work in advertising and you know what outlandish imaginations they have.'

Jiao nodded knowingly and the couple continued preparing the various dishes until a bell rang in the kitchen. Someone had entered the restaurant and Feng glanced at his watch. He removed the well-stained apron and after straightening the tie that hung down over his well-rounded figure he went through the swing doors.

Feng's hyperactive ten-year-old daughter was towing a good-looking man by the hand to a table whilst talking non-stop in Mandarin about what he should order to eat and drink.

'Welcome, James,' Feng greeted the tall slender man in English with an outstretched hand. 'You're a little early for your lunch today.'

James Goodfellow sat and accepted the massive menu that Lin-Lin had thrust into his hand. 'I've just finished an investigation and was returning to my office when I fancied one of your delicious *char siu bao*, pork-filled buns.'

'Jiao has just finished making the dough.' Feng smiled broadly as he hurried back into the kitchen to tell his wife what James, their tenant who lived and worked above the restaurant, wanted for lunch.

'Why don't you tell James about Han's phone call,' she said as she placed a steamer on the big range. 'He's a very good detective and he may be able to sort things out.'

Feng shook his head. 'We can't ask him to solve a problem when we don't even know what the problem is.' He took the freshly brewed pot of green tea and turned to leave. 'Let's wait until Han comes down from London and then we can discuss the best course of action.' Jiao nodded as she placed four of her finest Cantonese buns on the steam plate above the boiling water and closed the lid.

Lin-Lin raced into the kitchen laughing. 'I'll take the tea, let me take the tea to Mr James,' she squealed and grabbed the porcelain teapot from her father and raced back out again.

'Slow down, don't run,' he cried after her.

'She's still got a terrific crush on Mr Goodfellow,' Jiao said and smiled knowingly. Feng shook his head and went back to prepping more chicken.

Goodfellow watched the young girl slowly lower the teapot onto the table. The tip of her pink tongue showed between her lips and an expression of grave concentration was on her round pretty face.

'You did that beautifully, Lin-Lin. You'll be the very best waitress when you grow up,' he stumbled in expressing his thanks in Mandarin. He had picked up a little of the difficult language during the many times he had spent eating in the restaurant.

Annoyance suddenly flickered across the schoolgirl's face. 'I'm grown up already and I don't want to be a waitress. I'm going to be a world-famous detective just like you.'

'I'm not world-famous, Lin-Lin. I'm not even known in East Steading.'

'You are too.' Pulling herself up to her full height of fifty-four inches Lin-Lin turned away with long black hair swinging angrily and stalked back into the kitchen. Her parents noticed her changed mood and quietly went on with their work knowing that she would soon be her boisterous self again.

The art deco star-burst clock on the wall clicked noon and the restaurant was beginning to fill when Feng returned to take James's empty plate. Just then the postman entered the restaurant and handed Feng assorted letters and a small packet.

'Anything to go, Mr Choi?' he asked and Feng shook his head as he studied the packet with a London postmark.

'What's wrong Feng, you look as though you've just received terrible news,' James asked in a concerned tone of voice as he lowered his cup.

'It could well be James, it could well be,' the restaurant owner replied as he sat opposite the private detective and placed the mail on the table before him. The two men had been good friends for a long time and had faced extreme dangers together. Feng knew he could trust James and disregarding what he had told his wife he put the packet on the table between them and began relating what his brother had said.

'Two thousand pounds doesn't sound like bad news to me,' James said when Feng had finished talking and subsided into a contemplative silence. 'Open the packet and let's read what your distant cousin has to say in his note before we start believing the world is coming to an end.'

As Feng began tearing at the clear tape sealing the brown envelope Lin-Lin returned to offer James the dessert menu. She was smiling again and looking at James with hero worship showing in her eyes. James grinned, shook his head and seeing the mouth turn down asked for a fresh pot of tea. Lin-Lin grinned broadly again and almost skipped back into the kitchen.

'You do realize I will have to jilt Jenny and marry your daughter when she reaches twenty-one,' James joked but Feng didn't laugh for his mind had been elsewhere while opening the packet. A small tissue-wrapped item slid out onto the snow-white cotton tablecloth followed by a folded sheet of paper and a small fragment of wrinkled paper.

Feng carefully smoothed the paper on the table's surface revealing familiar Mandarin calligraphy that had been created with the tip of a fine writing brush. 'What does it say Feng?' James asked twisting his head to read the artistic strokes.

'I don't know James,' Feng said and frowned in concentration. 'When I was a young man in Beijing, I had known all the characters like the back of my hand. It has been so long that I will have to spend some time studying it before I can translate what it says.'

'What about your brother?'

'He would have sent me the translation if he had been able to read it,' Feng replied and clasped his hands in frustration. 'One thing puzzles me though.'

'What?'

'The cousin Han mentioned couldn't have written this. The paper used is extremely old and the ink seems to have faded as though written centuries ago.'

James reached across and carefully tested the paper between his thumb and forefinger and after sniffing his fingers he nodded.

'You're right Feng, this is old rag paper that wouldn't be out of place in a museum. It has that musty smell one generally associates with mouldy old books.'

'The style of calligraphy also seems to be positively medieval, unlike this letter,' Feng said as he unfolded the A4 sheet of modern photocopier paper.

'It's a letter to Han from someone who only signs himself as Huang. The only person I know by that name was a very distant cousin who used to live in the Jiangsu Province as a young boy. When Han and I were small our father told us that the whole family ostracized the boy because he wanted to be a policeman when he grew up. In those days of strict communism the police were always feared. He has to be the distant cousin Han referred to.'

'What does it say?' James asked and Feng read the message aloud slowly.

Dear Cousin, I enclose an ancient bi and some very old-style Mandarin writing. They both came to me quite by accident. I have been trying to interpret the characters and the marks scratched onto the bi. So far I have learnt that it is from the Bronze Age whereas the paper is much later –

'At least the tissue paper seems to be modern, what's in it?' James interrupted.

Feng picked up the object and unwrapped it until a heavy disc of pure white jade dropped into the palm of his hand. It was no more than three inches in diameter, flawless and covered with hexagonal patterns, exquisitely carved dragons and calligraphy characters.

'It's the Chinese funerary bi that Han spoke of and is mentioned in this letter,' Feng explained. 'They taught us all about these when I was at school, most of which I have long since forgotten. However, I do know that some of the motifs are of deities who represent qualities that the deceased wanted to invoke or communicate to Shang Ti.'

'Shang who?'

'Shang Ti is our Supreme Ancestor who has the power to give someone who has died the right to enter heaven.'

'A bit like our St Peter at the pearly gates,' James said with a light laugh as he took the disc from Feng's palm and held it up to the light. There were no air bubbles or tiny cracks and the lustre and delicacy of the craftsmanship clearly advertised a piece of superior quality.

'The ancients believed that jade is far superior to diamonds and gold as it is supposedly animated with a soul and also indicates that the individual is of high moral character. In other words, it's the perfect messenger for convincing those in heaven. In the Neolithic period one of these would have been carved out of stone and in a later period, cast in bronze. Then jade and glass followed,' Feng continued as he took the teapot from Lin-Lin who without being invited had sat down beside to her father.

James turned the disc over and looked more closely at the sculptured surface. 'Would these additional characters reduce the value of the piece?' he asked as he passed it to his friend.

Feng took the disc and scrutinized the surface until he saw the fine signs that had been crudely etched over one of the dragons. 'It doesn't seem to have been done recently but I agree, whoever scratched that has reduced the overall beauty of the jade but not necessarily its value.'

'Does the letter say anything else?'

'Yes, it goes on, *The marks on the bi* – which must be these – *are rough indications of where something was secretly placed during the Zhou dynasty* – that would be roughly 1,000BC – *and the old characters predate any formal writing. However, someone called Ji Hu did manage to interpret them and relocate what was hidden to another secret location. Ji Hu, thought to be a descendant of one of The Three Guards, had received the bi on the death of his father in the ninth century and written the cryptic note for his son Cheng Hu before he died of typhoid.*'

James held up a hand. 'Hold on for a moment Feng: You've lost me with all these names.'

'It gets easier to understand James,' Feng said and he continued reading:

'*The note resurfaced again in the nineteenth century and it was used to locate the unknown object. Subsequent family documentation uncovered that the precious object was being kept safe until ten years ago when a threat to steal forced them to send it to Europe. A special code was used to cover their tracks. I will be giving this to you very soon and you can investigate the European link further. You should be warned that a local triad organization and an Illuminati group have also been looking for it and have not hesitated to kill in their hunt. This makes me believe that the bi is only a step to something of far greater value. Take extreme care. Your cousin. Huang.*

Both men sat in silence for a moment before James handed some money to Lin-Lin. 'Keep the change Lin-Lin and tell your mother that she has done me proud again. The pork buns were delicious,' he said with a twinkle in his eyes and the girl skipped away happily to the amusement of the other diners. Feng rewrapped the piece of jade in the tissue paper and put it back in the envelope with the letter. He held the old piece of paper for a while to stare at it reverently.

'To think that's a note from the ninth century,' James said reverently as Feng put it in the envelope. 'It's amazing that it survived.'

Feng nodded slowly. 'I must get back to work James,' he said as he got up and shook the investigator's hand. 'I will let you know when Han arrives so that we can discuss this matter further.'

James nodded and went out of the Forbidden City and into the next doorway along the street that led to his office and flat upstairs. A small brass plaque screwed to the wall was engraved with two simple words, *Goodfellow Investigations*.

Feng returned to the kitchen to help his wife handle the sudden increase in orders and put the envelope on a top shelf where he kept his spare woks and saucepans.

'What's that, Feng?' his wife asked as she looked up without pausing in her chopping of a very large bunch of parsley.

'Something Han sent for me to hold until the next time he comes down from London to see us.'

'That's nice, we haven't seen your brother since the New Year celebrations.'

Feng nodded without smiling as he recalled Han's words: *I think the note and the bi are being followed.*

2

TWO WEEKS HAD PASSED since Feng last spoke to Han and he had become increasingly concerned for his brother's safety. He hadn't arrived in East Steading nor had he been in contact as promised. Feng tried phoning on a number of occasions but each time his calls were diverted to a messaging service.

Jiao took Lin-Lin to Worthing to visit her sister while the Forbidden City was closed for its annual cleaning. The thorough cleaning wasn't mandatory but Feng had always taken personal pride in having a spotless, hygienic kitchen and restaurant and the many award certificates displayed were the first to be dusted. He had just finished the high shelving and was busily scouring the wooden tops with wire wool when he heard rapping on the back door. James was waiting outside and Feng waved him into the kitchen.

'I'm not interrupting am I, Feng?' James asked in response to the slight frown on the older man's forehead. Since taking on the lease of the office and apartment upstairs he had been treated like one of the family and he regularly took breakfast in the Forbidden City, even when the restaurant was closed.

'No, no my friend,' Feng replied and waved James to one of the pine chairs by the freshly scrubbed table. 'The usual?'

'Not today Feng. I'm trying to watch my weight a little so I'm cutting out the fried food for a while.'

'Then I will prepare a traditional dish that my mother used to make when I was very small.'

'I can't believe you were ever very small Feng,' James joked and was pleasantly rewarded by a small smile before the worried look returned. 'Tell me what's happened. What's worrying you?'

Feng fired up the gas ring and placed a pan over the heat. 'It's my brother. He still hasn't arrived and when I call there's no answer. His phone rang for a while but now there's no sound and I think his battery has gone flat. I'm worried that something may have happened to him. On the phone he said that he was being followed and now I think that person may have wanted to harm him.'

'You think it's because of the jade disc and the old note?'

'I'm sure it is and I'm thinking of taking the train to London today to find out what is wrong.' Feng grated ginger and added it to the short and long grained rice, miso and rice wine in the pot. James looked thoughtful as he watched him prepare the traditional congee breakfast.

'I don't have any clients at the moment and Miss Lightbody wouldn't begrudge me a day or two to help a friend,' James said as he speed-dialled the office. 'I'll let her know where I'm going and as soon as we've eaten we'll go to the station together.'

Feng listened as James spoke to his secretary: she was a lady with a cold businesslike exterior but a warm heart, and as he stirred the pot he mouthed his silent thanks.

Two hours later the two friends arrived at Waterloo Station and caught a taxi to Han's apartment in Bedford Place. Feng pressed the buzzer beside the bright blue door but despite his insistent ringing there was no reply. They waited another two minutes before Feng sorted out a Yale on his tightly packed keyring and the door was opened.

'He gave it to me for when I come to town to visit the catering trade exhibitions. It's somewhere to stay and it sure beats paying the hotel prices round here,' Feng explained as they entered a brightly lit hallway. 'All the lights are on, that's unusual for Han. As I recall he was always very thrifty when it came to using electricity.' They went into the front room and the chaotic scene that confronted them came as a shock. Drawers had been pulled out of lacquered chests and their contents scattered across the floor. The upholstery on every single chair had been ripped open and the stuffing pulled out as though someone had been frantically searching for something. They hurried across the hall to the dining room where they found the same devastation. Ceramic willow-patterned plates had been shattered and hundreds of blue and white pieces were scattered across the carpet.

James immediately switched into professional mode and began using his smart phone to record the images of destruction.

'My God, where's Han?' Feng gasped and he rushed down the hall to the kitchen calling out his brother's name. James followed more slowly. He had paused to look up the stairs in the hope that Han would appear when a short curdled cry of grief made him rush into the kitchen.

Feng stood in the middle of the room looking down at the naked body of a Chinese man who was of similar build to him. James winced as he took in the scene of torture and mutilation: the man's body was covered in burns and deep cuts and his face had been completely destroyed by a blast from both barrels of a shotgun. Blood, bone fragments and brain tissue covered the tiles above the marble worktop and thin wire bound the ankles and wrists. Blood had flowed from where the cruel strands had cut into the flesh.

The ghastly details were seen in a flash and James grabbed Feng by the shoulders and twisted him away. 'We must leave the room and call the police,' James urged as he pulled his friend close to him and led the traumatized man into the hallway. He then turned and surreptitiously triggered a number of pictures as Feng stumbled towards the staircase.

'Who could have done that?' Feng croaked as he sat on one of the lower steps; recalling the image of his brother's mutilated body he threw up between his legs.

'Are you sure it's Han?' James asked as he handed him a clean handkerchief.

Feng wiped his mouth. 'When we were teenagers we dared each other to go into a tattoo parlour that was down by the gasometer. We had the same design, a small peacock, put on our buttocks. His was on the right side and mine on the left. You saw it James. It could only be Han.' Feng broke down and sobbed into his hands.

James returned to the kitchen and avoiding looking across the room he picked up a mobile phone that had clearly fallen from the table during the struggle and been kicked under a dresser. It had caught his eye while leaving the kitchen and he slipped it into his pocket. Returning to Feng he rested a reassuring hand on his friend's shoulder and speed-dialled the emergency number using his own smartphone.

It was only a matter of minutes before two police cars, sirens bleating, screeched to a halt at the blue door while two more sealed both ends of Bedford Place.

James opened the door just as Detective Inspector Cutler was climbing the four white-washed steps. Sergeant Mansfield was right behind and both men rushed past James before coming to a stop at the sight of the oriental sitting on the stairs, clutching his head as he stared down sightlessly at the puddle of vomit.

Another policeman entered and closed the door behind him. He was instructed to block the way should anyone consider leaving in a hurry. James introduced himself and Feng to all three officers before turning to his distraught friend.

'The police are here,' he said softly and waited patiently as Feng unbowed his head and slowly stood up.

'My brother is in the kitchen,' Feng said in a low voice that trembled and then fell silent as tears welled up again and rolled down his face.

Cutler nodded and hurried to the and stopped abruptly when he crossed the threshold. His face blanched at the scene and he waved to the other two policemen who hurried to join him. The sergeant managed to suppress his shock but the young constable gagged and turned away.

'Call for a full crime scene investigation team, Sergeant,' Cutler said to Mansfield. 'And I also want *you* to cordon off an area to keep the public and the media at a ten-metre distance from the front of the building,' he instructed the young constable. Both men nodded and thankfully hurried away from the horror in the kitchen to carry out their orders.

The inspector left the kitchen and walked back to where the two men were still waiting. 'I also want you and Mr Choi to go outside and sit in the back of my car until I tell you otherwise. Is that clear, Mr Goodfellow?' Cutler took a step closer to stare meaningfully into James's eyes.

'Understood Inspector, but why your car. Are we being detained for any specific reason?' James asked as he held the inspector's gaze while taking Feng by the arm. Cutler broke eye contact first and visibly relaxed as a slight smile betrayed his normally hidden sense of humour. 'Not at all, sir, but you do understand that a terrible crime has taken place and that I need to preserve the crime scene from any further contamination. There are also many questions I need to ask of you both. Most importantly, why are you here, you clearly do not live in this apartment.'

Detective Inspector Roger Cutler had built his career on a university degree and followed a disciplined protocol for all investigations. His first task was to check thoroughly the identities of the two men who were at the scene of a particularly nasty crime.

James had raised a quizzical eyebrow but finally accepted the officer's reasoning. Leaving the house he helped Feng descend to the police car, where Constable Merriwether was waiting for them.

'If you wouldn't mind waiting in here, sir, the inspector will be with you very soon,' he said with a compassionate glance at Feng.

The wait was a lot longer than the constable's 'very soon' and as they sat in silence a white forensic van arrived and offloaded half a dozen white-overalled men and women who quickly poured into the terraced house carrying an assortment of aluminium cases. Curious neighbours had spilled out onto the pavement to gawp and speculate and constables who had been sealing off the road were helping Merriwether to control the onlookers while he cordoned off the address.

One of the forensic team came to the squad car carrying a small aluminium case. 'I will need to take fingerprints, blood and DNA samples from you both,' he said. 'Purely routine for elimination purposes you understand,' he explained politely as he unclipped the case.

'Can you give my friend a few minutes?' James pleaded and the officer nodded and went back inside the house.

Feng gave James a thankful look as he dialled Worthing to give the bad news to Jiao while James called Miss Lightbody to ask if she could go downstairs and comfort Choi's wife on her return until Choi was back in East Steading. The two friends finished their calls at the same time and began discussing the motive for Han's murder.

They agreed that the jade disc, or what it signified, had to be at the heart of it and that a triad or member of the Illuminati organization had been trying to extract information from Han about the artefact. They didn't know if Feng's brother had broken under torture and told his tormentor that he had sent the bi to East Steading but both agreed that they had to get back to the Forbidden City as soon as possible. They also agreed that they needed a speedy translation of the ninth-century scrap of Chinese calligraphy.

Having exhausted all their ideas they were beginning to feel impatient to get going when the front door opened and Inspector Cutler descended the steps and approached the car.

'My apology for keeping you waiting, gentlemen.' Getting into the front passenger seat and removing the white forensic overshoes he pushed a button on the dashboard and a small red light died. 'No doubt the recording will fill in a lot of the gaps for me but in the meantime let's do the formal interview.' Cutler waved to the constable standing in front of the car.

Feng and James looked sheepishly at each other as Constable Merriwether climbed into the driver's seat and pushed the tiny button again. The little red light winked on and for the next twenty minutes they gave details of their identities, their relationship to the dead man and a vague reason for visiting him while the constable noted down their behaviour and body language.

Cutler finished questioning both men and asked Merriwether to put his notebook away. 'Now we will all listen and learn,' he said as he fiddled with some controls on the dash. James and Feng heard themselves discussing the murder and the ancestral artefacts and only when they talked of the weird calligraphy did Cutler stop the recording.

'Do you have the jade disc or the indecipherable note on you?' he asked and both men shook their heads. 'Where is it?'

'They're hidden in my restaurant,' Feng replied in an absent-minded tone while trying to block out the murder scene.

'I will need to see that and the original disc, whatever that is, before the persons who did that … ' he pointed up at the blue door ' … pay you a visit too.'

'That can be arranged, Inspector,' James said while looking at Feng who simply nodded. 'But can you provide some form of protection for Mr Choi and his family until the murderer is apprehended?'

'I will contact the East Steading police and see to that matter immediately,' Cutler said in a more kindly voice.

'Do you believe this unusual artefact will lead us to the killer?' Merriwether asked and the Inspector scowled at his junior officer's bold interruption.

'Not at all, Constable, but I do believe it is a clue to the whereabouts of something else that is more valuable,' Feng said in a soft voice. 'The disc is a way of communicating with Shang Ti, the Supreme Ancestor and therefore is priceless for a deceased person.'

'Just like a hotline to the hereafter?' the constable said with a laugh that he instantly suppressed when his superior's face darkened angrily.

'See to the crowd, Constable,' Cutler snapped as he gave Feng an apologetic look. Merriwether sheepishly left the car and went to stand at the orange tape where he made a point of ignoring the questions fired at him by the large group of curious bystanders.

'My apologies, Mr Choi, but youngsters can be rather insensitive at times. However, I do have to ask if this so-called bi has any monetary value.'

'An individual jade disc could fetch about £2,000 at auction, Inspector,' James said.

'I wouldn't have thought that would be enough of an incentive to murder,' Cutler said with a thoughtful expression.

'That's why we seriously believe it is only a clue to something of a far greater value,' James cut in and Cutler nodded slowly.

'Mr Choi, once again you have my sincere condolences and I will be in touch with you as soon as I have any news concerning this investigation. I will have one of the squad cars take you both to Waterloo Station as soon as you have given DNA samples and fingerprints to the crime scene investigators.' Cutler left the car and went to instruct the technical officer carrying the small case to return.'

The drive to the station was conducted in silence as the friends kept their eyes on the dashboard for any sign that their conversation was being taped.

Feng was quiet as their train sped non-stop through the suburbs to East Steading. He was lost in his own personal thoughts about his brother, their lives as children and how they drifted apart as they grew older. He was on the point of welling-up again when James exclaimed in a loud voice:

'Look at this Feng,' He turned his smartphone so that his friend could see the screen. It was a picture of the dining room in Han's house.

'What am I supposed to be looking at?' Feng asked as he studied the dozens of broken ceramic plates that once stood on a rail around the room but that now littered the floor.

'All the books are still on the shelves as are the English ceramic figures and plates.'

'So what?'

'Look at the shattered plates on the floor. They're all blue-and-white willow-pattern plates,' James said excitedly. 'Quite old by the look of them.'

'They are. Han specialized in collecting blue-and-white porcelain but the well-known willow pattern was first created for the export market only and it started becoming popular in England during the eighteenth century when Thomas Minton was inspired by the Chinese ceramic industry.'

'This is important, Feng.'

'It can't be, none of Han's plates were that rare or valuable.'

James pointed at the screen. 'But not everything here is willow pattern. On the plate rail there are a few plates with different designs that I've never seen before.' The image was enlarged as the investigator used his thumb and forefinger to zoom in on three untouched plates.

Feng studied the screen with a puzzled expression. 'So someone has deliberately smashed all the willow-pattern plates. Why do that, it doesn't seem to make any sense at all.'

'Unless that person was looking for a specific plate that was willow-pattern and broke them one by one to eliminate looking at the same plate twice.'

'I still don't understand,' Feng said.

'I do believe this is taking us somewhere.' James was looking at the phone he had found under the dresser in Han's kitchen. 'This must be the text Han received.'

'Is that my cousin's message?' Feng stared at the phone and James nodded. 'So, what does it say?'

James stared at the glowing screen silently before giving it to Feng to read the brief mysterious message.

C SALE 2 4350N1112E DCCIA

CHCKPL84DING. WRTH4TUNE. HUANG.

'Huang is definitely our cousin,' he said with a nod. 'I vaguely recall that he transferred from Beijing to work for the Hong Kong police just before the handover in 1997.' Feng gave the phone back to James. 'It still doesn't seem to make any sense.'

James held it closer to his face as if it would make the message clearer in its meaning. 'The second line is clearly text-talk for "check plate … worth fortune" but I can't guess what 4DING in the middle means and most of the first line is indecipherable,' James said as he read the cypher again. 'The plate referred to must be one in the blue-and-white collection that Han had and which the murderer smashed but I don't know what *ding* means.'

'We need to get the old bit of paper translated,' Feng said as he switched the phone off. 'It must contain the answer or at least a clue as to what the whole matter is about.' The train slowed and pulled into East Steading and the two men prepared themselves to face whatever lay ahead.

Miss Lightbody was waiting outside the station and as James drew near she held up the keys to his old Jeep. 'You had a rather harrowing time in London?' she asked and he nodded and opened the rear passenger door for his secretary. Feng went around the 4x4 and climbed into the front as James got behind the wheel. He had been declared safe to drive and his licence had been returned two months earlier and he waited until his companions had fastened their safety belts before starting the vehicle and heading for the Forbidden City.

James had suffered from narcolepsy since his twenty-first birthday and had suffered numerous unfortunate accidents until the doctors managed to control his condition with the right kind of medication. However, forgetting to take his morning tablet could still result in paralysis that always heralded the onset of a REM sleeping period that could last for seconds, minutes or even hours.

Extreme emotion wrought by a sudden shock or uncontrollable laughter could still trigger the symptoms and recalling the sight of Han Choi made him thankful that he had taken his tablets that morning. Feng knew of James's affliction for he had saved the investigator's life during a particularly nasty case he was working on. It had involved a drug-controlled would-be assassin seeking revenge.

Just as the street lights were lit James dropped Feng at the restaurant and without saying anything he gave his friend a squeeze of the shoulder before driving off to park in his usual spot.

'We have some work to do tomorrow, Miss Lightbody,' James said as they walked back to the office in a fine, misty rain. She could not understand why he was so reluctant to call her by her first name but Agnes didn't particularly mind the formality for she had a deep respect and fondness for the younger man.

'Do we have a commission?' she asked, ever the practical businesswoman.

'We have a friend who has –'

'We have a landlord, James,' she corrected.

'Very well, we have a landlord whose brother has been brutally slaughtered and I need to find out why. The subject of money doesn't enter into this at all.'

A pencilled eyebrow lifted and the thin lips clamped tighter as she envisioned the expression on the bank manager's face the last time she went to plead on James's behalf.

'I'm sorry, Miss Lightbody, but I saw Feng's brother and I cannot just sit back and leave it to the police. I must do a bit of digging myself.' He daren't reveal how intrigued he was with the whole matter of secret notes, coded text messages and an ancestral Chinese treasure. She wouldn't understand how these things could affect a grown man with responsibilities for running a business.

The slender, middle-aged woman leant against her reception desk and her ice-blue eyes softened as she watched her employer go into his office and slump into the high-backed chair.

James absently picked up a pen and began to doodle on the clean blotter. Miss Lightbody knew he would be lost to her while he pondered the case he had committed himself to solving. Feeling that it was the start of a very long evening she went into a small room leading off the reception area that was filled with cheap steel filing cabinets and a desk with a photocopier and coffee-making equipment.

Miss Lightbody had begun to make strong Blue Mountain coffee, the way James liked it, when the doorbell chimed. She hurried into reception and pressed the intercom switch.

Detective Constable Kent was waiting downstairs.

3

AS JENNIFER KENT OPENED the door and stepped into reception Miss Lightbody greeted her warmly. The two women had first met during a previous investigation when James had needed the help of the local police to uncover a child abduction ring. After they had hugged Jennifer was shown into James's office without any need to announce her arrival.

'Jenny, what a lovely surprise,' he declared as she kissed him on the cheek. 'What brings you to this neck of the woods?'

They had fallen in love some time ago but she insisted on retaining her independent lifestyle for a little longer. She had let James down gently when he proposed marriage and they agreed to postpone any wedding plans for a couple of years.

'I'm sorry James but I'm here on business,' she said as she sat and made herself comfortable. 'Detective Inspector Tilley –'

'Gerald.'

'Right, Gerald instructed me to ask you for the piece of paper and a weird artefact, his words not mine, that are pertinent to a horrific homicide in central London.'

'So, the items that nobody can decipher are now required by Gerald who will no doubt understand them even less.'

'I must take possession and make sure that they get into the hands of a certain inspector Cutler of the Metropolitan Police.'

'Feng and I met that officer at Han Choi's home.'

'Oh my God! The deceased was Feng's brother?'

'He was, didn't Miss Lightbody tell you? Someone took his life in a rather brutal fashion. Feng has the note and the bi but at the moment he is totally devastated and I suggest we visit him tomorrow when he's had a chance to come to terms with what has happened.'

'You're absolutely right, darling, and I'll make sure Gerald understands the delay. We'll get together in the Forbidden City at 10 a.m. tomorrow.'

'Make it 8 p.m. tonight and I'll treat you to one of Mrs Choi's famous Szechuan-styled chicken dishes.'

Jennifer laughed and stood up. 'I can't resist such a tempting offer. Shall we make it 8.30 p.m.?' They hugged and kissed before she tore herself away and Miss Lightbody blew her an air kiss as she went past and out of the door. James told Miss Lightbody to hold the fort and hurried down to the Forbidden City.

The private investigator ignored the closed sign and tested the door. It was unlocked and found the husband and wife were sitting silently in a completely empty restaurant. Contrary to her normal greeting Lin-Lin walked slowly towards him with a solemn expression on her pretty little face. James gave her a brief hug before going to embrace her parents to whisper words of condolence.

The four of them sat around the table in silence until Feng, who was struggling to control his feelings, finally said, 'What should we do now?'

'We will make a copy of the ninth-century note before we are compelled to hand it over to the police tomorrow morning. They are not aware of your cousin Huang's letter so we needn't give them that.'

'I will do it immediately and give you the copy to keep safe,' Feng said more resolutely as he rose to his feet. 'Will you do me a big favour and try to find out what it says. With all the police formalities and my brother's funeral arrangements I won't have time to seek someone who is familiar with medieval languages. If it is Mandarin it's not what I was taught at school.'

'If it's Mandarin at all,' James murmured. 'But I will definitely have it professionally translated so we can find out what makes it worth killing for.'

Jiao was still sobbing and Feng placed a comforting hand on her shoulder before disappearing into the kitchen. There was a whirring sound and Feng reappeared holding a single A4 sheet of paper that he gave to James. 'Good luck, James,' he said briefly before sitting down again. 'If you should want to eat later I will be opening as usual for my regular late evening customers. Jiao insists that we should do this in memory of Han and I agree.'

The investigator was surprised but said nothing and waved goodbye to the grieving family as he left to return to the office.

'We have a pretty difficult task, Miss Lightbody.' were the first words he uttered when he stepped into the reception. James held the ancient sheet of paper above his head as if he were Prime Minister Chamberlain returning from Berlin.

'What is it, James?'

'A message from an extremely distant past in a language that may not be possible to translate.'

Miss Lightbody took the paper and nodding her head slowly scanned the calligraphy. 'I think I can help you here, James,' she said with an optimistic tone to her voice that raised James's hopes. 'My uncle is a project curator in the Mexican gallery at the British Museum.'

'This was most probably written in an ancient city like Xiangzhou and not in the Sacred City of the Zapotecs,' James said disdainfully as he took the paper from his secretary's hand and strode into his office. 'It's a form of Chinese, not Mayan.'

'For goodness sake, James, I know that!' she called after him with an edge of annoyance as though addressing a small boy, 'but my uncle knows a lot of people in the various archaeological departments and I can ask him to help.'

James flinched inwardly and apologized rather sheepishly. Miss Lightbody took the paper and scanned it into her computer before composing a long e-mail letter. Night had been creeping up on them and the constant chattering of roosting sparrows was fading when James switched on the lights. Miss Lightbody attached the PDF file and e-mailed the letter to her uncle's address at the museum.

'We won't get an answer until tomorrow so I suggest you finish for the day and go home,' James said. 'Thanks for your help and for staying so late, Miss Lightbody, I'm sure it will be much appreciated by Feng.'

His secretary smiled, slipped her coat on and left, closing the door quietly behind her. James slumped back into his chair and taking a bottle of The Glenlivet from his desk drawer he poured a large nip. As he slowly sipped the smooth single malt he went back over the events of the day, trying to make some sense of them until he was unable to keep awake. Napping two or three times a day had been recommended by his doctor as his narcolepsy had a habit of keeping him awake at night. Without daytime napping he ran the risk of falling into a deep REM sleep when he least expected it.

It was late-evening when a slight noise disturbed him and he was fully awake in an instant. James sat up slowly, his ears straining to separate and identify all the night sounds. The low rumble of traffic was unchanged as was the creaking of ceiling joists and floorboards of the cooling building. Suddenly he heard the sound again, a brief rattling of metal on metal. Reaching into the kneehole of his desk he gripped the handle of the aluminium baseball club that he kept there for emergencies.

The noise increased and he realized that someone was picking the outside door lock. James speed-dialled Jennifer's number at the police station before creeping into reception and standing by the door with his head tilted to one side to cradle the mobile by his ear while he gripped the bat with both hands that had begun to sweat.

There was a loud click and the door opened slowly. James looked through the gap between the jamb and the door and briefly saw a dark shadow as the intruder entered on silent feet. Suddenly the silence was broken by a loud 'Hello James'. Without realizing it James had pressed the speakerphone button with the side of his head and Jennifer had answered his call.

The door was flung back against him and James staggered to one side, hitting his head against a tall filing cabinet. The mobile fell to the floor as he tried to remain upright and fight the paralysis creeping up his legs. James crumpled to the floor and fell asleep.

With a small hiss of surprise the intruder glanced down at the motionless man and the phone with its screen glowing colourfully in the dark; he hurried into the office where, after a quick search, he found the calligraphic letter he had come for.

'What is it James? What's happening?' The frantic sound of Jennifer's voice continued pleading for an answer as the dark-clothed figure raced down the stairs and out into the night.

Zijin Cheng, the Forbidden City, was awash with loud conversation and the crimson light from the table lamps when the squad car braked hard outside. The flashing blue-and-red light bar drew curious looks from the diners inside. Feng finished serving a regular diner and went out into the street to satisfy his curiosity. He was surprised to see Detective Sergeant Briscoe rushing into Goodfellow Investigations followed by Constable Shawcross who used to be rather unpleasant to James when the investigator first started courting Jenny.

'What's going on,' Feng called out but he was ignored. He was about to pass through the open doorway and climb the stairs when the squad car driver stepped before him.

'Sorry sir, you can't go up there.' The brusque tone of the constable's voice brooked no argument and Feng returned to the restaurant with a concerned look on his face. Jiao met him at the kitchen door and questioned him silently with a raised eyebrow.

'There's something happening upstairs but I'm not permitted to go and see what it is,' he said as they both entered the kitchen. 'I'd put Lin-Lin on watch but it is far too late and she must finish her homework before going to bed.'

'Call Jennifer, she may be able to let us know,' Jiao said as she swiftly chopped a cabbage into narrow strips. Feng's eyes lit up: the Choi family had been close friends of the policewoman since James's last case when she had helped to save them from a disastrous situation. Feng crossed the kitchen and used the old Roladex to find the number.

'What's going on at James's place,' Feng said the moment Jennifer answered the phone. The reply was muted and difficult to understand through the ambient noise of traffic.

'I'm on my way there now, Feng,' she said while negotiating a midtown roundabout. James called me ten minutes ago but all I heard were the sounds of something crashing and falling. He didn't respond even though I kept on asking what was wrong. I then called the station and they should have sent a car by now.' There was a pause during which Feng confirmed the squad car's arrival. Jennifer blipped her siren to overtake a car. 'I'll give you a call as soon as I have something positive.'

Feng thanked her and put the phone down and related the gist of what had been said to Jiao before going out into the restaurant to attend to his customers. He moved about the room with a strained smile for each diner as his brain raced and he kept one eye fixed on the police car.

The staircase was in darkness as they climbed to the first floor. Detective Sergeant Briscoe approached the open door with caution. The reception beyond was dimly lit by neon lights shining through the office window and Constable Shawcross hung back until his superior had switched the main lights on.

The dark huddled shape of James Goodfellow was the first thing to catch Briscoe's eye as he stepped through the open door. He quickly knelt beside the investigator and waved at a nervous Shawcross to go and check the inner office.

It didn't take the sergeant long to discover that James was suffering from one of his spells of narcolepsy that was the cause of his retirement from the police force. Taking a cushion he made the sleeping man comfortable before joining Shawcross who was standing in the office with a puzzled expression.

'Nothing seems to have been touched, Sergeant,' he said, looking round to make his point. 'Is Goodfellow dead?' he asked with restrained eagerness.

Briscoe gave Shawcross a hard look then swept the room with a professional eye before going back to the reception where James was beginning to stir. He tried to open his eyes but was forced to wait until the numbness had faded from his legs and finally the rest of his body. The first thing he saw was the familiar chunky features of his old boss.

'Hello, Sarge. Fancy meeting you here.'

'What happened, James,' Briscoe asked as he lightly touched the bruise that had formed on James's forehead.

The investigator winced. 'I was working late and dozed off. I woke up when I heard someone trying to break into the office. I called Jenny … Constable Kent, and waited behind the door until it started to open. Suddenly Jenny's voice came loud and clear and that's when everything went black. That's all I can recall except for the part when you woke me from my enchanted sleep with a kiss.'

'Very funny,' Briscoe growled as he bent to study the door lock. 'However, we've looked everywhere and nothing seems to have been disturbed.' He grunted knowingly as he looked closer at the lock. 'Except there is evidence that someone crudely picked this.' He gave Shawcross a pointed look of dissatisfaction for not noticing the bright scratches on the metal.

James staggered to his feet and quickly looked round the reception and his office. 'Whoever it was got what they wanted,' he said pointing to the top of his desk. 'I left a piece of paper lying there and now it's gone.'

'Valuable?' Shawcross demanded to know.

'Not in itself but possibly invaluable in its meaning.'

'And what the heck does that mean?'

'It was evidence required by Detective Inspector Cutler in London as part of his investigation into the death of Feng Choi's brother.' James had avoided directly answering the question. 'That's valuable enough isn't it?' he asked in an innocent tone of voice that prompted Briscoe to look at James with some suspicion.

'It seems you are now unable to send it to the inspector which could be inconvenient for you,' the sergeant said and the sarcasm wasn't lost on James. 'Or is it?'

'It's very inconvenient, Sergeant, because I'm now in a lot of trouble with the Metropolitan Police. They could accuse me of making the whole thing up.'

'And did you?' Shawcross scoffed. He hadn't stopped disliking James since the very first day that Jennifer had shown more interest in the ex-policeman than himself.

'No, Roger. I did not.'

Shawcross didn't like the familiar way he had been addressed and he frowned. Before becoming a private investigator James had been a trainee police constable who Jenny had helped when narcolepsy brought about his compulsory retirement from the force. Shawcross had made a point of teasing him about his medical condition making James more determined to prove that he could be the better detective.

The room fell quiet as the two officers stared at James waiting for him to say something more but James remained silent with a slight smile creasing the corners of his hazel-flecked eyes. It was Briscoe who broke the gravity of moment.

'There doesn't seem to be anything we can do here, James. You are completely unable to give a description of your assailant and apart from the slightly damaged lock and the disappearance of a mysterious piece of paper your company has suffered very little loss; as a formality we'll send a crime scene technician to check for any prints. Apart from this the case is closed unless we find a match on police files. In the meantime I suggest you get your locks changed.'

James nodded his agreement as he shook the man's hand and then smiled at Shawcross knowing how much the man disliked him doing that. The officers had turned to leave when Briscoe suddenly had a thought.

'Did the thieves also break into your apartment?'

James slapped his forehead and hurried out of the door and raced up the next flight of stairs. The police followed him to the next landing where James was using his key to open the door.

'Anything missing?' Briscoe called out as James disappeared inside. Shawcross made a point of studying the lock as Briscoe entered the living room. James emerged from the normally untidy bedroom and shook his head.

'Nothing has been disturbed and I seriously doubt if they would have bothered to come up here. They most probably didn't know that I lived on the premises.'

'It's that or they tried your office first and having found what they wanted they didn't have to look any further,' Briscoe said holding James's look. James knew full well that the sergeant meant the piece of paper. The officers took their leave and went back down the stairs and left the building.

Seconds later Feng arrived at the front door. 'Are you alright my friend?' he shouted in Mandarin.

'Everything's fine, Feng. However, someone broke into the office and stole that piece of calligraphy.' James then reassured him that a copy had been made and sent for translation. The round friendly face broke into a broad grin and he gave a wave before closing the door and returning to his restaurant.

James had only just stepped back into the office when Jennifer used the intercom, asking to be let in. This is turning into a musical farce, he thought as he pushed the lock release button and Jennifer ran up the stairs and into his arms with a small cry of relief. She almost immediately pulled back with a frown when she saw the developing bruise on his face.

'Are you quite alright, what happened to you?' and she lightly touched the sore bump. 'All I heard was a big crash and then everything went mysteriously quiet.'

'I'm fine, Jenny.' James pulled her back into his arms. 'I fell asleep that's all.'

'But I thought you'd sorted out your narcolepsy.'

'I have but being hit by a large piece of wood can overwhelm the effects of a Xyrem tablet.'

'A piece of wood?'

'The door, Jenny. Someone broke in, heard your voice, flung the door open and my face just happened to be in the way. Xyrem couldn't possibly handle it and I collapsed. Luckily the intruders thought they had knocked me out and were in so much of a hurry to find what they wanted that when they did they had no need to wake me for questioning and left before Briscoe arrived.'

'They had heard my voice?'

'I had accidentally switched my mobile to speakerphone.'

Jenny tut-tutted at his carelessness as she walked into the office and made herself comfortable in the visitor's chair. 'What was it they were looking for?' she asked as she crossed her long legs. This made her tight skirt ride up and it took maximum self-control for James to focus on her question.

'It was that strange piece of ninth-century writing that Feng received from his brother.'

'So we'll never know what it said.'

James sat down. 'Luckily Miss Lightbody had already taken a copy and e-mailed it to her uncle who works at the British Museum.' As he spoke he couldn't help admiring her auburn hair and the symmetry of her high cheekbones before being drawn to her beautiful green eyes.

'You seem to have recovered quite rapidly judging by the way you're looking at me,' Jenny said and she laughed in a low, sultry manner that never failed to rouse him.

Slightly embarrassed at being caught out James stood up, his mind racing to change the subject. 'How is Claudiu?' he asked, referring to the eight-year-old German boy that Jenny was in the process of adopting.

'You know full well that school is out and that he's staying with Alice in Bournemouth for two weeks while I study for my promotion *and* you're deliberately changing the subject.'

'I think I'd better check my apartment. The intruders may have gone there first,' James said quickly as he strode from the room and climbed the stairs. When he reached the door Jenny was right behind him and he went through the pretence of searching the living room and kitchen once more for any missing items. Entering the bedroom he found Jenny had arrived there while he was in the kitchen and she was sitting on the bed, her eyes fixed upon James.

'Can I stay with you tonight? I can be your bodyguard.'

'You can guard my body at anytime,' he said as he went to lock the front door. For the last six months the couple had been amorously involved and on his return to the bedroom and despite the painful bruise on his face James leant over and kissed her.

A full hour later the couple reluctantly rolled apart and James voiced the need for some form of sustenance. Jenny was also hungry and as they both dressed she suggested that they go downstairs to their usual haunt. They had just entered the virtually empty restaurant when Lin-Lin, her eyes red from crying, disappeared into the kitchen and Feng Choi hurried out.

'What have you been doing? You've been so long in coming down Lin-Lin was worried that something terrible had happened to you. I was on the point of closing up shop for the day and coming upstairs to check on you again.' Feng then became aware of Jenny standing behind his friend and he blushed. 'I'm so sorry, James. Don't listen to this foolish old man's gripes. We can discuss the matter of the stolen paper later.'

Jenny was also blushing and James passed her a mammoth menu behind which she hid and pretended to read the columns of regional dishes. The couple fell silent as they read until Feng bent slightly to speak quietly to James.

'The police have contacted me. They've finished the autopsy and other investigative studies and my brother's body will be released in four days so I will be able to arrange the funeral for the following week. It would honour me and my late brother if you would be able to attend.'

'We both will, Feng,' Jenny said, her voice breaking slightly as she lowered the menu to look at him compassionately.

'That is most kind of you both. Now, what can Jiao, Lin-Lin and I tempt you with?' A trio of smiles dissipated the pall of sadness that had begun to gather over them. James gave both menus to his friend.

'Surprise us, Feng.'

'And let Lin-Lin choose the dessert,' Jenny added thoughtfully.

4

LONDON

THE MUSEUM WAS CRAMMED with boisterous groups of school children when James entered and checked the museum floor plan. The Mayan exhibits were in room twenty-seven and James strode across the Great Court and walked along the gallery displaying themes of *Enlightenment* and *Living and Dying*. Walking through a decorative archway he found himself surrounded by glittering ceremonial belts, blood-letting instruments, double-headed serpents and a group of fourth-formers with i-Pods attached to the side of their heads. A short man with the archetypal appearance of a scholar in a tweed jacket with patched elbows and tan corduroy trousers was droning on about the bare-breasted statue of the Huastec Goddess while the class members, who weren't texting lewd messages to each other, sniggered behind hands and cupped imaginary breasts.

James crossed the room and touched the man on his arm. 'Excuse me, are you the museum guide for this room?'

The man shook his head and went back to lecturing his boys.

James shrugged, saw a man in a smart blue blazer sitting by the doorway and asked him if he knew a staff member called Lightbody.

'You'll find him in the Stevenson Lecture Theatre preparing for a talk on this display.'

James thanked the guide and after many twists and turns of the corridors he came upon the museum's theatre where a tall, elegant looking man with a milk-white goatee beard was sitting at a table studying a set of papers.

'Mr Lightbody?' James asked and the man nodded with an inquiring expression as he put his chipped mug of tea down.

'Do I know you young man?'

'James Goodfellow, I am –'

'Ahhh! You're the private investigator, my niece's employer. My name is Robert.' The Curator rose from his seat with a broad smile on his face and extended his hand. 'Which you undoubtedly know already.' The two men briefly shook hands before sitting at the table that was littered with books and bound documents.

'I don't know if you're aware of it but Agnes talks a lot about you,' the middle-aged man said with a twinkle in his eyes.

'Good things I hope, Mr Lightbody.'

'Especially so, James. Ever since you rescued those poor children last year your praises have been regularly sung to high heaven.'

'I was hoping you might be able to help me with another case that has cropped up. Your niece, Miss Lightbody, sent you a –'

'Do you normally use the family name when talking to her?' Robert had a bemused expression on his face.

'It's an old habit that I find hard to change.'

Robert shrugged, considering the investigator to be a little on the young side to be so formal. 'Well, I hope you'll break your habit with me.'

James smiled as he continued. 'Your niece sent to you a copy of ninth-century Chinese calligraphy that we hoped someone in your department would be able to translate,'

'My secretary gave it to me early this morning and I spoke to my colleague in charge of Oriental studies. He was most intrigued and has been very busy on your behalf. He reads most Chinese languages including various official and non-official dialects of Mandarin. However, the note goes back a lot further than the ninth-century as it is primitive logographic writing which puts it in the region of 400 BC.'

'Oh wow!' it was all James could say and he waited for Robert to continue.

'According to my friend Tristram the origin of the logographic characters is possibly Hanzi and had proved rather difficult to accurately interpret but having spent more than three hours in archival research he was able to identify the characters despite the crude brushwork and put them into a logical order. He was then able to create some form of poetic order.'

While talking Robert had been randomly shuffling bits of paper about on the table that were covered in hastily scribbled notes until he seemed satisfied with the displayed order. He then took the top sheet and passed it to James.

'After breaking it down – ' he waved at the small stack of notes before pointing at the sheet James was holding. ' – that is Tristram's final attempt and although I said he understood the words it doesn't mean they made the message clearer when put together.' Robert reclined in his chair with his fingers steepled on his waistcoat as James read the neat, cursive handwriting.

'It seems to be in two parts but Tristram was unclear as to their relationship to each other,' the curator added.

Children of Huo of Cai,
declare true purity of heart.
Speak with a thousand tongues
on meeting the Ancestor Supreme.

To seek your path to heaven
circle the lowly vessel
that lies within the darkness
of Wangzui.

James put the paper down and looked at the curator with his bewilderment clearly showing. 'This is clearly a set of directions to find something but what does it mean?'

Robert sat upright slowly and read from one of the scribbled notes. 'The Supreme Ancestor was the only true god during the Bronze Age. Certain offerings were buried with people that could be shown to this god to show the true worth of the deceased so he could gain entry to heaven. This may be the meaning of the line 'declare true purity of heart'.

Tristram told me that the offerings were called bi and generally took the form of small discs.' He paused and busily flicked through the stack of papers as he spoke. 'They are not dissimilar in concept to the *Indulgences for the Dead* that were sold to gullible European peasants during the Middle Ages.'

Robert finally found what he was looking for and James saw that it was a photograph of an intricately carved disc. 'The bi were meant to act as envoys to the supreme being and the words 'thousand tongues' written in the message you gave me may have meant a thousand bi although according to Tristram this would be very unusual as the ancient burial sites have revealed that one *bi* was all that was needed to describe a man's true character. This was placed on the chest with five jade plugs in every orifice of the body. The Supreme Ancestor would then know the true character of the man.'

'But why so many burial discs in one place?'

'They may have been gathered from different families during the three-year war at the beginning of the Zhou dynasty when villages and towns were constantly being sacked by the dukes and noble warriors. In fact, the name Huo of Cai is very significant because he was one of the Three Guards who rebelled in 1026 BC against the Duke of Zhou, who was their own brother.'

'So he and his two other blood-thirsty warriors rampaged across China doing all the pillaging, raping and gathering of other people's bi?'

'Not quite the picture I would have drawn. Firstly, it wasn't China in those days and secondly, they were trying to reclaim what had been rightfully given to them by a king and Huo may have been gathering the bi as legitimate spoils of war. Families often gave them as a sign of total surrender. This piece of bronze-age history was spoken of many centuries later by Tang dynasty poets in the *jintishi* regulated verse. The poets claimed that Huo and his brothers were honourable nobles whose lands had been stolen by the Duke on the death of King Wu.'

'And the rest of the meaning?'

'A mystery to me although I personally tracked down a lake that's one of China's five great lakes called Hung-Tse or Hongze. It is 65 kilometres long by 24 kilometres wide. It's very beautiful and is only one hundred kilometres from Nanjing.'

'Is there anything else you can tell me?' James said as he pocketed the translation and started to rise to his feet.

'Yes, there's a bit of bad news actually. I have scrutinized old scrolls which faithfully record that in 1194 the Yellow River changed its course to the south to join the Huai river which had no outlet to the sea. This sudden increase in water volume caused it to spill into the Hung-Tse Lake that subsequently grew to more than twice its original size. If anything had been hidden in a lakeside village it would now be under three- or four-metres of water.'

James thanked Robert profusely for his meticulous help and left the museum a trifle depressed by the way his investigation had reached a watery dead end. On the train back to East Steading James took his notebook out and flipped it open. The last entry was now the only chance he had of finding Han's killer and it was the first line that intrigued him the most: C SALE 2 4350N1112E DCCIA.

His pencil notation teased him with its ambiguous message. 'See sale to,' he muttered and then stopped. Who had Han been selling to and what was it he sold? he thought until he remembered what Han was most interested in. Plates!

James slapped his forehead. Of course! Han had sold a plate to the person referred to in the reference number and that person was most probably the one he needed to find and question. The second line confirmed this train of thought: CHCKPL84DING. WRTH4TUNE. HUANG.

Now all he had to do was interpret the letters and numbers to make any positive progress. The train came to a stop and James hurried back to his office.

Agnes raised a quizzical eyebrow when he entered reception. 'How was Uncle Robert?' she asked. 'Helpful?'

'Your uncle was most kind and was able to give me some interesting research results. You must remind me to send him a Christmas card.' James showed her the neat copperplate translation.

'To do this so fast Uncle Robert must have performed miracles and done a great deal of the research himself. He has often told me how it can take weeks, even months, to get a historic search implemented by his colleagues. He must have bribed someone to jump the queue so you'll have to send him more than just a card. I suggest a large bottle of 12 year-old malt whisky and don't even think of using the company's petty cash.' The last instruction was delivered in a crisp no-nonsense tone of voice.

James winced but nodded his complete agreement. He was unaware of the slight smile on his secretary's face. 'I'm still stumped and all I have is a text message from Han and Feng's cousin who never turned up at Heathrow as promised.'

Agnes held out her hand. 'Let me have a look. Maybe a fresh pair of eyes will be able to see something you've missed.'

James gave her his notebook and went into the office to call Feng downstairs. The restaurateur answered on the second ring. 'Yes James, you have some good news?'

'The note was successfully translated but gives a rather confusing message which may involve bi that had been hidden beside a lake over 2,000-years ago but is now somewhere else.' James read out the poetic lines and then tried to explain the meaning of the cryptic text message. 'It has something to do with your brother's interest in Chinese porcelain. I believe he sold a piece to someone quite recently not knowing that it held an answer his murderer was seeking.'

'Is this becoming a treasure hunt?'

'There's a very good chance it has something to do with a lot of those discs which we're told are worth £2,000 each.'

'You think the answer is on a plate?'

'I'm not sure about that, Feng. What I do believe is that those who killed your brother are also trying to find the same piece of porcelain and they're the bastards I want to find.'

'What can we do now?'

James shrugged. 'I don't know but I'm not giving up. The letters and figures in the text message are sure to be a clue that Huang sent to Han knowing he would immediately understand, whereas any casual reader would remain in the dark.'

'Like we are.'

'There's always light at the – '

'No cliché's James, please, or there'll be no supper for the super sleuth and his beautiful moll tonight.'

James grinned and hung up.

The following day James arrived at the office to find Miss Lightbody had already begun her day as usual. She was poring over a large map of Italy with the tip of her tongue showing at the corner of her mouth. She didn't acknowledge his presence as she ran her fingers along the two rulers she had laid on the outspread map.

'I have it, James!' she declared. 'I've cracked the code and it was no more than two sets of figures to give a global location.'

'What do you mean?' James asked as he looked over her shoulder at the map and saw that the intersection of the rulers was close to the city of Florence.

'Longitude and latitude,' she declared triumphantly as she leant back in the chair, bumping her head against her employer. '43° 50' N by 11° 12' E is right on –'

'Sesto Fiorentino,' he completed as he read the name printed in gothic capitals on the map. He kissed his secretary on the cheek before hurrying into his office and switching on his laptop computer. 'I'll see if I can find any reference to DCCIA in that town,' he called out as he rapidly tapped the keys with two fingers. Miss Lightbody was still blushing from the kiss as she raced to solve the puzzle before him. She had already worked out that the second line concerned a plate and she entered the words ceramic and Sesto Fiorentino into the search window. The choice of sites flashed up and she scrolled down until one particular address drew her attention.

'I've found it!' she cried out a split second before her boss appeared in the doorway holding the laptop on his arm, his expression revealing his excitement.

'DCCIA stands for Doccia,' Agnes pointed at her screen that showed a photograph of a long low building set amongst trees. 'And it's a museum. The Chinese gentleman in London must have sold his plate to this museum.'

James had been tapping away furiously and his eyes lit up further when he found what he knew would be there. 'Doccia was founded by the Marchese Carlo Ginnori who used to manufacture porcelain as early as 1735 but in 1896 the company was incorporated into the Società Ceramica Richard of Milan.'

Agnes was listening intently, her interest growing as she realized why James had been so fascinated with taking the case, even without taking any commission or the normal advance fee.

'Richard Ginnori now maintains the museum in Sesto Fiorentino and it is open to the public on request.'

'I think I know what you will want me to do now James. You'll next be asking me to dip into our dwindling petty cash again.'

'You read my mind, Miss Lightbody, as you always can.' James laughed at his secretary's look of frustration and then he left the office to visit the Forbidden City.

The closed sign was on the glass door but a light tap brought Feng out of the kitchen and he was soon inside telling him about Miss Lightbody's discovery and where it had led them.

'I shall be flying to Florence to see if I can locate the plate that was sold by Han as I believe it holds the key to his death.'

'If you are going to this museum then I will be joining you,' Feng said as James's excitement became infectious. 'You will not pursue this matter at your own cost either my friend. The tickets and all expenses are on me and I insist you tell Agnes that not a penny must depart from her precious petty cash.'

James smiled for he knew that Feng too was amused by Agnes's combative defence of her petty cash. He wanted to protest at the man's generosity but knew that it would prove fruitless to argue with him and Miss Lightbody would kill him if he did. Feng was more determined than James to bring the killers to justice for he had made a silent vow to avenge his brother's death on that fateful London street.

'What about the restaurant Feng? You cannot just leave Jiao to run it by herself.'

'Jiao has a very close friend in Guilford who can help us –'

'He means Martin Lei,' Jiao interrupted as she emerged from the kitchen where she had been listening to the men's conversation. She was wiping her hands on a clean tea towel. 'He is a young man we put through catering school and trained for two years before he left us to become a sous chef at a gastro pub in Surrey.'

'He'll jump at the chance to help us when he learns of my brother's death,' Feng added and James smiled at the big-hearted couple before leaving to instruct Miss Lightbody to book two seats to Aeroporto Di Firenze.

When he entered the office Agnes was holding up a slip of paper. She had already booked two seats on the evening flight from London

Heathrow. 'I knew Feng wouldn't let you go by yourself,' she said and then fought to suppress her look of delight when James informed her of the financial situation. 'First he feeds you better than his other customers and then he buys you a holiday in the sun. Now that's what I call the most generous of friends,' she said with mock surprise.

'I have the distinct feeling, Miss Lightbody, that despite being in the sun it will be far from a holiday.'

5

HONG KONG

Z HU WEN STOOD STOCK-STILL with legs slightly bent and ready to react instantly to any move made by his opponent. His left arm was pressed across his body, double-edged sword pointing down at the sprung floor to his right. Wen relaxed both hands that gripped the silk-bound hilt as he calmly looked through the coarse mesh of his helmet into his opponent's eyes and then at his menacing sword being held aloft with both hands.

As Zhu Wen's employee, Chi Lee was obliged to lose but he had to do so in a convincing manner so that his boss did not lose face. He watched the ancient sword, last valued at $4.7 million, being held casually to one side in one of the many textbook fighting positions and slowly lowered his own weapon until it pointed straight at Wen's chest in preparation for the first strike.

The *jian,* long sword, Wen was gripping lightly was reputed to have belonged to Wang Shih-ch'ung who had deposed the Sui puppet prince at Lo-yang in the spring of 619 AD and proclaimed himself emperor. Wen's researchers had traced its history over the last fourteen centuries but that was as far back as they could go. The archaic legend engraved along the length of the magnificent blade had been of no further help in discovering its true origin. The translation read *Dragon's Breath Is The Last Touch Felt*

By Men Judged Evil and this led scholars to believe that the sword had once belonged to, or had been used by, a public executioner.

Lee's replica *dao,* however, had been forged the previous year in Beijing for the tourist market and the swordsmith had used inferior steel. It was already considerably chipped along its dulled single edge.

When Zhu Wen converted two levels of the new Wimex Consolidated head-office building for his personal use he installed a military-styled gymnasium, a *Wu Guan,* that incorporated an eleventh-century bathhouse. All the floors had been engineered in matured cedar wood to emulate the Japanese *nightingale* system that was used hundreds of years ago in Nijo Castle to betray professional assassins. Special nails in the cedar floors chirped in reaction to yhe slightest change in foot pressure.

It was those unavoidable sounds that advertised Lee's next move and Wen stepped back the moment Lee stepped forward to lunge with his blade. With lightning speed Wen moved to his right and Dragon's Breath glittered in a horizontal sweep to strike Lee in the waist with a satisfying thud.

The sword sliced through the thick leather with an edge that had not lost its keenness for twenty-one centuries. Fortunately Lee had taken the precaution of wearing a Kevlar-lined vest beneath the ancient corselet. He staggered, instinctively drew back and then lunged once more at Wen, the tip of his sword striking and slipping between the turtle shells covering Wen's medieval leather coat and he staggered back with eyes flashing angrily.

'You dare to strike!' Wen ripped the protective helmet from his head and threw it across the large room. 'My first hit would have cut you in half. You were mortally struck and therefore would have been totally unable to retaliate.'

'My sincere apologies, sir. It was a natural reaction to your hit and the point is yours?' He looked across the room to where a beautiful young woman was seated at a desk with an abacus before her. Jing flicked a carmine-tipped finger and a counter slid along the wire to click to a stop. She looked up to nod at Chi Lee and then gave her master a satisfied smirk.

'That was the final point and it makes you the winner of the match, sir,' Lee added lamely as he sheathed his sword.

Wen had hardly been listening to the personal trainer. While stripping off his armour he discovered a tiny drop of blood that had soaked through his expensive silk shirt. He summoned Jing with a crooked finger and she hurriedly left her desk to take a first aid box to the wounded man and tend to the tiny cut. Wen stripped off his shirt revealing the green-and-red dragon that coiled about his body. A small trickle of blood had run from the wound in a scaly tail that looped around Wen's navel.

'Congratulations Lee, you've drawn first blood,' the CEO of Wimex Incorporated said quietly as he pointed his sword at the younger man. Lee's crestfallen expression had turned to fear when he saw the red stain on the shirt and then the blood being dabbed with cotton wool. Jing used a strong disinfectant before applying a small plaster. She then took the sword offered by her master and stepped back a pace to await further orders.

'My apology, sir, my apology,' Lee stuttered as he watched Wen refasten the buttons of his shirt before taking Dragon's Breath back from the girl. There was a short scream as Wen lunged to push the tip of his sword between the side fastenings of the leather armour and into Lee's body.

'Second blood to me Lee and your apology is accepted,' Wen said casually while wiping the blade on a piece of clean linen before turning away and striding to the door at the far end of the *Wu Guan*. 'Don't be late for the next practice session.'

The willowy secretary picked up the medicine box and hurried after her employer, leaving the personal trainer clutching his side with fingers that dripped blood onto the immaculately polished cedar wood.

Wen stripped off every piece of sweat-stained clothing as he made his way along the corridor to the changing room and his secretary picked up each item as she followed, admiring the coils of the dragon writhing on the muscular body that strode ahead. A powerfully built man in a white robe was waiting at the door to the bathhouse. Zizhou bowed as Wen handed him the sheathed sword. The door opened automatically and he went into the bathhouse where two young girls wearing nothing but shameless smiles greeted him.

As Wen was being shampooed and bathed by the girls his secretary returned to the main office where she checked the latest incoming mail on her computer. Her almond eyes raced over the jumble of indecipherable e-mails with cool indifference but when she picked up Wen's mobile phone and checked the last text message she felt an icy chill run down her spine. She unlocked the safe and taking the numeric codebook she decrypted all the other messages from Wen's agents who were located in key organizations worldwide. None was important and she replaced them in the tray on Wen's desk.

With shaking hands Jìng reread the last message. She pocketed the mobile with the message from Hong Kong still glowing on the screen and hurried to the bathhouse. The bodyguard was still standing by the door but seeing the urgency of the girl's approach he triggered the remote control and the door swung open.

Wen was stretched out on the marble table while the two masseuses expertly kneaded his naked back and thighs. He turned his head at the interruption and looked at the woman with half-closed yet quizzical eyes.

'My sincere apologies Mr Wen but a situation has arisen in Hong Kong.' She held out the mobile phone and Wen wiped the sweat from his brow before taking it and reading *Huang on 18.30 BA 2 Lndn.*

He sat up with a shout of anger and threw the phone into the plunge pool. 'Get me Seán O'Rourke now!' He screamed at Jìng and the girl hurried back to the office. Wen sat on the edge of the marble slab deep in thought while the two girls stood waiting uncertainly.

'Dry me,' he suddenly commanded and then pointed to one of them: 'Fetch my clothes.' The girl raced to do his bidding and Wen was soon marching down the corridor in a dark three-piece silk suit followed by Zizhou who carried his sheathed sword.

Wen's quick brain and criminal associations had made him a multi-millionaire but now he was confused and seemingly unable to save a situation that had gone beyond his control. He had just lost the chance of possessing the bi and an ancient message that were the sole clues leading to the recovery of property belonging to his ancestor's greatest enemy. Drastic counter-measures were called for.

Jìng was waiting by Wen's desk as he stormed into the office. She had already dialled the number when she handed him the phone and it was already ringing when he took it from her and settled into the high-backed leather chair.

'Seán O'Rourke,' said a lilting baritone Irish voice.

'I have a job for you, O'Rourke,' Wen said quietly. 'It involves travelling and the recovery of certain items that were among the personal effects of a man who travelled from Hong Kong to London yesterday.'

'Is Mr Shing aware of this matter, sir?' O'Rourke was referring to the principal triad leader who controlled the city and was Wen's immediate superior.

There was only the slightest hesitation. 'Naturally.'

'The usual fee plus expenses?'

'Yes. I also want you to visit one of my men in Hong Kong who made a fatal error.'

'His own?'

'Yes.'

'Text me his name, address and a picture.'

'Jing will send that now and I expect results within twenty-four hours.' Wen rang off and nodded to his secretary who immediately began sending information from her laptop that would terminate the triad member who had failed to prevent Inspector Xiao Shi Huang leaving the country.

Zizhou placed the sheathed jian on the lacquered side table and with his hands clasped behind his back waited silently by the expansive mahogany desk for his orders. Wen ignored him and began reading the decoded e-mails that had been placed discreetly near his hand while he had been talking to his enforcer.

The latest e-mail drew his attention. It was a brief message revealing that Inspector Huang had been shot in the back yet had survived long enough to board his flight to London. He died during the flight and was found by a flight attendant when the plane was halfway to Heathrow. Wen made a note of the sender's initials so that O'Rourke could be informed.

Wen dearly wanted to keep all knowledge of the items he wished recovered to himself but in order for O'Rourke to find them he was compelled to send a text message from his own phone.

FLORENCE

James and Feng left the terminal and took a taxi for the five-kilometre drive to the Museo Di Doccia, a long contemporary building that looked more like a factory than a museum. When the two friends entered the building their breath was taken by the displays of exquisite porcelain perfection artfully lit by hidden spotlights. Life-size nudes vied with giant vases and miniature figurines but it was the array of plates within the glass cabinets that fascinated the two men.

Senor Paulo Ambrosini watched the two strangers closely as they entered the museum carrying light overnight cases. He was intrigued by their apparent interest in the plates and approached them with a broad smile of welcome.

'Buon pomeriggio, signori! Parli Italiano?' he asked politely while studying them for clues as to their origins and reasons for visiting such a specialist museum.

'Scusi, non capisco,' James replied, virtually exhausting the phrases he had gleaned from his Italian pocket book.

'My name is Paulo Ambrosini and I am one of the senior curators. How can I help you, gentlemen?' he said taking the hand that had been offered and shaking it lightly before taking Feng's hand.

'This is Mr Feng Choi and I am James Goodfellow. We phoned from London to make an appointment for a viewing. We are very interested in looking at an item that was sold to your museum a short time ago by Mr Han Choi who lived in London.'

'I would like to know why you wish to see that particular piece before I can fully answer your request,' Paulo said as he held James's gaze.

'My friend was Mr Han's brother and we are curious about the plate that was disposed of only days before his death.'

'My condolences, Mr Choi,' Paulo said with a more sympathetic tone of voice as his gaze switched to Feng who was holding out his open passport as proof of his identity. 'Would you kindly follow me to the upper level where we store the more valuable pieces of early porcelain and china.'

The three men ascended the stairs at the end of the long gallery and Paulo led them into a private office. A uniformed security guard was sitting at a plain steel desk and he eyed the two strangers with professional suspicion until the curator nodded.

'Where are you from?' Paulo asked while taking a key from his waistcoat pocket and unlocking a heavy door.

'As I said, we've just come from London,' James answered as the door swung open and the lights came on automatically in the strongroom. They followed Paulo inside and were surprised at the beauty that suddenly dazzled them.

Shelves crammed with eighteenth-century coffee pots, cups and saucers covered in gilt and fine illustrations lined the walls. Paulo took them to a small lacquered display case in the far corner and using one of the many keys he kept on a ring he unlocked and raised the lid. The two friends looked over his shoulder and saw the plate Han had once owned.

'Our tests have shown that it is of the Ching dynasty. That was when blue-and-white wares were being fired at a very high temperature to give them a more brilliant look than the enamel glazes of the Ming dynasty,' Paulo said and putting on a pair of silk gloves he held the plate up to the light so the two friends could see it more closely. 'The tri-colour wares of the seventeenth-century had been replaced by the blue-and-white and polychrome approach of the eighteenth-century and this is a perfect example that we have attributed to a brilliant ceramicist called Ogata Kenzan.'

James was only half listening to the curator for his imagination had been caught by the scene captured by the brush of an old master. Mountains and trees followed the meandering path of a river that was crossed by a tiny arched bridge of stone. The sweeping motion of the brush tip had captured the spring season for the three blossoms in the foreground were fully open.

'May I take a picture?' James asked and Paulo gave a nervous grin, nodded and held the plate steady.

Using the new i-Pad that Miss Lightbody had bought for him James recorded many angles and close-ups of the Chinese characters that flowed around the lip of the large dish. Paulo then turned it over to show the maker's seal plus one other beside a column of characters.

'We have translated this to read *"Beneath the high place seek the stone dog for heaven's gate"* and one of the seals is that of Kenzan himself but the other is impossible to decipher,' Paulo continued after James had finished taking pictures. 'On close analysis we are of the opinion that the script beside the seal is of a much later date.'

'You mean the cryptic phrase?'

'Yes, the calligraphy is by a modern hand but the rest of the plate including Kenzan's seal is original.'

'That's a mystery,' Feng murmured and all three men nodded in silence.

'I do hope that this is the plate you came to see and that your trip hasn't been a waste of time.' Taking great care Ambrosini placed the plate back in the display case and locked it.

'One final question, where was the purchase finalized?' James asked and was puzzled by the curator's answer.

'It was arranged for payment to be made and the plate to be given to the museum's representative at the Rialto hotel in Venice.'

'Thank you Signor Ambrosini, you have been very helpful,' James said as he scrolled through the pictures rapidly before closing the tablet. 'Is there anything else you'd like to see Feng?' James asked turning to his friend who was deep in thought.

'I think we've seen all we want to see James. Let's go home.'

Ambrosini escorted the two men to the main entrance, formally shook hands with them and gave a tentative wave as they walked down the long drive to the main road where they managed to hail a passing taxi. The visitors had disturbed the curator with their questions and he had begun to think of ways to protect his investment.

The flight back to London was uneventful and the next morning Miss Lightbody, delighted at being presented with only a few inexpensive receipts, put out extra bourbon biscuits with the morning tea.

After Feng had checked that Martin Lei, the temporary chef, was coping in his absence he went back upstairs and the two men studied the pictures James had taken in the Museo Di Doccia. James had lowered the blinds and was projecting the images onto the only clear white wall in the office.

'Beneath the high place seek the stone dog for heaven's gate,' Feng murmured as he studied the photo of the base. 'With a reference to a stone dog it has to be in China somewhere. Could you show me the front again James?' Feng rose to his feet and slowly walked to the wall, his eyes fixed on the delicate brush strokes that had been applied several centuries ago.

'This looks like a very big river,' he muttered to himself as he drew curves in the air with his finger, matching those on the plate. 'I should be able to recognize it. It was not unusual for these blue-and-white plates to be painted with representations of real places but this is very unfamiliar. I've spent many holidays in the homeland and seen all the major rivers like the Yellow River, the Yangtze, the Zhujiang and –'

'What if the artist didn't actually paint a river but a sea?' James interrupted and went to stand beside Feng. 'I learnt somewhere that the

Zhujiang River is the largest river in south China and that it flows into the South China Sea between Hong Kong and Macau.'

Feng was silent as he stared with new eyes at the porcelain antique. 'You may be right James. Some of the trees along the banks look very much like mangrove trees and they can only survive in tidal environments.'

'Exactly. Somewhere on a coast.'

'But there is that strange-looking bridge and we know that Hong Kong island could only be reached by crude ferries when this was hand-painted.'

'Maybe it's not a bridge. Look closely at the ends of the bridge: though the construction is sharply arched the ends seem to be shaped and decorated like those of a dragon boat,' James said. 'It may purely be symbolic of travel over water.'

Suddenly feeling very excited James rushed out of the office and in seconds was back followed by Agnes who was carrying a large rolled-up piece of paper. 'I picked this up years ago when I was planning to take a holiday in the region,' James explained as they unrolled it on the floor and weighed it down with books taken from the shelves. Feng leant over and realized he was looking at a detailed scale map of Hong Kong, Macau and the New Territories regions. He could clearly make out the Zhujiang river estuary and the many small islands that cluttered its widening mouth.

'I don't understand,' he muttered as he knelt down beside James who was bent over the map and running a finger over a particular group of tiny islands. 'Why are we trying to understand an ancient ceramicist's artwork when the calligraphy, done much later, has to be the answer?'

'Because I don't believe it's just a painting but a very clever way of showing where something of great value may be hidden. This was painted long before the willow-pattern design was created. The now familiar image of three figures crossing a bridge and the lovers' tragic tale was created later to satisfy the taste of eighteenth-century Europeans.' James smoothed the map and pointed to a very small island midway between Macau and Lantau Island where Hong Kong's international airport was located. 'A number of people seem to be interested in what lies at the end of this trail. So much so that they have been willing to kill two people so far. One being your brother.'

'But could it have simply been the plate in the museum?' Miss Lightbody asked. 'That has to be worth a small fortune in itself.'

'There must be something else that's even more valuable or Huang wouldn't have sent the coordinates for the Museo Di Doccia halfway round the world.'

'And you think the answer is here?' Feng stood and pointed at the map with the toe of his shoe.

'Sanjiao Mountain Island,' James declared firmly as he sat back on his haunches. 'It's the only one with the word mountain or high place in its name and it is equidistant from two large land masses that would have been disease-ridden swamps when the plate was first produced.'

Feng looked up as the pastoral scene appeared on the wall again and for the first time he saw a streak of white through the foliage on the left-hand side of the plate. 'You may be right James. This could be illustrating an island and Sanjiao does translate as hill or mountain.' He waved his hand to encompass the left half of the plate. 'That bright streak could be the estuary on the other side but why choose that island. There are any number of islands lying nearby and as I recall they all have pretty high elevations?'

James stood up and scrolled back through the pictures until the under side was showing again. 'Beneath the high place –,' he read as he pointed to the characters. 'I'm assuming that refers to a mountain or at least a very high hill and there is a very good chance that a shrine with a stone temple dog to guard it is nearby.'

Miss Lightbody looked pensive as she left the room to make two fresh pots of tea. Indian Assam for James and herself and Chinese *Lung Chin* for Feng. They always kept a stock of the traditional green tea from Hangzhou which was much appreciated by their landlord. While switching on the kettle she thought about what they had been discussing and for a brief moment a feeling of dread swept through her and she shuddered. She had sensed that the worst was yet to come and her hand shook as she spooned tea into the two pots.

6

HONG KONG

O'ROURKE CHOSE A DISUSED rotting warehouse in the old dockyard to interrogate Wen's inept assassin. Discarded fishing nets and fraying ropes hung from the beams and swayed slightly in the draught as he painfully extracted an account of Inspector Huang's escape before quietly disposing of the man in the dark waters of Aberdeen Harbour.

One unsettling fact O'Rourke had learnt was that another agent was interested in what Huang had been carrying and it was that person's ill-timed interference that had caused the policeman to panic and make a run for it.

The agent was a member of a small-time triad group that had migrated to the city to compete aggressively for the city business. It was a splinter group off the same criminal organization to which Wen and O'Rourke owed their allegiance. Any encounters inevitably ended violently and O'Rourke had an uncomfortable feeling that there was an unknown triad member within that rogue group who had his own agenda for the recovery of Wen's property.

It had taken very little of O'Rourke's style of questioning to extract the number of the British Airways flight that Huang had taken and he booked himself on a flight that left at the same time of day. He knew that he was gambling on a possibility that international flight attendants kept to the same schedule and that those on Huang's plane would also be on his. O'Rourke was quietly pleased when his hunch paid off and during his flight to London he learnt the final piece of information he needed.

Julia Simpson, flight attendant, was a little shy and very naïve when it came to men. Repetitive rejection had given Julia a rather lonely life which made her the perfect target for O'Rourke's adept flattery.

O'Rourke first thanked her for the complementary champagne and then admired her hair, pulled back in a formal French Twist, and the colour of her eyes. She found this irresistible and began lingering by his seat more ferquently.

'Would I be right in saying that you had a bit of a kerfuffle on the plane last week?' O'Rourke casually asked as they crossed the Bosphorus at 30,000 feet and flew out of Asia and into Europe.

'It was terrible,' she said in an excited whisper. 'I found a man who had been shot. He had actually died not far from this seat but I'm sure you read about it in the newspapers.'

'To be sure I did, Julia,' O'Rourke said softly while thinking that his lucky day had arrived. His drawling accent hypnotized the girl into becoming more forthcoming.

'I was so shocked that I came close to fainting at the sight of all that blood. Can you believe it, a dead man on my plane.' She had bent down to whisper in his ear. A colleague passed with a tray of drinks and a smirk on her face and Julia pulled away but O'Rourke continued with his questioning.

'When you landed at Heathrow do you know where they took the poor fellow?'

'Well, it was extremely inconvenient. Everyone had to be kept on the plane at Heathrow because the police had declared it a crime scene. An officer told us later that the death was being treated as "suspicious" which isn't surprising when you consider the man had been shot in his back. At least that's the rumour I heard.'

'But where did they take the body?' O'Rourke pressed.

A call button chimed and Julia stood up and brushed her skirt down. 'Back in a moment, don't go anywhere.' She giggled softly at her own little joke and went to attend to impatient passengers who were insisting on another free bottle of wine. She listened to their alcoholic demands but her thoughts were on how she could go about seducing the attractive Irishman. It was her friend Margaret who whispered, 'Take him to the staff toilet, love. It's hardly ever used and I'll make sure to keep an eye out for you.'

Julia nodded with an embarrassed grin and took the bottle of Merlot to the slightly merry couple who were travelling home after their grand tour of the Orient. O'Rourke cursed silently at the delay but resigned himself to waiting for an answer to his question.

'Ashford Hospital,' Julia whispered as she returned and slipped into the empty seat beside him. 'I overheard one of the paramedics say that the police wanted the corpse to be taken there for a closed-door autopsy, whatever that means.'

'It's a security expression,' O'Rourke said quietly. 'Nobody other than those performing the autopsy can be present and only the homicide team working on the case get to know the results.'

'It sounds terribly exciting but what about next of kin?'

'They get to know the results much later and only if the case is declared closed,' O'Rourke whispered as his hand suddenly crept beneath her skirt. Julia's breathing rate increased and she stood up, looking down expectantly at the charming man with inviting eyes.

'Do you want me to follow you?' he teased.

Oh yes, she thought. I want you so much, and she furtively crooked her forefinger.

'Have you done this before, Julia.' His voice was a deep sexy whisper as he closely followed her past the galley section. The brunette flight attendant was taking sugar sachets from a locker and she looked askance at the tall handsome man with the suspicion of a grin.

Julia shook her head and mouthed 'no' to O'Rourke before shyly entering the vacant staff cubicle. O'Rourke winked at the brunette who was busily pouring coffee and, somewhat jealous, she winked back at the Irishman as she watched him follow Julia into the tiny restroom and close the door.

It's still four hours to Heathrow, she thought.

O'Rourke collected his overnight bag from the carousel and using one of the three passports he always carried he cleared immigration and customs in a matter of minutes.

Giving precise instructions to the cabbie he was soon dropped off outside the dazzling white, four-storeyed hospital on London Road with a grunt of displeasure from the driver. When ranking at Heathrow Airport cabbies anticipated picking up gullible tourists going into London and charging them over the going rate. O'Rourke's ten-per-cent tip seemed hardly worth the effort.

O'Rourke spent some time slowly walking round the building to inspect every entrance and every fire exit. Having studied all the information he could find on the Internet he knew that it was a premier training hospital with a state-of-the-art lecture theatre and a tight security system; once inside he would have to go on instinct to reach the mortuary as the Internet hadn't given any floor plans. Once there he hoped to find the corpse of Superintendent Xiao Shi Huang.

The carbon-fibre knife was comfortably strapped to his calf – after many trials at museums, art galleries and airports it had proved the perfect weapon for it always failed to register on any detectors. Anticipating the CCTV in the hospital he had applied a false beard with gum arabic and now wore a flat cap pulled down to cast a deep shadow over the top half of his face. The small magnetic device held tightly in the palm of his hand could scramble entry phone keypads and activate any ward or departmental lock.

O'Rourke shuffled into the reception area and kept walking as though he knew precisely where he wanted to go until he came to a bank of lifts. He knew from experience that mortuaries were usually in the basement and pushing the down button he hoped that Ashford Hospital would not be the exception.

The white-tiled corridor was empty and he slowly walked along reading the nameplates on every door he passed until he saw what he was looking for. O'Rourke wasn't surprised to find the mortuary door locked as it was lunchtime. He held the device against the face of the keypad and switched it on. There was a slight clicking sound – gently putting his weight against the door it opened soundlessly to reveal a simple reception area with a neatly kept desk and rows of locked filing cabinets. Peering through two swing doors with circular windows he saw a similar set of doors facing him on the other side of a passage.

Without any hesitation he went through and noticed a large window that was curtained on the other side halfway along the passage. O'Rourke assumed that this was intended for the next of kin to discreetly view and identify their beloved's remains and he went through the second set of doors and into the mortuary itself.

A quick reconnoitre of the large L-shaped room showed that he was alone and he hurried to the line of glinting stainless-steel drawers covering the end wall. These had ID tags hanging from the handles and O'Rourke assumed by their smaller size that they contained the personal effects of the bodies that lay in the larger cabinets.

Running his eye over the labels he soon located *Xiao Shi Huang (Superintendent – Hong Kong Police)* and he opened it and pulled out the contents, untidily scattering them on the floor: a bloodied shirt, dark slacks with mud streaks, scuffed loafers and a lightweight raincoat that was heavily stained on the inside; a wallet that contained very little apart from a few Chinese Yuan, 500 Euros and a picture of a handsome Chinese woman holding a small boy. He read Huang's official warrant card and ignored the small bunch of keys on a Ninja Turtle keyring as well as the mobile phone.

O'Rourke ran through the items again but there was no indication of any *bi* or ancient letter. He cursed, pocketed the phone and hurried from the room. As he went through the outer set of doors he almost ran into a petite woman wearing a white coat. She stepped back with a startled expression and a wordless 'O' on her lips as O'Rourke smiled grimly and hurried on to stop the lift doors that were starting to close. The woman's exclamation of surprise and then her loud cry of 'wait' failed to halt the closing doors. The Irishman rose to the ground floor and was about to get into a cab at the hospital rank when the security alarm sounded.

Much later, in the privacy of his hotel room, O'Rourke activated the mobile phone and ran through Huang's message history. The majority related to a few friends, his office contacts in Hong Kong, his wife and Lee Sing Primary School. When he came to the last message O'Rourke realized that the date coincided with Huang's flight to the UK. The name Han Choi meant nothing to him but he made a note of the name and the number.

When he read the message that was sent he quickly made sense of *See sale to* and *Check plate for Ding worth fortune* and knew that he was on the right trail although the coded numbers and letters meant very little to him.

O'Rourke read *4350N1112E DCCIA* over and over while downing a large quantity of Irish whiskey until his befuddled mind vaguely focused on the *N* and *E*.

'North and East coordinates,' he muttered. 'They're bloody map coordinates. That's what they are damn it.'

Reception was unable to provide an atlas and he quickly flung on his clothes and went to Foyles bookshop in Charing Cross Road.

The reference section was on the fourth floor and without any regard for the other customers he squatted in the aisle and opened a large atlas. Using the longitude and latitude figures he had scribbled down earlier he soon pinpointed Florence and the town of Sesto Fiorentino. Moving to the travel section he found a popular guide to Florence and gave a grunt of satisfaction when the Museo Di Doccia was listed. The reference to a 'plate' in the cryptic message suddenly became very clear. O'Rourke placed both books on the same shelf and strode past the frowning woman assistant who had been watching him and left the store. Back in his hotel room he instructed the receptionist to place a call to the museum in Italy and lay down on the bed to wait.

'Paulo Ambrosini, senior curator. How can I help you?' A friendly voice said as O'Rourke picked up the receiver.

'Bon giorno, I am seeking a little information about a friend who I believe donated a Chinese ceramic plate to the Doccia museum recently.' O'Rourke said.

'My goodness, yours is the second inquiry for this particular plate, senor,' Paulo replied and O'Rourke detected hesitancy in the man's tone. 'And unfortunately it wasn't donated, the Museo Di Doccia had to purchase the item for a considerable sum of money.'

'Ah! The other inquiry you received would have been from my brother. We are both trying to find the same plate. Could you tell me if he has seen the actual plate?'

'Mr Choi and his English colleague who may have been your brother were here yesterday and took a number of photographs of the plate,' Paulo said. 'You will be able to see if it is the right plate after looking at his pictures.'

'Thank you, Senor Ambrosini. You have been most helpful.' O'Rourke quickly broke the connection in case Paulo realized that the English visitor to his museum didn't have an Irish accent. So, a relative of Han Choi was in Florence, he thought. I need to talk to this man now. Picking up the phone he had stolen in the mortuary he dialed a number.

James Goodfellow spun round in his office chair to stare at Han Choi's smartphone. Vibrating loudly it was slowly moving towards the edge of the mahogany desk when James snatched it up to check the caller.

The photo identity was that of a Chinese policeman and James waited with bated breath after tapping the photograph to receive his call.

'To whom am I speaking,' a strange voice asked with a lilting accent that clearly originated in Limerick and not Beijing.

'A Chinese cop with an Irish accent. That's a novelty, who are you and where did you get the phone from?' James countered and waited while the line fell silent for a moment.

'I was given this number as belonging to Mr Han Choi. You are not of oriental origin yourself, who are you?'

'I'm a close friend of Mr Choi and he is very busy and cannot come to the phone right now. However, I need you to tell me your name and how you came by Mr Huang's phone. I can then get Mr Choi to call when he is finished for the day or you could give me a message to pass on if your call is urgent.' Once more James waited while O'Rourke thought.

'Can I call him on another line?'

James was becoming tired of playing games. 'Do you honestly expect me to give you any information when you're using somebody else's phone?' he snapped.

'I'm sorry for any confusion but my own battery went flat and Inspector Huang kindly loaned me his phone so that I could make a couple of business calls before we began our descent.'

'You're on a plane?'

'Tell Mr Choi I will come and look for him.'

'What is your name?'

Click.

James closed the phone with a puzzled expression on his face. A complete stranger with an Irish accent had used the policeman's phone and lied about being airborne. This meant that Feng's cousin had been travelling to London when he sent the cryptic message to Han. James called directory information and asked for Heathrow Airport Flight Information and once connected enquired if a Mr Xiao Shi Huang had recently flown to London.

'You will have to check with the airlines,' was the only answer he could get and James tried British Airways Passenger Information.

'Nobody of that name has entered Britain with BA today,' the woman said in a polite, even-toned voice.

'In the last week?' James asked hopefully and there was a long pause as the computer was consulted.

'Are you a relative of the gentleman?' she asked warily.

'No, just a friend of a friend.'

'In that case I unfortunately have to inform you that the passenger travelling by the name of Mr Huang was taken ill on a flight from Hong Kong and sent to Ashford Hospital on the London Road four days ago. I cannot help you any further. Please contact the hospital for any more information.' The apology hung in the air for a few seconds before a surprised James thanked her and rang off.

He called the hospital and once again no information could be given over the phone. However, if he were related to Mr Huang he could present himself to the hospital authorities in Ashford. With a thoughtful expression he cut the connection and then speed-dialled.

'Detective Constable Jennifer Kent,' Jenny said in mock seriousness. 'How can I help you?'

'Jenny, a man called Huang was admitted to Ashford hospital and I have a feeling he may have encountered a problem while flying to England. He is Feng's distant cousin and I'd like to make sure I'm not going to be the bearer of bad news.'

'Just because the hospital staff refuse to give information to a civilian you expect me to be the bad cop?' she moaned with a mock pout he could only imagine. 'You only want me for my useful connections, James.'

'Your body makes me pretty happy, too.'

'So, you'll show your appreciation tonight then?'

'That's not all I'll show you,' James laughed and rang off.

Thirty minutes passed before his smartphone gurgled and Jenny came on the line. 'Bad news I'm afraid, James,' she said. 'Mr Xiao Shi Huang had been admitted to the hospital but was found to be dead on arrival.'

'How did it happen?' James whispered.

'This is the truly awful part. The poor man had been shot in the back and Homicide Division are now in the middle of a full investigation because it seems he was shot during his flight.'

'How did you find that out?'

'With difficulty and now I'm being investigated too. They wanted to know why I was asking questions about the deceased and said that I should keep my nose out of an ongoing investigation. I think you've dropped me into a lot of hot water James.'

'I'm sorry, Jenny.'

'It seems a flight attendant found him when the plane was flying over the Bosphorous and our chaps are now liaising with the police in Hong Kong because Feng's cousin was a police superintendant.'

James winced at the news. 'If someone is going to all the trouble to assassinate a senior Hong Kong police officer while he is flying with a major airline then this is a lot bigger than I thought.'

'There is another theory,' Jenny interjected.

'Tell me.'

'The coroner said that the bullet may not have killed the man instantly as several arteries had been severed in the chest cavity which would have caused the man to die a more slow, agonizing death.'

James thought for a while and then speculated that Huang may have been shot prior to boarding.

'New evidence has surfaced, James, and the new theory is that Huang may have been trying to escape from a number of gunmen on his way to catch the flight and that he was mortally hit during the road chase.'

'That makes more sense to me than firing a gun on an aircraft.'

'That's right. I was told that nobody heard any shots and the passengers and aircraft were searched thoroughly before anybody could deplane. The forensic team didn't find a weapon or any gunshot residue in the region of Huang's seat which is evidence that the shooting took placed before the poor man arrived at the airport.'

'Then the man who used Huang's phone could well be the killer,' James thought out loud.

'What!' Jenny exclaimed. 'You received a call from Inspector Huang's phone? That's not possible. It had been bagged, tagged and filed by forensic in the Ashford Hospital mortuary at the time of the body's arrival.'

'Sorry. I should have mentioned it earlier,' James said and recounted his conversation with the stranger who spoke with an Irish accent.

'That must mean that the killer stole the weapon from the hospital. I'll pass that on to homicide while you go down and break this latest news to Feng,' she said softly and then hung up.

James locked the office door and reluctantly went downstairs to the Forbidden City.

7

A LITHE FIGURE DRESSED in a black skin-tight catsuit and silk hood that partly hid his dark, glittering eyes leapt down from the high wall to land lightly on the immaculate lawn. Fountains hissed in the wide moat that surrounded the building and he swiftly slipped into the water to join the beautiful *coi* carp inhabiting the darkness.

After seven strokes he slowly slithered out to lie alongside an ornamental stone dragon that stood before the mansion. Pingzi lanterns, hung equally spaced but unlit in the loggia. Ironically, their sky-red colour was symbolic of good fortune.

A movement and a flicker of light in the shadows beneath the overhanging roof made the trespasser freeze until he was able to identify a guard lighting his cigarette. With infinite patience he waited until the man had strolled past the dark shadow of a tall shrub that he had used to camouflage his presence. He silently rose to his feet and moving up behind the guard he broke his neck. The killer pulled the dead man down the slope and into the water before returning to the loggia encircling the mansion.

Like a shadow he flexibly flowed up one of the many columns and flittered across the roof to the wooden balustrade of the higher verandah. He paused to check for any sounds and then nimbly climbed over and went to the open window that he had identified the day before with a powerful telephoto lens.

Two frogs noisily competing for mates ended the heavy silence hanging over the estate. The still figure emitted a slight sigh, recognizing this good-luck sign, and filled with renewed *yin* energy he slipped through the window and into the inkiness that lay beyond.

As he flattened his body on the floor his eyes slowly adjusted to the gloomy interior and he was able to see that the room was unoccupied. Leaving a trail of wet prints he crossed to the door and cautiously tried the handle. The door opened on well-oiled hinges but as he took one step into the corridor there was a brief yet highly distinctive sound and he froze, recognizing the nightingale floor alarm.

After five minutes of complete stillness the man began to move again. He took a long step to the other side of the corridor and as he anticipated there was no sound. The part of the floor that was hard against the inside wall wasn't sprung and with his back pressed firmly against it he sidled along the passage until he reached the staircase.

Faint light showed at a partially open door on the ground floor and using the waxed handrail he slid down the stairs. A tentative foot placed on the floor revealed that it wasn't sprung. He stepped lightly to the elaborately carved door and looked through the gap.

Zhu Wen was dressed in a yellow silk robe and sitting before three giant flat-screen televisions. Each was showing a different programme and Wen's attention constantly shifted between an American baseball match, a Japanese quiz show and a pornographic movie involving two heavyweight women. Zizhou was half reclining on a settee by the window while a slender girl in a diaphanous gown that barely concealed her nudity mixed whisky and sodas for both men at an ivory-inlaid table.

The intruder's gaze swept the room until it settled on the long sword that the bodyguard had brought from the Wimex Consolidated building. The weapon was never too far from Wen's side and was cradled on a small coffee table close to the open door. There were also two automatic weapons next to the sword and he suspected that they belonged to Wen and his careless bodyguard. The dark figure made rapid calculations in his head before moving into the room.

Zhu Wen became aware of the dark shadow when it had already reached and unsheathed Dragon's Breath. Zizhou leapt up but was unable to take more than one step before he lost his head to a scything blur of steel. Jing screamed but was silenced as her master's blade swept across her windpipe.

Wen leapt to his feet horrified by the death of his servants but a tae kwon do kick to the chest sent him flying back into the armchair with the sword stopped millimetres from his throat.

'Do you know who I am?' Wen exclaimed as he gasped for air and stared up into the emotionless black eyes.

'I do,' the intruder whispered, his voice muffled by the damp silk hood. 'But I represent someone more powerful than you. He is the one who is your master.'

'You've been sent by Pengfei Shing, the *Mountain Master,* into my home to do violence? What have I done that warrants the killing of my bodyguard and my secretary?'

'I come to teach you that betrayal is not acceptable to my master. I am here because spies in your household have told the *Mountain Master* that you have secretly been seeking something of great value and that you plan to keep it for yourself. You should know that such items of wealth belong to the triad leader, our master, and are not for you to keep.'

'What I am looking for does not rightfully belong to anyone other than my own family members. We've been hunting for these things over many centuries. We were taught since early childhood that it guarantees peace for the souls of our ancestors who have been waiting a long time.' Sweat had begun to trickle down Wen's face and yet he felt an inner calm and was prepared for what he knew was about to happen.

'Then I suggest you tell your ancestors in person that they can stop waiting.'

The unblinking dark eyes hypnotically held Wen's attention as the sword was plunged through his throat and into the plush cushions beyond until only the words *Dragon's Breath* could be read on the blade. Wen's thrashing legs were soon still and the assassin withdrew the sword and cleaned it on the yellow silk of Wen's gown before sheathing it. He glanced around the room and gave a grim nod of satisfaction before using a match to set fire to one of the heavy silk drapes. The figure in black then slipped silently out of the mansion and into the concealing night.

The *Mountain Master* snipped the end carefully with a silver cutter and rolled the cigar between his thumb and forefinger. He had acquired the taste for expensive Cuban cigars while working in America and had recently made a successful bid for 100 Gurkha Black Dragons in hand-carved chest of camel bone. Each rich leafy masterpiece cost $1,150 and the young girl nervously struck a wooden match and held the flame cupped in her palms while the triad leader took his time to create a steadily glowing tip.

'The task has been completed, sir.' The man standing before his smoke-shrouded master bowed slightly before reverently placing Dragon's Breath on the floor with both hands. 'I also attended to the personal bodyguard and his secretary as they may have known what Zhu Wen was looking for.'

'Does anyone else know of Wen's treachery?'

'I recovered his mobile phone to check the latest contacts and found a message that had recently been sent to a man called Séan O'Rourke. He had been given details of a strange container and its contents.'

'Who else?' Another stream of pale blue smoke issued from between fleshy, slightly feminine lips that seemed out of place in the face of a cruel triad leader who held the fate of thousands in his hands.

'The secretary's phone listed the number for a *Straw Sandal*, one of our minor soldiers in Hong Kong, who was found in the harbour with a broken neck and signs of having been tortured, and the number of another who is operating in London,' the assassin said quietly.

'Then you will have to deal with both the western *gweilo* and our triad member in England.'

The man nodded and without saying another word left. It appeared to the girl watching that he dematerialized like a spirit and a shiver ran through her body. Fingers clicked impatiently and Shing pointed to the cold teapot. As she hurried from the room to fetch fresh tea he flung his gown open to be ready on her return.

Shing was able to trace his history back to one of the eight most powerful families in the history of China. They had been named the Eight Immortals by the firm of Bloomberg, the world's most reputable financial analysts who are based in New York. Adored as being revolutionary warriors at the forefront of China's economic birth after Mao Tse-tung's demise the families were soon controlling the fastest growing economy on the planet.

Shing was 52 when he inherited political influence and a staggering amount of wealth that had been amassed by his grandfather. Like his father he continued to ensure that all business dealings were cloaked in total secrecy; to further this he created complex corporate shields to exploit every capital-generating opportunity and increase his power.

By the time he was 57 he had become bored and began investing in triad criminal activities. He was obliged to drink a mixture of animal blood and wine and take the thirty-six oaths before being appointed as a triad *White Paper Fan*. His new role was as a financial and business adviser to all members of his own specific triad. Within weeks he was exposed to the unbelievable profits that could be acquired from drugs, prostitution, counterfeiting, extortion and human trafficking.

Shing had found his true vocation and he rapidly climbed the hierarchal ladder to become the triad's *Incense Master*. The inclusion of deadly aconite leaves in a dish of mushrooms finally cleared his path to becoming the *Mountain Master*. This gave him total control of the whole organization and the power of life and death over every triad member and his family. Shing immediately began to increase the organisation's revenue by leasing container ships and filling them with billions of dollars' worth of luxury cars, cigarettes, chemicals as well as young under-aged girls for the Asian sex market. Within three years he had acquired his own fleet to become one of China's most influential and wealthiest men.

The original aim of all triads was to overcome every obstacle and avenge the triad Five Elders by defeating the Qing and bringing the seventeenth-century Ming dynasty back into power. However, this was of no consequence to Shing for like most contemporary triads he was focused solely on accumulating the most money and achieving total political control of the nation. To this end he demanded total loyalty and obedience from everyone within his control.

Failure to support and adhere to Shing's strategic plan to gain supreme power of the nation was to invite the *Mountain Master's* anger, crippling fines and possibly fatal accidents.

The *Red Pole* is a triad military commander who controls offensive and defensive operations. Although Shing had many men like this his principal enforcer was known only as Xun. His name meant 'fast' or 'sudden' and he lived up to his name with the speedy execution of any man or woman who showed lack of respect and was disloyal to Shing; his dispatch of Wen was an example of his cold-hearted efficiency.

The *Mountain Master's* instructions to terminate the Irishman and the triad member in England had been imprinted on his mind and he was determined to carry out his order or die. On leaving Shing's fortified mansion he was driven by a triad chauffeur to the airport.

When he entered the airport Xun scoured the busy concourse seeking any out-of-the-ordinary activity as he stood near to the British Airways check-in counter. His ticket was scrutinized by the check-in attendant as three of his 'soldiers' moved amongst the milling crowd of travellers. When he finally received his boarding pass he turned and was given the agreed 'safe' signal by each member of the triad team. Xun went through the gate to immigration control and customs and was satisfied that he hadn't been seen or followed.

ENGLAND
While travelling to London on the Heathrow Express O'Rourke used Huang's mobile phone to call directory enquiries and ask for Han Choi's address. A stiff-voiced woman informed him coldly that such information could not be given. After ten minutes of elaborate of lies, delivered with soft roguish charm, O'Rourke finally softened the woman and elicited a street name in central London.

His laptop computer spewed out scores of people called Choi but only one in that particular street. The taxi dropped O'Rourke at the end of Bedford Place and as he slowly walked past Lancaster Hotel he spotted an unmarked police car parked in front of the address he sought. He was within twenty paces of the steps leading up to the bright blue door when a woman emerged from the house next-door. The moment she drew near O'Rourke switched on his most boyish charm.

'Is there some trouble in Han's place?' o'rourke asked innocently, the woman paused, eager eager to gossip with the tall handsome man in the well-cut suit. 'I hope my friend isn't in any trouble,' he continued.

The woman had been reassured by the Irishman's apparent familiarity with Han and she sympathetically explained that his friend had been 'Done away with. Awful like.'

O'Rourke feigned surprise and then shock as she continued. 'It was a terrible thing for his brother to find him like that.' She dropped her voice and moved closer and began describing the scene as told to her by the constable she had befriended.

O'Rourke raised an eyebrow. 'His brother found him?' He was genuinely surprised that Han Choi had a brother.

'Yes, Mr Feng Choi and his friend came to visit Han and they discovered the body in the kitchen.'

O'Rourke had noticed that one of the policemen had got out of the car and was now leaning against it and looking their way. He could be the constable that the woman had befriended and he was reluctant to be drawn into any further conversation.

'I know Feng very well,' he said, cutting short any further gory descriptions of the murder scene that she had to be imagining. He started walking in the direction the woman had intended to go and she kept pace with him. 'He has a business in Limehouse.'

The cherubic-faced woman paused and then hurried to catch up. 'Are you sure you know the Chois?' She was suddenly suspicious of the stranger. 'Mr Feng's restaurant is in East Steading and if you had been a close friend of Han you would have known that.'

The Irishman realized that she knew the family better than he had at first thought; he was skating on thin ice. 'Hadn't you heard,' he said in mock surprise. 'Feng is planning to expand his business further and has decided to open up a take-away branch closer to the former Chinatown in Pennyfields to capitalize on all the bankers in the area.'

The woman stopped with a look of puzzlement. 'Han never mentioned that to me.'

O'Rourke kept on walking. 'Feng wanted to keep it a surprise until the day of the opening night,' he said over his shoulder as he increased his pace to move ahead of a very puzzled woman who was now considering mentioning her conversation to the constable guarding the blue door.

With lengthening strides O'Rourke soon turned the corner and was passing the imposing gates of the British Museum when a thought struck him. It would be impossible for the item Zhu Wen had wanted to already be safely tucked away in the museum. He gave a low audible laugh that amused a passing couple.

O'Rourke took the Northern Line to Waterloo Station and was soon on the stopping train to East Steading. As they rattled from station to station through the lush countryside he took out the smartphone and tried to contact his master but found that his line had been terminated. He felt a shiver of alarm. The next call he made was to a Peter Ming, a triad of *White Paper Fan* rank. Ming, as an administration officer and non-combatant, lived in Knightsbridge where he could present himself as a legitimate businessman. He had been located in London with the sole task of monitoring a team of drug distributors and the grooming of the new girls. He personally reported to Zhu Wen on the financial aspects of all transactions made in the United Kingdom.

O'Rourke was of the higher *Hung Kwan* rank, sometimes also referred to as *Red Pole* and had the right to command fifty fighting men. However, when he identified himself to the triad, Ming immediately became offhand in his manner. 'What do you want, *traitor*?'

'Why can't I contact Zhu Wen,' O'Rourke snapped ignoring the man's accusation.

'He is no more and you are kindly invited to join him,' the man jeered and O'Rourke felt a chill. 'The *Mountain Master* had found him and all his servants guilty of the highest treachery. A head has been taken and yours is to follow.'

'What treachery does Shing accuse me of?'

'It was found that you seek a vast wealth that you wish to keep for yourself which is contrary to the tenth oath you took,' Ming snarled.

O'Rourke immediately recalled the evening at Wen's mansion when he drank blood and wine and made the thirty-six binding oaths. The tenth oath immediately sprang to mind – *I shall never embezzle cash or property of my sworn brothers. If I break this oath I will be killed by myriads of swords.*

'I have embezzled nothing,' he declared.

'Tell that to Xun when he catches up with you.' The phone went dead and O'Rourke knew that he had been thrown out of the brotherhood and into the metaphorical wilderness. He was now fair game for Shing's top wolf or any ordinary triad member who liked hunting men and women. Xun was no ordinary triad for he was a *Red Pole* like himself and his skills as an assassin were legendary throughout Hong Kong and Macao. When Xun was sent on a mission his target had little chance of survival.

O'Rourke left the train when it pulled into East Steading and asked for directions to Choi's restaurant. The stationmaster had never heard of the name Choi but he did know of a very good Chinese restaurant in the High Street and he gave directions. O'Rourke preferred to use his long legs to get there as this gave him the opportunity to think of his next move. He assumed that Han knew of the *ding* and the *bi* and that meant there was a very good chance that his brother, Feng, also knew. He had to convince Feng that it was in his best interests to cooperate and give him any information regarding their whereabouts. If he could get his hands on them and give them to the *Mountain Master* he would be able to redeem himself and possibly be accepted back into the brotherhood.

'Oh damn,' he muttered as he recalled the *Paper Fan's* words. 'I still have Xun on my back.' He turned into the high street and saw the distinctive colours of a Chinese establishment next to a greengrocer. As O'Rourke passed the displays of fruit and vegetables that spread out onto the pavement he also passed a door right beside the restaurant with a brass plaque that read *Goodfellow Investigations*.

O'Rourke paused outside the restaurant and looked through the window at the traditional décor inside. There were very few diners and as he went in he was immediately greeted by a small girl in a check shirt and cut-off jeans.

'Would you like to eat, sir?'

He looked down at the eager face beaming up at him and he nodded. Lin-Lin led the way to a table against the wall and as soon as he sat down she presented him with a menu that was half as tall as herself.

'My father will be with you soon to take your order.' She disappeared into the kitchen and within seconds an oriental man emerged and walked across the restaurant with the mandatory smile of greeting.

'Good afternoon, sir, may I offer you a drink while you choose your meal?'

'Do you have Tsingtao?'

'Ahh, a true connoisseur! I always keep a good stock of my homeland's finest beer for my more discriminating guests. You have been to China recently?'

'I live in Hong Kong,' O'Rourke said sharply in perfect Mandarin and Feng, although surprised by his linguistic skill, sensed the man was in no mood to discuss anything more and he hurried back to the kitchen to fetch the drink.

The chilled amber bottle with its distinctive gold foil neckband and streaming with condensation was placed at O'Rourke's elbow along with a refrigerated glass and Feng stepped back with pencil poised as the Irishman read the list of familiar dishes.

A Kuang Pao chicken stir-fry was chosen and as Feng wrote the order down O'Rourke studied the short man with the round ruddy cheeks and came to the conclusion that he didn't present any physical threat. He was content to let the chef return to the kitchen before asking any pertinent questions.

The tempting aroma rising from the plate put before him galvanized O'Rourke and he spent the next ten minutes engrossed in savouring the delicate flavours until he had finished and laid down his chopsticks. He waved to Feng who was standing by the coffee machines.

'May I have a chat with you, Mr Choi?' O'Rourke said in his friendliest tone and he pointed to the seat opposite. 'Please sit down.'

'The chicken wasn't to your satisfaction, sir?' Feng asked in Mandarin with a mixture of concern and puzzlement as he looked down at the plate that had been completely cleared.

'It was delicious. You are to be commended on the authenticity of your recipe and the presentation.' O'Rourke dabbed the corner of his mouth with a napkin and sat back to look at Feng with a hint of amusement showing in his eyes. He raised his glass and saluted the oriental.

'I have had Kuang Pao prepared by some of the best chefs in the Sichuan Province and I can honestly say that when it comes to Sichuan cuisine you are their equal.'

Feng beamed with delight at such praise and he relaxed. 'Thank you, sir. I am honoured by your praise. It is rare to receive such a compliment in this part of the world and in Mandarin too. I fear the subtlety of China's spicy tastes are lost on the Western palate. When they've finished in the pub and come in here the food, like the Anglo/Indian takeaways, has to burn the tongue to a cinder before it gives any satisfaction.'

'You have my sympathies but perhaps now, Mr Choi, you will honour me and tell me a little about Chinese artefacts. You must be quite an expert on a particular object I seek.'

Feng stopped smiling as he looked into the blue eyes that had become an icy stare. 'I do not know what you are referring to, sir. I think you have me confused with someone else,' he said with a stutter which instantly communicated his nervousness.

'Your brother Han knew how to find the artefacts I am talking about but as it is no longer possible for him to tell me what I wish to know I have come to ask you the same questions, Mr Choi.' O'Rourke was talking softly but with an edge to his voice. Feng looked wildly around the restaurant as though seeking help but apart from two elderly pensioners and a young art student he was alone.

'What is this artefact you refer to, Mr –'

'Just call me Hung Kwan, Mr Choi.'

Feng froze briefly as fear gripped him when he recognized the triad title and he began to stand up.

'Stay!' O'Rourke commanded and Feng sank back down. 'The items I want are a *ding* and a *bi*. You know of what I talk otherwise you wouldn't be so frightened of me.'

'All sensible Chinese are frightened by the triads and you've just declared yourself one of the brotherhood enforcers.'

'Then be frightened and tell me where I can find the objects,' O'Rourke demanded as he suddenly reached across the table and grasped Feng's hand in a vice-like grip. 'If you do not tell me the little girl by the sweet trolley may suffer an accident.' The soft brogue was no longer pleasing to Feng's ear. The man's Mandarin had become the grating sound of an evil monster, a *mogwai*, and it was threatening little Lin-Lin, his beloved daughter.

'All we learnt from Han was that there's something on Sanjiao Mountain Island between Hong Kong and Macau in the Zhujiang River Estuary. I don't know what it is and I don't want to know if it's going to put my family into any danger,' Feng said hurriedly. 'Now leave us in peace.'

'That's not enough, chef! How did you learn of Sanjiao?'

'I told you, from my brother.'

'Your brother had been killed before he could tell you.'

Feng remained silent.

'You also said "we" and I want to know who else knows of this matter?'

'I do!'

The strident voice behind O'Rourke caused him to spin in his chair. A handsome man holding a heavy walking cane was poised on the balls of his feet and his expression unsettled O'Rourke.

'And you are?'

'James Goodfellow, private investigator and a friend of Feng's, who are you?'

O'Rourke stood and saw that he was an inch taller than Goodfellow. As he reached inside his jacket James stepped back and gripped the stick in readiness for any offensive move by the Irishman. O'Rourke calmly took out an expensive calfskin billfold and tossed some banknotes onto the table.

'That should cover the Kuang Pao plus a handsome tip for the excellence of the cooking,' he said and strode from the Forbidden Garden. 'You will be hearing from me soon, Mr Choi,' he concluded without looking back. 'Give your daughter a hug for me.'

8

'WHO THE HELL WAS THAT?' James exclaimed, aware that the Irishman had upset his friend.

'A guy who was claiming that he was a triad from the old country,' the chef muttered, trying to stop his hands from shaking as he looked across the room to where Lin-Lin was happily folding table napkins in readiness for the evening trade.

'His Chinese sounded authentic but can there be such a person. I thought that the brotherhoods were restricted to Orientals only.'

'That's true but I have heard it whispered on the Internet that there is a Chinese secret society called the Green and Reds who have six million members.' Feng sat at one of the tables and pointed to the seat opposite. A trifle puzzled by Feng's news James sat down and waited for him to continue.

'The Green and Reds regularly use Western-looking assassins to carry out contracts in the West where an Oriental face could draw attention. I believe that I was talking to one of those killers and that the man knows all about the artefacts we're now looking for.'

'Did you mention anything?'

'He threatened me by saying harm would come to Lin-Lin if I didn't answer his questions truthfully so I told him that we thought the *ding* and *bi* could be on Sanjiao Mountain Island.'

'You did right, Feng. If anything happened to you or any member of your family I wouldn't be able to forgive myself.'

'You cannot blame yourself for it was Huang who started it all, not you, James.'

'I know but it was I who found the whole thing exciting and a challenge that couldn't be turned down; now, due to my foolhardiness, it's brought this dangerous man to your restaurant and a threat to your family.'

'You don't know that for sure James. However, the big question now is what should we do about it. He thinks we have all the answers to the whereabouts of the items which means there's a good chance he will return.'

'Well, he knows that Sanjiao is our last clue and as I certainly wouldn't be able to convince Miss Lightbody to break open the piggy bank for a trip to Hong Kong I'm sure this treasure hunt will be ending in East Steading.'

The two friends were in silent meditative thought, trying desperately to come up with an answer to their situation when the door burst open and three armed and armoured police officers stormed in with Heckler & Koch sub-machine guns at the ready. The elderly couple just looked round at the disturbance, noted the armed response officers and carried on sipping their coffees as though it happened every day. The art student wisely ducked beneath her table with a spring roll in one hand and her iPad in the other. James rose to his feet and spread his hands as if to say, 'what the hell is all this about?'

'It's okay James, it's me,' a familiar voice called out and Jenny, wearing a Kevlar vest that was two sizes too big for her, emerged from behind the three burly men.

'Are you and Feng okay?'

'Why wouldn't we be?' James said as he watched the officers spread out to check the occupants of the restaurant and the kitchen.

'Ashford police did a check on Huang's missing mobile phone and found that it was still alive and active. It was then traced to this spot only fifteen minutes ago which means the person who stole it from the hospital is, or had been, in Feng's restaurant,' Jenny explained.

'He was,' James answered. He then gave a quick description. 'Roughly 35 years of age, six foot two, black hair cut short, blue eyes and wearing a dark blue business suit.'

'He also spoke with a strong Irish accent,' Feng added as he put his arm around his wife who had come out of the kitchen. 'He had recently flown in from China, speaks excellent Mandarin and has impeccable taste when it comes to Chinese food.' His nervous laughter stopped when he recalled the cold way in which O'Rourke had threatened Lin-Lin.

'He also claimed that he was a senior member of a triad organization,' James said, he completing what Feng had told him.

Jenny frowned. 'According to that information he has to be a professional assassin. That makes him very dangerous and an undesirable visitor to our shores. I'll check with Sergeant Briscoe to see if this doesn't justify a country-wide alert to apprehend him.'

'I would prefer it if he was caught, tried and locked up for life for he may have been my brother's killer.'

'Why do you say that, Feng,' Jenny asked as the other police officers returned from searching the premises. One officer approached their group while the other two left the restaurant and James recognized the friendly face showing beneath the helmet and visor.

'Hello, James,' Detective Sergeant Briscoe greeted the investigator and then turned to face Feng. 'Yes, why do you say this man killed your brother, Mr Choi?' He removed the helmet and ran fingers through his ruffled hair while waiting for an answer.

'Firstly, he had somehow got hold of Huang's mobile phone and secondly, he said Han couldn't tell him anything about the artefacts because he was dead; he wouldn't have said that unless he had been to Bedford Place and possibly killed Han.'

'That's only conjecture on your part but you could be right.' Briscoe turned to Jenny. 'You have my permission to issue that alert Constable, but make it regional. Let's catch the suspect before he has a chance of doing away with any more people.'

'So you do think this man was also the killer of Huang Choi on the London flight?' James asked.

'Not at all but I am beginning to have my suspicions even though there was no record of a man of Irish descent on Huang's flight.'

'This damned man is making a point of killing all of my family, you've got to catch him, Sergeant.'

James touched Feng on the arm to calm him down and get his attention. 'I suggest you lock up well tonight and have my speed-dial number to hand,' he said softly, not wishing to upset the man any further.

One of the armed officers re-entered the Forbidden City and spoke quietly to Briscoe who turned to James. 'I will leave D.C. Kent with the Choi family tonight. Further tracking of the mobile phone has put its location only half a mile from here and I will be taking the team to investigate. Hopefully we can end this affair tonight.'

Jenny nodded and Briscoe briefly waved to the two men before leaving the restaurant. They heard the tyres of the police van squeal as it accelerated away.

Feng disappeared into the kitchen while Jiao went to console the art student who had just emerged from under her table and was dusting herself down with a clean napkin. The elderly couple had finished their coffee and the man was waving his hand to get Lin-Lin's attention.

James moved close to Jenny and murmured in her ear, 'I'll be eating all alone tonight as you seem to prefer the company of a Chinese family.' James brushed a lock of hair away from her eye.

'I'm sure they'll be a lot more entertaining than an investigator with sex on his mind,' she teased.

James laughed and tapped her nose lightly. 'Take the advice I gave to Feng and be ready to speed-dial,' he said without any humour in his voice. 'The Irishman may not be found by Briscoe tonight and he may yet come back to continue his conversation with Feng.' They kissed briefly and the intimate mood evaporated as Jenny's phone rang.

She replaced the phone in her bag and sighed, 'That was Briscoe and you were right, they found Huang's phone in a street litter bin nine hundred yards from here but there wasn't any sign of an Irishman.'

Jenny was reassured that James would be only two floor above her but she knew in the time it would take to wake up and rush down to the Forbidden City a great many things could happen.

O'Rourke had only walked a short distance before he heard a screech of brakes outside the restaurant and the clatter of boots as the armed response team rushed inside. How did the police discover his whereabouts so fast, he wondered, until, he realized that the phone he had stolen from the mortuary had undoubtedly been traced.

Walking swiftly for another five minutes he discreetly dropped it into a bin attached to a lamp-post and then circled back using the service streets running behind the shops. Arriving back in the high street he was in time to see the police leaving the restaurant and speeding off in the direction he had originally taken It wouldn't be long before they found the phone.

The sun was setting and the light fading fast when the assassin slowly walked past the restaurant on the opposite side of the road and glimpsed the policewoman inside. She was standing close to the tall man who had confronted him with the cane.

I'll talk to the owner when those two have left the restaurant, he thought and walked on to the nearest public house where he could while the time away without drawing attention to himself. He ordered a pint and picked up a discarded newspaper that he read in detail until he felt a sufficient length of time had elapsed.

Streetlights were casting their yellow light when O'Rourke walked down the high street to the Forbidden City. The last diners had left and the restaurant was in darkness. He peered through the glass but the gloomy interior revealed nothing and he decided to try another way to gain entry.

The service street he had used earlier was in poor condition and he took each step carefully, feeling his way in the dark to the plain wooden gate at the rear of the restaurant. O'Rourke took a small can from his jacket pocket and dribbled some WD40 onto the hinges. After a few seconds he pushed the gate open without making a sound and stepping lightly he made his way to the back door. O'Rourke brushed his fingertips over the lock and with a satisfied grunt took two lock picks from his pocket. After only a minute he heard a satisfying 'click' and the door swung open.

O'Rourke crept through a small lobby and into the restaurant kitchen where he paused to orientate himself. He could hear liquids simmering on the huge range – someone was preparing a dish and could be returning at any moment. He bent double and made his way to an open door that stood across from the swing doors leading into the restaurant. A glimmer of light showed under the door at the end of a passage and oriental music could be heard – the closed door muffled the Chinese singer's falsetto voice.

'Don't move an inch if you value your life,' a deep voice said behind O'Rourke and he felt the pressure of something sharp in the small of his back. He was taken completely by surprise and froze on the spot. He was suddenly blinded as the person behind him tripped the hall-light switch; his attempt to turn round was aborted by another painful jab of the weapon.

'Don't even think of moving again,' the voice instructed before shouting out, 'Feng! Come out. We have an intruder.'

The door at the end of the passage was flung open to reveal Jenny who looked at O'Rourke in amazement. 'Looks like you were right, James, he did come back.'

O'Rourke realized that the person behind him was the man he had seen earlier and that the woman confronting him with a pair of handcuffs dangling from her right hand had to be the policewoman he had seen in the restaurant with a man she had called Goodfellow.

'I think the expression is, fair cop, guv,' O'Rourke said with an attempt at humour. And then he laughed. 'You have a very light step,' he added half turning his head to catch a glimpse of the weapon being pushed into his back only to receive another painful jab.

'Stay perfectly still while the lady puts the handcuffs on you.' James instructed and Jenny moved forward, indicating that O'Rourke should extend his wrists. As Jenny reached to take his hand O'Rourke grabbed hers and spun round to use her as a shield. He glimpsed the potato peeler in James's hand and laughed as he put his arm around Jenny's throat and pulled her close to him. The other hand had swiftly retrieved a short throwing knife from inside his sleeve and he held it to her throat.

Feng was behind O'Rourke and had started to advance when the Irishman turned sideways to reveal the threat to Jenny's life. Feng stopped with a look of horror and looked at James with a silent question.

'What now?' O'Rourke laughed as he read both their minds. 'I'll tell you what now. You will both back away and let me leave but not before you've told me where to find the artefact.'

'Artefact, what are you talking about?' James asked while trying to disguise his dismay.

'Play with me and I'll play with your friend's throat,' O'Rourke hissed. 'I want the *ding* and it seems every other person in the world is looking for it too.'

'You're the one who killed my brother,' Feng shouted.

'You are quite misinformed there. I was visiting Han Choi to ask him about the *ding* when I found the police hanging about outside. I then learnt about his death from a woman who lives next door and knew your brother well enough to have tea with him on many afternoons.

'I don't believe you,' Feng shouted. 'Han would have told me of any friends he had.'

'I couldn't care less whether you do or don't accept my word. All I want from you is the location of the *ding*.'

'People are being killed for this bloody museum piece which can't be worth a man's life. Is it the *bi* it contains?

'*Bi*?' O'Rourke looked puzzled. 'What *bi*? I'm not bloody interested in honey.'

'*Bi* is a sacred disc and the *ding* contained a great many of them,' Feng said with a furrowed brow. He was equally puzzled that the man didn't know of the precious jade discs.

'I don't care about ancient crap. I only want the *ding* and the object that was hidden in it. Now where is it?'

'It's on Sanjiao Mountain Island.'

'And that's all we know,' James said as he studied the man holding the knife. 'You told my friend that you were a triad yet you don't look like one to me.'

'Then you would be correct for although I took the oaths and professed loyalty to Zhu Wen, the triad leader in Hong Kong, I really owe my allegiance to a completely different organisation in Europe.'

'IRA?'

'Good God, no!' O'Rourke exclaimed. 'Just because I'm Irish is no reason for you to jump to conclusions and assume I belong to the Republican Army. You're wasting my time so just tell me how you found out that the cauldron is on Sanjiao?'

'A decoration on a blue-and-white plate depicted the location.'

'The plate in the Doccia Museum?' O'Rourke exclaimed in frustration. 'We've known all about that for a long time and we've also been to the island and searched it from top to bottom. We found nothing there. No *ding*, no *bi*, whatever you call them, and no bugs.'

Feng tried another approach. 'If you're not a member of a triad organization that's interested in the *bi* and you're clearly not Chinese why do you want an ancient pot that has ancestral value only in China?'

'You're still wasting my time and it is obvious you haven't a clue as to where the *ding* has now been hidden.' O'Rourke suddenly propelled Jenny towards James. They both staggered backward enabling O'Rourke enough clear space to slip into the kitchen and through the double doors into the restaurant. He ran to the front door that James had neglected to lock and he darted out and disappeared into the damp darkness beyond.

James steadied Jenny and ran after the Irishman. Light rain and bad lighting made it impossible to see very far. O'Rourke had vanished and James went back into the Forbidden City and locked the door behind him.

'Well, we learnt one thing tonight,' Jenny called across the restaurant. 'Our mystery intruder didn't kill Han and doesn't have the artefacts which must mean that someone else is roaming about out there and waiting for the opportunity to do the same thing to Feng.'

'Thanks a lot, Jenny,' Feng mumbled. 'That bit of news does wonders for my confidence.'

'Sorry Feng, but we have to face facts. It's not just the triads who want to get their hands on the *ding*. There's another group of people or an organization competing for the same prize.'

James held up his hand and the two fell silent. 'My biggest concern is not who's chasing this pot of gold at the end of the rainbow but O'Rourke's complete ignorance concerning the rare *bi* the *ding* is supposedly filled with. He seemed to be more anxious about something else that has been put in the vessel that he referred to as bugs. Where the fortune in jade has gone is anyone's guess.'

The trio fell silent as they considered the implications of his words.

'If the *bi* have been removed and replaced with something else then that must be worth a great deal of money,' Jenny said before taking a sip of the green tea that Lin-Lin had put before her.

'Correct, Jenny, and that something has to be a lot more than the estimated £2 million at auction that the *bi* could fetch.'

'The word "bugs" seems to be our only clue and that could mean anything from nasty beetles to advanced listening devices,' Feng said as he watched Lin-Lin placing napkins on the tables. 'It may even be something to do with advanced military technology, some kind of weapon which would explain why so many different organizations want to get their hands on it first.'

I wonder what the hell it is, Jenny thought, and she shivered.

9

MAJOR HUGH WATERSTON ENTERED the drawing room by the French windows and limped across the Hafiz, Maku and Kashmar carpets to answer the phone on his desk. He had taken a rifle bullet in his left leg five years ago while gathering military intelligence along the Lhasa River in Tibet. A Chinese border patrol had caught up with his four-man team and a sniper had knocked him off the path and into the river where he was swept to safety as his sergeant and two privates were pinned down and eventually killed. This incident had subsequently left him with one leg shorter than the other and he was invalided out of the army on a modest disability pension.

A year after his full recovery the Secret Intelligence Service, MI6, offered him the position of a training officer to teach field operatives everything he knew about the intelligence service of the Chinese military and their methods of operation.

The major also held another position that he considered much more important: he was the Chairman of the UK branch of a secret society called the Illuminati. Adam Weishaupt in Bavaria founded this organization in 1776 with the sole purpose of opposing any prejudice over public life including abuses of state power.

As a secret society it was outlawed by the Bavarian ruler Karl Theodore and disbanded only to fragment across Europe and emerge as a number of different societies with the same name but very diverse goals. It has even been claimed that the Illuminati was the secret force behind the French Revolution.

The major stroked his moustache in both directions while picking up the receiver. 'Major Waterston,' he said briskly.

'We have a small problem, sir,' a familiar voice said.

'What is it, O'Rourke?'

'The object I've been hunting is no longer where it should be and our contact in London who could pinpoint its latest whereabouts has unfortunately been terminated.'

'This is quite a problem. Say no more on the phone and meet me at the usual place in thirty minutes.' Waterston replaced the receiver without waiting for any confirmation and went upstairs to change.

The electric doors lifted with scarcely a sound revealing a raven-black Lamborghini Gallardo, a Silver Range Rover and a dark green Fiat 500 that hadn't been washed for a year. The major always made use of the filthy-looking car when he wished to keep a low profile and his scuffed boots, baggy cords and patched tweed jacket completed the desired image to give him complete anonymity.

Regardless of its appearance the small car had been modified with a 280bhp turbocharged engine capable of achieving 135mph and on the seldom police-patrolled country roads the major was able to travel from his country house to the Six Bells in Crawley in under twenty minutes. He slowed on approaching the quaintly thatched inn in order to reduce the exhaust note and maintain the car's run-down appearance.

O'Rourke had yet to arrive and although fine malt whisky was the major's normal tipple he opted for a pint of bitter and went to sit in a settle that occupied a dimly lit corner of the bar. He casually surveyed the other drinkers over the rim of his glass and was satisfied that none of them presented a threat. For security reasons Waterston only ever used the Six Bells for clandestine meetings. The Green Man was his normal watering hole as it was only one hundred yards from his own house. The short distance plus the length of his long, tree-lined drive provided him with a reasonable form of exercise after any evening meal.

The major had almost drained his glass when the tall Irishman entered the inn bringing in a flurry of damp russet leaves. He ordered a pint of Guinness and then lowered himself into one of the chairs opposite the major so that his back was to the room. Normally he would have faced the room but this suited him as he preferred to take the precaution of foiling any possible lip-readers at the bar.

Waterston nodded slightly towards his empty glass and O'Rourke rose and went to get him a refill. This gave him the opportunity to survey the whole interior of the inn again. When he had given the major his drink he sat down and took an appreciative sip of the smooth black stout as only an Irishman could. O'Rourke then began relating in a low undertone every detail of what had happened since his return from Hong Kong.

'You are aware that Zhu Wen was found wanting and removed from his position by Shing?' the major asked quietly when O'Rourke came to the end of his report.

'Yes and I also know that Shing has ordered Xun to give me an equally early retirement too.'

Waterston leant forward over his beer glass. 'Now think carefully, Seán. Does Xun know you are a member of our society?'

'No, thank God. He and Shing only assume that I'm a traitor to the triad's main cause so I think you and the committee –'

The major held his hand up to prevent O'Rourke from going on. 'I understand that we are safe for now but very soon that could all change so your task is to neutralize this man you call Xun in an inconspicuous manner and as soon as possible. I have heard his name before and I know what he is capable of. He could prove to be the biggest threat to our end game if he finds the article first.'

'I will do what you order sir, the moment I am able to find him.'

As Waterston took another draught of the bitter he examined his agent over the glass. 'This private investigator, James Goodfellow, do you see him as any kind of a risk?' He put his glass down.

'In my opinion he's an amateur who's more at home looking for lost cats and errant husbands who have roamed from their nuptial beds than solving murders.'

'Make use of him,' the major rasped, ignoring O'Rourke's attempt at humour. 'Keep your eyes open because even private investigators can inadvertently stumble over surprising facts. He may not recognize the significance of what he has found at first but you will. If he was clever enough to break Huang's code and trace the ceramic plate to Italy then he may be clever enough to give you a lead.'

Waterston put his glass down and was ready to leave when O'Rourke gestured for him to wait as he looked around at the sprinkling of customers. The major slowly lowered himself down and looked at O'Rourke with hard, questioning eyes.

'There is a chance that if I get too close to this Goodfellow chap I will be setting myself up as the proverbial tethered goat for Xun.'

'Good! That will give you the opportunity to find him sooner and to take him out of the game.'

'Or vice versa, sir,' O'Rourke said, knowing that it was what the major had planned all along, and he looked into the older man's pale watery eyes without flinching.

'I would suggest that I become more circumspect and let Xun do most of the finding for us. He undoubtedly has orders to recover the *ding* and its contents for Pengfei Shing and if I wait until he has it before I strike then I will be killing two birds with one stone, so to speak.'

'You also take the risk that he could elude you and manage to take the object or its contents back to his master. It's not a chance I would willingly like to take but I have to admit there is some logic in your argument.'

'Is there a chance the rest of the Illuminati council will accept this course of action?'

Waterston's eyes suddenly blazed with anger and his head snapped upright. 'What did I tell you?' he hissed beneath his breath as he leant across the table to bring his face close to the Irishman who had, once more, taken a brief look round to see if anyone had overheard their conversation. 'Never mention our name in public again!'

'My apology, Major. It was a mere slip of the tongue and it won't happen again.' O'Rourke adopted a contrite expression but he seethed within as he watched the major rise to his feet.

'I'll tell you of the committee's decision regarding our next move,' Waterston said as he bent over O'Rourke. The SIS major then left the inn while his most trusted agent cursed beneath his breath. O'Rourke knew that he had made a basic mistake which he wouldn't have accepted from any of his trainees.

As a double agent for the Illuminati he had managed the impossible and infiltrated the infamous Green and the Reds who were their sworn enemies. O'Rourke had gained their trust by carrying out a number of tasks that involved removing awkward triad business competitors without drawing undue attention to their deaths. Traffic accidents and accidental drowning were his favoured methods but he knew that Xun would need to be handled in a totally different manner.

In one smooth action he tipped his glass to finish the contents and left the inn with a friendly wave and a smile for the landlord's cheery wife.

The drive to East Steading gave him valuable time to think and he had formulated a plan by the time he had checked into a quiet backstreet hotel called the Bunch of Grapes. It was an unpopular public house that offered a grubby bed-and-breakfast service for budget-conscious travelling salesmen and O'Rourke knew it would be unlikely that anyone would notice his coming and going from the place.

'Welcome to my humble hotel, Mr O'Grady,' the landlord said as he read the completed check-in form and compared it against O'Rourke's forged passport details. Frankie's face suggested that he knew it was a fake identity. 'Will you be staying long sir?'

O'Rourke took the Yale key that was attached to a block of beer-stained oak with four links of chain. 'I'll be here for a couple of days or until I've finished my business in this town,' he said as he began walking to the unlit staircase.

'What business are you in, sir,' Frankie asked nosily.

'Extermination.'

'That's interesting.' The landlord couldn't help thinking of the numerous cockroaches in his hotel kitchen but thought it wise not to mention them. 'Can I help you with your bags, sir?' Scraping his two-day stubble with the palm of his hand he looked pointedly at the small overnight case and computer in O'Rourke's hands.

The Irishman ignored the man's sarcasm and went up to the room where he dropped his case onto the bed and unzipped the laptop. He switched it on and tapped in the wi-fi code he had seen scrawled on a sticky note stuck behind the counter. In no time he was on line and looking for Goodfellow Investigations.

The major returned to the manor and changed into his favourite dress shirt, silk smoking jacket and navy twill trousers. On the last day of every month the six influential and very wealthy members of the committee gathered here to talk about trivial matters over barons of sirloin before taking port and cigars in the billiard room. It was only then that the servants were dismissed for the night, doors were locked and the real business of the Illuminati was discussed.

'Right Waterston, what's this about the Green and Reds?' Eustace Hinkman, a QC with chambers close to the Royal Courts of Justice asked bluntly. 'Your text stated that they are making a move that could be a danger to us all.' The tall, silver-haired man, formally dressed in a dinner jacket and bow tie, was staring at the major across the large coffee table.

'My dear Eustace, it's quite simply this: Pengfei Shing who heads up the Green and Reds in Hong Kong has sent one of their best assassins to England with the sole objective of recovering the bronze vessel we seek and eliminating my own personal enforcer.'

'We cannot afford to lose the container, but more importantly, the bugs it contains,' Lawrence, one of the older committee members exclaimed.

'Lawrence worries too much,' Waterston said to Forster, a Member of Parliament. Forcing a smile onto his face he continued, 'My aide will find the container first and then if it still contains what I put there five years ago we can use it to initiate the first step of our plan.'

There were a few grunts of approval from the six men and Waterston drew heavily on his cigar to camouflage his nervousness behind a dense cloud of blue smoke.

'Does this assassin know anything about the Illuminati members?' Forster asked.

'As far as I know Xun's knowledge is confined to triad business,' Waterston replied confidently.

Rackman, a small, rat-faced man who headed the local council tapped on the mahogany coffee table next to him. 'I am unfamiliar with this new threat you call the Green and Reds, would you please enlighten me, Hugh.'

Waterston disturbed the smoke with a wave of his hand and fixed the councillor with an impatient look. 'I thought you were briefed at the January meeting,' he grunted.

'I was in Helsinki at that time helping our Finnish brothers with a local by-election.'

'Then I will enlighten you.' Waterston leant back in the leather armchair and began his discourse. 'The Manchus invaded China in 1644 and the Ming army became an underground society with the sole objective of destroying the Manchus and restoring order.

'They even tried to assist the Boxer Rebellion but failed thanks to foreign imperialistic intervention. Support came much later from outside China and the Ming overthrew the last Emperor and Sun Yat Sen took his place. They became known as the Green Gang and the Red Gang who tried to fight the communists in Shanghai. They were thoroughly defeated in 1949 and became an underground organization once again.'

'But what of today?'

'Patience, Rackman, I'm coming to that,' the major snapped. 'After 1949 their influence increased and their members infiltrated the Chinese government although they are not officially political. They also have connections with the Japanese Yakuza even though they still profess to abhor criminal organizations.'

'Their hatred of the Illuminati, how did that arise?'

'The Green and Red society were thrown into chaos during the time of the Bush administration when the subject of race-specific biological weapons was mentioned.'

'And that's the subject of our search.'

'Correct. They believe we are looking for that weapon to use against the people of Oriental ethnicity to reduce the rapidly rising population levels in that part of the world by fifty per cent.'

'I wish I had that in my hands right now so I could make that percentage much greater,' Rackman muttered icily and there was a rumble of assent around the table.

'We believe that such a weapon existed a few years ago and that it was used experimentally on specific targets. Those who were in possession deliberately put the blame on the Illuminati. The Chinese warned us that the weapon must never be used within their borders or there would be global reprisals on a magnitude beyond comprehension.'

Waterston looked up at the portrait of himself that hung over the stone fireplace. It depicted a slightly younger man in oriental clothing standing before the Tibetan mountains.

'We were reconnoitring Chinese troop positions on the Tibetan border near a small village called Zhalaxiang when by chance, while hiding from a military patrol, I discovered a prehistoric bronze pot, a *ding,* in a small cave. The pot was filled with what appeared to be flat discs that I presumed to be the coinage of the age. Much later I discovered that they were *bi*-discs symbolic of heaven and earth and placed in graves as a means of conveying messages to the ancestors and an even greater spirit. On closer inspection I found one of the discs to be a modern, sealed petri dish with some kind of red-and-black growth. This worried me as the Chinese army was stationed close by and the dish may have come from our secret research centre that had been completely destroyed by the troops. It may have been saved and hidden amongst the *bi*-discs to be collected later by the Illuminati biochemists.'

'What did you do with it?' Rackman asked totally fascinated. His small eyes had widened and were fixed on the storyteller.

Waterston took a sip of Courvoisier from the lead crystal glass. 'As it was too heavy for me to carry by myself and I didn't want to involve my men I did the most sensible thing and left it where I had found it with the idea of recovering it later.'

'Why didn't you take just the petri dish for analysis and leave all the rest?' Rackman asked. 'Surely it was worth a great deal more as a weapon than the value of a few Bronze Age trinkets.'

'Because I knew if I had been captured carrying it they would have assumed that I was one of the research scientists and shot me on the spot. I decided to collect the petri dish with the pot later because I was also aware that the *ding* and discs would fetch a princely sum in the antiques markets to help with our cause.'

Having heard the major's story many times before the committee had fallen into quiet conversation and newspaper reading as Rackman, a newcomer to the committee, persisted with his questions.

'Where did you hide the pot?'

'Exactly where I found it in a cave near Zhalaxiang yet when I returned two years later on an intelligence operation the cave had been entered and the *ding* was gone. It was while we were returning on a narrow mountain path that I was hit by a Chinese sniper and fell down a ravine and into the river.' He took another sip and luxuriated in the warmth of the spirit trickling down his throat. 'The rest you know.'

Rackman gave a small sigh like a child at the end of a bedtime story and relit the cigar that he had forgotten about while he was listening to the major.

'Using his MI6 contacts the major discovered that his treasure had been found by a local goatherd sheltering from a snowstorm. Thinking that it might be worth a few yuan the goatherd tried to sell it in the nearest marketplace,' Hinkman explained. 'It was immediately taken from him by a local triad leader and passed on to Pengfei Shing who treasured it as an ancestral vessel. He became convinced that it held a connection to his own ancestors and was unaware of the petri dish.'

'Then the *ding* was stolen again and hidden once more,' Waterston interrupted. 'Weeks later vague rumours began to surface in many quarters of the city placing the *ding* somewhere in Europe. Through a senior officer in the Hong Kong police we learnt that a superintendent called Xiao Shi Huang had learned of the location. He was questioned by this senior officer but denied any knowledge which subsequently led to him being hunted for this knowledge.'

'That's the man who was found shot on the British Airways flight to London,' Rackman said. 'Was he assassinated by the Illuminati?'

'Of course not!' Hinkman exclaimed angrily.

Waterston raised a hand to calm the man. 'The triads also have police contacts and they foolishly killed the officer before he could lead them and us to the *ding* and that brings you up to date.' Waterston rose to his feet. 'I will now propose that my agent bides his time and does not make contact with the private investigator until Shing's assassin has shown his hand.'

'Can't you use the SIS facilities to trace and find this Chinese killer?' Lawrence asked. 'Surely they have the power to check docks and airports at will.'

'I'm an adviser not a supervisor or field agent. If I ask for information like that it will raise questions that could be embarrassing for the Illuminati as I only have a few of our members working in the service.' Waterston was beginning to lose patience. 'All those in agreement with waiting for the assassin to make the first move and exposing himself to our man please raise their hands.'

Six men, including the major, raised their hands.

10

THE WORDS THAT READ *Beneath The High Place Seek The Stone Dog For Heaven's Gate* kept repeating in James's and kept him awake. Untreated narcolepsy tended to cause extreme insomnia and he quickly checked to make sure that he had taken his medication. James slowly rose from the bed not wanting to disturb Jenny and went into the kitchen.

Three coffees and repetitive scrolling through the pictures of the porcelain plate in the Doccia museum vault increased his frustration; he switched the laptop off and began aimlessly doodling round *The Times* crossword while thinking. Reading through the clues for the tenth time he was suddenly struck by one in particular.

'Brit-pop band adds Arabic note to saxophone?' He muttered and he began running through all his childhood heroes. 'Oasis, Pulp, Shed Seven, Rialto, Supergrass –' He paused and the answer clicked. 'Ri-alto!' he cried out as he recalled Paulo Ambrosini's words to him in Sesto Fiorentino: *It was arranged for payment to be made and the plate to be given to the museum's representative at the Rialto Hotel in Venice.*

Jenny appeared at the door yawning having been wakened by James's cry of surprise. 'What's wrong?' she asked and then yawned again. Jenny had that warm inviting fragrance that only a woman can have after a good sleep and James was briefly distracted.

'Nothing, it was just my noisy eureka,' James replied. He opened the laptop and waited for the system to start. 'I think we've been looking in the wrong part of the world entirely.'

Jenny began filling the kettle with growing interest. 'What do you mean we've been looking in the wrong place?' she prompted as she spooned a measure of instant coffee into each mug.

'The curator said that the sale of the blue-and-white plate took place at the Rialto Hotel in Venice. Soooo, why there of all places?'

'Why not?'

'No reason at all if the person selling the plate was already in the city and didn't want the inconvenience of travelling to Florence.'

'I don't think Han Choi had an apartment in Venice.'

'Correct, so we can assume that it wasn't him who did the deal and that he had never owned the plate in question. However, Huang did have it and was staying at the Rialto when he arranged to meet Paulo Ambrosini's representative in Venice. Obviously this happened before Huang was forced to make his escape from the Hong Kong triads a few days ago.'

'So the triad chasing him assumed he had given the plate to Han in Italy so that he could retrieve it from him in London.'

James nodded as the aroma of strong coffee filled the kitchen, overwhelming Jenny's perfume.

'That must be why they ransacked his place in London. They were looking for it there.' Jenny poured the milk and stirred vigorously.

James stared at the lit screen for a few seconds before saying boldly, 'Find a way of having a look at Huang's passport. It would confirm my theory if you discover that he has a fairly recent Italian visa.'

'James! You know I could get into a lot of trouble if I start poking about in an ongoing investigation.'

'Please, please Jenny!' James pleaded.

Jenny handed one of the steaming mugs to him. 'I'll see what I can do but don't go holding your breath as you could be following a false trail.'

'You're a treasure,' he said and stood to give her a kiss on the cheek.

The policewoman mumbled something disparaging and strolled back to the bedroom with her coffee. After a few quick taps on the keyboard he had a satellite view of the Rialto Hotel next to the famous bridge crossing the Grand Canal. James then brought up the controversial blue–and-white plate in a separate window, took a quick sip from his mug and settled down knowing it would be a long search.

O'Rourke studied the private detective's website and the short biography that had been written to reassure prospective clients before clicking on to each of the services being offered. Finding little to interest him he closed the site and brought up a street map of East Steading. The Forbidden City was clearly marked and to his surprise the private investigator's office was right next door to the restaurant.

That's convenient, he thought as he shut down and closed the laptop. With practised efficiency he swiftly dressed, slipped a thin stiletto into the wrist sheath beneath his leather jacket and left the hotel fully prepared to satisfy his curiosity.

Frankie Trist had been serving behind the bar when he saw his suspicious guest leave and he waved to his wife to see to the customers. Taking the master key from the little cupboard beneath the bar he hurried upstairs and unlocked the second door in the poorly lit corridor.

It was a small room with only a single bed and slightly off-white linen. A laptop had been placed on the cigarette-scarred bedside table and a small overnight case was lying on the bed. Frankie tripped the catches and lifted the lid, carefully peeling away each layer until he reached the crisp white underwear at the bottom. It was there he came across a small brown paper package. Two elastic bands held the wrapping together and he removed them and to unfold the stiff paper.

Frankie couldn't prevent his sudden intake of breath when he saw two bundles of money. He expertly flipped the corners of one bundle and quickly noted that they were all £50 banknotes. Must be close to ten thousand, he thought and then another tempting but dangerous thought ran through his head, prompting him to carefully peel off five banknotes from each bundle and rewrap the package. He'll not miss them, he rationalized as he put the money back in the case and carried on checking the rest of the contents. He froze when he discovered a Beretta Nano 9mm wrapped in a T-shirt. O'Rourke couldn't bring a weapon with him from Hong Kong and had instructed the triad agent in London to get him one. The Nano was all she could obtain given such short notice. The dull matt-black finish of the micro-compact pistol belied its lethal capability and Frankie gingerly touched the lethal weapon with his fingertips before replacing it. A pocket inside the lid contained a note covered with Chinese characters and he slipped that back, no more the wiser and closed the case.

Knowing a password would be required Frankie didn't bother with the laptop and after a brief glance around the room for any clues about the occupant he left the room. The discovery of the gun momentarily caused him to consider replacing the money but parting from the ten crisp notes was contrary to his nature and he stuffed the notes into his hip pocket. His wife gave him a questioning look when he entered the bar but he ignored her and began polishing wine glasses with his mind in a whirl.

It was after midnight when O'Rourke casually walked past the Chinese restaurant and glanced through the window into the dark interior. Satisfied that the Choi family had retired to their apartment at the rear of the building he walked past to study the side door with the brass plaque. O'Rourke snapped upright in frustration: he had hoped to search the investigator's office while he was at home but the plaque clearly showed that Goodfellow lived above the shop. He decided to make a subtle entry the following day once Goodfellow had left the building. The lock was a common design and he whistled his favourite Enya song *'My! My! Time Flies'* very softly to himself as he strode back to the hotel. He caught sight of the proprietor looking his way before ducking into the back office and closing the door. O'Rourke shrugged, took his key from the rack, and went directly to his room.

The first thing he noticed was that someone had been there while he was away. The paperback was no longer meticulously aligned with the edge of the bedside table, a partially opened drawer had been fully closed and there were greasy smudges on the two locks of his case. As a final precaution he always carefully wiped such surfaces with his handkerchief before leaving a hotel room. Small things, that instantly alerted him to any visitors in his absence.

With care O'Rourke opened the drawer and checked the contents before going to the bed and releasing the catches of his case. He lifted the lid three centimetres and checked for wires; finding nothing that posed a threat he opened the case.

Everything seemed exactly as he had left it except for a single black sock that was now on top of a blue pair. The Beretta seemed to be untouched until he took it out and held it up to the light. Faint smudges were on the matt-black finish and O'Rourke immediately presumed that Frankie

Trist had interfered with his property. He made a mental note to severely reprimand the hotel owner.

With the same care he double-checked the security of the packets and soon spotted that the elastic bands had been replaced in the wrong colour order and that the top serial number of each stack of banknotes no longer ended with 9 – he had been robbed.

It took O'Rourke only a matter of seconds to calculate that he was five hundred pounds short. Oh, Mr Trist, you'll pay for that later, he thought as he rewrapped the money and replaced everything in his case except for the weapon. The human hair he had placed on the laptop's lock was still in place and he knew his secrets were safe for none of his files could be read without knowing a very complex set of passwords.

He undressed down to his boxer shorts, set the alarm on his wristwatch to 5 a.m. and lay down. He slid his hand beneath the pillow where he had placed the Beretta; touching the cold metal reassured him and he instantly dropped off into a dreamless sleep.

Xun checked the telephone number again before dialling and he waited patiently for his call to be acknowledged.

'Hello, who is this?' a woman asked in poor Mandarin.

'My name is inconsequential,' Xun replied in English. 'Just tell the gentleman sitting beside you that I speak for Mr Pengfei Shing and that I wish to have a word with him.'

'He is very busy at the mome –'

'Now!' Xun snapped.

The line fell silent and he waited, lightly tapping his fingernails on the tabletop until a man spoke with a nervous edge to his voice.

'I am Peter Ming, what does Mr Shing want?' he asked. Xun recognized his accent as being from the Chongqing region.

'Your master, and mine, wishes me to meet with you to discuss matters of extreme urgency,' Xun said quietly. 'You must choose an isolated location where we can talk without fear of being overheard.'

'We can meet in my office tomorrow at 7 a.m. None of the staff for any of the other companies in the building arrive before 8.30. That will give us the privacy you require. I frequently arrange my more delicate transactions at that time of the day.'

'What about your own personnel?'

'Sheila is my confidential secretary and the only staff member I have,' Peter said slyly. 'She only speaks a little Mandarin but you can trust her to keep her mouth shut.'

'Do you sleep with her?'

After a little hesitation Peter said, 'Yes.'

'Good, ask her to be on time as well. What is your exact address.'

Xun wrote down the details rapidly in Mandarin and without another word he rang off.

The underground journey from Waterloo mainline station to Knightsbridge via Green Park took little time as it was a full hour before the daily rush began. Wearing a dark suit and carrying a black briefcase Xun drew very little attention as he strode the length of Sloane Street until he reached the tall Queen Anne-styled townhouse.

The door clicked open three seconds after he had pushed the button with a gloved finger and he entered by pushing the door with his shoulder. The latticed gate opened and the lift rumbled upward at a snail's pace until it reached the top floor. The attractive woman who opened the door was in her late twenties and wore a charcoal suit that set off her trim figure nicely. Hazel eyes looked him up and down, approving his expensive taste in clothes.

'You are Mr Shing's representative?' Sheila asked with a cute sideways smile and Xun nodded and inhaled a cloud of Bulgari as he walked past her to enter the offices. Xun's eyes strayed down briefly to appreciate the exaggerated rhythm of her bottom as she clicked ahead in her four-inch heels, not unlike a runway model, to lead him into the large oak-panelled boardroom.

A thin man with an equally thin moustache rose to greet him. His suit had been impeccably tailored yet still managed to hang like a damp rag from his bony shoulders to create the image of a scarecrow with lotto winnings in the bank. 'Good morning, I am Peter Ming and you must be … ?' he asked extending his hand.

Xun ignored the gesture and sat down to face him across the large redwood table. Brushing an inkstand and calendar to one side he placed the briefcase before him and stared at Peter in silence as his secretary began grinding Blue Mountain coffee beans. Xun waited until she had finished before speaking. 'I do not drink coffee,' he said in Mandarin with an imperceptible shake of the head.

Sheila did not understand what the handsome Chinese had said but she took her cue from the head movement and offered tea.

'Water,' Xun demanded in English

'What can I do for the Mountain Master?' Peter asked, realizing that his guest wouldn't be volunteering his name. He fiddled nervously with a pencil and a plastic sharpener until the lead tip broke.

'I need to know the exact whereabouts of Seán O'Rourke. You are familiar with the name?' Xun said, keeping the conversation to Mandarin while removing his gloves.

Sheila's attention was caught by the Irishman's name and she tried to learn more as she continued to prepare Peter's coffee for she had carried on a secret affair with O'Rourke every time he visited London. She knew he only slept with her for the information he could extract but he was sensitive to her needs when love-making and therefore she was quite happy to satisfy him in more ways than one.

'Yes, he is – was, my controller for all matters concerning drug distribution and payment,' Peter confirmed. 'I met with him quite often and when I was unable to make contact I used Sheila for the less sensitive matters.'

'Then you know why I want to talk with him,' Xun said in a soft sibilant tone that reminded Peter of a cobra before striking.

'I have heard that he is a traitor to our sacred cause and should pay a penalty.'

'And?' Xun sipped from the glass silently put beside his elbow.

'I also know that he is tracking a restaurant owner called Feng Choi who he believes will lead him to a secret weapon that will reinstate him in Shing's favour.'

'You also know about the ancient *ding*?'

'O'Rourke mentioned it to me on the phone.'

Xun sighed when he learned that the man now knew about the ceremonial items. 'That was very foolish of him. And where is he now?' He tripped the catches on his case, suppressing his excitement as he waited for an answer.

'Choi has his restaurant in a town called East Steading. I believe O'Rourke is in that area waiting for Choi to make the first move,' Peter said as he acknowledged the coffee the woman put beside him. She remained standing behind her rich lover with one elegant hand resting intimately on his narrow shoulder.

'What do you mean, in that area?'

'He is staying at a hotel called The Bunch of Grapes.'

The SWR silenced Walthar P22 appeared from behind the open lid of the briefcase and a red rose bloomed on Peter's forehead. As his head was thrust back against the shocked woman she looked down and realized the same missile had entered her stomach. Before the excruciating pain began to fully register her left temple disintegrated, spraying scarlet over the wall behind her. Sheila crumpled to the floor; her startled hazel eyes wide open in death. Peter had slumped sideways, his body held by the chrome armrest of his chair.

Xun unscrewed the silencer and placed the weapon back in the briefcase. The Mountain Master had ordered the death of any who knew about the ancestral artefacts and in Xun's eyes O'Rourke had condemned Peter Ming when he made the decision to confide in him. Xun considered the woman's execution as a tactical move that prevented his description being passed on to the police. He also presumed that she learnt a great deal about Ming's dealings from their pillow talk and Xun couldn't take any chances that she could survive the first bullet.

Taking an unused cotton handkerchief from an inside pocket he polished the water glass as well as the arms of his chair before rising. He put on his gloves, locked the brief case and left the office. The building was still silent and awaiting the first office workers and the bodies probably wouldn't be discovered until the evening cleaners had begun their shift. Nevertheless, Xun used the staircase and as a further precaution he kept well away from the walls until he had shouldered his way through the front door and left the building.

Xun strode along the Brompton Road and boldly went into Harrods as though he knew exactly what he was looking for. He attracted the attention of a well-dressed sales assistant and inquired about various pieces of luggage. As the young man enthusiastically listed the features of top-of-the-range Louis Vuitton cases Xun casually lowered his own to stand amidst similar looking briefcases.

'You have been most helpful, young man,' Xun said with a winning smile. 'I will speak to my wife and ask her to come and talk to you about a complete set as we are planning a vacation in the Bahamas this year.'

Xun bent to pick up the case standing next to his own. 'In the meantime I would like to purchase this excellent case.'

The sales assistant beamed, all memory of the charming Chinese man arriving with his own case completely wiped by the promise of a sale. After the cash sale had been completed Xun shook his hand. 'I will tell my wife to ask for you personally.'

'Thank you, she will be most welcome, sir. Do tell her to come at any time and to ask for Harold.'

Xun nodded, left the department store and imperiously signalled to the doorman to hail him a taxi. He then loudly asked the driver to take him to the Ritz Hotel, ensuring the doorman overheard him. He changed the destination to Gerrard Street in the Chinese quarter once the taxi was under way.

The taxi stopped outside the SeeWoo Supermarket as requested. Once the taxi was gone Xun left the supermarket and walked through to Lisle street where he found the address Pengfei Shing's secretary had given him. He opened the door and was faced by a steep unlit staircase and a giant of a man. Contrary to his oriental origins he was over seven feet tall and had the musculature of a professional wrestler. A hand the size of a dinner plate was placed against Xun's chest.

'You have an appointment?' The man rumbled in Cantonese.

'No, but I am here to make peace with the Two-Headed Dragon.'

The password was accepted, the hand dropped, and the man stepped to one side. 'Second door on left at top of stairs,' he said and turned to face the door once more without saying another word.

Xun went up the stairs and two triads who were much shorter than the doorman confronted him. They were stripped to the waist and their heavily tattooed torsos glistened with oil in the light of the red lanterns.

'The Two-Headed Dragon expects me,' he said softly and the men stood to one side, revealing the most beautiful woman Xun had ever seen. She was reclining on a plush divan with her legs pulled up and hidden beneath an exquisite hand-made gown of charcoal grey silk. Long jet-black hair framed an oval face with high cheek-bones and exquisite almond-shaped eyes. Full lips glowed bright red against her unblemished pale skin.

'Welcome Xun,' she said, languidly extending a long-fingered hand in greeting. 'I am Sying.'

Xun took the hand briefly, thinking how apt the name 'star' was to someone so radiant. Acknowledging her gesture to sit he chose the armchair facing her. 'I am here on a very special mission for the Mountain Master,' he said. 'And it will require your full cooperation and a weapon.'

'You came with no weapon?' The husky nature of her voice stirred feelings in Xun that he had thought he could never feel again. His eyes drifted south, taking in the shapely form that refused to be disguised beneath the robe.

'It was used and had to be disposed of.' His eyes returned to Sying's face to find faint amusement reflected in her eyes. 'I now need a replacement for the task that lies before me.'

'That can be arranged. I am also pleased to tell you that your package was picked up at Heathrow as you requested without any complications at customs.' She said this with a casual wave of her hand towards the corner of the room.

Xun turned his head and saw the familiar four foot long wooden crate that lay upon the parquet floor. It was plastered with official-looking seals and notifications stating that it was British Museum property and had to be handled with extreme care.

'Good, I have a feeling that I may have need of that to complete this mission in the most appropriate manner.' He rose and walked across the room to break all the seals before producing a small key to unlock the two padlocks. The two bodyguards became fully alert and raised their weapons only to lower them again on a silent gesture from Sying.

The Red Pole lifted the lid and noisily removed a layer of bubble wrap and the two bodyguards craned their necks to see what lay beneath. Their eyes widened at the sight of the magnificent scabbard and sword hilt of 'Dragon's Breath.' Xun picked it up and there was a light snicker of steel on steel as he withdrew the blade. They gasped as the keen edge glinted and reflected the crimson light of the lanterns overhead.

'A very pretty toy, Xun,' Sying said disdainfully as he slid the weapon into its ornate sheath.

'A toy that has played with many a neck,' Xun whispered as he sat down with the sword lying across his thighs.

Sying's eyes widened in pleasant surprise and she sat up. For a moment Xun caught the briefest glimpse of a perfectly moulded breast before the silk flowed back into place like a slow-moving stream of water.

'Now what about my request?'

Sying nodded to one of the two men standing behind Xun. He went behind the woman and after depressing a hidden catch a section of the wall swung open to reveal a brightly lit room racked with guns of all descriptions on all three walls.

'Take your pick Xun. They are all untraceable but remember, if you lose it you must pay for it.'

'Understood,' he said as he rose to his feet and strode into the armoury. His first choice was a Heckler & Koch sub-machine gun that was only 15 inches long and could accurately fire 900 rounds per second over 220 metres. He put the compact weapon into the new briefcase plus 2 detachable magazines.

'Are you planning on starting a war?' Sying asked with a grim smile.

'I just like to make sure that what goes down stays down.' He then selected a Colt hammerless semi-automatic and four Australian F1 grenades from their respective shelves and closed the briefcase. Xun went and sat in the same armchair as before while the bodyguard closed the vault. He smiled at the beautiful 'star' who was now stretched out on the divan. One hand was behind her head that had the effect of emphasizing her firm breasts.

'I have heard a great deal about you, Xun,' she said. 'Your reputation for having Death as your sole partner precedes you everywhere.'

'That is not good news, Sying. I prefer to remain anonymous as it lets me get on with my work more effectively.' As he spoke in Mandarin he had had been looking at the bodyguards who were reflected in one of the many mirrors hanging in the room. There were no signs that they could understand what he was saying.

'They don't speak Mandarin,' Sying said and she waved to the two men. They both nodded and quickly left the room. 'I prefer to have Cantonese staff as that gives me a certain measure of privacy when I desire it.'

'You desire it now?'

'I desire you now.'

Xun went and knelt beside the divan that was wreathed in the intoxicating scent of sandalwood. He ran a finger down her cheek and her breathing rate increased noticeably.

'How many men have you killed?' she asked between quickening breaths as she looked into his dark soulless eyes with a passion that had the power to arouse the cold-blooded assassin.

'I no longer count.'

She sighed deeply with eyes closed and he knew that she was ready to be taken.

The Forbidden City was brightly lit and golden light was spilling out and glistening on the wet pavement when Xun arrived in East Steading later that night. He instructed the taxi driver to drive past the restaurant slowly and then to continue for another hundred yards before stopping at the town square.

After he had paid the driver, who scowled at receiving a meager tip, he got out and strolled casually into the concealing shadow of a life-size cavalry officer cast in bronze and mounted on a tall granite plinth. Xun sat on the bench donated by a loving war widow and placed the laden briefcase on his lap.

He had come prepared for a long tedious wait and it was two hours before the last diners had left the restaurant and the lights were extinguished. Midnight chimed on the town clock and after shifting his backside on the hard wood for the umpteenth time he saw a tall figure in a dark trench coat approaching the restaurant.

Somehow the way the person moved reminded him of someone he knew he had seen in Hong Kong. The figure paused at the restaurant to look through the window and then strolled on to stop at the next door. Xun saw the person bend as though trying to read before straightening up and striding away. As the dark figure turned a corner Xun hurried across the park and onto the high street. He hurried to where he had seen the figure pause and read the inscription on the brass plate.

'Goodfellow Investigations,' he muttered and then shrugged for it meant little to him. The person in the rain-coat did, however, and he sped down the road in pursuit. As he turned the second corner he caught up with his quarry and was just in time to see him opening the door of a public house. The light inside illuminated the man and Xun exhaled in surprise for he had recognized the man immediately.

O'Rourke went inside and locked the door behind him without realizing he had been found by his executioner.

11

THE PALE LIGHT that preceded the rising sun was smudging the dismal sky when James finished googling the sea-cradled Italian city. His meticulous search had covered the sixteenth-century church of San Sebastiano and eventually spread across to the Sant' Elena monastery. He still hadn't been able to match the ceramic painting with any of the Venetian landmarks although the tower of San Giorgio Maggiore Church and St Mark's Campanile were the closest to the 'High Place' mentioned in the text. He stretched his leg muscles and rose to get a coffee from the kitchen when the doorbell rang.

'Morning James,' a very wide-awake Jenny shouted as she bounded up the stairs and without a by-your-leave took the coffee cup from his hand.

'Is it?' James mumbled through a yawn that threatened to dislocate his jawbone.

'Who got out of bed on the wrong side then,' Jenny replied with a laugh as she sipped his much-needed stimulant.

'What bed? I haven't seen one for twenty-four hours,' he complained as he poured a fresh cup. 'I've been working through the night on the theory that the damned plate would show me the whereabouts of the *ding* in Venice.'

Jenny made a sympathetic face as she sat at the table and studied the Google map of Venice that was still on the screen. James had zoomed in on the area around the Doge's Palace and she changed the satellite scene to the simpler graphic map and read some of the street names as he sat beside her.

'That seems new,' she muttered after taking a sip. 'It wasn't there when my aunt took me four years ago. We had to use a much crowded stop at San Zaccaria.' She was pointing at the vaporetto dock that was close to St Marks Square.

'It is fairly new,' he replied and zoomed in on the new landing stage and changed the screen back to satellite to reveal the glass and steel construction that seemed so out of place in the ancient city. 'It was opened last July. That must have been after your holiday.'

'Look! It's just around the corner from Harry's Bar. That's where I had my first Bellini.' She recalled the heavenly taste of the puréed white peaches and sparkling prosecco with a twinge of sadness for her favourite aunt who took her on so many exciting holidays had passed away earlier in the year.

'Are you okay, Jenny?' he asked when he saw her face sadden.

'I'm fine. Just miss that cheery face terribly,' she replied and resumed studying the streets of Venice more closely.

James went to sit in the old, threadbare armchair he had discovered in a local charity shop and closed his eyes. In no time he was drifting off and was soon lost in a deep sleep. Jenny looked up to gaze at the recumbent, unshaven man and told herself to remind him to take his medication on waking. As she glanced back at the screen something stirred in her subconscious and she looked closer, homing in on one particular street. 'James!' she cried out excitedly and quickly crossed the room to shake his shoulder. 'Wake up, I think I'm on to something.'

He stirred and opened his eyes.

'Didn't you say that part of the translation was something about a stone dog?'

'"Seek the stone dog," yes, that's right. What of it?'

'What was the whole line?' Jenny said enthusiastically.

James closed his eyes again and thought for a few seconds before sitting up. *'Beneath The High Place Seek The Stone Dog For Heaven's Gate,'* he recited.

'Then come and read this.' Jenny went back to the computer and when James wearily joined her she pointed to the road running past the vaporetto landing stage.

'My Italian is pretty well non-existent, Jenny. You'll have to be my translator.'

'This street is called Riva Degli Schiavoni which loosely translated means the dock of the Dalmatians. They were a group of famous artists of Slavic descent who were nicknamed Schiavoni because of their origin.'

'How does this help us?' His expression showed his puzzlement.

'Dalmation is also a breed of dog and the road is lined with stone!'

It seemed as if a very bright light had been switched on in James's head. His eyes snapped open with realization and a smile appeared that matched her own. 'Stone dog!'

'Beneath High Place must refer to the Campanile, the bell tower in St Mark's Square,' Jenny added and found herself a trifle breathless from the excitement of the moment.

'Now all we have to find is a tiny humpback bridge and all those bloody oriental cypresses that are illustrated on the plate.' James clicked up one of the photographs of the ceramic art. His attitude had become one of hopelessness again and he slumped back into his seat.

'Let's zoom out and look along the Riva Degli Schiavoni for something that might possibly match the illustration,' Jenny said cheerfully, hoping to rekindle his interest in what had been revealed. With a resigned expression James moved his chair closer and together they studied the road running beside the Grand Canal.

'There's only one measly little park,' James said morosely.

'And a little bridge close by!' Jenny pointed excitedly and for the first time James looked more closely and saw the small arched bridge crossing a very narrow waterway feeding into the Grand Canal after it had circled the little park. Clicking to satellite view he was amazed to see a symmetrically arched bridge that seemed to belong more in a Chinese formal garden than in Europe. The brilliance of the red brick tower caught his eye and he realized that the Campanile was only a stone's throw from both bridge and park.

'Oh, my God, this must be the place,' he said, his voice breaking as Jenny's excitement proved to be contagious. 'The elements have all appeared to come together. It must be where the cauldron was secretly brought and hidden so long ago.'

'The eighteenth-century?'

'No, much later,' James explained. 'I believe someone saw the similarity in locations between Sanjiao Mountain Island and the park here at

Vallaresso. He judged the description could act just as well as a guide to both places.'

'But who?'

'We will never know but a wild guess would be that a Chinese friend of Han Choi had deciphered the phrase when the plate was in Han's possession. He may have travelled to China on business and then come into some information about the fabulous wealth of the artefacts and had worked out the Sanjiao connection.'

Jenny looked doubtful about the theory but James went on, lost in thought. 'This man then found the cauldron, saw how valuable it was and shipped it to Europe for disposal later.

'Venice? That sounds too incredible.' Jenny zoomed in and changed to the street view to be able to walk through the park by the San Marco-Vallaresso landing stage.

James swept his hand to encompass the whole screen. 'I think it's credible. Venice is a vibrant cosmopolitan city where works of art are changing hands at an incredible rate every day. He or she could occasionally dip into the *ding* and cash in the *bi* one at a time so as not to attract too much attention.'

'You think that person is still doing it?'

'Could be.' James studied the screen as Jenny clicked along the pre-recorded pathways. 'Now all we have to do is scour five-thousand square metres of shrubbery to discover what remains of this mysterious Chinese pension.'

'I suggest you spoil yourself with a brief holiday in the most romantic city in the world,' Jenny said coyly and fluttered her naturally long eyeslashes.

'Are you trying to get me to invite you along?' James found it difficult to keep a straight face.

'Would I do that? Anyway, I don't think I can get the time off.'

'It's Friday, don't you have this weekend free or would you rather stay at home and do some laundry.'

'Damn you, James. Ask Me!' Jenny exclaimed as she lightly punched him on the arm.

'OK, will you join me in the most romantic city for a rather dirty weekend?'

'Of course I bloody will, you idiot.'

'And by dirty weekend I mean digging up a city park with a trowel.' His lips abruptly stifled her laughter and she went limp in his arms before she kissed him back.

O'Rourke rose early and braving the stiff wind that was driving fine rain along the high street he cautiously approached Goodfellow Investigations. The door opened as he approached and he hesitated for a second as a young woman stepped out into the street and opened a bright yellow umbrella. A hand briefly waved from the doorway and then the door was closed behind her. O'Rourke assumed that Goodfellow was still upstairs; Xun, watching the Irishman from the lee of the statue knew James was in for he had seen a shadow pass one of the windows upstairs. He watched O'Rourke continue along the road past the restaurant as the woman hurried on in the opposite direction with thoughts of a wonderful weekend ahead.

Xun was biding his time: O'Rourke wouldn't be interested in the private investigator unless he was able to lead him to something of great importance. He watched the Irishman duck into a cake shop that advertised tea and coffee and settled himself down on the wooden bench to await further developments.

The constant misty rain had begun to penetrate his light raincoat when the door to Goodfellow Investigations opened and James emerged, opening a black telescopic umbrella. Almost in the same instant O'Rourke came out of the coffee shop and began trailing the investigator who was on his way to meet his secretary in his travel agent's office.

'Good morning, Miss Lightbody,' James said cheerily as he entered the Global Entertainment agency. She was primly seated before Mr Teddington's desk with one leg crossed over the other and an officious-looking black briefcase resting in her lap.

Miss Lightbody looked up from the sheet of A4 paper she had been reading and glared at her employer. 'This is most inappropriate James. I could have done all the planning and the various bookings on my arrival at the office. Why are we meeting here in Mr Teddington's office?'

The travel agent remained quiet while he observed the usual banter between his friends with some amusement.

'It was simply more convenient, Miss Lightbody. This gives Teddy the opportunity to show me all his lovely catalogues about Venice.' James ran his finger down the glossy surfaces of the racked brochures until he came to one for Venetian tours and packaged holidays. He removed it from the display as Miss Lightbody held up her sheet of paper with an expression of triumph.

'You may look all you like, James, but I've already booked the flights, selected the hotel, made out the cheque and I have been awaiting your signature to finalize the matter.'

Miss Lightbody's efficiency never failed to amaze James but on this occasion disappointment spread across his face. 'I was hoping to have a browse through this and make my own shortlist to finally choose from,' he said holding up one of the colourful booklets.

'I've already done that for you.'

'You did include Jenny, I trust.'

'Naturally. Did you think I would let you go to that place un-chaperoned by the person with the most interest in you?'

'I thought you had the most interest.'

Miss Lightbody tried to prevent herself from smiling as she took the brochure from his hand and turned to one particular page. 'Would this be suitable for your romantic tryst, James?' She passed it back and James looked at the magnificent full-colour spread showing the Rialto Bridge.

'You want us to sleep under a centuries-old bridge like a couple of down and outs?' he teased as he admired the Rialto Hotel standing beside the world famous landmark. 'Well, if that's all your petty cash can run to it will have to do for a couple of nights.'

Ronald Teddington could no longer suppress his laughter. 'You have one of their better suites, James,' he managed to say. 'Miss Lightbody has only just come off the line. She managed to twist the hotel manager's arm to get you and Miss Kent a special deal.'

'It's that time of the year, James. It was very simple, no trouble at all.' Miss Lightbody gave a small dismissive wave of her hand as she slid the chequebook under his nose and magically produced an ancient fountain pen.

James saw the two Easy-Jet tickets in her hand and couldn't help smiling: she had managed yet again to soften the blow to her precious petty cash with the cheapest seats she could find and he signed the cheque with a flourish.

'I also recalled, James, that the plate exchange took place in a hotel called the Rialto and I have assumed this is the same one. You may be able to do a little checking with the staff to discover who were involved in the transaction.'

James once more he gave silent thanks for his secretary's sharp mind.

'I will now give Miss Kent a call and give her the good news and the bad news,' Agnes said as she passed the cheque to Teddy.

'Bad news?' James asked, concern creeping into his voice.

'The good news is that she will have a very romantic weekend in Italy's most beautiful city but the bad news is that when she finishes work this afternoon she must meet you at the Easy-Jet check-in desk at Stansted Airport.'

'Where's the bad news in that?'

'She will only have forty minutes to get there.'

The three people were so engrossed in all the travel arrangements that none was aware of a tall man peering at them through the rain-dappled glass.

As he looked through the window O'Rourke wiped the raindrops from his eyes with the side of his hand and instantly saw the Venice brochure that was in Goodfellow's hand. He also saw the Easy-Jet tickets lying on the desk in front of Miss Lightbody before turning away and walking down the street. That destination puzzled him as he naturally assumed that if Goodfellow were considering revisiting the Museo Di Doccia then he would have flown to Florence.

O'Rourke walked faster to avoid being noticed by the couple should they emerge from the travel agency. 'Why Venice, what's the connection?' he mused beneath his breath as he turned his collar up against the light rain being driven into his face by the chill wind. He returned to the hotel with his unwelcome executioner trailing behind and using the landline in his room he checked for flights to Venice. When he learnt that there was a flight at 7.40 p.m. he used one of his many credit cards to book a seat in first class. This was on the premise that if Goodfellow was on board the same flight then he would undoubtedly travel economy. O'Rourke had simply reduced the chance of them meeting or even seeing each other.

Xun saw O'Rourke looking through the travel agent's window before suddenly hurrying away and he followed the man at a discreet distance. When he recognized the street they had turned into he knew that his target was returning to the hotel.

The taxi left East Steading and sped through the countryside until it filtered onto the M25 motorway and was compelled to slow down. The sides of heavy articulated transporters were all round, blotting out the sun and creating a shadowy canyon that often slowed to a complete standstill. James checked his watch apprehensively as time melted away and the deadline for the last check-in rapidly approached.

'Sorry about this Guv,' the cab driver said. 'It's the same every day at this time and the extra lane they're going to spend millions on ain't gonna help either.'

'Not your fault, mate,' James replied as he looked at his watch once more. 'It's not too far to the terminal now and the traffic seems to be picking up a little.' He was wondering if Jennifer would be able to make it in time but remembered that her current posting was at a police station that was closer to Gatwick than East Steading.

True to his words the lanes began to increase in speed and soon they were taking the off-ramp and heading into the airport. James was alighting at the drop-off point when a very welcome voice hailed him.

'James, you're late!'

He spun round and was hit by an excited missile with wildly flying auburn hair.

'We only have five minutes to check-in.' Jennifer was wearing a smart blue skirt topped by a crisp white blouse beneath a blue-and-white striped jacket. She trotted away and James hurried to catch up with her.

'How did you get here before me?' he asked. 'I was more worried that you wouldn't make it here at all.'

'Agnes gave me the flight time and I told the inspector I wasn't feeling too well and he said I should go home,' Jennifer said over her shoulder as she stepped onto the bottom step of the escalator. High above a tall man in a dark raincoat was just stepping off the escalator and hurrying across the departure hall to the First Class check-in.

Like a migrating swift O'Rourke swept through the ticket, passport and baggage checks and was striding through the jet-bridge to board the plane by the time James and Jenny had been issued with boarding passes.

The flight was completely uneventful and being in the right class meant that O'Rourke could be cleared by the various authorities to enter Italy long before the couple was able to begin walking along the seemingly never-ending covered footpath to where the water taxis were moored.

The Irishman sat inside the cabin of a small motorboat he had chartered and waited until he saw James respond to a board bearing his name and a few others. After waiting a few minutes for everybody to board the water taxi started its engine and went out into the Laguna Veneta.

O'Rourke gave instruction to his boatman to follow it and sat back in his comfortable leather seat as he watched the taxi ahead cutting through the small wind-raised waves to leave a white wake that his motorboat stayed in at a distance of one-hundred yards.

The fresh smell of ozone filled his lungs and he breathed deep and long, knowing from experience that it would all change in a matter of minutes.

The boatman glanced back at O'Rourke from time to time as he speculated on why the stranger was following the other boat; was he a policeman, secret agent or a thief targeting innocent tourists? He continued imagining outlandish scenarios of high intrigue to overcome the boredom as they passed Isola di San Michele and, leaving the open water, entered the Rio del Gesulti basin. The freshness of the sea changed to become humid and tfaint smells of rotting fish and diesel fuel hung in the air.

The boatman expertly navigated deep into the city where strong aromatic cooking smells began to prevail, reminding him that he hadn't eaten on the plane. Every sounds was amplified by high-rising terracotta buildings lining the sides of the claustrophobic waterways.

O'Rourke looked up disinterestedly as colourful shirts, dresses and sheets strung on lines above the canal moved in brief but welcome breezes and gave a sigh of relief when they emerged into the wide-open water of the Grand Canal where the air instantly changed back to cool freshness.

They chugged into view of the famous Rialto Bridge. The boatman throttled back slowly in preparation for mooring on the opposite side to the Rialto Hotel. As his taxi gently nudged into a mooring O'Rourke looked across the water to see Goodfellow's water taxi jousting with two gondolas in an effort to tie up first.

O'Rourke stayed seated and watched his quarries disembark until they finally entered their hotel – a deep terracotta-coloured building adjoining the bridge. Removing a large sum in Euros from his wallet he asked his boatman to recommend a reasonably priced hotel on their side of the canal. 'Would you also remain here and let me know when that young couple come out and where they have gone?' he asked in perfect Italian once a hotel had been pointed out.

The boatman counted the wad of notes and his black bushy eyebrows flicked up further and further in surprise. He nodded slowly and O'Rourke took his small overnight case and stepped ashore.

Walking along the quayside amongst tables and chairs set out by a restaurant he approached the hotel entrance. It was mildly inviting but not too salubrious and suited his needs. At the reception desk he was informed in no uncertain terms and with much hand waving that the hotel was fully booked. However, when he mentioned his boatman's name he was immediately taken to a small room on the top floor. His first action was to go to the window and check the precise location of the small powerboat before scanning the windows facing him.

VENICE

Carrying their small overnight bags James and Jennifer registered in the Rialto and a porter, anticipating the usual large tip, was dismayed by the lack of any heavy luggage. He took them to their room which involved passing through the main body of the hotel and out into a narrow alleyway. Fifty metres along this gloomy passage they reached a set of dark green iron doors which lead to a near vertical flight of stairs that seemed to rise forever.

'Is this the same hotel?' Jennifer panted halfway up and the porter gave a sardonic grin. He finally opened one of the three doors at the top.

They were immediately dumbfounded by the splendor of their room. A large silk-canopied four-poster bed dominated one side of the suite while the other had a chaise longue and an elegant writing table. All the furniture, including an assortment of chairs, dated from the seventeenth or eighteenth century. Gilt-framed mirrors and delightful paintings of Venetian scenes decorated most of the walls.

'This is so beautiful James. How did Agnes manage to book this romantic gem in such a short time?'

James went to one of the three windows and opened it. 'How did she manage this as well?' he said as Jennifer joined him and they gazed out over the Grand Canal. The busy Rialto Bridge was to the right and the magnificent Universitá Cá Foscari was to the left on the bend of the canal. It was the Venetian rush hour and boats of all descriptions were hurrying to and fro while the slower-moving gondolas dodged and weaved amongst the traffic. Screeching seagulls wheeled above boats laden with fish being delivered to the famous Rialto Mercato on the other side of the bridge.

'It's so romantic James,' Jennifer murmured and leant her head against his shoulder. The neon lights were beginning to flicker on as the red-streaked sky grew dark and they both watched in silence as the busy waterway began to twinkle prettily.

James adjusted his watch to European time and nudged Jenny. 'It's getting late. We should cross the bridge and eat at the Marconi Hotel before all the tables are taken.' He pointed across the canal to the canopied tables that were attractively placed at the waters edge beyond the traditional blue-and-green-striped mooring poles jutting out of the water.

The Irishman took a small pair of binoculars from his case and stepping back from his open window he focused on the hotel opposite. As he slowly panned across the windows he suddenly saw James Goodfellow who was standing with the young woman at an open window on the second floor. Goodfellow was pointing directly at him and a shocked O'Rourke stumbled further back into the room even though he knew that he couldn't be seen in the dark void of his window.

O'Rourke waited until they both disappeared before realizing that the man had been pointing at a slight downward angle. Cautiously approaching his window he glanced down and immediately understood what had attracted Goodfellow's attention: the restaurant was clearly a popular venue and was already beginning to fill up: early arrivers were selecting the most desirable tables at the water's edge first. As he looked across the canal he was in time to see the couple exit and make their way to the bridge. They were clearly going to dine at his hotel and that considerably cramped any movement on his part. O'Rourke decided to use the room service and stay put until the morning.

The phone on the bedside table rang and the switchboard operator put through an outside call.

'The couple you are interested in have just left the hotel and are crossing the Rialto,' the boatman's gravelly voice said. 'What do you want me to do?'

'Nothing. You were a little late in letting me know but let me know when they return to their hotel.' O'Rourke hung up and dialled the kitchen to order a simple pasta dish and a bottle of Chianti.

Tomorrow was another day.

12

JAMES WAS WOKEN by the sounds of traders unloading their boats and the loud voices of the commuters greeting each other while they waited for a vaporetto to take them to work. Even the seagulls' screeching failed to stir Jennifer and as he lay, propped up on one elbow, he watched her sleep. Soft auburn curls lay on the snow-white linen pillowcase framing her face and her long dark lashes lightly rested on a flawless skin.

An alien wailing that rose and fell grew louder as the waterborne ambulance sped along the canal to slice into the general hubbub below their window. Jennifer's long lashes flicked up and startled green eyes looked up at him.

'Good morning,' he said as he stroked her cheek.

'What's that noise,' she muttered irritably as she threw the duvet back and sat up.

'It's either a fire engine or an ambulance.'

Jennifer went to the window where the morning light was spilling through and he admired her silhouetted figure beneath the light nightdress.

'An ambulance,' she murmured. The sight of the emergency vehicle fascinated her as it sped away, leaving a white wake that violently rocked the ranks of moored gondolas. 'It's so weird to see something like that on water and he does seem to be in a bit of a hurry.'

'As we should be,' James said and he leapt out of bed and went into the attractively decorated en-suite.

They decided to be a trifle extravagant and after a ten-minute stroll they were in the expansive piazza enjoying an expensive continental breakfast at the Florian Café in St Mark's Square.

'Miss Lightbody will have a fit when she sees the receipts for this place,' James said as he sipped his orange juice. Jennifer could only nod as she began making short shrift of her Colazione del Doge, a breakfast of warm croissants, natural yoghurt, Venetian sausages and cheeses.

Their appetites fully sated they both sat back to savour their caffelattes as they admired the beautiful stone frontage of St Mark's Basilica and the fluted red brick shaft of the Campanile rising 160 feet above them.

'Do you really believe that's the 'High Place' described on the Chinese plate?' Jennifer pointed up at the cube-like design that sat above the belfry near the top of the bell tower. The Lion of St Mark was carved on each of the four sides.

'I think so and we'll know after we've had a chance to explore the park gardens which lie somewhere behind us.'

'It's such a beautiful sight and yet so old.' Jennifer's neck was beginning to feel stiff and yet she couldn't stop looking up at the four-arched stone loggia that surrounded the belfry.

'Not so old, Jenny,' James replied. 'The original Campanile collapsed in 1902. It was a miraculous event because fortunately nobody was killed apart from the caretaker's cat. It was only in 1912 that it was completely reconstructed to exactly the same design.'

'Is it safe to sit so close to it now?' Jennifer looked at James and then back at the tower with mock terror on her face.

'It's perfectly safe, you silly thing. The new tower had additional reinforcements built in to ensure the same thing didn't happen again.' James placed a small sheaf of Euros on the bill. They walked around the square until they reached a road called Riva degli Schiavoni.

Traders were in the act of unlocking a row of small conical-roofed kiosks. They hung brightly coloured souvenirs on the shutters and unfolding walls in time for the expected flood of tourists. As they walked towards the entrance to the small park Jennifer's eye was caught by the varied skills of the artists who were unpacking their canvases and standing them in their own allotted spaces.

'Some of them are quite lovely,' she murmured as she paused before a scene depicting a moored gondola in a minor canal. 'There's a lot of atmosphere in this one.'

'And a lot of euros on the label,' James said softly as he pulled on her elbow and they continued on to the high wrought-iron gates that were being unlocked by an attendant. They joined the small band of tourists entering the park and began a subtle search for their proverbial needle.

Jennifer put what they were both thinking into words. 'How on earth are we going to find a bronze cauldron in here and if it's so easy to find how come it hasn't been found already. Gardeners must work in here every day and the chance of them overlooking something as obvious as a 3,000-year-old bronze cauldron would be very slim indeed.'

James was about to agree when he saw a familiar face in the crowd. 'Quick, come this way,' he hissed and taking Jennifer's arm he led her away from the main group and down a small path.

'What's wrong,' she asked when they were beyond earshot.

'Ambrossini is what is wrong.' He peered through the foliage to where the group was beginning to thin out as people went down various paths. 'It's a very strange coincidence that Signore Paulo Ambrossini, a curator at the Museo Di Doccia, should also choose to do his sight seeing in this place.'

'Was he the man you saw in Sesto Fiorentino?'

'That's right, he showed us the ceramic plate at the museum and I can only assume that he has also been working at interpreting the message and has come up with the same answer.'

'He may have had the solution before you came asking your questions and taking pictures of the plate.'

'I didn't think of that. If he knows all about the ding then he may be here now with plans to hide it somewhere else or at the very least empty the vessel of its contents.'

'Those *bi* you mentioned would be worth quite a lot of money, wouldn't they?' Jennifer asked.

'Millions,' James murmured as he spotted Ambrossini striding purposefully towards the far end of the park. 'Let's follow and see if our latest assumption is correct.'

The couple retraced their steps and went the same way the curator had taken. The trees were growing more dense as were the boxwood hedges lining the pathway they were on – there was no cover should Ambrossini turn round. Fortunately the man seemed too engrossed in reaching his goal to notice anyone behind him.

Red benches lined the path where it turned abruptly to the left but the curator went straight on to where a maintenance shed stood behind a temporary barrier. James stopped and turned and taking Jennifer in his arms he kissed her.

'Stay where you are – ' he whispered when she instinctively tried to pull back. ' – he's going to check if he's being followed and he knows my face.'

Jennifer understood immediately and like the archetypal hot-blooded Latin lover she eagerly pressed her lips to his. 'What's he doing now?' James managed to say. She ended the kiss and looked over his shoulder. Ambrossini was pulling the barrier to one side to give him enough space to slip inside.

'He is putting the barrier back in place and going round behind the shed,' she whispered in his ear.

James turned and hurried down the path with Jennifer close behind. He looked round and seeing that it was clear in all directions he pulled the wire barrier to one side as the curator had done and they both squeezed through. James held a finger to his lips and indicated that Jennifer should stay where she was and then crept round the shed slowly to find Ambrossini kneeling by a small pit. A wooden cover, a small heap of soil and old leaves revealed how the pit had been concealed.

As James approached a twig snapped and Ambrossini jumped up to face him. 'What do you want?' he snapped nervously before realizing that he knew the person creeping up on him. 'It's Mr Goodfellow isn't it?'

James stepped closer and looked down into the hole to see a small piece of canvas pulled to one side to reveal a metal container set into the soil. The interior was dark and as he moved slightly he could catch a glimpse of something light in colour.

'You cracked the code, Signore Ambrossini?' James said unnecessarily. 'When did you first find this?' and he pointed down to the cauldron.

'It was the day after you came to the museum. I was fascinated by your interest and spent some time studying the picture and the text. I then chanced it and took the train to Venice. I hid in the hedge until the gates had been locked for the night and began searching the whole place when everyone had gone. I managed to find the item during the second evening.'

'And how many *bi* have you taken?'

The curator cast a sheepish look at James. 'Only two and I sold both of them to a dealer I know in Venice who doesn't ask questions. These would have been the third and fourth.' The two small discs were made of white jade with inscriptions carved into the precious mineral.

Drawn round by their voices, Jennifer went round behind the shed. Ambrossini gasped, 'Good God, you brought a woman with you!'

'And why not,' James said.

'There are many seeking these objects. Men who think nothing of resorting to violence to get what they want.'

'You think I don't know that,' James snapped. 'My friend's cousin was shot to death and his brother was tortured and slaughtered for this.' James gestured towards the artefacts and spat out the last word like a bad taste in the mouth.

'I had no hand in those unfortunate deaths, I just wanted to retire in reasonable comfort and the Chinese plate showed me how that could be a reality. The museum doesn't exactly pay me a fortune every month and I'm no longer a young man.'

'So you decided to become a thief.' Jennifer frowned at the curator as she gripped James's arm.

'How can I be a thief when these belong to nobody.'

'They are historic relics that belong to a particular Chinese family, Signore Ambrossini,' James said firmly as he held out his hand until the ashen-faced man dropped both discs into his palm. 'I will make a point of returning them.'

'There are so many of them, a few would not be missed,' Ambrossini protested as he watched James drop the discs into his jacket pocket.

'There's no moral argument in your words, sir,' Jenny snapped before turning to James. 'What can we do now, the *ding* looks so heavy and obviously this man cannot be trusted.'

'We will put the lid back on and disguise the site we are able to return with the right authorities to perform the recovery.' James paused before flipping the canvas back into place and replacing the wooden lid for he had seen something in the dark interior that seemed out of place. He moved a few of the stacked *bi* and took the object very carefully and slipped it into an inside pocket. As he scattered soil and dead leaves over the rotting lid Jenny tapped him on the shoulder.

'What about Mr Ambrossini?'

James finished the camouflage and stood up. 'Sir, we will forget that you have already disposed of two items or were ever involved in this matter but only if you agree to leave this place and these curios alone and return to Sesto Fiorentino. You must never come back to this park again.'

The curator stared into James's eyes and could only see an honourable offer, a lifeline being handed to him and he swiftly nodded. 'Thank you, Signore Goodfellow, you are being most generous and forgivi – ' the man stopped abruptly as his forehead disintegrated and he fell forward. James instinctively grabbed Jenny and pulled her to the ground.

'We must move away quickly before the shooter comes looking for us,' James whispered close to her ear. 'Keep low and follow me as quietly as you can.' He began crawling through a gap in the hedge and then along the wire fence until he found a point where two fence panels joined. He inched one of the panels outward until there was sufficient space for them to crawl through. They left the gardener's service area and crouching low they hurried through the shrubbery and trees until they reached a pathway thronged with visitors.

'What now?' Jenny gasped as they hurried through the gateway. They fought the urge to run, fearing a bullet in the back at any moment and kept to a steady walking pace that wouldn't draw too much attention to themselves despite the obvious muddy state of their clothing.

'We have to find the nearest Polizia before the gunman finds us,' James said ignoring the looks they were getting from tourists and locals alike.

'I seem to remember walking past a police station further along that way when we were coming,' Jenny said pointing to the Museo di Palazzo Ducale. James followed her lead and they walked fast along the Riva degli Schiavoni, past the Hotel Danieli and over the Rio de Vin that was thronged with back-packing tourists.

'There was something else apart from *bi* in the *ding*,' he said in a low voice and he slowed his pace and led her to the water's edge. 'This was amongst the jade; in size and shape it seemed very similar until I studied it closer and saw that it was made of glass.'

He removed the item from his pocket and shielding it with his body from any casual onlookers he showed it to Jenny.

'It's a sealed petri dish and seems to have something growing inside.' He pointed to the green stain that had formed a dirty smudge in the clear gel.

'Why on earth would someone hide a laboratory petri dish in an ancient *ding*?' Jenny asked as she puzzled over the appearance of the growing bacteria.

'I don't know but I fear that this is the main reason why so many people are being killed.' James placed the dish back in his pocket.

'You think that may be a new type of a biological weapon?'

'Something like that; it's possible, and until we know more we must keep this to ourselves. Agreed?'

'Okay, but when we return to England you must hand that over to Inspector Tilley or at least to the right authorities.'

James nodded while continuing to glance back, trying to spot anyone giving the appearance of following them. They had crossed a total of four little stone bridges when Jenny suddenly pointed to the familiar green, white and red flag fluttering limply over the entrance to what appeared to be an official-looking building.

'I think that must be the place,' she said and stopped to read the plaques on the wall beside the stone entrance. It was festooned with CCTV cameras and James gave one last look behind them before following her into the cool, dark interior. A police officer was on the point of leaving the station when the dishevelled couple caught his attention.

'I wish to report a murder,' James said abruptly.

The junior officer stopped dead in his tracks and grasped James's arm as he fumbled for his holstered gun.

'No! I haven't murdered anyone,' James protested when he found himself looking down the barrel of a Beretta semi-automatic. 'We've found a body.'

The officer backed away with his weapon still pointing and he shouted something that James was unable to understand. In an instant doors were flung open and officers flooded the corridor with similar-looking pistols that were all aimed at the couple. James stepped in front of Jenny who moved in close behind him. Suddenly there was a sharp instruction shouted over the general hubbub and the uniforms parted, making way for a tall man in a light cream suit.

'I am Commissario Cinghiale. Who are you and what is it you wish to tell the police about someone having been murdered,' he said in excellent, lightly accented English.

'My name is Goodfellow and my friend is Jenny Kent. We're in Venice on a short holiday and when we were walking around the park along the Riva degli Schiavoni we heard a strange noise.'

'And what was that strange noise, signore?' The commissario asked as he looked round at his men and patted the air. The ring of men holstered their weapons.

'I went through a gap in the wire fencing on the right hand edge of the park and found a man lying on the ground behind a small work shed.'

'He had been shot in the head,' Jenny added.

'You went with your friend to investigate this noise?' Cinghiale said in an incredulous voice. 'Did you not think that would be a foolish thing to do?'

'I am a detective police constable in England and therefore familiar with investigating situations that could prove to be dangerous.' Jenny drew herself up to her full height and the commissario smiled and gave her an appreciative look before issuing rapid instruction to his men in Italian. Three assistente capos hurried out into the bright sunlight to verify the report.

'There was nobody around at the time? You didn't see the killer?' Cinghiale asked as he waved them through a doorway and they entered a spacious office containing one very large desk. Jenny and James sat down in two of the plain chairs that stood before the desk.

'Not at all,' she said as she watched two more officers file into the room and stand against the wall with eyes fixed on James.

'So it was purely by chance that you happened to be in the park at the same time the man was killed?' He had picked up a pen and was writing something down in a small notebook.

'That's right, Commissario,' James said crossing one leg over the other and fixing the senior officer with a steady gaze. 'We were getting a little tired of the usual tourist trail and the park appeared to be cool and restful.'

The officer looked pensively at the two facing him and then closed his notebook. 'We will wait for my men to report what they have found before we go any further.' Cinghiale looked at Jenny with a concerned expression. 'You have seen something very ugly and must be a little shocked, no matter what you say about being a tough policewoman.'

'It wasn't very nice,' Jenny agreed.

'Then would you like a little grappa in your espresso.' It was a rhetorical question as Cinghiale was already pouring a generous tot of the fiery spirit into the three steaming cups an officer had placed on his desk.

They both nodded and accepted the proffered cups. While they were taking their second sip of the powerful brew that an assistente capo entered the room and whispered in his superior's ear.

As the man left the office he gave the couple a sympathetic look and Cinghiale confirmed that he had found what they had claimed. 'Not only did he find the body but there was a recently excavated hole in the ground beside him that had contained something round.'

'Something round?' James said innocently.

'Yes, there were clear signs that the large hole had recently been used to conceal a receptacle of one kind or another. Do you have any idea what that may have been?' Picking Jenny as the easier target Cinghiale leant forward to look into her eyes. 'If you know what was taken it may help us to find the killer faster.'

Jenny didn't break eye contact as she calmly replied. 'There was no hole when we found the body, Commissario.'

'The killer must have come back and dug up whatever the item was,' James added, confidently.

'That could have been why the poor man was killed,' Jenny said which put into words precisely what the commissario was thinking.

'Possibly,' he said as he opened his notebook again. 'Where are you both staying?'

'The Rialto Hotel. We anticipate being there for at least another day and then we planned to return to London,' James said.

'With your permission, Commissario, naturally.' Jenny was familiar with police procedures and anticipated being asked to stay in Venice for a little while longer. She produced her police identity card and slid it over the desk for Cinghiale to take down the details and without being asked James did the same. The policeman's shaggy eyebrows rose when he saw the details.

'You are a private investigator?' he said with a touch of suspicion in his voice.

a calf muscle with a 7.62mm bullet. In spite of his pronounced limp the Secret Intelligence Service, formerly MI6, immediately recruited him for the knowledge locked in his head. He was encouraged to join the local council to create a perfect cover.

Rackman's first section chief at the Vauxhall Cross headquarters was Major Waterston with whom he had served in Afghanistan. When the major retired Rackman had become his intermediary with various intelligence officers in the SIS.

Two years elapsed before the major introduced him to the fundamental aims of an organization Rackman had only ever encountered in fanciful novels. After being fully briefed over two weeks by Waterston he was so excited by the aims of the organization that he secretly became a member of the Illuminati and was the major's prime information highway out of SIS headquarters.

With his high level of security clearance Rackman had direct access to intelligence being gathered within the country and overseas and on this occasion he made use of his position as a Business Support Officer to covertly do the airline check himself.

With meticulous care he slipped the 9mm Beretta 92 that he had liberated in Afghanistan into a calfskin shoulder holster and buttoned up his British Warm against the night.

It had been a simple matter of checking all the airlines with flights from Venice to establish that a certain Mr S. O'Rourke had returned to London that morning. With a degree of reluctance Rackman dialled the agent's apartment in Soho as though dialling a leper. His own house was in Chelsea on the Thames and he despised O'Rourke – he felt the combination of being Irish and living in a seedy Greek Street flat was far below the standards he had expected of an Illuminati. Whenever he complained to the major about this lowering of standards he had been ignored; Waterston knew O'Rourke had to be close to his triad associates, the major's enemies in the Chinese sector, if he was to gather reliable intelligence.

'O'Rourke,' was the curt response when the phone was lifted.

'This is Rackman, I need to talk to you urgently on an important matter that the major has raised with me.'

'Be here at ten o'clock sharp.'

'It wasn't very nice,' Jenny agreed.

'Then would you like a little grappa in your espresso.' It was a rhetorical question as Cinghiale was already pouring a generous tot of the fiery spirit into the three steaming cups an officer had placed on his desk.

They both nodded and accepted the proffered cups. While they were taking their second sip of the powerful brew that an assistente capo entered the room and whispered in his superior's ear.

As the man left the office he gave the couple a sympathetic look and Cinghiale confirmed that he had found what they had claimed. 'Not only did he find the body but there was a recently excavated hole in the ground beside him that had contained something round.'

'Something round?' James said innocently.

'Yes, there were clear signs that the large hole had recently been used to conceal a receptacle of one kind or another. Do you have any idea what that may have been?' Picking Jenny as the easier target Cinghiale leant forward to look into her eyes. 'If you know what was taken it may help us to find the killer faster.'

Jenny didn't break eye contact as she calmly replied. 'There was no hole when we found the body, Commissario.'

'The killer must have come back and dug up whatever the item was,' James added, confidently.

'That could have been why the poor man was killed,' Jenny said which put into words precisely what the commissario was thinking.

'Possibly,' he said as he opened his notebook again. 'Where are you both staying?'

'The Rialto Hotel. We anticipate being there for at least another day and then we planned to return to London,' James said.

'With your permission, Commissario, naturally.' Jenny was familiar with police procedures and anticipated being asked to stay in Venice for a little while longer. She produced her police identity card and slid it over the desk for Cinghiale to take down the details and without being asked James did the same. The policeman's shaggy eyebrows rose when he saw the details.

'You are a private investigator?' he said with a touch of suspicion in his voice.

'Even a private investigator needs to take a romantic break from work from time to time, Commissario.'

'Si. I understand. And naturally all private detectives in England take their vacation with a police officer?' His voice lacked all humour.

Cinghiale stood up and indicated they could do the same. 'I will have one of my men take you to the hotel by launch. I would appreciate it if you would remain there until I am satisfied with your story; then you will be able to continue with your vacation.' His brusque tone clearly showed his dissatisfaction with the couple's version of the events.

'Thank you, Commissario.' James extended his hand but it was ignored and the couple followed the officer allocated to take them to the Rialto Hotel. As they crossed the road outside the police station and descended the steps to the moored boat they were unaware of the tall man leaning against the balustrade of a small bridge nearby. O'Rourke was using his cellphone to talk to an Illuminati team member who, with two others disguised as gardeners, had recovered the *ding* and transferred it to a small boat that would take it to the airport.

He nodded with a look of satisfaction and made the decision to leave the investigator and the policewoman alone. He no longer found it necessary to tidy up the loose ends unless Major Waterston instructed him otherwise.

O'Rourke watched the couple sitting arm in arm like a pair of lovers in the back of the launch as it powered away from the quayside and sped towards the entrance to the Grand Canal.

'Arrivederci, signore Goodfellow. There is a chance that we may meet again, especially if you continue to annoy me.'

13

ENGLAND

MAJOR WATERSTON HAD JUST replaced the phone and was furiously crushing out his Havana cigar when Rackman entered the room.

'The stupid fools haven't recovered the formula,' he shouted across the room and Rackman winced at his tone. 'They went to great expense and sent the whole thing back by charter plane instead of taking it out of the *ding* and sending it to me by special courier. The bastards even neglected to check whether the dish was still hidden in the damned pot.'

'The dish is gone?' Rackman asked with a puzzled look as though he hadn't quite understood the significance of what had been said and the major glared at him as though he was an idiot. 'What I meant was,' Rackman mumbled hastily. 'Who could have taken it in Venice? Has O'Rourke turned double agent or did the Chinese get to it first?'

'That's for you to find out and you'd better do it soon. I want the sample and the formula worked out before the week finishes or heads will roll.' The major glowered and gave a dismissive wave of his hand. The councillor left the room knowing he would have to find O'Rourke if he was to have any chance of learning who had taken the petri dish.

Second Lieutenant Richard Rackman had been invalided out of the counter-terrorist squadron of the SAS after a Taliban sniper had shredded a calf muscle with a 7.62mm bullet. In spite of his pronounced limp the Secret Intelligence Service, formerly MI6, immediately recruited him for the knowledge locked in his head. He was encouraged to join the local council to create a perfect cover.

Rackman's first section chief at the Vauxhall Cross headquarters was Major Waterston with whom he had served in Afghanistan. When the major retired Rackman had become his intermediary with various intelligence officers in the SIS.

Two years elapsed before the major introduced him to the fundamental aims of an organization Rackman had only ever encountered in fanciful novels. After being fully briefed over two weeks by Waterston he was so excited by the aims of the organization that he secretly became a member of the Illuminati and was the major's prime information highway out of SIS headquarters.

With his high level of security clearance Rackman had direct access to intelligence being gathered within the country and overseas and on this occasion he made use of his position as a Business Support Officer to covertly do the airline check himself.

With meticulous care he slipped the 9mm Beretta 92 that he had liberated in Afghanistan into a calfskin shoulder holster and buttoned up his British Warm against the night.

It had been a simple matter of checking all the airlines with flights from Venice to establish that a certain Mr S. O'Rourke had returned to London that morning. With a degree of reluctance Rackman dialled the agent's apartment in Soho as though dialling a leper. His own house was in Chelsea on the Thames and he despised O'Rourke – he felt the combination of being Irish and living in a seedy Greek Street flat was far below the standards he had expected of an Illuminati. Whenever he complained to the major about this lowering of standards he had been ignored; Waterston knew O'Rourke had to be close to his triad associates, the major's enemies in the Chinese sector, if he was to gather reliable intelligence.

'O'Rourke,' was the curt response when the phone was lifted.

'This is Rackman, I need to talk to you urgently on an important matter that the major has raised with me.'

'Be here at ten o'clock sharp.'

The hissing on the line stopped and Rackman was left holding a dead phone. Bastard, he thought as he replaced the handset in the base unit. Who the hell does he think he is to give *me* orders.

Rackman had only limped a dozen yards from his front gate in the chill wind when he spotted a cruising taxi and was able to climb into its welcome warmth. He alighted in Soho Square and walked briskly down Greek Street until he was outside a door that was beginning to show its age. A trio of nameplates glowing bright yellow against the peeling black paint listed two photographic models, Candy and Scarlet, and the top plate simply read S. O'Rourke.

The door clicked open seconds after he had pressed O'Rourke's name and he hurried up the narrow staircase to the top floor. The door on the first floor opened to his heavy tread and he glimpsed a plump, middle-aged woman wearing a transparent negligee and little else. She leered at him and then shut her door with a disappointed slam as he continued on climbing the stairs.

A shadow darkened the peephole before the safety chain rattled and two bolts were withdrawn. O'Rourke was muffled in a large, dark-blue dressing gown and wearing green slippers. Rackman couldn't help noticing his hairy legs as he was waved past and in to a small living room.

'Welcome to my humble abode, *Lieutenant*.' O'Rourke greeted him with an element of sarcasm in his voice. He had always detested British army officers and disliked the major's sycophant as much as the man disliked him.

Rackman selected one of the two armchairs and without being asked sat down and stretched both legs. Without wasting words on polite greetings Rackman got straight to the point. 'The petri dish wasn't in the delivery and the major is bloody furious,' he snapped. 'Where is it?'

O'Rourke raised an eyebrow and poured himself a whisky without bothering to offer one to his visitor. 'I can only assume that someone had taken it from the *ding* without my knowledge. It may have been one of the boatmen or anyone else who handled the crate between Venice and London.'

'How can I believe you?'

'You have to take my word, the word of an Illuminati.'

'The word of a triad, you mean.'

O'Rourke put his glass down slowly and turned to face the man. 'Are you inferring that I stole the dish?'

Rackman moved in the armchair on the pretext of getting more comfortable but in fact was giving himself easier access to the weapon under his left arm. 'That was not what I said, O'Rourke.'

'What *did* you mean? You know I infiltrated the Hong Kong triad to help our cause.'

'It's missing. The culture is missing and we have to find it quickly and get it analyzed or we will be in real shit with the major.' He paused for breath while watching O'Rourke's face. 'I know all about the reasons given for you becoming a member of the criminal class but where does your true loyalty lie?' Rackman's tone clearly revealed his lack of faith in the Irishman.

O'Rourke ignored the question and picking up his glass he took a sip. 'Ambrossini or Goodfellow must have taken it from the *ding* before I went back to unearth it with the team who took it to the launch.'

'Ambrossini? Goodfellow? Who are they? Why would these apparent strangers be interested in our affairs?' Rackman countered. 'For whom are they working?'

'The Italian was a harmless museum curator and Goodfellow is a private investigator. Both became involved because someone killed the brother of a Chinese restaurant owner. The brother had owned an old ceramic plate that contained clues to the whereabouts of the *ding*. He had sold this to an Italian museum and Goodfellow traced the plate and followed those clues. Ambrossini had also seen the answer and purely by chance, the two men located the hiding place of the *ding* in Venice at the very same time.'

'And now one of them has the petri dish?'

'I do not know. However, I was able to eliminate Ambrossini but when I returned to recover the cauldron I didn't have time to go through his pockets.'

'So you're telling me that this man Goodfellow may also have taken it and if *he* didn't then the dish could now be classified as evidence in a Venetian police station where they are currently investigating the murder of an Italian curator?'

'That's about the size of it, yes.'

'You'd better hope that Goodfellow took it.'

'Or what, Rackman?' O'Rourke opened the dressing gown, revealing a well-toned muscular body and a fully automatic Glock 18 tucked in the waistband of his undershorts.

Rackman admired the weapon, interlaced his fingers beneath his chin and looked up into O'Rourke's eyes. 'It looks like we will both need to watch our backs.'

The Irishman grinned before closing his gown and sitting in the armchair facing Rackman. 'I'll check Goodfellow to see if he took it and what he has done with it. There's a good chance he had no idea what it was, got bored and tossed it into the Grand Canal.'

'If this investigator doesn't have it then you will have to get that piece of evidence from the Venetian police yourself.'

'Hold it right there Rackman, why can't you help me. Doesn't SIS have an understanding with the Italian police in all cases concerning acts of terrorism?' O'Rourke watched Rackman's eyes closely as he waited for an answer.

'There is no way I can use any of my resources at Vauxhall Cross. Any action on my part, and that includes international inquiries, would automatically flag a warning and put a red tag against my name. This would then focus attention on my activities and those of the major as my relationship with him is well known in the department.' Rackman's eyes had begun to flick left and right like a cornered rat in a chicken coop seeking a way to escape.

'What is the good of being an SIS officer if you can't use the powers given to you?' O'Rourke pressed.

'With power comes responsibility and what you're suggesting lacks any responsible thought. This could terminate the major's source of first class intelligence by putting me away at Her Majesty's Pleasure for many years.'

'Not a bad thing, Rackman.'

Xun had the patience of a cat waiting beneath a bird feeder. Three days after setting up camp in a boarding house opposite the Bunch of Grapes he finally caught sight of O'Rourke getting out of a taxi and going into the hotel. From his vantage point in the poorly furnished bedroom he looked down upon the tall man striding into the hotel. He gave a satisfied grunt and he only had to wait a further few minutes before a light appeared at a first-floor window. O'Rourke soon appeared and after peering down at the street below he drew the heavy curtains.

It was as he entered the hotel reception lobby that O'Rourke collided with Frankie Trist. 'Mr Trist!' he exclaimed. 'How nice to see you again. I've been to Italy for a short break and now I'm a little short of cash. You know how expensive Venetian holidays can be. I was wondering if you would return my £500 before I remember that it should be locked in my case upstairs.' The charming Irish lilt had rapidly deteriorated and the landlord blanched at the harshness, knowing too well that his theft may lead to painful consequences.

'Very nice to see you too, sir,' he stuttered. 'If you would give me a few minutes I'll bring it to your room.'

'No problem, take your time Frankie. You have three minutes.' O'Rourke went up to his room and after closing the curtains he turned slowly, examining every aspect of the room and his belongings until he was thoroughly satisfied that nothing had been disturbed this time.

The international news was just finishing without any mention of a murder in Venice when there was a light tap at the door. O'Rourke switched the television off and called for Trist to enter. As soon as the man had closed the door behind him O'Rourke grabbed him by the shirt collar and lifted him up off his feet, pinning him to the wall. Trist struggled vainly as he felt himself being choked. The banknotes he had been carrying fluttered to the ground as he tried to remove the big man's fingers from his throat.

'The next time you decide to take money without asking be prepared to lose the hand that took it.' O'Rourke dropped Trist and he fell to the floor where he lay gasping for breath. The toe of a Jack Jones leather boot punched into his back and he felt a sharp, searing pain in the kidney area.

'Now pick it up and give it to me.'

Trist crawled to where the money lay scattered, gathered up the notes and held them up to O'Rourke. It was not something he fancied explaining when his wife would undoubtedly challeng him later.

'Please, don't hit me again,' Trist pleaded and O'Rourke grabbed him by the arms and roughly pulled him to his feet.

Trist yelped. 'You wont tell the police will you? You can stay rent free for as long as you like. I'll clear that with the wife.' Shit, I'm really up to my neck in it, he thought as the incensed man brought his face close to Trist's.

'I have no need of the police.' O'Rourke pushed the wheezing man towards the door. 'If I judge you need punishment I'll do it myself. Do you fully understand me, Frankie?'

The use of his first name gave even more credibility to the threat and Trist nodded vigorously with terror in his eyes. He clutched at the searing pain in his side with one hand as he struggled to open the door as quickly as he could.

'Don't forget, Frankie. If anything goes missing from this room again you wont know what hit you. You had also better tell those who clean my room to keep their itchy fingers away from my property. Make sure of that because I will hold you responsible.'

Trist nodded wordlessly and O'Rourke slammed the door in his face and returned to sit on the bed to ponder his next move. Goodfellow was on his mind and if that investigator had found and kept the petri dish he would need to question him before he made any decisions about what to do with the culture. That's if he had taken it from the *ding* and also if he hadn't already disposed of the dish.

After a quick shower and change of clothing O'Rourke slipped the Glock beneath his belt and locked his room. He left the Bunch of Grapes without any sign of Trist in reception and walked quickly through East Steading until he was outside the door to Goodfellow Investigations. It was still very early; the restaurant was closed and appeared to be empty. He pushed the buzzer beside the well-polished brass plate and announced himself to the tinny voice on the intercom.

'My name is O'Grady. I would like to speak with Mr Goodfellow about the case he is currently working on.'

The hiss of the speaker ceased, the door clicked and he climbed the steep flight of stairs to enter the reception.

'How can I help you, Mr O'Grady?'

O'Rourke replied with his most winning grin and the gentle lilt of his voice instantly Miss Lightbody at ease. 'I would like to speak to Mr Goodfellow about a certain item that was recovered in the city of Venice. I believe he returned from Italy yesterday.'

Miss Lightbody couldn't contain her curiosity. 'You know who has it and where it is now?' she said hoping to tease an extra tidbit of information from the man.

'I'm sorry, madam, but this is a highly confidential matter and I can only speak directly to your employer.'

'One moment, sir,' Miss Lightbody replied as she reverted to a cut-glass tone that implied she wasn't normally excluded from her employer's private matters. She tapped on a door marked private and indicated that he should go in. O'Rourke made a point of closing the door behind him and Miss Lightbody frowned at the snub. He seemed such a pleasant young man, too, she thought.

When the door closed firmly James looked up from the mail he had been opening and instantly snatched at the metal baseball bat under the desk.

'Good morning, Mr Goodfellow. I note that you're pleased to see me.' O'Rourke had seen the investigator's reaction and he stopped short of the desk and eyed the bat James was gripping.

'What do you want this time?' James asked.

'I went on a little trip to Venice last week where unfortunately you and your bit of skirt found something that I have been looking for. I say unfortunately because I have to inform you that you stepped into a minefield the moment you put your sticky fingers into the honey pot.'

'What the hell are you talking about?' He had avoided the direct lie and James was able to keep a straight face without the betrayal of a stutter.

'For God's sake, man. I was there and I saw you and the woman cop. You were at the place where the bronze cauldron had been buried and you were with the man from the museum.'

'What man are you talking about?'

'The one I killed,' O'Rourke growled ominously as he took the Glock from behind his back and pointed it at James's head. 'And you'll be next if you don't hand over what I want.'

'What is that?'

'The dish. Don't play dumb with me; you're the only one who could have taken it.'

'If by chance I did have this dish you talk about and don't give it to you what will you do then?'

'I'll go out into what you call reception and blow your secretary's head apart with this.' O'Rourke waggled the barrel of the heavy weapon.

James looked into the man's ice-blue eyes and realized he was quite capable of doing it. 'Very well, you can have it but you will have to give me two days to retrieve it.'

'Where from?'

James could see that O'Rourke was puzzled. Why was the dish not kept on the premises why would it take so long to get it?

'For safety's sake I sent it to an address that's up in the north, deep in the countryside.'

O'Rourke stared suspiciously at James. 'Go and get it and return here in two days at the same time precisely. Make sure you bring only the petri dish or the life of your employee *and* your girlfriend will be forfeit.'

James nodded grimly.

'Remember, Goodfellow,' he snapped. 'If I see the police or anybody else within a mile of your front door you'll be advertising for a new secretary and buying a hot water bottle to keep you warm at night. Do you understand?'

James nodded and went into reception to speak briefly to Miss Lightbody. She had clearly understood the situation before James told her about O'Rourke's ultimatum and after slipping on her jacket she left the office with a determined expression on her pallid features. James had always admired her courage but he nonetheless whispered that she should immediately go and visit her sister on the coast until he gave her the all clear.

James closed the door behind her with his fingers mentally crossed and returned to the office where O'Rourke was ominously tapping the glass of his wristwatch. The Irishman warily aimed his gun at James and gave a derisive wave before leaving the office and hurrying down the stairs.

James ran upstairs and quietly crept back into the bedroom to discover that Jenny had already left for the police station to make her report to Bristow.

Thank God she left without visiting me in the office, he thought.

Two days later and on the hour O'Rourke returned as arranged. Miss Lightbody, who had told James that she refused to be intimidated by 'some cheap hoodlum' greeted the man icily. She showed him into the office and asked him to wait. She returned to her desk and unobtrusively pushed a button beneath the edge of her desk to alert James. James put his slice of buttered toast down – breakfast would have to wait.

Carefully unpicking the lining of his travel case he inserted the petri dish he had been keeping warm in the airing cupboard. He then re-stitched the lining and after dousing his hair under the shower he went downstairs to the office.

O'Rourke was still sitting in the investigator's chair with the Glock loosely pointing at Miss Lightbody. 'Took your time, Goodfellow,' he said as James entered the office carrying a small well-used case. He watched James like a hawk as the case was placed on the desk.

'You caught me taking a shower.' James flicked the catches to open the case and O'Rourke raised the automatic threateningly.

'No tricks, Goodfellow. That case had better be empty.'

'It only contains one thing and I believe that's what you came for.' James gripped the corner of the silk lining and tore the fresh stitching. The petri dish fell out into his hand and he held it up for the Irishman to get a good look at the colourful bacterial culture.

'Not the most original hiding place.'

'Packed with dirty laundry and smelly trainers it was good enough to deter any curious customs officer,' James said. 'Now I want you to let Miss Lightbody leave the premises before I hand this over to you.'

'You're in no position to tell me what to do,' O'Rourke snarled, raising the automatic and pointing it at the secretary. 'This will fire thirty-four rounds in less than two seconds and remove her head completely. Do you think you can get to me in that time, Goodfellow?'

'No, but in those same two seconds I can drop this and crush it into the carpet with my heel,' James replied as he held the dish out at arms length making O'Rourke blanch and slowly lower the weapon.

'You shouldn't do that, Goodfellow! You don't know what it's capable of. Just hand it over to me and I'll leave without any need for further violence.'

When the automatic had been fully lowered James nodded towards Miss Lightbody. The Irishman briefly hesitated and then waved her from the room.

'Go home and don't tell anybody what's happened here otherwise your employer will die needlessly,' O'Rourke said brusquely.

The woman looked from the Glock to the mysterious petri dish that seemed to have such a hold over both men. 'I am concerned about what will happen to you, James,' she whispered, her eyes troubled but James shooed her to the door; as she reluctantly left the room he whispered: 'Your sister, don't forget your sister.' He returned to stand on the other side of the desk.

'Now you're showing some sense, Goodfellow,' O'Rourke pointed the gun at the dish in James's hand. 'I would advise you to treat that with extreme respect and to put it down on the desk very gently.'

James ignored the instruction, walked across to the window casually and opened it wide while keeping his eyes fixed on O'Rourke who was aiming the weapon at his head.

'No stupid mistakes,' O'Rourke warned.

James waited until he heard the front door slam shut and the heels of Miss Lightbody's sensible court shoes clicking away on the pavement before turning and placing the dish on the desktop.

O'Rourke kept the automatic steady as he went to the desk and slipped the dish into an inside pocket. 'Move left and give me plenty of room to leave,' he instructed as he slowly moved to the right of the office and the two men circled like a pair of pugilists.

O'Rourke was well beyond James's reach when he left the office and closed the door behind him. The investigator listened to the big man descending the stairs and hurried to the window to watch him leave the building before heaving a big sigh of relief and collapsing into his chair.

James didn't see the figure who slipped from the shadows of a doorway across the street and was now following the Irishman.

14

XUN WATCHED THE IRISHMAN leave the detective's office and began trailing him as the morning light grew brighter and the early commuters increased in number. People hurrying to bus stops and the railway station provided natural cover for the stalker.

The triad enforcer had been O'Rourke's shadow for the last two days. He had wondered why the man hadn't made any move from the Bunch of Grapes and the only conclusion Xun could come to was that O'Rourke had yet to take possession of the *ding* and that the investigator was involved.

Xun had decided to question Goodfellow and was on the point of crossing the high street when O'Rourke appeared and entered the building. Xun waited and his target soon emerged and took a direction away from his hotel. The pattern had been broken and Xen's hunter instinct told him that he was getting close to the *ding*.

O'Rourke was setting a fast pace but the athletic triad easily kept him in sight and they soon arrived at East Steading railway station.

'Where is that tall man going?' Xun asked the bored-looking man behind the grille.

'What's it to you, mate?'

'I'm a private detective and his wife thinks that he is cheating.'

'Not my business. Where do you want to go?'

'Same place as him,' Xun pointed across the track to where O'Rourke was purchasing a paper from the news-stand.

A ticket was flicked under the bars and the twenty-pound note Xun had put down disappeared. 'You should let the poor bugger have his bit of fun. His wife's most probably a killjoy anyway,' the ticket clerk said sullenly as Xun walked away pocketing his change.

Xun made his way up the steps to the footbridge, careful not to alert O'Rourke. He waited until the train was pulling in before going down swiftly to board the last coach.

Midday came and so did the rain as Xun followed O'Rourke from the underground station in Sloane Square to one of the Victorian terraced houses that surrounded Cadogan Square Gardens. Iron railings enclosed the small residents' park in the centre but an open gate allowed Xun to slip through and sit down on a wooden bench that gave him a perfect view of the address through the lush foliage. A hastily purchased umbrella barely kept him dry and water constantly dripped down the nape of his neck.

Xun had been waiting five minutes when another man scurried down the road with an umbrella angled against the inclement weather and entered the same house. He had been limping heavily and was a complete stranger to the triad. Then a number of men in raincoats arrived. They were admitted the instant they pressed the doorbell and announced themselves. He was unable to hear what was being said, the thrumming of drops on his umbrella masking every sound in the square.

O'Rourke went to stand at the second-floor window. He was waiting for Major Waterston to finish his phone call and he whiled time by studying the trees and shrubbery filling the garden. He had become aware of the Oriental as he was leaving the tube station and had taken a circuitous route to confirm his suspicion. Now he studied the suspicious figure that was sitting on the bench and rather foolishly becoming wetter with each passing minute.

The door beside him opened and Lawrence Forster beckoned to him. O'Rourke entered the oak-panelled room lined with portraits of stern-faced military men from every armed service. Their eyes seemed to follow him as did those of the men seated around the large polished table that reflected their faces as he went to the only vacant seat.

'Welcome Sèan. I believe you have some good news for us all,' Major Waterston said waving to the chair as an invitation to sit.

'I have indeed, Major.' O'Rourke took the sealed petri dish from his pocket and sent it sliding across the table where it was stopped by the hand of the startled major.

'Take care, man. This is too dangerous to play with,' Waterston said as he picked the dish up gingerly and studied the culture through the thick glass. 'Have you had it analyzed to check it's strength yet?'

'I'll be taking it straight from here to Guildford as my first priority.' It had been ten months since O'Rourke had told the major that he had developed a reliable contact who worked in a research laboratory and that they should consider purchasing the company should the Illuminati have need of such an operation – the time had come and the organization now had their own research facility.

The major drew on his Cuban and the rising blue cloud joined the pall of cigar smoke hanging like stratocumulus beneath the elaborately stuccoed ceiling. He held the dish up for the others present to see and then held it out for O'Rourke to take.

As the Illuminati agent left the house Xun prepared to follow for it was clear that he wasn't struggling under the weight of a *ding*. To his amazement O'Rourke didn't turn to walk down the street but walked directly across and through the open gate. Xun leant forward and held the umbrella lower to hide his face. A pair of black shoes entered his field of vision, stopped and turned to face towards him.

'Well, if it isn't the *Red Pole* from Hong Kong. What a coincidence,' O'Rourke declared and he sat beside the triad enforcer. 'I'm surprised you haven't made your move yet. What are you waiting for?'

Xun raised the umbrella and folded it before answering. 'I need to know where the *ding* is before I carry out the Mountain Master's orders,' he said slipping one hand into his pocket to feel the cold grip of the Colt semi-automatic.

O'Rourke burst into laughter. 'Is that all you want, Xun?' he exclaimed with surprise.

The *Red Pole* raised his eyebrows at the man's reaction. 'You have it and the *bi* that fill it?'

'I know who has it now and if you want it that much I will point you in their direction but as for myself I couldn't care less about those trinkets.'

The rain had completely stopped and the clouds were beginning to clear as Xun waited for O'Rourke to give him the answer that would end his search. His finger tightened on the trigger in preparation to eliminate the triad traitor.

O'Rourke was reading the Oriental's mind and he held his hand up. 'If you think I'm going to tell you everything now and then sit calmly while you pull the trigger of the gun you have in your pocket then you have another thought coming.'

Xun's eyes narrowed.

'I will lead you to the *ding* tomorrow and not before.'

'Is it far?'

'No. It is hidden not far from where the small freighter I used to ship it here is docked. Meet me at nine o'clock in the morning and we'll go to the old Spillers Mills building near Royal Victoria Dock. The items were transported from there to the derelict mill.'

'Thank you Sèan,' Xun said as he took the Colt from his pocket and jammed it into O'Rourke's side to muffle the sound od any report.

'I wouldn't do that Xun. The mill is twelve-storeys high and there are thousands of square metres on every floor. There are also hundreds of rooms crammed with machinery which would take you more than a year to search.'

The gun remained pressed into O'Rourke's side while Xun tossed a mental coin.

'I should also mention that there are three armed men who have a vested interest in the value of the cauldron and its contents,' O'Rourke added quietly.

The triad replaced the Colt in his pocket and stood up, his hand still gripping the butt. 'Where shall we meet?'

'I suggest that you take the Docklands Light Railway to the Pontoon Dock station where I will meet you and take you on by car to the mill building.'

Xun waited until O'Rourke had walked to the gate on the opposite side of the park before he turned and headed back to the tube station. At this stage of the search a bullet or knife in the back wouldn't be too welcome.

James knew that it was only a matter of time before O'Rourke discovered he had been given a substitute petri dish. Feng had made a hot water solution of agar-agar that he used frequently in the kitchen to set dishes. A minuscule drop of chicken blood had been added to act as food for the bacteria. The dish had been set to a jelly-hard consistency in the refrigerator before a final press of his finger on the surface. Then two days in a dark, warm part of the kitchen had completed the transformation.

'What have we grown?' Feng asked his friend as he lifted it down from the top shelf and stared in amazement the bright green, yellow and purple spores that emulated the original sealed petri

'Damned if I know, Feng, and I don't want to,' James said strongly. 'However, we must never unseal it as those spores may do us some harm if they got into a small cut or were breathed in. Only a chemist will be able to determine whether it's safe or not and that will take some time in a professional laboratory.'

'What are you planning to do with the time until the Irishman comes back looking for the original culture?'

'I will spend it looking for a safe hiding place and then I'll need to identify the right people in government to talk to.' James laid a hand on Feng's shoulder. 'I have the distinct impression that the culture growing in the dish I found is far more dangerous than I first thought. It may even be deadly and if released into the atmosphere could be carried vast distances by the slightest breeze.'

Feng looked round and stopped chopping the vegetables he was prepping. 'Now you've got me really worried, James. Where is the bloody thing now?'

'Don't worry, it's upstairs in a sealed bag and I'll be sending it away from here tonight.' James patted his friend's shoulder once more and turned to leave. 'Give my apologies to Jiao for not staying to enjoy her food and I wouldn't say anything about this to her. We wouldn't want to worry her needlessly.'

Feng waved to the investigator as he left and shuddered. Why had the original culture been created?

Returning to the apartment James immediately took the original petri dish from his wash bag. He held it up to the light over the washbasin and was alarmed to see that the culture now covered the whole disc. He placed it in a zip-lock sandwich bag and tightly wound tape around it until it was a airtight as he could make it.

A padded envelope seemed to be good protection for the glass dish and with a large felt-tip pen James addressed it to Detective Constable Jennifer Kent, East Steading police station. A short note was enclosed and an adequate number of postage stamps were applied to guarantee first class delivery.

James concealed the envelope beneath his jacket and after checking the street he left the building and walked rapidly to the post office in the next street. Another quick check showed nothing unusual in the daily routine of the street and as the brown packet dropped into the security of Her Majesty's mail James gave a sigh of relief and headed back to the office to plan his next move.

Xun alighted at Pontoon Dock railway station and went down the stairs to ground level where he found O'Rourke waiting. He was standing beside a small blue van with a trade name emblazoned across the side.

'Plumber's Mate? So you've got a real job at last.' Xun's mirthless laugh didn't reach his ice-cold eyes as he got in on the passenger's side with one hand firmly placed in his coat pocket.

'I picked it up in Wandsworth so we have approximately forty minutes to collect the ding and take it to wherever you want before it becomes too hot to drive.'

'Why steal? You could have hired a car.'

'I'm in this country temporarily and spreading my name around while I'm here wouldn't be very clever.'

'Why, are you planning to kill someone today?'

O'Rourke laughed briefly, fell silent and after a few seconds turned sharp right to head towards the Royal Victoria Dock. The road was lined with semi-detached homes that soon thinned out until they were confronted by a single brick chimney standing by itself on a roundabout. Rising one hundred and twenty feet high it was a lone monument to the industrial activity that once dominated this part of the river Thames.

The car circled and took a right turn to be faced by plain concrete walls on both sides and ahead. One side of a double gate was open and O'Rourke drove through and into a wasteland that was overshadowed by a monumental derelict building.

Xun looked up as they drew closer and his grip tightened on the Colt in his pocket. The multi-storeyed face of Spillers Mills was patterned by scores of large crittall windows. They all lacked glass and the blackness presented to the world was ideal for any hidden sniper.

The van stopped outside an entrance and O'Rourke got out and without any hesitation walked into the darkness. Xun followed, his eyes searching for any sign of a trap as they entered the main lobby. They soon became used to the gloom and were able to pick out a staircase and doors that led to the ground floor offices.

'We have to climb to the third floor,' O'Rourke said and his loud voice echoed through the dust-enshrined building.

'You hid the *ding* that high?'

'The local kids play in here quite often and it was a way of preventing inquisitive eyes from finding it too easily.'

The two men started climbing, Xun keeping ten steps behind the Irishman. When they reached level three, indicated with a large figure three painted in black on the wall, O'Rourke suddenly vanished through one of the two wooden doors; the triad was caught unawares and whipping the Colt from his pocket he raced after him.

Xun entered a long corridor with dozens of unmarked doors on both sides. He tried the first door and stepped into an unfurnished office with a single naked bulb hanging in the centre of the room, his feet stirring up billowing clouds of dust. As he retreated into the corridor a deafening sound raced towards him a split-second after the 9mm bullet perforated the sleeve of his coat. The sudden sting across his bicep galvanized him into action and Xun leapt across the corridor and through the next doorway. As he crouched down, feeling his arm to explore the damage, he looked around and saw that he was in a complex machine room. Tangled cables looped down from the decaying ceiling and were connected to strange, unfamiliar machines. A scuttling sound alerted him to the presence of rats as he finely tuned his hearing to detect any human movement.

The creak of a door slowly opening on the far side of the wide room alerted Xun that he wasn't alone and he removed his loafers. With the stealth of a stalking cat he moved amongst the machines in the direction of the sound until he heard a soft thud nearby; an accidental knock against one of the machines? He froze and crouched down as he put the pistol back in his pocket and unsheathed two short throwing knives. Xun had always preferred the sword or keen-edged knives to guns for any close-quarter fighting. He began to minimize his breathing as he waited for his opponent to draw closer. Despite the line of broken windows along the length of one wall the room still remained gloomy and Xun stared down at the dark floor to improve his vision. A shadow moved in his peripheral sight and he saw a pair of legs through gaps in the machine behind which he was waiting.

As the man crept round the large piece of machinery holding a heavy automatic Xun grabbed his extended arm and locked it under his armpit. Then, chest-to-chest he plunged the blade four times into the man in a savage blur of glinting steel.

The skill of the strikes passing between the third and fourth ribs shredded the man's heart causing instant death. With the collapsing man's arm still held tightly Xun lowered the corpse to the floor as quietly as possible. As he wiped the blade on the man's shirt he turned his head and stared into the face of a total stranger.

The puzzled triad stood upright and caught a glimpse of the far door closing. He sprinted across the room, zigzagging amongst the machines and threw the door wide without going through. Heavy calibre bullets splintered the doorframe where he had stood and he crouched down and waited. He had held his position for a full two minutes before he heard soft footfalls approach the open door. It was someone who didn't have the same patience and training as Xun. He backed to one side and ducked behind a lathe-like machine with a throwing knife balanced in each hand.

The doorframe darkened and a figure jumped into the room and put his back against the machine Xun was crouching behind. The triad slowly stood up and then swiftly reached across the greasy equipment, grasped the man's hair and jerked his head back. Before Xun's stalker could raise his weapon he became stalked and a keen edge flowed across his neck to neatly sever the carotid artery. Once more Xun was disappointed to find that it wasn't O'Rourke but another sent to assassinate him.

With extreme caution Xun descended the stairwell and stepped outside. The blue van was gone. He had no doubts now that the *ding* had been hidden elsewhere and that O'Rourke had selected the old mill building to be an excellent killing ground. Air hissed between his teeth as he considered what he would do when he caught up with the treacherous Red Pole.

A quick search on the other side of the building revealed the vehicle the two gunmen had arrived in. The smart Audi had been hidden behind an old generator shed. With a lifetime of skilful practice it was a simple matter to start the car without a key and soon Xun was driving across London to Gerrard Street where he disposed of the car. He walked past the See Woo Supermarket to the address beyond and after polite greetings were exchanged Sying, the Two-Headed Dragon, gave him the long silk bag tied at one end with silken cords.

As far as Xun knew the house in Cadogan Square was the only place linked to O'Rourke and he was determined to make that address his own killing ground, the traditional way.

15

EUSTACE HINKMAN QC had planned to work late on a defence case involving an elderly man who had suffocated his wife after discovering she had been sleeping with the milkman for twenty-eight years.

The defendant told the police that his wife claimed she did it to reduce their milk bill. Hinkman yawned, put the file down and took a sip from the brandy snifter as he tried to justify extreme provocation in his mind with very little success.

A melodic door chime woke him from his brief musings. Hinkman went to open the front door and was irritated to find nobody there. Taking a pace out onto the top step he looked both ways but apart from two of his neighbours walking away there wasn't a soul to be seen in Cadogan Square.

The sun had long set but the streetlights were quite adequate and Hinkman could see that the gates to the private gardens were locked. With a shrug of his shoulders the lawyer went back inside and shut the door against the chill night air. He had just started reading the prosecutor's findings when he was summoned yet again and he hurried to fling the door open, hoping to surprise the mystery doorbell ringer.

'Do you normally answer your door in that uncouth manner, Eustace?' Waterston said as he pushed past the open-mouthed silk.

'My apology, Major, but I've just been subjected to a childish prank and I was hoping to catch the offender in the act.'

The major nodded even though he couldn't possibly care about such a trivial matter and strode into the study ahead of Hinkman. 'I've come at this late hour as a very big problem has arisen.'

'Concerning the petri dish?'

'Yes. The analysis has just been completed at the lab that O'Rourke made use of and the results are downright nauseating.' The major slammed a computer printout onto the desk with the palm of his hand. 'That bloody Irishman got his hands on a culture that could be no more virulent than a bad head cold.'

'That can't be right.' Hinkman opened a folder and flicked through the papers to pull a single sheet out. This is a summary of the sample's specification that was saved by our agent in China. It definitely claims that the culture has the ability to alter the DNA of people of a certain ethnicity.'

'Namely all those in the Far East,' Waterston said grimly. 'That was the weapon we originally briefed and paid for. It had to be able to rewrite the information within the DNA to eradicate the immune system in the next generation. From the first moment they are exposed new-born children should be unable to survive the viral onslaught.'

Hinkman scowled as he took photographs from the folder and spread them on the desk. 'We were told that airborne spore tests were carried out over a tiny farming community and that every infant expired within days of their birth. Do you believe that these pictures sent as proof were forged?'

'No, they're genuine enough as I was there when they were taken by the scientists.'

'How long will it take them to regenerate the product?'

'They can't. Unfortunately the laboratory was burnt to the ground with complete loss of the key personnel and we have no evidence to refer back to. The petri dish was the only one to survive and if we are to redevelop the weapon we must recover it so that we can start growing more.' Waterston slammed his fist down making the brandy snifter jump.

'You do realize what this means? Sometime during the delivery someone switched the culture dishes.'

'Of course I do and our first suspect has to be O'Rourke.'

'He made contact and recovered the petri dish. It would have been a simple matter for him to make the switch and cash in by selling it back to the Chinese for them to destroy.'

'It seems the culture is now on the triad grapevine which is something O'Rourke didn't put in his last report. The authorities have leant all about the virus and will pay a billion US dollars for the dish and as much as I trusted O'Rourke, when he worked undercover within the triad organisation, I don't know if I can now. That level of temptation is far too great.' Waterston picked up the telephone.

'Who are you calling,' Hinkman asked as he took a cigar from the humidor and rolled it between his fingers.

'Rackman of course. This is how he can rightfully earn an honoured place in Illuminati society.' Waterston finished dialling and listened to the ring tone. 'I'll get him to trace O'Rourke and bring him to us for interrogation.'

'You'd bring him here?' The barrister registered his disbelief.

'I'm not a bloody fool, Hinkman. I have a special safe house in Surrey for this purpose. Rackman knows where it is and once SIS hand over O'Rourke he'll take him there and then give me a call.'

'Won't SIS be asking questions?'

'Naturally. However, Rackman has the ear of a particular commander who does a lot of covert work with a squad of six ex-SAS operatives. They can be trusted to be extremely discreet in matters such as these.'

'Illuminati?'

The major shrugged and walked across to the brandy decanter. 'How is Mrs Hinkman,' he said, changing the subject.

'Evelyn is very well and the last I heard she was actively intent on depleting the stock of every Knightsbridge store.'

Waterston laughed politely, his mind still contemplating what to do if O'Rourke had defected with the petri dish. He finished his drink and picked up his coat.

'You are leaving, Major?'

'I have a lot of things to prepare for the arrival of my reluctant guest.' The major left the room and Hinkman shrugged and continued reading his papers.

The man sitting half hidden in the residents' park watched Waterston leave the house and walk along the street, his eyes searching only for the familiar orange light of an available taxi.

After a long complicated run that avoided all main roads being monitored by police cameras O'Rourke abandoned the blue plumber's van in a lay-by three miles from East Steading and took a local bus to reach the town centre. It was beginning to get dark and had started to rain again. With his collar turned up he went directly to Goodfellow Investigations.

'You were expecting me to return,' he said as the intercom hissed after pressing the button.

'Yes I was but not quite so soon,' James's tinny voice replied. There was a click and the door opened as the lock was released.

O'Rourke hurried up to the office and noticed straightaway that there was no secretary in the reception area.

'They are both beyond your reach,' James stated calmly as he waved to the big man to enter his office.

O'Rourke cautiously walked in and saw that they were the only two present. He threw himself down into the leather club chair reserved for clients, tossed the counterfeit petri dish onto the table and made a point of placing his empty hands on the arms.

'I've just been sent that along with a lab report that says it's not the real thing. My boss will also receive the same report and that puts me in a rather awkward position. I am not here to threaten but to discuss rationally why you should give me the real dish.'

'Can there be a rational reason why I should hand over a deadly weapon of mass destruction?'

'The only reason I can mention is that by doing it you will be saving the lives of two billion people or, to put it another way, a third of the human race.' O'Rourke indicated that he wanted to reach into his jacket pocket and James nodded suspiciously, his hand tightening on the handle of his faithful baseball club beneath the desk.

The Irishman took out his cigarette case and after offering it to James who shook his head he lit one up and took a deep draw.

'You may find it difficult to believe what I am now going to tell you but on my mother's grave I swear it is the whole truth.'

James remained silent.

'It started six years ago,' O'Rourke began. 'I was working for a trading company in Hong Kong when I was recruited by the Chinese government to help them put a stop to the smuggling operations that affected companies such as my own. I was able to obtain a certain amount of information that helped in ending some of the smaller triad operations. They then asked me to infiltrate a major triad group run by a man called Pengfei Shing. By organizing a couple of smuggling trips through my company for that man I was accepted and became trusted; I was given the position of *Red Pole* with a minor triad leader called Zhu Wen.

'What the hell is a *Red Pole?*' James asked.

O'Rourke gave a tight-lipped smile. 'I'm an enforcer, a kind of weapon used by triad leaders to punish those who misbehave within the clan and therefore fall out of favour.

'An executioner?'

'Sometimes, but only those within the clan are chastized. I do not punish those I loosely refer to as civilians.'

'What about myself?'

'I'm not about to kill you, your secretary or your girlfriend as I'm still an operational agent working for a legitimate government.'

'Not a democratic one, though,' James said bitingly.

'I'll give you that but we are digressing from the main point. The main reason for hunting down the petri dish is to return it to the Chinese for them to destroy. The culture growing in the dish is the sole remains of a ghastly experiment to alter the human genome by tampering with the structure of the DNA in all orientals.'

O'Rourke took a deep breath. 'I don't want to sound like I'm lecturing you, Goodfellow, but the double helix is like a twisted ladder and the base pair of rungs carry the main instructions for the DNA to copy itself exactly. Affect those rungs and exact reproduction is unlikely to happen and extreme mutations can occur.'

'Feng and I guessed that it had to be something terrible but what you are saying is downright terrifying,' James said having gone pale when realizing the full implication of what the Irishman was saying.

'Terrifying isn't the word because this new virus is airborne. There is no defence against it if sprayed from a plane like a crop-duster. The main thing is that it only affects those of oriental origin causing a loss of every natural defence in all newborn babies. The Chinese and dozens of other races of similar ethnicity in that part of the world will come to an end in the span of one generation.'

James felt the paralysis growing in his legs and he relaxed back in the seat aware of what was about to happen.

'Excuse me but I'm going to sleep for a minute … ' he managed to mumble before the narcoleptic condition took control and his eyelids dropped. James had been unable to prevent the attack from happening and the last thing he saw was the Irishman's expression of incredulity.

O'Rourke stared at the unconscious man in amazement as James's eyelids flickered agitatedly and his head lolled forward. 'Hey! Wake up!' he called out as he stood and leant across the desk to shake James by the shoulder. 'Is this some kind of trick? What the hell are you up to?'

There was a slight twitching reaction to O'Rourke's rough handling and James's eyelids began to flutter less before they suddenly snapped open.

'I'm sorry about that,' he slurred before recovering full control of his speech. 'I forgot to take my medication this morning and the shock of what you've just told me was too much.'

'What's wrong with you?'

'I've had narcolepsy since leaving university but I can control it if I take my morning pill; I forget – well, you've seen what happens, but please, do go on.' James took a small white box from his desk drawer and swallowed a Xyrem tablet.

O'Rourke waited until he had finished sipping from a glass of water before continuing: 'You know now why I have to recover the dish and take it back to China. They have to analyze it to create an antidote should anyone else come up with the same formula. Only then can it be fully destroyed.'

'I can't believe anyone would ever want to grow such a virus,' James whispered, putting his hands together as though in prayer.

'They have done so and the Illuminati members will try again,' O'Rourke said solemnly. 'That's why you and I must help the Chinese in one way or another.'

'Who are the Illuminati?'

'It's a secret European organization that I infiltrated and was accepted as a trusted member.'

'You're an Irish Chinese government agent, a triad assassin and a member of a secret society. My God, what's happened to the old-fashioned import-export business and 007?'

O'Rourke's infectious laugh made James grin until both men recalled what they had been discussing and suddenly stopped as though on an unheard cue.

James broke the silence first. 'Can you give me some more facts about the Illuminati?'

Before O'Rourke could fully explain the intercom interrupted and James went to release the door downstairs.

'It's a close friend,' he explained as he sat behind the desk again. 'She may also be interested in what you tell me about Chinese gangsters and secret societies.'

'I don't think that would be too wise,' O'Rourke said getting to his feet. They heard someone climbing the stairs and Jennifer entered the office.

James smiled and gave her brief hug before turning to introduce the stranger. 'Jenny this is – ' He stopped and was at a loss to continue.

'Sèan O'Rourke. I'm very pleased to meet you again, Jenny. This time I promise not to hold a kitchen knife to your throat.'

'He's an extraordinary character.'

Jennifer caressed her neck. 'Now you tell me.'

'That's right, and he was about to tell me everything he knows about a secret society called the Illuminati.'

Jennifer raised a quizzical eyebrow and sat down eyeing the Irishman who had begun to tick off items one by one as he spoke.

'The name which goes back many centuries was considered heresy and therefore an enemy of the Catholic Church. More recent history indicates that in 1776 a Bavarian called Adam Weishaupt revived the Illuminati with the object of opposing all prejudice and abuses of state power. It was outlawed by the government and the Catholic Church and was eventually forced underground in order to avoid being vilified by those who held the Illuminati responsible for the French Revolution.'

'Good grief, were they?' Jennifer exclaimed in surprise.

'It was never substantiated but since then the Illuminati splintered into many different societies and chapters who became associated with scores of conspiracy theories. Notable figures such as US Presidents have been claimed as members and some assassinations have even been blamed on the many fictional Chapters of this organization.'

'So they don't really exist,' James said as he went to a cupboard and removed three glasses and a bottle of whisky.

'Oh! They exist all right and I'm a bona-fide paid-up member of the London Chapter,' O'Rourke said with a grim expression. 'The society in this city is run by Major Waterston who is an ex SIS operative. He chairs a board of directors, one of whom was also an SAS officer and SIS operative.'

'SIS?' Jennifer asked.

'Secret Intelligence Service or, as it's widely known, MI6,' James murmured, realizing how complicated and possibly deadly the case had become.

'As a Detective Constable I should have known that,' Jennifer muttered as embarrassment coloured her cheeks.

O'Rourke jerked upright and nearly spilt his drink. 'You're a policewoman?' he cried.

'Relax, O'Rourke. Yes, she's a cop and a very clever one who has helped me on a number of occasions,' James said calmly. 'Jenny knows all about the *ding* full of *bi* and the death of Han Choi in London.' James's eyes narrowed slightly. 'By the way, did you have anything to do with that killing?'

'Christ no! That was Paulo Ambrossini.'

'The Italian curator who was shot in the Venetian park?'

'That's the one and I'm the one who shot him.' O'Rourke spoke in such a relaxed manner that the sense of his words didn't sink in for a few seconds.

'You murdered that poor man in – ' Jennifer started to say.

'Poor man! Fiddle-faddle! He had found the hiding place of the petri dish and had to be stopped because he was also an Illuminati, albeit a very greedy one.'

'Why do they want it so much?' Jenny asked as she sorted each thread of information in an effort to make some kind of sense.

'A hidden war has broken out between the Chinese secret societies who the world refers to as the Triads and various chapters of the Illuminati. It started on the misguided perception that new kinds of depopulation weapons were being investigated that had the specific capability of isolating and decreasing the Oriental population. At first these rumours were dismissed as being ridiculous and fanciful. Then Chinese whispers, excuse the pun, began to spread. They concerned a small group of Illuminati biologists who had been able to perfect a viral strain that could be wind-borne across the whole country. It would stop all chances of successful childbirth. To summarize, it would terminate a complete race in one generation.'

'Are you saying that it is a form of birth control and that no children can be conceived?'

'No. Children can be conceived but they will be born with an inoperative immune system and will contract every known disease and die in a number of horrific ways.'

Jennifer raised a fist to her mouth in horror. 'That's inhuman,' she whispered and both men nodded gravely.

James spoke first. 'But Ambrossini legally purchased the ceramic plate in Venice. Why would he come to England to kill Han Choi?'

'Who told you that he bought it in Venice?' O'Rourke asked with a half smile.

'Ambross –'

'Precisely. That was *his* story to *you* when in fact he had been seeking the dish long before you knew of its existence. Ambrossini knew the *ding* had been shipped from Hong Kong and hidden somewhere in Venice. When an Illuminati agent in China informed Ambrossini that Inspector Xiao Shi Huang had recently visited Han Choi in London and given him a ceramic plate he realized that it could be lead to the exact whereabouts of the *ding* and of course the petri dish hidden amongst the *bi*.'

'This was before Huang's fateful flight?' Jennifer muttered.

'Yes.' O'Rourke's face dropped. 'He was meant to contact me if he had any trouble but he chose to go to London and locate the petri dish alone.'

Sensing James's puzzlement he continued, 'I know all that because Huang was my undercover partner.'

'Partner?' James said.

'He also worked for the Chinese government, not just as a senior policeman but as a go-between. Any information I was able to gain from Zhu Wen in Hong Kong I passed on to Huang.'

'I'm sorry for your loss,' Jennifer said softly. She could understand what the death of a partner could do to a surviving police officer.

O'Rourke gave her an appreciative look before continuing. 'Ambrossini visited London to obtain the plate but Han Choi said that he was unable to sell it to any museum as it belonged to his cousin called Huang and that he was coming to collect it.

This enraged the curator who then killed Han, took the plate and broke all the others in Choi's collection to divert attention away from the solitary theft. He also sent a message to his agent in Hong Kong to remove Huang from the scene.'

Understanding appeared on James's face. 'So it wasn't the triads trying to kill Huang but Illuminati agents?

'Correct.'

'But I don't understand why the curator would bother to say that the payment was made and the plate collected at a hotel in Venice.' James emptied his glass.

'You met Ambrossini at the Doccia Museum. Naturally he didn't want you to think he had made the purchase locally as that would have made it too easy for you to check his story. He also didn't count on you working out the location of the ding from your cursory look at the plate in the vault.'

James sighed. 'It was lucky we took photographs to study later or we would never have found the petri dish.' He relaxed back in his seat. 'I'll go down now and put Feng's mind at rest by telling him that we know who killed his brother and why.'

'I wouldn't do that yet,' O'Rourke said. 'I forgot to tell you that I took oaths with both a Triad organization and the Illuminati in London who now believe that I have betrayed them all. Don't involve your friends at this stage of the investigation as they may be in mortal danger.'

'Surely this is the time to bring in my colleagues.' Jennifer took the mobile from her handbag but the Irishman held his hand up to stop her.

'Apart from yourself, involving the police is not such a good idea, Jenny. First of all, although I have an Irish passport I'm still a Chinese agent and if the local boys get involved it will only slow my departure to Hong Kong. They'll want to interrogate me every which way for days by which time new research could be well underway to replicate the culture.

'Can't we simply take the dish to the Chinese embassy so that they can send it back to Beijing in the diplomatic bag?'

'There are two Illuminati agents working in the embassy building who are willing to sacrifice their lives to acquire that culture for Major Waterston.'

'So we have to believe your fantastic tales and simply hand a third world war weapon over to you.' Jennifer searched O'Rourke's eyes for a sign that she could trust the man.

'Yes.'

'No. It is my duty to give it to the right authorities in London.'

'And who would that be?'

'Scotland Yard, SIS or even the Prime Minister.' She almost stamped her foot in her determination to do the right thing.

'Do you have the dish that I sent to you, Jenny?' James asked in an effort to gain time and calm her down but before she could say anything O'Rourke grabbed her arm and pulled her down to the floor.

'Get down, Goodfellow,' he shouted pointing at the window. 'We're being watched and I have a feeling they're Illuminati.'

James dropped out of his chair and shuffled back until he was under the window where he carefully raised his head to look down into the street. The usual traffic was flowing back and forth and nothing seemed out of place except for a matt-black car with tinted windows. It was illegally parked on the double yellow lines and a patrolling meter maid had ignored the offence and was walking away shaking her head.

A heavy-set man in a dark raincoat was leaning against the top of the vehicle and staring up at the window. The ranks of storm clouds and steady rain had failed to shift the sunglasses from his face.

'They've found me,' O'Rourke muttered. 'They must be Waterston's tame SIS men which is why the meter maid didn't bother to ticket their car.'

For safety's sake James took the white box from his pocket and swallowed another tablet without the assistance of any water. 'What's our next move?' he asked.

'I'll make the next move while you stay here.' O'Rourke leapt to his feet, snatched Jennifer's handbag and ran from the office. Before they could rise to their feet he was pounding down the stairs and the door crashed open below.

Watching from the window James saw O'Rourke running straight to the man leaning against the car and downing him with a vicious rugby tackle. Two men leapt from the car and began firing after O'Rourke who went darting down an alleyway and disappeared from sight.

'We've got to go upstairs immediately,' he said. He took the fake petri dish from the desk and slipped it in his pocket before tugging at Jennifer's arm. 'They could come for us next and I want to be prepared.'

'If they are SIS there's nothing we can do,' she said as they left the office and hurried upstairs.

James shook his head. 'If they were on official SIS business they wouldn't be firing guns in the high street of an English town. I believe they are following orders given by Major Waterston just as O'Rourke said.' He closed the apartment door and securely locked it before hurrying into the bedroom.

'What are you doing, James?' Jennifer asked when she saw him on his knees and looking under the bed.

James slid a small suitcase out and snapped the catches. He removed a bundle from a cardboard box and unwound a stained oilcloth to reveal a large pistol and a number of military full-metal-jacketed bullets.

'That's your dad's old revolver,' Jenny exclaimed. "I thought you had got rid of that after your last case.'

Captain Richard Goodfellow of the Royal Engineers had last used his Webley .38 in 1944 to save his own life on an airfield in Tobruk. The temporary airstrip had been laid for a Spitfire squadron en-route from Malta and the troops had been the target of many enemy infiltrators. James inherited the gun on the day he announced that he was starting a private investigation company but had never got round to applying for a licence.

He checked the cylinders were empty and dry fired to ensure nothing had corroded since he last put it away. The cylinders had a six-millimetre rotational play but he was sure this would reduce when the gun was cocked and the trigger pulled. James knew that it was a reliable weapon even after sixty years and he broke the gun to load it.

'Are you sure this is wise, James?' Jennifer asked as she watched him carefully place the bullets into the chambers and snap the pistol it shut.

'I will only use it to let them know that I am armed and prepared to defend us,' James said as he put his arm around her shoulders. 'I won't shoot to hit anybody.'

'Thank God for that. Can I now call the station and get some help?'

'I'd rather you didn't because Waterston may use what clout he has in Vauxhall Cross to have us taken somewhere on the pretext of it being a security matter. Even Inspector Tilley and Sergeant Briscoe haven't the clout to prevent that from happening.'

They heard someone climbing the stairs and a fist pounded on the apartment door making it shake in the frame. After a short pause the fist renewed its attack on the thick panel. The couple waited without saying a word; there was the sound of a mobile phone and the banging ceased. A murmuring voice could be heard and then footsteps retreated back down the stairs.

'They're leaving,' Jennifer whispered.

James relaxed his grip on the revolver and wiped the sweat on his trouser leg. 'Don't be fooled, they could come back.'

16

KEEPING TIGHT TO THE railings and in the shadows cast by the dark garden Xun circled Cadogan Square to study every possible avenue of escape should the need arise. He had just rung the doorbell at the address he had seen O'Rourke leaving from when a woman exiting the adjoining house forced him to move on and circle the square once more.

Xun shifted the silk bag from under his arm and swung it over his back using the silken cord as a sling when he spotted a solitary figure enter the square and walk towards the house. Although the rain had ended the man still had his raincoat collar turned up and a fedora pulled down to shield his face.

'O'Rourke?' Xun murmured uncertainly as he waited until the man had climbed the two steps and after a brief wait had entered the house. With a graceful loping stride Xun went to the door but hesitated to press the bell. What if it was O'Rourke, he thought and decided to wait for the man to show himself at one of the windows. The gates to the central gardens had been padlocked for the night but a lithe leap cleared the railings and Xun strolled to the bench he had used before and sat down.

Studying each window in turn he saw nothing but an occasional passing shadow on the net curtains. After thirty minutes the front door opened to throw a shaft of yellow light across the road and into the shrubbery. Xun ducked down and crept closer to the railings to catch a brief look at the same man who had entered earlier. This time light fell onto his face before he put his hat on and as he turned Xun could see that it wasn't O'Rourke but a complete stranger.

This must mean O'Rourke is still inside, he thought. When the portly man disappeared round the corner he checked both ways and left the gardens to sprint across the road and ring the bell.

As the door began to swing open Xun heard someone say, 'Did you forget something, Major?' He thrust his weight against the door. The man opening it was thrown backward to land heavily on his backside.

'What the hell!' Hinkman yelled as Xun slammed the door shut. 'Who the blue blazes are you?'

The triad reached over his shoulder and unsheathed his sword. 'Where's Mr Sèan O'Rourke?' he said softly as he placed the tip of the sword against Hinkman's chest.

The QC realized who Xun was and his face paled. 'O'Rourke doesn't live here.'

'That wasn't the question.' The point tore the shirt to touch bare skin. 'Where is he?' Xun moved the sword point and Hinkman felt a stinging sensation move across his chest. He looked down to see the white cotton staining red.

'I don't know, I really don't know,' he stuttered with eyes fixed on the gleaming sword point. 'We are hunting him ourselves.'

'Who are *we*. Who else wants to speak to O'Rourke?'

'The SIS, Major Waterston and Rackman. In fact, the whole damned organization want his head on a plate.'

There was a second stinging sensation as the blade cut the other side of Hinkman's chest.

'And what is the name of this organization?'

'The Illuminati.' Hinkman looked up into the merciless eyes. 'Please believe me, I'm telling the truth when I say I don't know where he is.'

'I believe you,' Xun said softly. 'Tell me, are you a member of this organization?'

'No, not at all,' Eustace Hinkman whispered in fear.

'And who was the man who just left your house?'

'That was Major Water – ' Hinkman suddenly stopped, realizing his mistake.

'Major Waterston! You said he was an Illuminati and yet you say you're not?'

'No, please, I'm just his legal representative – '

'LIAR!' Dragon's Breath rose to fall swiftly and the Queen's Counsel fell to the floor dead.

After cleaning and sheathing the sword Xun swiftly searched the whole house before quietly leaving the premises and the square to merge with the shadows of the night.

Xun now knew that the people who could directly lead him to O'Rourke would be the three mentioned by the lawyer. The major called Waterston who has a link with the SIS and another man called Rackman. As he sat on the platform bench waiting for the underground train he sent a coded text message to Pengfei Shing asking if he knew of any Illuminati called Waterston and Rackman. As the train thundered into the station preceded by a warm blast of air his phone 'pinged'. He boarded the train and as it raced into the darkness of the tunnel he read the reply.

Major Hugh Waterston ex SIS adviser – Chairman of London Illuminati Society. He seeks what we seek. Eliminate.

James unlocked the apartment and they went down to the reception. All his case files, of which there weren't too many, lay scattered over the floor. His office was in a similar state. I'm going to get it in the neck from Miss Lightbody, he thought as he picked up the chairs and made an attempt to tidy his own desk.

'They weren't too house-proud in their searching,' Jennifer said in an attempt to lighten his depression.

'Luckily the petri dish was in your handbag,' James said grumpily.

'That's where we were really lucky. If they had apprehended and searched us they would have found it right here.' Jennifer reached into her pocket and showed James the dish still sealed in its sandwich bag.

'That means O'Rourke will return the moment he's had a chance to search your handbag. As much as I want to believe what he had told us we will still need to get a head start on him.'

'Why?'

'Because the SIS will be close on his heels and if they catch him they'll catch us, too.'

James took the dish and slipped it into his own pocket. Taking Jennifer by the hand he led her out of the office and down the stairs. He opened the door cautiously. Spotting nothing unusual in the dark street outside they left the building and went next door to the Forbidden City.

Feng saw the couple entering and hurried across the restaurant as they deliberately chose a table at the rear. 'What has been happening, James,' he asked uneasily. 'Lin-Lin saw a man leave your place in a hurry and run down the street after he had knocked down a man standing by a car. Two other men then started shooting at him before getting in their car and driving off.'

James quickly brought his friend up to date and then told him the news about his brother.

'So in helping our distant cousin by keeping the plate safe Han became a target, and he wasn't killed by a triad gangster but by one of these strange Illuminati people.'

James nodded. 'And now we have to leave before the police turn up with a lot of awkward questions or O'Rourke decides to come back to claim what he believes is rightfully his.'

'Where will you go?'

'We will first hide the culture in a safe place and then find a place to hide out until the furore dies down.'

Feng took James's hand and looked into his eyes searching for some kind of reassurance that his friend had the confidence to carry out his plan successfully. 'Good luck, my friend.' He stepped back as Lin-Lin rushed up and threw her arms about James.

'You must come back soon,' she said as she bravely tried not to cry. 'We will make you a special *luo buo gao* cake.'

James gave the little girl a hug. 'Delicious,' he whispered in her ear and then turned to say goodbye to Jiao while Jennifer embraced Lin-Lin. The couple left the restaurant and hurried to where James had parked the car. Checking for any strangers in the immediate vicinity they got in and with lights dipped drove out of East Steading, taking the road leading to the motorway.

The magnetic tracking device on the manifold faithfully went with them.

O'Rourke sprinted to a row of parked motorcycles and ignoring the bigger, more powerful sporting machines he hotwired a Honda 250cc. By the time the two pursuers had come round the corner the Irishman had disappeared down a narrow alley. The dark SIS pool car cruised East Steading for ten minutes before racing off into the night in the direction of London. They had missed the departure of James and Jenny by three minutes.

With the motorcycle lights off O'Rourke checked the contents of Jennifer's handbag and cursed when he couldn't find the petri dish. He started the engine and slowly pulled out of the alley and rode the machine round the block to park within sight of the Forbidden City. He didn't have long to wait before James and Jennifer emerged from the restaurant and got into Goodfellow's car. As it pulled away O'Rourke began to tail it discreetly and soon the two vehicles were on the M25 motorway heading east.

The lack of a crash helmet concerned O'Rourke and although it was dark he knew that the first patrol car to spot him would pull him over. He took a chance and pulled into a service centre and stopped by a collection of bikes. The owners were obviously members of a club and looking through the brightly lit windows he could see the group of bikers had stopped for refreshments. Four of them had left their helmets on their bike seats and on the second try he found one that fit snugly and he was soon back on the motorway. He had taken a gamble on being able to catch up with Goodfellow and wound the throttle up to the max, hoping the speed cameras wouldn't be able to monitor him in the darkness.

O'Rourke was planning to cross the M1 interchange when he spotted the car up ahead. It was taking the slip road leading to the motorway and he managed to peel across all three lanes and take the M1. Where on earth is he going, O'Rourke thought as they sped north. He throttled back to cruise at the same speed.

With number plate recognition cameras hanging over the M1 traffic lanes O'Rourke knew it wouldn't be too long before his registration was flagged as a stolen vehicle and he sighed with relief when the car ahead took the off-ramp into Toddington service centre. He followed them to the fast-food forecourt and stopped the bike a hundred yards behind. O'Rourke watched James get out of the car and waited until the couple had walked away and entered the Costa coffee shop before cruising closer to park the bike. With his back to the coffee shop he walked up to the car and surreptitiously tried the rear door.

'Where are we heading?' Jennifer asked when they finally settled themselves into a booth.

'I plan to hide the culture in a safety deposit box with a company in Milton Keynes. That way no one will be able to access it without the duplicate key held by the bank.

'Couldn't they simply present the key if we're attacked and robbed?'

'That's not enough, they would have to have identical features including fingerprints and retinal authentication before the bank uses the duplicate key. They're pretty thorough which is why I chose the place.'

After satisfying their hunger with cheese croissants and cappuccinos James led Jennifer back to the car and as they closed the doors a familiar voice greeted them from behind.

'Now that wasn't very nice of you, Jennifer,' O'Rourke said sitting upright on the rear seat and tossing the handbag into her lap. 'What did you do with the dish?'

James looked in the mirror and saw O'Rourke's smiling face. 'Where did you spring from?'

'Since leaving your friend's restaurant I've been trailing along behind and from now on I'm sticking to you tighter than superglue until you give me what I need.'

'That would only happen if you could tell us what happened to the ding and all the *bi* that was supposedly inside.'

'Oh, it was full of *bi* alright.' O'Rourke laughed. 'That's the irony of it all. The bloody cauldron and the ancestral discs are most probably worth millions of dollars yet the most valuable item is a single laboratory dish.'

'Who does the treasure really belong to,' Jennifer asked in a curious tone.

'Once again, a rather weird twist of fate, my dear.'

'If you don't mind, I'm not your dear and please answer the question.' Jennifer had fixed the smiling man with a cold stare as she reverted to being the investigative police officer.

'Simple, Feng Choi is the owner now that his brother is dead.'

'FENG!' The couple shouted together as they twisted round to look at the Irishman.

'Yes. I learnt in Hong Kong from Inspector Huang that his family tree goes back a very long time. It would appear that he was related to one of

The Three Guards who was defending some king or other and his lands well over 1,000 BC.'

'I recall Feng telling me months ago that he could trace his lineage back to some guys called the Red Guards,' James said excitedly. 'I thought that was just fanciful dreaming on his part.'

O'Rourke continued. 'On the death of the king there was a bloody war during which two of the Guards were killed and the third escaped. It is said that the one who escaped took a bronze cauldron filled with jade discs to a far part of the eastern province.'

'Are you saying that Feng's cousin had been able to trace his lineage back that far?' Jennifer said with disbelief on her face.

'In China they kept far better records of their family histories than we were capable of because they had the beginnings of a written language. However, Huang discovered more than that. He also learnt that Zhu Wen, a triad in Hong Kong, who owed his allegiance to the *Mountain Master* had also traced his own ancestry back –'

Jennifer interrupted. 'A mountain master, what on earth is that?'

'That's a top triad leader called Pengfei Shing.'

'Nice fellow?'

'If you can call a man who has personally killed over a hundred people *nice* then I suppose he could be. He is the difference between a clan member comfortably feeding his family or being uncomfortably fed to sharks.'

'You were saying something about this other triad's ancestry?' Jennifer turned her head a couple of times to ease the stiffness from looking back all the time.

'Zhu Wen claimed that his ancestor was the Duke of Zhou who won that long-ago war I was telling you about and as the victor he was entitled to all the wealth. Wen therefore lays claim to being the owner of any ancestral artefacts associated with his family.'

O'Rourke took a quick drink from the mineral water bottle and continued, 'Pengfei Shing had Wen assassinated two days ago for being greedy and planning to keep the treasure instead of giving it to his leader for distribution within the clan. Shing also believed that I was guilty of betraying the triads which is why he has sent the same *Red Pole*, Xun, to England with the express orders to retrieve the artefacts and to kill me too.'

'There's that title again: *Red Pole*,' James spat out the words as though a nasty taste was in his mouth.

'It's the triad title for an enforcer,' O'Rourke explained to Jennifer. 'As I told James, when I was undercover and working for Zhu Wen I was also promoted to *Red Pole* status.'

'You killed people for that man?' Jennifer's icy stare had returned.

'I terminated nobody who didn't deserve to die.'

James studied the Irishman's face in the rear-view mirror. 'Do you still have connections with this Shing now that your boss is dead?'

'As I explained, Wen was executed by a professional killer called Xun.'

'And this Xun is now going to kill you.' It was an unemotional statement of fact by Jennifer.

'Not if I can kill him first.'

'Better still, you could leave the whole matter to the police.'

O'Rourke looked at Jennifer as though she had gone mad. 'You must be joking, Jenny. You obviously have no idea how strong the triad organization is in Britain. Xun has undoubtedly been to the *Two-Headed Dragon*, the local triad armourer, to get the weapons he needs and he will also have a network of spies alerted across the whole country.'

Jennifer fell silent and James took the opportunity to return to the original point being discussed.

'As I understand it, the older brother Han would have inherited but on his death Feng would then become the sole heir to items that have no provenance apart from word-of-mouth over many centuries.' James started the car engine. 'What do you plan to do now?'

'I can take you to the cauldron if you give me the petri dish to take back to China.'

'Then do so, O'Rourke,' James said engaging first gear.

'Right. The first thing is to drive back to East Steading.'

'You hid it there?' Jennifer asked in astonishment.

'In the safest place where nobody would ever think of looking.' James pulled away wondering about the smug manner of the man as he said that and they were soon speeding back the way they had come.

They had barely covered five miles when O'Rourke turned to look out of the rear window for the fifth time. 'You do realize that you've picked up a tail.'

'What do you mean,' James said glancing in the mirror.

'The black car lingering three cars back has been there since we left the service centre.'

'So what's unusual about that. We're on a motorway. I expect he'll be in the same place for quite a while or at least until we reach the M25 ring road.'

'You'll find they'll be with us much further than that my friend. When oncoming lights lit them up I recognized their registration as being that on the car outside your office. They are definitely the same SIS agents.'

Jennifer looked round but her view was obstructed by the glare from the lights of a large articulated Mack truck that was tailgating them. 'How could they know where we were so soon?'

'Knowing the resources of the SIS they accessed your car details from the DVLA and had police help in monitoring all the major roads by using the traffic cameras.' O'Rourke pointed up as they passed under one of the many gantries crossing the motorway. 'It's that or the car's bugged.'

'I'll check the moment we get off this damned road,' James said. 'In the meantime what shall we do about the car behind us?'

'Lose them when you can without drawing too much attention so that we can gain some time to find and lose the tracer.' Jennifer was flicking through the old oil-stained road atlas she had found beneath her seat. 'They may expect you to take the off-ramp for the M25. Don't. The next junction will give us a suburban area that will make it a lot easier to give them the slip in the dark.'

'You've done this sort of thing before?' James teased.

'It's my job to know how the criminal mind works.'

James laughed as the illuminated blue signboards indicated the filter for the M25. He moved over to the left and glancing in the mirror saw the bright lights of a large limousine also move over into the filter lane. Before the car could close the gap an articulated truck pulled over blocking the pursuer's view and lighting up the inside of their car again.

'You're taking the off-ramp James?'

'He thinks I'm taking the off-ramp; that's the important thing,' James said watching the next set of road signs flash past. As the lane was separated from the major motorway by white chevron markings he jerked on the wheel to rejoin the M1 before they hit the grass divider. The truck sounded its klaxon as it thundered away towards the M25 interchange followed closely by two surprised SIS agents.

'They'll rejoin this motorway within a few minutes by which time we should reach the next slip-road. That will take us onto the North Orbital road into Watford where we can stop and look for the tracer,' Jennifer explained as she dropped the map.

O'Rourke had been lost in his own thoughts and as he considered the next step he would have to take James left the motorway and they were soon in the suburbs of a big town. He turned down a small street and parked the car.

'Let's do this quickly before they pinpoint us on their screen,' he said and they all began searching. It was Jennifer, using a small penlight torch, who found the magnetized tracer on the bottom of the fuel tank. She rose triumphantly and brushing the dead leaves from her jacket and skirt gave it to James. 'What now?' she asked as she got back into the car.

'We have to dispose of this so that it gives the impression that we are still on the move. If it remains stationery for too long they will know that we've found it.' James tossed the small metal oblong box from one hand to the other as he looked round. Suddenly he smiled to himself and joined the others in the car. He quickly drove round the corner to where a sign had been pointing and stopped opposite a bus stop that was outside a railway station. A bus was waiting for late-night train passengers and the driver was preoccupied with reading his newspaper.

'This will do nicely,' James murmured as he left the car and strolled across the street. Passing the back of the bus he bent down briefly to place the tracer before returning to the bemused couple.

'That will keep them running around for a while,' James said as he drove on. The three laughed fleetingly.

'I suggest we take a circuitous route back to East Steading and I'll take you to the treasure which I will exchange for the petri dish,' O'Rourke said quietly and James nodded.

'I'll be glad to be rid of it,' he muttered grimly and Jennifer readily agreed.

17

South Street was an elegant tree-lined address in Mayfair that exuded a quiet air of wealth and self-contentment. After considerable research, Sying, the *Two-Headed Dragon,* had supplied Xun with Major Waterston's home address in that street. Sying had then spent a pleasurable evening with the enforcer after he had slaughtered a minor servant in Soho for offending her. This was to be payment in full for her services.

Xun had walked briskly from Hyde Park station in the chill night air to stand outside the attractive Georgian residence. The black tracksuit with hood pulled up blended into the darkness of the street as he studied the lit windows. A figure appeared at a mullioned window on the first floor and Xun studied the small photograph in his hand that one of Sying's spies had taken. It showed a portly man of military bearing with a full moustache and receding hairline. Another man was descending the steps outside the house but Xun ignored him – the portly man in the window was now closing the curtains and he seemed to be a perfect match for the photograph.

At midnight Xun carefully crossed the street and turned to check the office windows opposite. There were no curtains and all the lights were out. He waited motionless for a full five minutes before lithely jumping up onto the railings outside the house and then using the stone casement windows raised himself up to grasp the first-floor balustrade. He swung himself over on to the narrow balcony and froze to look for any indication that his swift actions had been spotted. The street remained silent and

Xun raised his head to peer through one of the windows. A small gap in the drapes revealed a wood-panelled room with a Queen Anne writing desk behind which Major Waterston was sitting. He was using a laptop computer that seemed out of place in such an antiquated environment.

Xun soundlessly moved to the end of the balcony where a slightly smaller window was partially open, allowing him to slip into the dark, unoccupied drawing room. Treading lightly he made his way across the room and checked the hallway. He then made his way to the next door, opening the long leather bag as he went. The keen blade slid silently from its oiled scabbard.

Years of practice enabled Xun to open the door, cross the room and have the tip of the sword at the major's throat within two seconds. The surprised man sat back in his chair but the sword tip followed him and he stopped every movement fearing the stranger would cut his throat.

'Who are you. What do you want?' he managed to croak between dry lips.

'Major Waterston, there is nothing I want from you but a little information.' Xun stepped back a pace but kept the blade levelled at the man's face. 'Firstly, you are the chairman of the Illuminati, yes?'

'I don't know what you're tal –'

Xun stepped forward and the tip drew a drop of blood. 'Don't play games with me. Answer my questions truthfully and you will not suffer needlessly.'

Waterston had felt the sudden sting in his neck and he flinched. 'Very well.'

'Are you a member of the Illuminati?'

'I am the Chief Executive of the London Chapter.'

'Do you know of a Mr Sèan O'Rourke?'

'Yes. He is a member of this chapter.'

Xun hissed angrily on having O'Rourke's duplicity confirmed. 'How do I find this man?'

'He keeps moving around. I have to contact him by phone and arrange any meetings at another member's house.'

'Mr Eustace Hinkman's place?'

Sweat was beginning to gather on Waterston's forehead and the pencil he was holding snapped. 'Yes. I organize my meetings at his place as my wife does not want anything to do with the Illuminati in this house. However, I do have O'Rourke's number but I have to warn you that he may not answer as he no longer trusts me.'

'You had better hope that he does as I want you to arrange a meeting with him here for tomorrow morning. Now call him.'

'It's after midnight!'

'Call him!' Xun hissed and Waterston scrabbled for the mobile lying on the corner of the desk.

All three stiffened when they heard the ringtone of O'Rourke's mobile. He took it from his pocket as the warbling sound increased in tempo, emphasizing the urgency of the caller.

'Who would ring you at this time of the night?' James asked.

O'Rourke shrugged and answered the call. 'O'Rourke. Who's this?'

'It's Major Waterston, Sèan. I have to discuss something with you tomorrow morning. It's of extreme urgency and concerns the culture that you are carrying.'

'I do not have any culture, Major,' O'Rourke said truthfully.

'No matter, I have to see you and you are to come to my own house in Mayfair.'

There was a long silence before the Irishman spoke. 'I haven't anything for you, Major. Why do we need to meet?'

'I cannot tell you on the phone; you will have to come to me in South Street so that we can talk face to face.'

'Mano-a-mano, Major. That sounds like a challenge which is something I usually cannot resist. What time in the morning?'

'Ten o'clcock . . . ' there was a brief pause in which O'Rourke thought he heard somebody whispering in the background. 'No! Make it eight o'clock.' The line went dead before O'Rourke could object.

'Will you go?' Jennifer asked when O'Rourke explained what the call was about.

'Sounds too much like a trap,' James said quietly.

'That's exactly what it is, my friend.'

The major put the mobile down and stared back at the Chinese gangster. 'What now?' he said in a clipped voice.

'We wait until the morning for O'Rourke to come and then you will – ' Xun was interrupted by the sound of a woman's cut-glass voice in the hallway.

'When are you coming to bed, Hugh?' his wife asked rapping on the door. 'Do you know what time it is?' she persisted.

'If she comes into this room she will die,' Xun whispered. 'Do you understand?'

The major nodded furiously. 'I've got a lot of work I have to catch up on, dear,' he called out. 'You go ahead and get some sleep and I'll see you in the morning.'

There was the sound of an irritated 'hrmmph' and a heavy tread going away until a distant door slammed and the house became silent once more.

'Good, now we will wait.' Xun pulled a chair close to the desk and sat with his eyes fixed on Waterston.

'For seven hours?'

'Naturally.'

James cruised quietly into East Steading and he took the service road that ran behind the Forbidden City and Goodfellow Investigations to park behind the restaurant. James got out with Jennifer followed by O'Rourke who then led them in the opposite direction into the allotments.

James was surprised when O'Rourke led them to Feng Choi's gardening shed. He had visited the neat rows of well-tended vegetables and soft fruits a few months before and had used the small shed to escape his own assassination. He now watched in fascination as the Irishman expertly picked the heavy padlock.

The door opened noiselessly on well-oiled hinges and O'Rourke disappeared inside. The couple followed to be enveloped in darkness and Jennifer reached for her small torch. The sharp beam of light flashed across the clutter to reveal O'Rourke blindly fumbling with boxes and empty potato sacks in the corner. He finally gave a grunt of satisfaction. His muscles straining beneath the thin cotton shirt he lifted a small crate and staggered backwards before placing it on the mud-caked floorboards in the centre of the shed.

'Voilà!' he exclaimed. 'Your precious treasure.'

'The ding is in that?' Jennifer whispered. 'It seems rather small. I remember it looked bigger in Venice.'

'The ding isn't that big and you were judging its size by the hole it was buried in. It's only twelve inches in diameter and about fourteen inches high.' O'Rourke took a rusty claw hammer from one of the many shelves to lever off the short boards on the top.

The last board was pulled up and O'Rourke ripped away the bubblewrap that was packed around the bronze cauldron. The metal gleamed in the torchlight and James knelt to peel back the piece of leather that covered the pale discs stacked inside. The *bi* reflected the light, giving the pitched pine roof an eerie wash of colour.

He picked up one of the jade discs and as Jennifer pointed her torch at it the delicate engravings to life. They all leant forward to study the details with bated breath.

'The last times I saw those was when Feng received a letter from his brother and when Ambrossini gave two to me before he was shot dead by you.'

'Each one is worth approximately £3,000,' Jennifer added. 'And there's a few hundred in there.'

'And they all belong to our friend Feng,' James added. 'Let's go and tell him now.'

'I wouldn't do that, Goodfellow.' O'Rourke had removed a small revolver from his pocket. 'Before you take possession of this I need the petri dish.'

James was about to reach into his pocket when the shed door burst inward and a powerful beam of light blinded the occupants.

'Don't move! I have a very sharp knife and . . . ' the shouting voice suddenly ceased. 'Oh, it's you James,' Feng said in surprise. 'And Jenny, too. I saw a light flickering in the window and came expecting to catch the person who has been raiding my carrots. I never expected to find you in my shed. Why *are* you here?' He suddenly became aware of O'Rourke standing silently in the gloom and pointing a gun at James. 'You!' he shouted. 'Put that down or I cut you into very small pieces and serve you as sushi in my restaurant.'

'He will too,' James chuckled. 'He's not too worried about the health and safety officers.'

'How dare you, James. You know I keep the cleanest kitchen in the whole of the south of England,' Feng spluttered.

James and Jennifer burst into laughter and as O'Rourke put the gun back in his pocket even he began to laugh. Feng looked from one to the other and then he joined in.

'Can we now get back to more serious matters,' the big man said with the grin still on his face.

James took the sandwich bag and handed it to O'Rourke. He couldn't help noticing that the usual colouration of the culture had changed. It was now a deep purple all over.

'It doesn't look quite so pretty,' he observed. 'More menacing than I saw it last.'

O'Rourke held it up in the torchlight and his eyes narrowed with concern. 'It has definitely changed; who knows what it means.' 'It looks a lot more lethal,' James said.

'Destroy it, Sèan,' Jennifer whispered as though fearing that the virus could hear her.

'I cannot do that, I must take it back to Beijing.' O'Rourke slipped the polythene bag into his jacket pocket and started to leave the shed.

'Will you go to the Chinese Embassy first?' Feng asked.

O'Rourke paused. 'I cannot trust anyone there. The triads are everywhere so therefore the safest plan is to collect my things in Soho and then go direct to the airport where I'll book an immediate flight.'

'So, it's goodbye?' Jennifer said, overcome by a feeling of thankfulness.

'Yes.' O'Rourke gave a brief wave of the hand and disappeared into the darkness.

Feng shrugged at the man's abrupt departure and as his torch swept from the doorway he saw the cauldron standing behind James.

'And who does that belong to?' He went to take a closer look as James bent to pull back the leather cover.

'It's your legacy, my friend. It's the ancestral ding filled with the *bi* discs that your distant cousin was trying to give to you.' James said with a broad smile.

'You're a multi-millionaire, Feng,' Jennifer said with a smile and hugged the man. 'Your brother was murdered for these and your cousin died on the plane while trying to reach you.'

Feng picked up one of the *bi* and studied it with a degree of curiosity. 'It's very much the same as the one Han sent to me,' he murmured.

'I think it would be safer if you left them hidden in the shed until such time as other matters have been cleared up and there is no longer any threat to you or your family.' James flipped the leather cover over the *bi* and started replacing the bubblewrap.

'What other matters?'

'The package I gave to O'Rourke is a petri dish with a growing culture. It had been hidden amongst these ancestral discs and it could prove to be the worst weapon of mass destruction ever created.'

'Many times worse than the hydrogen bomb,' Jennifer added sombrely. 'Possibly the end of the entire Oriental race on the planet.'

Feng looked puzzled and he remained silent as James nailed the wooden slats back in place to seal the crate. Feng hurried to help him carry it to the corner of the shed and disguise it with sacks and seedling boxes.

'Why the Oriental race?' Feng asked. 'Doesn't the virus affect everyone?'

James gave an abridged explanation. 'This particular virus has been deliberately designed to alter the Oriental DNA structure only. After exposure there would be no next generation and China would rapidly depopulate.'

'Who would do such a terrible thing?'

'The Illuminati has a great fear that China is steadily moving towards destabilizing world economies and the triad organizations, without realizing it, are helping the Chinese government by making it their sole mission to eliminate all Illuminati members.'

'And who was O'Rourke really working for?'

'The Chinese government,' Jenny said. 'He infiltrated both the Triad and the Illuminati to find the virus and destroy it after an antidote had been developed.'

Feng shook his head in disbelief, relocked the shed and invited the couple to adjourn to the Forbidden City's kitchen where he had left a pot of green tea hanging over the dying embers of an open stove.

The ghostly image of a barn owl silently flashed overhead as they entered the restaurant. That's a bad omen, Feng thought. An evil spirit can only mean a death.

The sun was streaming through the windows on South Street when Waterston heard the sounds of his wife stirring above them.

'She will want to know if I'm coming for my breakfast,' he said to the motionless man who had watched over the major like a hovering hawk as he slept slumped in his chair.

'I will stand by the door and you will ask for coffee only. Say you still have an urgent report to finish,' Xun whispered. 'When she brings it you will take it at the door.'

The major nodded his understanding and stood to open the door. 'Shall I ask her to get you a cup too?'

'Don't be a bloody fool. If she even suspects you have a visitor or enters this room you will both die.' The sword was raised threateningly and the major stared at the glittering edge. He cracked the door, shouted for coffee as instructed and then shut it again.

Waterston had finished his coffee when the mantel clock softly chimed. Xun looked at his wrist to check its accuracy and found that with typical military precision it was precisely on time.

'He is late, Major,' Xun said, his eyes glittering dangerously. 'You had better pray that he comes within the next hour or . . . ' he left the threat unsaid and the major felt his hands shake as he clasped them together.

At quarter to nine Mrs Waterston called out that she was going to do some shopping in Knightsbridge and the bang from the front door reverberated in the hallway making her husband wince. He glanced up at the mantel and an icy hand gripped his chest.

'What will you do if he doesn't arrive on time?' he mumbled.

'What do you think?'

Before Waterston could start thinking of the consequences the phone on his desk rang to jar his nerves. He reached out but his hand was stopped by the sword tip.

'You will say nothing, do you understand?' Xun growled. 'If it is O'Rourke you will simply listen very politely to his excuse, find out when he will arrive and then hang up.'

Waterston nodded and picked the receiver up. 'Rackman?' He sat upright and listened intently before thanking the person at the other end and hanging up.

'Well?'

'It wasn't O'Rourke. It was my second in command.'

'That's unfortunate.'

'I don't know where O'Rourke is but Rackman has the address of his apartment in London.' Beads of perspiration were gathering on Waterston's forehead.

'Call him back and get the address now!' Xun snapped and the major snatched at the phone and pressed recall.

'Rackman. What's O'Rourke's address?' he said in a voice tinged with panic. He picked up his pen and scrawled on the notepad lying before him. As the major replaced the phone Xun swung Dragon's Breath and the pen fell from the dead man's fingers.

Xun sprung back to avoid the geyser of blood from the neck and snatched up the notepad. He cleaned the blade on an antimacassar and returned it to the scabbard before removing two of the F1 grenades from the small satchel he carried. He pulled the firing pins and dropped them both into the lap of the corpse.

The triad hurriedly left the room and made for the front door; finding the street empty he jog-trotted down South Street. He had just turned a corner when a tremendous roar announced the detonation of the grenades.

The sound rolled away through the streets of London setting off dozens of car alarms; Major Hugh Waterston and all forensic evidence that Xun may have inadvertently left behind was incinerated in the explosion that also destroyed the front of the old building in one tremendous fireball.

Xun swung the leather bag over his shoulder and after memorizing the address on the blood-splattered notepaper he made for Soho.

If the *gweilo* won't come to me I'll go to him, he thought and then laughed.

18

O'ROURKE EYED EACH PEDESTRIAN with suspicion as he walked along the poorly lit Greek Street. Late-night revellers lurched past him arm in arm as lone men guiltily sidled out of doors with illuminated nameplates that promised loveless pleasure. It was two o'clock in the morning and he was dog-tired and in need of sleep before leaving for the airport.

He entered the building and crept up the stairs to his apartment where he quickly stripped, climbed into bed and fell into a deep but troubled sleep.

A solitary shaft of bright sunlight slowly crept across the bed until it illuminated the face of the sleeping man. Coincidentally, the alarm clock on the bedside table began ringing and O'Rourke's eyes snapped open. He leapt from under the covers and instantly felt the chill air on his naked body as his feet hit the cold linoleum.

'Bloody hell,' he exclaimed looking at the time. It was ten o'clock and he had only intended to catnap for a couple of hours.

He painfully shaved and then showered in the tepid water from a tap that the landlord had amusingly labelled HOT and dressed in a hurry. He had just boiled water for an instant coffee when there was a timid knock at the door.

O'Rourke took the Glock semi-automatic from under his pillow and slipped it under the waistband at the back of his slacks. He looked through the spyhole and saw a heavily made-up face. There were three locks and it took O'Rourke a few moments to turn each one before yanking the door open.

The blowsy prostitute called Scarlet from the room below stood before him in a thin cotton housecoat that barely covered her knees. Hair that had once been light blonde had been changed over time by peroxide to a brassy yellow that hung in lank locks across a badly bruised face. O'Rourke could see terror in the woman's eyes before she was propelled towards him by the man standing behind.

O'Rourke stepped to one side as she tripped on the edge of the carpet and fell. There was a dull sound as her temple struck the corner of the bed rendering her unconscious but the tall man's eyes had remained fixed on the figure standing in the doorway.

'Xun! This is a pleasure,' he said. His eyes narrowed as he watched the immobile man and internally readied himself for the next move. 'I heard a lot about you when I was in Hong Kong and I expected Shing to send someone of your quality. Are you here on his orders or are you following your own agenda?'

'Pengfei Shing requests that you give me the ding to auction in Europe. I have already contacted Sotheby's to confirm interest in the items. Money accrued from the sale will be wired by the auction house to Shing's account in Hong Kong.'

'Is there nothing else you want?'

'Such as?' For a brief moment O'Rourke could see that the man was a little puzzled by his question and he immediately knew that Shing was unaware of the petri dish and the culture growing in it.

'I would imagine you want the *bi* as well.'

'Naturally! What else would I be interested in,' Xun snapped as he took a step into the room and closed the door behind him.

'You cannot have either as they have all been returned to their rightful owner,' O'Rourke said as he took a step back to maintain a respectable distance between them. He had already spotted the long leather bags slung across the triad's back and guessed correctly that it concealed the triad's favoured weapons. But why did he carry two? he thought.

'Who would that person be?' Xun reached over his shoulder and with a quick, hissing movement produced a sword. 'It cannot be Superintendent Huang or Han Choi as they are both dead.' He tossed the sword onto the bed casually. 'It can't be Major Waterston who I know is your other master, traitor!' Xun spat out, 'because I've just taken his head with this.'

He reached back and Dragon's Breath appeared in his hand. 'Yours will join his if you don't tell me where the ding is.'

'That will remain a secret until my dying day, Xun.'

O'Rourke smiled to deliberately antagonize the triad who gave a grunt of anger and raised his weapon to attack the big man. 'Pick up the sword and show me how you can die like a triad.'

O'Rourke glanced at the weapon and then grinned at Xun. 'I prefer to die like an Irishman,' he declared and in one fluid movement he produced the Glock, aimed at the man's head, flicked to fully automatic and squeezed the trigger.

Xun had only taken two steps forward and begun the blade's downward strike when his head was shattered by the impact of five high-velocity bullets. The assassin was flung backwards and the sword completed its downward strike harmlessly. O'Rourke strode across the room and pulling the carpet to one side he slipped the still smoking gun under a loose floorboard for possible future use.

Wrenching Xun's fingers from the hilt he took Dragon's Breath. I'll return this to the person who sent it, he thought as he slipped it back into its beautiful sheath. He grabbed the travel case and gave one sympathetic look at the sleeping woman, knowing that she would have a lot of explaining to do on awakening, and left the room.

As he hurried down the stairs all the doors in the building remained firmly closed. The high-priced tenants did what came naturally when they hear any gunfire: they bolted their doors. Involvement in a brothel fight had to be avoided at all costs and clients were in full agreement as they fearfully wilted and wished they were somewhere other than a tart's boudoir.

O'Rourke stepped into Greek Street with the sword slung across his back and hailed a black cab parked down the street. The cab stopped alongside and as soon as he had closed the door and sat down with the sword case across his knees the door locks engaged. O'Rourke went on full alert and feeling at a loss without the Glock he undid the leather case and gripped the hilt of the sword.

The driver turned to face his passenger and smiled through the safety glass without any humour in his eyes. 'Mr Sèan O'Rourke. It's so nice to see you again. I believe you have something that Major Waterston needs.'

'Major Waterston is dead, Rackman.'

'And who told you that?'

'A triad *Red Pole* before I blew his head off.'

Richard Rackman didn't respond but did a U-turn and they were soon heading towards the Mayfair area and South Street. The door-lock lights glowed steadily and O'Rourke had to be content with sitting back and waiting for the ride to end; he knew the barrier between him and Rackman was shock resistant and he didn't fancy trying an ancient sword on bullet-proof glass.

Rackman knew his way around London as well as any other cab driver who had studied *The Knowledge* and they soon arrived at the end of South Street where they came to a dead stop. Fire tenders, ambulances and police cars blocked their way and armed response officers in full body armour and carrying Heckler & Koch machine guns were diverting the traffic. Winding his window down Rackman asked one of the men why they couldn't enter the street.

'There's been some terrorist activity, sir. A bomb in one of the houses,' he said briefly before waving Rackman on and O'Rourke was driven to Berkeley Square where the cab parked opposite Morton's, a private club that Rackman had been introduced to by the Major.

'So the major *has* been killed,' Rackman said over his shoulder. 'I suggest we go in here and discuss the situation like two civilized people.'

O'Rourke could feel the sword reassuringly pressing on his thighs as he nodded. The cab doors unlocked and he climbed out to follow Rackman across the street. The SIS man didn't seem to be too concerned by the long leather case that O'Rourke had swung round to hang down his back.

Once seated at a table in the long bar Rackman ordered Grey Goose vodkas for them both and as they waited in silence for the drinks the rat-faced man studied O'Rourke.

'You have recovered the culture?' he asked in a soft voice after the waiter had left and without waiting for an answer he went on, 'You have it on you now?'

There was a long silence during which O'Rourke took a sip of the ice-cold spirit. 'I also have a rather sharp sword on me that says the Illuminati can't have it.'

'You do realize that I can mobilize the SIS to hunt you down, take the culture forcibly and make you disappear. But only if it becomes necessary as I would rather you give it to me now so that we part on more peaceful terms.'

'If you involve the SIS, Rackman, there will be questions about the culture; who, how and where it was developed and its ultimate purpose.' O'Rourke leant forward to emphasize his next point. 'You'll find I can be very forthcoming with answers when threatened. If I expose you as being a member of a secret society it could prove to be embarrassing for you and a number of government people in key positions.'

Rackman sat back and scowled. 'Don't you realize that the Chinese nation is planning to engulf the rest of the world. They will very soon control our financial and personal lives to the point that Britain may well join the Third World nations asking for aid. Poverty and disease will become commonplace throughout the Home Counties. Places like Tonbridge Wells, Windsor and Cheltenham will become ghettos and –'

O'Rourke had been sipping his vodka while Rackman became increasingly agitated by his own words until he held his hand up to stop the man's ranting. 'Rackman, wake up and smell the Liu'an tea, will you? You can't stop China from wanting to deal with the rest of the world and you certainly can't stop their desire to become more of a consumer society. One thing you should understand is that they will now be learning all the daily problems that arise from trying to satisfy ever-increasing consumer demands on heavy and light industries. In the meantime the West have to make an effort to understand their culture and to learn to trade with them. We'll find they have as much to offer us as we have for them and a balance will be reached that gives mutual satisfaction.'

Rackman compressed his lips and glared across the small table. 'How can you speak like that to me? You are Illuminati, you cannot renege on your oath to stay on the enlightened path,' he whispered.

'I also took a triad oath; so what if I am a double-agent? Joining both societies was essential to ensure that I am successful in my mission.'

'Your mission?'

'I was instructed to stop the culture from falling into irresponsible hands such as your own. I have succeeded and it is now on its way to China by courier,' O'Rourke lied, feeling the small packet in his pocket grow heavy with the responsibility it held. 'Thank you for the drink, Rackman, but I think it's time I left. Do not bother to follow me as nothing will come of it but a lot more trouble.'

'Where is the *ding* and all the *bi*? At least give something back to the Illuminati.'

'They have all been returned to the rightful owner and I wouldn't attempt to take them for yourself.' O'Rourke prepared to walk towards the exit as Rackman jumped to his feet.

'I *will* have that petri dish, O'Rourke. Mark my words. I *will* take it even if I have to go to the ends of the earth to get it,' he hissed through his teeth, his face revealing his hatred of the Irishman.

O'Rourke shrugged as he picked up his bag and the sword case. 'Then you will have to declare war on the Chinese government to get it, Rackman.'

The Illuminati glowered. 'Before you go, O'Rourke, just remember that I want those ancestral pieces and that I know Han Choi had a brother. Would *he* be the rightful owner?'

The two men stared at each other for a full five seconds as O'Rourke's absorbed the threat. His face became thunderous and he pointed a long finger at Rackman. 'Touch anyone in East Steading and you'll be as dead as your ex-master.' He turned on his heel and left the club.

Miss Lightbody had heard the phone ringing while climbing the stairs. She hurriedly unlocked the office door but as she reached to lift the receiver it stopped. A quick glance at the wall clock confirmed that she was ten minutes early and it wasn't until it showed nine o'clock that the phone rang once more.

'Goodfellow Investigations, how can I help you?' she said.

'Is James there, Miss Lightbody?'

'Good morning, Mr O'Rourke. No, he hasn't arrived yet. Can I take a message?'

'Tell him I've delayed my flight and I am now at East Steading station. I should arrive at his office within the hour and it's vitally important that he is there to hear what I have to say.' O'Rourke hung up and Miss Lightbody immediately rang the mobile number of her employer but it was switched off. Knowing James she guessed it was a dead battery. James was extremely forgetful when it came to recharging his phone and taking his Xyrem.

At precisely ten o'clock the door opened and a familiar voice greeted Miss Lightbody. She quickly gave him the gist of O'Rourke's message and as he went into his office James wondered what was so important to cause the Irishman to cancel his flight to Hong Kong. Freshly brewed coffee was placed at his elbow just as the main door opened and O'Rourke entered. Without waiting for an introduction he rushed into James's office.

'Bad news, Goodfellow,' he exclaimed, panting heavily as he threw himself into a chair. 'Can I too have one of those, please, Miss Lightbody, milk no sugar? I didn't want to alarm your secretary,' he continued in a quiet voice when the door was closed behind her. 'There's an Illuminati who is out to cause us a lot of trouble.'

'In what way?'

'Not only was he after the virus, he now wants the cauldron and everything it contains. He has learnt what it's worth and as he is now the new chairman he wants to use that money to fund more Illuminati research into the viral weapon.'

'Exactly who is this person?' James asked in a puzzled tone.

'His name is Richard Rackman and he was the right-hand man of Major Waterston who was the UK chairman of the Illuminati.'

'They are the ones who want to use the virus against the Chinese nation, aren't they?'

'Yes and now Waterston is dead . . .'

'How?'

'Assassinated by Xun last night.'

'And Xun?'

'Killed by me.'

'What makes this Rackman fellow so dangerous that you'd cancel your mission to get the virus back to China?'

'Rackman wants the cauldron and he has already worked out that Feng Choi is next in line to the inheritance and has it.'

'How did he get to know that?' James said incredulously.

'That was my mistake. I told him that everything had been returned to its rightful owner which means he will be coming to East Steading to question Feng Choi.'

There was a long silence during which James sipped at the scalding liquid. As his gaze drifted across his desk his attention was caught by the red light glowing on his landline phone. His secretary had been listening to the conversation.

'You might as well come in, Miss Lightbody. Maybe you have the solution to our problem.'

The door opened and his secretary entered rather sheepishly. 'My apology, James, but the urgency in Mr O'Rourke's voice caused my curiosity and I couldn't help listening. I was horrified to hear that Feng and his family may be at risk and I would like to suggest that they all stay with me until the police can put an end to this terrible threat.'

'That's extremely generous, Miss Lightbody, but Feng has a successful business that he can't just shut down and walk away from. At least, that's what he'll say in response to your offer.'

'We could ask him.'

James shook his head. 'There's no point. We cannot tell the police for we do not know whom we can trust. The only people we might mention this to would be Sergeant Briscoe and possibly Inspector Tilley but if the nation's secret service has been infiltrated by the Illuminati then you can be sure that the upper echelons of the police force have also been infected.'

O'Rourke shifted his weight in the leather club chair and the squeak of leather drew their attention. 'You're right, Goodfellow, and as Rackman's an SIS intelligence officer he has resources at his fingertips that is going to make locating Feng a walk in the park.'

'Then I must go and warn him now.' James stood, followed by Miss Lightbody. 'Alone,' he added while giving her a meaningful look before turning to O'Rourke. 'You can't afford to put that petri dish at risk so I suggest you avoid every chance of ever meeting Rackman again and that you get it out of this country as soon as you can.'

The big man nodded as he shifted the sword case to a more comfortable position on his back. 'What will be *your* plan?' he asked out of curiosity.

'The less you know the better. Good luck in Hong Kong.' With a swift shake of the hand James left the office and hurried down the stairs. O'Rourke waited until he heard the lower door slam before bidding farewell to Miss Lightbody and leaving.

She suddenly felt very alone. Sitting at her desk she doodled on her notepad while considering all that had been discussed. When she had completed the third abstract shape that the phone broke the silence, startling her.

'Goodfellow Invest –'

'I know who you are,' a voice rudely interrupted. 'Just tell your employer that his friend will have his china doll returned in exchange for a few old memories. Tell him to call this number before noon or I will go ahead and test the fragility of the doll.' The string of cellphone numbers was quickly transferred to the notepad before the connection was abruptly broken.

Miss Lightbody hung up and rushed from the office to clatter downstairs and into the restaurant as fast as her court shoes would permit. James and Feng in a corner booth, both leaning forward over the table with their heads close together, were discussing O'Rourke's latest news.

'Excuse me, James. I've just taken a weird call,' she panted as she slumped down into the seat beside Feng. She rapidly gave the message and handed him the sheet of notepad paper.

James jerked upright. 'Where's Lin-Lin?'

Feng stood and looked round the room with wild eyes. 'She should be at school. Jiao dropped her off at nine o'clock before going on to the vegetable market to get some supplies for the restaurant.' He rushed to the kitchen while James grimly clenched his hands. Miss Lightbody had never seen her employer look so agitated.

Feng reappeared shaking his head with a troubled look on his face. 'Miss Williamson, her teacher, said she had been brought to school by Jiao but that a friend of mine had come to collect her because I had been taken very ill.'

James pounded the table with his fists making the crockery and water glasses bounce noisily. 'She's been taken, Agnes,' James said in a low, wrathful tone.

'Kidnapped?' she whispered fearfully.

James said nothing with Feng facing him, trembling like the leaves of a silver birch in the wind. He placed a hand over his friend's to steady the shaking. 'We will have to give him the *ding* and the *bi*; Lin-Lin is far too precious to try any clever tricks.'

Feng nodded rapidly and James began dialling the number given to Miss Lightbody.

'James Goodfellow,' he said softly. 'To whom am I talking?'

'That's irrelevant, Goodfellow. What is relevant is that I want you to take the cauldron and its contents to Lydd Airport. You must rendezvous with a small white van at 6 a.m. tomorrow. It will be parked near a small bridge that you'll find on the access road to the airport.'

'Will you bring the girl with you?' James asked.

The voice ignored the question. 'If you bring anyone with *you* the doll will be broken. Do I make myself clear?'

'As crystal.'

The connection was broken and James shook his head as he looked into Feng's frightened eyes. 'I think that was the man I told you about.'

'Richard Rackman?' Feng asked.

James nodded. 'I believe he plans to fly the cauldron across the Channel to put it beyond our reach should we try to recover it later when Lin-Lin is freed.'

'Recovering them would be the last thing I want. The damned things can be lost for another three thousand years as far as I'm concerned.'

James gripped the man's hand and stood up. 'I had better take my car to the garden shed and get the damned thing loaded. I don't envy you the task but you'd better tell Jiao what has happened.'

'I'll do that,' Miss Lightbody suddenly said with a hand half raised to stop Feng from rising. 'It will sound less alarming coming from a woman.'

Feng thanked her with a grateful look that spoke a thousand words and then watched her weave between the empty tables and enter the kitchen.

James patted his friend on the shoulder before leaving the restaurant. Feng remained seated, his head in his hands, his eyes glistening with tears.

James backed the car until it aligned with the wicket gate leading to the allotment and opened the rear door. He hurried into the garden shed to uncover the cauldron. Carrying the heavy bronze *ding* brought sweat to his forehead as he staggered to the car and placed it on the rear seat. After draping an old potato sack over it he started the engine and pulled away.

Using the hands-free system James called Jennifer at the police station and gave her a quick summary of events before asking her if she could join him on the run to Lydd airport.

'After the exchange Lin-Lin will most probably need the immediate comfort and sense of security that only a woman can give,' he explained and Jennifer instantly agreed, trying to disguise the fear she felt. As soon as James had collected Jennifer he took the southbound road out of East Steading.

'Is the man violent?' were her first words as she settled herself for the long drive.

'Rackman is SIS which means he's capable of pretty much anything in order to get what he wants.'

'He'd hurt Lin-Lin?'

'He may. That is why Feng and I have agreed to make the exchange without any police interference. There is also the possibility that certain high-ranking police officers may learn of the situation and assist Rackman in his plan.'

Jennifer fell silent for a moment, keeping her eyes fixed on the road ahead. 'I'm sorry James, but I told Sergeant Briscoe everything.'

'What!'

'I didn't tell him it was at Lydd. As far as he's concerned I don't have that information yet and he expects me to call him the moment I know the location.'

'Thank God.' James slumped back in his seat. 'If a SWAT team had turned up then I wouldn't give two pennies for Lin-Lin's chance of survival.'

'So, it's just the two of us?'

'We're only giving Rackman what he wants. I do not anticipate any undue violence if we behave ourselves.'

The Ford smoothly ran down the highway and soon turned off onto the minor road that took them to Lydd. James planned to stay at a hotel close to the airport to guarantee making such an early rendezvous and as soon as they approached the small town he spotted an inn that promised good food and a comfortable bed.

'Isn't there something a little more salubrious?' Jennifer asked.

'Possibly but it won't be as close to the airport turn-off as this.'

They went in and were immediately assailed by the smell of old cooking fat and beer-stained carpets. Jennifer gave James a disapproving look as the surly-faced landlord approached them without any sign of welcome on his face. He looked them up and down and when James requested a room for the night his lip curled. He had noticed the absence of luggage and had jumped to the worst conclusion. He introduced himself as Ken and produced the visitors' book, quoting a ridiculously high rate. As James picked up the pen Jennifer produced her warrant card and thrust it under the man's nose.

'How much?' she asked sharply.

'Sorry, that was the high season rate,' he mumbled, giving a price that was fifty per cent lower.

James smiled and deliberately signed the register with a flourish as Mr and Mrs Smith. The landlord gave James a key with a large wooden tag and with a final sniff of disapproval he disappeared into the back room and resumed watching *Who Wants To Be A Millionaire*.

Entering their first-floor room they immediately saw that there was no television, radio or tea-making facilities. The en-suite bath was stained rust-yellow and James was reluctant to check the colour of the water.

'I suggest we find somewhere else to have a late lunch. I'm sure we can find a warmer, friendlier place than this,' Jennifer suggested with a crinkled nose and James laughed.

'Not quite the honeymoon suite, is it?' he said after they had left the inn and got into the car. They slowly cruised through Lydd until James spotted a small restaurant.

'Do you like Indian cuisine?' he asked.

'I can eat anything. I'm really starving.' As if to add emphasis to Jennifer's words there was a distinct rumbling in the region of her stomach and James grinned.

They lingered over the meal to help pass the time but when the staff started putting chairs on the tables they felt obliged to pay the bill. They bought magazines from a small nearby newsagents before driving back to the shabby inn. The afternoon dragged by as they read their magazines from cover to cover. There was a moment when James wanted to make love but peeling ceiling paper, rising damp and the smell from the en-suite plumbing dampened any romantic thoughts.

They slept fitfully and were easily woken by James's wristwatch alarm at five o'clock. They combed their hair with open fingers and took a chance on the water to douse their faces before dressing and going down stairs. It was far too early for any kind of breakfast and when there was no answer to the bell James left the key on the bar.

Rain had been falling steadily and the sky was only just beginning to lighten when they left the inn and drove the short distance to the turn-off leading to the airport. The surroundings suddenly opened up to become flat grassland with very few buildings in sight. As they followed the winding road with sprouting winter wheat on either side they could vaguely see the tops of hangars rising above the morning mist ahead.

'We're getting close,' James murmured as he slowed the car.

Glancing at her watch Jennifer realized that they only had three minutes to make the deadline. Suddenly they passed a speed limit sign that also carried a culvert sign.

'This must be it,' she confirmed pointing to the white van that had materialized from a passing bank of mist. It was parked on a farmer's access road only fifty yards from the airport road.

James slowed down to a crawl and turned into the road before coming to a stop. With bated breath they waited for someone to appear. Five minutes passed before the driver's door swung open and a short, dark-suited figure climbed out and limped to the rear of the van. He stood looking at the Ford as he waited for a burly man in dark glasses to finish getting out on the passenger side.

'Goodfellow,' Rackman shouted. 'Get out and tell that person with you to get out too.'

James turned to Jennifer with a grim expression. 'Let the show begin,' he murmured and opened his door.

19

O'ROURKE WAS AWARE that he was being shadowed and was sure that the two men in black fly-fronted overcoats were SIS agents acting on Richard Rackman's orders. He boarded the underground train and kept an eye on the men as the sliding doors began to close. Both suddenly leapt forward into the next carriage, clearly intent on staying with O'Rourke all the way.

He changed at Paddington Station for the Heathrow Express and the men did the same. *Unless they have airline tickets for Hong Kong they are going to be very disappointed*, he thought.

At the airport he watched as they followed him through passport control. They simply flicked open official passes and from noting the respectful response that they received O'Rourke was now quite certain that they were SIS officers.

They fingered perfumes and aftershaves in the duty-free area while a security officer delayed O'Rourke with an over-sensitive metal detector. He had put Dragon's Breath into hold baggage with his small travel case. It had been professionally boxed and covered with counterfeit official seals of the Chinese government by Sying. She hadn't heard of Xun's demise but did wonder how the Irishman came to be in possession of the sword. The all glass petri dish was still in an inside pocket of his jacket and naturally it didn't register on the security machine.

Finally he was allowed to proceed and O'Rourke lingered in the bookshop. He bought a Clive Cussler novel and going to the bar he pretended to read while sipping an indifferent pint of bitter. When his flight was called he briskly strode to Gate 27 sensing them close behind.

As he entered the jet-bridge to the Boeing 777 he glanced back to see the men stop at the boarding gate. O'Rourke then knew that he had been followed only to ensure he was really going to take a flight. This could only mean that they planned to have someone waiting for him when he arrived at Chek Lap Kok Airport to take over the surveillance.

The twelve-hour flight to Hong Kong was one of long periods of boredom interrupted by short snatches of sleep and despite the comfort of the business class seat O'Rourke was extremely thankful when the announcement was made that they were making the final approach.

HONG KONG

He cleared immigration and customs swiftly thanks to the official government identification he had been given in Beijing at the beginning of his mission. He climbed into the taxi and waited for the long box and travel bag to be placed in the boot.

Looking round O'Rourke saw an Illuminati agent talking to the driver of the next taxi. The lanky twenty-something was wearing a cream linen suit that looked as though it had been slept in. Aviator-styled sunglasses and a wispy goatee completed the disguise. O'Rourke smiled for he had instantly spotted his new shadow in the arrivals hall by the tall man's attempt to blend in with the Chinese crowd who were considerably shorter.

As they pulled away O'Rourke turned his head to see the young man leap into his taxi and gesture for his driver to follow. He'll look for the first opportunity to take the dish, O'Rourke thought as he faced front. He smiled smugly knowing that the most suitable place would be his own apartment.

They made excellent time despite the heavy traffic and soon crossed the amazing feat of engineering called Tsing Ma Bridge. With the Illuminati close behind they sped through the Cross-Harbour and the Aberdeen tunnels to cross the island. As the taxi came to a halt outside Hoi Chan Court O'Rourke glanced back to see the cream linen suit get out of the taxi that had double-parked a fair distance behind.

The normal flow of mini buses packed with early-morning commuters flowed back and forth on Chengtu Road and O'Rourke was thankful for the throng of people that poured from each to hinder his shadow's progress. He took possession of the long box and travel bag and hurried down the passage between the two high apartment towers and entered the lobby. Not wanting to reveal that his flat was on the eight floor O'Rourke ignored the bank of lifts and took the stairs.

After five flights of rapid climbing he paused, gasping for breath. and put the box down. Unlocking the wooden box he used the penknife he kept in his travel bag to sliced through all the official seals. Polystyrene pellets that had protected the sword spilt out onto the steps as he lifted the lid. He took the leather bag from the box and slung it over his shoulder. He now had a silent means of defence to hand and continued to climb to the eighth level.

O'Rourke's follower cautiously entered the building. Lights above two lifts were moving in a downward direction while the other two remained stationary. He glanced towards the door leading to the stairwell and then walked over to the tenant listing on white plastic plaques affixed to the stone wall.

Unaware that O'Rourke spoke and read Mandarin fluently he ran his eyes down the columns checking the English names. Two precious minutes were lost before he discovered his error and strode across the lobby to the stairwell to start climbing. At each level he looked in both directions but could see no sign of O'Rourke. Reaching the fifth level he came across the mysterious wooden box the Irishman had carried and leaving it where it lay he went on climbing.

The small polystyrene pellets that O'Rourke had dropped on the stairs guided him to the eighth floor. The last pellet was lying outside a door numbered 86 in both English and Cantonese. As there was no spyhole in the door he took the Smith & Wesson .38 from inside his coat and knocked on the door.

The bearded old man who opened his door was shocked to be looking down the barrel of a gun. The man holding it was no less surprised and he quickly holstered the weapon, made rapid mispronounced apologies in Cantonese and fled. The agent knew that the Chinese tenant would soon raise the alarm and he raced down the stairs, left the building and walked down Chengtu Road to the corner where he planned to wait for O'Rourke to show himself.

The Irishman smiled as he watched the man hurrying out of the building. He had deliberately dropped the polystyrene pellets to confuse his shadow and now the tables were turned; he was the stalker and he planned to follow the man to see where he went.

From his vantage spot in the window of the Café de Coral he was able to watch the man as he lingered on the corner, occasionally looking towards the entrance of the tower block. After O'Rourke had finished three coffees and two coconut-filled cocktail buns the man in the linen suit became impatient and walked towards the harbour where scores of fishing boats were moored. O'Rourke left money on the table and quickly followed the man who stood head and shoulders above everyone else. Knowing how tall he was O'Rourke stayed well back to avoid detection.

Using the footbridge to cross the Aberdeen Praya double highway O'Rourke's stalker met with another European. They were having a rather heated discussion and the new man, a short-haired, equally thin man in an open-neck white shirt and faded jeans, kept jabbing his finger in the direction of Chengtu Road – O'Rourke guessed that linen suit was being instructed to keep a close watch on the apartment building. He was soon proved right when his shadow suddenly turned on his heel and headed back to the long ramp leading up to the footbridge. O'Rourke went down the steps on the other side and when he was sure that linen suit had not spotted him he began following the second man along the waterfront.

With the long gait of an athlete the man was soon at a white cruiser moored well away from the serried ranks of fishing vessels. The man knew his own vessel for he confidently jumped aboard and disappeared below deck. The Macau registered vessel was showing her age and the thin skin of deck varnish was beginning to peel not unlike that of a sun worshipper who had lazed in the sun far too long.

O'Rourke tossed his travel bag onto a wooden bench beside the water and using it as a pillow he lay down and waited for the sun to set. He lightly dozed with his senses alert for any sounds of danger. He wanted to know more about the Illuminati in Hong Kong but he had the patience to wait until the sun had set behind Lantau Island.

ENGLAND

James stood beside the car staring at the dapper stranger in the murky morning light as Jennifer got out and went round the back of the car to stand beside him. Rackman turned to signal the heavy-set man who reached into the van with a hand as big as a baseball mitt and pulled Lin-Lin out by the scruff of her neck. She briefly squealed with pain before she was put down and a gun placed to her head.

'Make a wrong move, Goodfellow, and the girl will cease to exist. Do you understand?'

James nodded.

'Now take the cauldron out of the car and bring it to me.'

With considerable effort James lifted the bronze *ding* and staggered towards Rackman. When he had covered half the distance the SIS man held up his hand. 'Stop right there and put it down,' he snapped.

There was a dull thump as the bronze legs hit the tarmac and James stepped back. 'Now the girl,' he called out.

'Return to your car and I will send her to you.'

James backed slowly until he felt Jennifer take his hand and squeeze it hopefully. Rackman went to the *ding* and pulled the top slats off and flipped the leather cover back.

'There is something missing, Mr Goodfellow,' he shouted angrily.

'All the *bi* are there,' James replied, fully aware of what the man was referring to.

'The virus, I want the virus or Brian will use a knife to redecorate the girl's face.'

James reached into his jacket and withdrew the fake petri dish. He held it up for Rackman to see. 'Is this what you want?'

'You know it is so place it in the cauldron.' He backed away to keep some distance between them, his eyes glittering greedily as he watched the dish being put down. James returned to where Jenny was looking at the terrified girl, trying to reassure her with a tentative smile.

Rackman took the dish and whispered something to the man called Brian. The man moved his grip to Lin-Lin's shoulder and forced her to walk towards the cauldron.

'Do not try anything when my man releases the girl as he has orders to shoot her in the back,' Rackman called out and the couple remained perfectly still, their eyes fixed on Lin-Lin.

The big man reached the ding, released Lin-Lin and picked the cauldron up as though it weighed no more than a kilogram of sugar. Rackman had opened the back of the van and the cauldron was placed inside.

'You may have the girl, Goodfellow,' he called out as the two SIS men got into their van. The lights came on, briefly dazzling them, and the engine roared as the van rushed past and turned onto the road to head for the airport.

Jenny ran to kneel by Lin-Lin and hugged her tightly. 'Are you all right, Lin-Lin?' she asked as she gently tilted the girl's head back so she could inspect her tear-stained face. Lin-Lin nodded and gave a brave smile.

'You're safe now, dear. The men have gone and we'll soon get you back home to your mum.' Lin-Lin scrubbed the tears from her face with her knuckles and still smiling she pulled away from Jennifer and ran to James.

'I didn't cry when they took me from school,' she said as he also gave her a tight hug.

'That's because you're a very courageous young lady,' James said as he helped her onto the back seat. During the journey back to East Steading James kept her spirits up by giving a very poor imitation of Elvis Presley, singing songs in a manner that startled every dog they passed. It was not long before Lin-Lin joined in the laughter and put her hands over her ears.

Feng gave a cry of joy when Lin-Lin ran into the restaurant and into his arms. He picked his daughter up and carried her to his wife with the hint tears in his eyes.

Jenny moved close to James and said in his ear. 'You do know that as soon as they have tested the culture and discovered it's as deadly as a bout of diarrhoea they'll be coming back for the real thing.'

'I'll be ready,' he whispered, knowing full well he had only delayed the violence that would descend on East Steading.

HONG KONG

The sun had long gone to be replaced by a dull yellow moon that cast very little light on the moored cruiser. O'Rourke waited on the bench until a light came on and shone through a single porthole below deck before walking silently towards the vessel. A door slid open suddenly and a man emerged to stand in the stern his face briefly illuminated as he lit a cigarette. O'Rourke immediately recognized his quarry. He paused behind a stack of empty fish boxes and watched until he was sure that the man was alone before crossing the promenade and jumping onto the gunwale.

The man spun round and reached beneath his jacket but was too slow for the big Irishman. The edge of the sword case caught the side of his head and he fell to the deck senseless. O'Rourke crouched and listened for any movement below deck but the regular slapping of water against the hull and a radio playing the latest Cantonese hit on a nearby fishing boat were the only sounds disturbing the tranquility of the evening.

O'Rourke gripped the man under his armpits and dragged him into the deeper shadows of the stern well. After retrieving his bag and the sword case he entered and closed the door and dropped the blinds before switching on the light. After a quick search in the lockers beneath the seats he found a neat coil of thin rope that he used to hogtie the man.

The cruiser was completely empty even though dirty crockery and glasses indicated that others had shared a recent meal. O'Rourke assumed they had left for the night or were seeking female entertainment in the local bars.

The esplanade was deserted and he pulled a rust-covered plough anchor from a locker and attached it to the Illuminati's ankles just as the man started coming around.

O'Rourke slapped his cheeks until his eyes flicked wide open with fear. 'Who are you working for? Who was the man you met on the esplanade this evening?' he demanded.

The thin man wriggled and discovered how well he was bound before spotting the piece of flaking ironmongery tied to his feet. He opened his mouth to scream for help and O'Rourke stuffed it with an oily rag which caused him to choke.

'If you keep quiet and simply answer my questions nothing will happen to you,' he instructed. 'Do you understand?'

The man nodded vigorously and O'Rourke removed the rag. 'I'll ask you again, who do you work for.'

He coughed and spluttered before answering, 'Pengfei Shing.'

'You owe your allegiance to the *Mountain Master*?' He nodded again.

'But you're an Illuminati how can you work for the triads?'
'Like you I am a double agent,' the man spluttered.
'What do you and your friends want with me?'
'Pengfei demands that his ancestor's sword be returned. We were also to extract information from you as to where the old *ding* is hidden.'
'And the man who was following me, the one you met, he is a renegade Illuminati, too?'
'Yes.'
'And you work together?'
'Yes.'
'Then you can expect to be together again very soon.'

The man was confused by O'Rourke's remark but before he could say anything the rag was pushed back into his mouth. Panic returned to his eyes as he was lifted onto the bulwark. He shook his head in protest as he was rolled over the side. The heavy anchor quickly followed him and the sharp sound of the double splash soon faded, as did the expanding ripples that twinkled in the weak moonlight.

O'Rourke retrieved the sword and travel case and retraced his steps to the apartment where he fully expected to encounter the man in the linen suit. As he turned into Chengtu Road he spotted the lanky figure outside the entrance to Hoi Chan Court. O'Rourke was within twenty paces of the man when he was seen and with a quick flash of cream the shadow disappeared into the passageway. The Irishman smiled coldly as he turned the corner and walked towards the lobby. He immediately saw the man entering the poorly lit entrance and within seconds he had entered himself and walked past the night watchman who had been dozing at his desk.

Halfway between the first and second floor O'Rourke caught up with the man. Sensing someone close behind he turned with an automatic pistol in his hand and it was lost to Dragon's Breath. Clutching at the spouting wrist he screamed and turned to run up the stairs but the bronze blade sliced through his throat cutting the high-pitched sound down to a low gurgle. O'Rourke dodged the falling body and then raced up to his apartment to collect the few items he always stored there.

He cleaned and resheathed the blade before putting it in a fishing rod case. He checked himself for any blood splatter before descending to the ground floor by lift. At no time had he been seen by any of the other residents and the night watchman was still snoring loudly as he went past and left the building.

The old-style Longines on his wrist showed that it was two o'clock in the morning. He hurriedly drove through the tunnels to the other side of the island and when he reached the waterfront at Victoria Harbour he drove to the Excelsior hotel and into the car park. He took an official government identity card from the glove compartment and placed it on the dashboard before locking the vehicle.

The night clerk in reception recognized his regular guest and nodded as O'Rourke entered and went straight up to the suite that was permanently reserved for official use. He hid the petri dish in his toiletry bag before showering and then climbed between the cool, crisp sheets.

20

ENGLAND

THE COUPLE LEFT the Choi family to their happy reunion and retired to get some well-earned rest. Insomnia was one of the effects of narcolepsy yet despite the special medication that was supposed to restore his sleep cycle James was still unable to drift off. Lying in the dark listening to Jennifer's soft breathing he tried to outguess Rackman until he arrived at the only conclusion: Once Rackman knew he didn't have the real virus he could use the same tactic and threaten Feng's family again.

If Jennifer told Inspector Tilley and Sergeant Briscoe the whole story they would run the risk of alerting the Illuminati who had infiltrated the force at a high level. James knew that Rackman must have been working independently from the SIS as Britain's secret service wouldn't condone an organisation that endorsed the genocide of any specific ethnic group.

He and Jennifer were on their own and apart from his father's old Webley and any weapon that Jennifer could get her hands on the odds were stacked heavily against them.

James moved closer until he felt the warmth of her body and as they cuddled he came up with an idea that would protect Feng and his family. He decided to go far away from East Steading and the restaurant and make himself the live bait in a trap.

Jennifer stirred in her sleep as he worked out how he could become the tasty tethered goat. A message on the office answerphone would act as the first prompt to lure Rackman out of town on a wild-goose chase. This would give O'Rourke more time to deliver the original virus safely into the Chinese authorities' hands. Having reached that decision he went into a shallow until the alarm clock sounded and a sleepy Jennifer rolled into his embrace.

She listened to the plan with a deep frown creasing her forehead as she made them breakfast. It was only when Jennifer was pouring the coffee that she spoke. 'I think it's a damned idiotic idea and one that's bound to get you killed.' Without realizing what she was doing she repeatedly spooned sugar into his cup. 'I suggest you forget it this instant and come with me to Inspector Tilley. I'm sure he can be trusted. He can't possibly have anything to do with any secret society.'

'I didn't say he did but even an inspector has to get permission from above before he can instigate protective steps or armed response.' James took his cup to the sink and poured away the heavily sweetened drink before refilling it from the percolator jug. 'It's the higher ranks we can't trust and I'm not going to jeopardize Tilley's career or your own just to save my hide.'

Jennifer watched him butter a slice of toast for a few moments before she suddenly burst into tears. 'I don't want you killed either,' she cried and James went and put an arm around her shoulders. She turned to bury her face in his chest and he felt wetness seeping through the thin cotton.

'I have a pretty good plan that will keep Feng and his family safe but it will need your support and a little help.' James hugged her to him. 'It's a bit outside the law but I am hoping the result will never come to light.'

She looked up, inviting him to explain the mysterious plan he had in mind.

'Can't tell you right now, but I will need you to appropriate a good rifle and a pistol. Can you do that for me?'

'I don't know what came over you, James,' she said in astonishment, 'but I can't just break into the police armoury and help myself to weapons like that, or anything like that. Rifles and pistols are all accounted for and have to be signed in and out. It's impossible to beat the system.'

James read the concern on her face. 'Not from the armoury, Jenny, but you may be able to take them from the Evidence Room. I doubt that anybody would miss two pieces of evidence until they are required for the actual trial involved. That's the only time they will have to be produced for the purpose of prosecution.'

'Fair enough, but I can't guarantee there's anything like rifles or pistols on the premises. Another thing, if you are forced to use them then you will be contaminating the existing forensic evidence. You'll be charged with obstructing justice and lay yourself open to any number of criminal charges.'

'Let me worry about that, Jenny, just take a look, please,' he murmured and kissed her on the forehead.

Detective Constable Jennifer Kent entered the police station intent on committing a serious crime and her hands were shaking as she went into the detectives' common room and placed a long florist's cardboard box on her desk.

Sergeant Briscoe grinned when he saw her. 'What's your lad been up to, Jenny,' he called out.

'Pardon, Sarge?'

'It's not unusual for chaps to buy expensive flowers from a fancy florist when they're trying to hide something.'

'I usually get my bunch of daffs from the petrol station,' Constable Shawcross said without looking up from his keyboard. 'A lot cheaper and seems to get 'em going just as well after a bottle or two of Chilean vino.'

'You're just a mean chauvinist pig whose mind rarely rises above his belt,' Jennifer replied sharply.

'You're also married, Shawcross,' Briscoe reprimanded.

The constable smirked. 'Get it when you can is my motto,' he said and Jennifer turned on her heels in disgust and left the room. She hurried down to the basement where the Evidence Room was located as she needed to scan the logbook. Jennifer went straight to the counter and stretched her arm under the grille to turn the large book round. She began flicking through the pages and it was only a matter of minutes before she discovered that no rifles or shotguns had been handed in and the only pistols were a matched pair of John Mantons. These were antique percussion pistols commonly used for duelling in the eighteenth century that had been recovered during the arrest of a suspected burglar.

'Looking for something in particular, Jennifer?' a voice said behind her and she spun round with a guilty expression on her face. The duty officer stood before her with a labelled polythene bag in his hand that contained two flick knives and a short length of lead pipe.

'Sorry, Geoff,' she stuttered. 'I was just wondering if the raincoat I lost in the pub last week had been turned in.'

'You know this room is strictly for evidence and that all lost property is kept upstairs,' he said with a suspicious glance at the last page she had been reading. 'I don't know what you were really looking for and I don't want to know.'

'I'll ask upstairs, someone might know if it was handed in,' Jennifer mumbled and she hurried from the room before the officer could ask any more questions.

She entered the detectives' common room and Sergeant Briscoe gave her a strange look and crooked his finger as he went into his office. Jennifer followed and closed the door behind her.

'You were in the Evidence Room. Why was that, Constable?' he asked brusquely.

Jennifer frowned until she saw the Sergeant point at the small CCTV camera that was monitoring the detectives' common room. In her haste she had completely forgotten the security cameras positioned throughout the police station including downstairs.

'I was in the Security Room talking to Inspector Tilley when I saw you taking a long look at the evidence book on one of the screens. What on earth were you looking for?'

Jennifer gave the same lame excuse she had given the duty officer and then instantly regretted it when she saw Briscoe's expression change.

'You've never lied to me before, Jenny. It must be something very important for you to start doing it now.'

She nodded slowly and sank into the chair. 'It's something so secret that I cannot possibly tell anyone without jeopardizing their careers and possibly their lives.'

'Yet you would risk your own?' He raised a quizzical eyebrow.

'I have to for James's sake!' Jennifer exclaimed.

'Ah. So it's that Goodfellow again,' he said as he nodded his head knowingly. 'What is it he wants you to do this time?'

'I told you, Sergeant, I can't tell you.'

'After the last case that involved James and myself I had hoped you could always trust me to be a good friend to you both at all times of trouble.'

'I do, Sergeant. However, if you insist then what I'm going to say must remain within these four walls.' Jennifer had said this so adamantly that Briscoe found he had no option but to nod his agreement and the young woman began telling him the whole story. Without any interruption from the spellbound sergeant she started with Feng Choi receiving the first *bi* to the threat that now existed and the need for James to defend the Chois and himself from the rogue SIS officers. In her lengthy explanation she neglected to tell the sergeant that the petri dish was now in Séan O'Rourke's hands.

When she had finally finished Briscoe sat for a moment in total silence, completely dumbfounded, and was about to speak when the door opened and Constable Shawcross entered.

'Inspector Tilley asks if you have determined the reason why Constable Kent was reading the evidence book entries?' he said looking at Jennifer, seeking signs that she was in some form of trouble.

'I will be discussing this with the Inspector in private later. In the meantime, close the door on your way out,' Briscoe growled waving his hand and the constable beat a hasty retreat. As the door shut the sergeant turned to fix his gaze on the white-faced detective.

'If Goodfellow has the dish we must give it to the right people as soon as possible. I will talk to someone I know in the Secret Intelligence Service and ask for his advice.'

'We cannot trust anyone, Sergeant. That's the problem,' Jennifer said and Briscoe could see the woman's distress in the way she twisted a handkerchief between her fingers.

'I will make very discreet enquiries as to whom we can trust and in the meantime you must protect Goodfellow and the bacteria sample. We must also find a good excuse for you being in the evidence room without anything else reaching the ears of anyone in the station,' he said as he began drumming his fingers on the desktop. Suddenly he stopped and said briskly. 'I will tell Tilley that I asked you to check on something concerning the rape in Walding Park and to keep it confidential as I may have been given false information by an informant.'

Jennifer nodded. 'If asked I will refer whoever it is back to you.'

'Good girl! Now the question of what James should do next is quite simple. I cannot condone the idea of supplying him with lethal weapons as that would be tantamount to being an accessory to murder should it come to a confrontation and someone is killed.' Seeing Jennifer's face fall he continued, 'On the other hand I can tell Inspector Tilley that there have been threats on Goodfellow's life and that I wished to provide an armed police officer to act as a bodyguard until the threat passes.'

Jennifer sat upright, suddenly looking more hopedul. 'That would be an excellent solution but will Tilley … Inspector Tilley, accept that?'

'He will if I say it involves triads who are trying to muscle in on Mr Choi's restaurant business.'

'Brilliant … and I can give my automatic to James and …'

'That is impossible. The weapon stays with you and you stay with James and the petri dish twenty-four-seven.' Briscoe's eyes took on a playful sparkle. 'Which I'm sure will suit you both down to the ground.'

'If that's an order then I guess I must do as you say, Sergeant.'

'Don't play the prissy miss with me, Jenny,' Briscoe said with a grin. 'I know that you two have been an item for quite a long time.'

She laughed and then became serious. 'James did say that he would need a rifle as well if he were to be successful after he had led Rackman and his SIS cronies away from the Choi family.'

'I'll make out the requisition for your usual automatic plus an HK417. You have already passed all designated marksman tests at police college and I'll explain that the triads are quite likely to use long-range sniper tactics to take him down.'

Jennifer flinched at his words but was able to leave Briscoe's office feeling lighter of heart than when she first entered. Shawcross scowled across the room at her and bent over a formidable stack of paperwork as she left to bring James up to date with the latest development.

Jennifer winked at James as she opened the mobile and speed-dialled the number for Goodfellow Investigations.

'I'm sorry, I cannot take your call as I am out of the office taking case notes to clients on the coast – please leave your message after the beep.' BEEP!

James picked up the landline handset and then replaced it. 'That should do it.'

'How can it,' Jennifer asked. 'If they're thinking of following you they'll find Britain has a very long coastline.'

'But my parents bungalow is in a place that's quite isolated and unpopulated at this time of the year and SIS have the resources to enter bank accounts and solicitors' files to discover something as simple as mortgage details and the address for any property purchased by myself and my family.'

'What about your parents? How will you keep them safe?'

'The bungalow on Camber Sands is their holiday retreat which they never use in autumn or winter. That's when the weather becomes too inclement for my mother's arthritis.'

'Quite convenient that it's so close to Lydd Airport,' Jennifer said, her suspicions aroused. 'That's where we made the exchange with Rackman for Lin-Lin.'

'I believe he used the airport to fly the virus out for discreet analysis in an anonymous French laboratory and he'll undoubtedly return the same way; that's why I chose Camber. As you said it's close to the bungalow and very close to the beautiful Cinque port town of Rye where you'll be staying. I've already booked a warm, cosy four-poster bed and it's waiting for you.' James beamed encouragingly hoping she wouldn't argue about their separation.

'So, you'll be Rackman's clay pigeon in the bungalow while I'm safely tucked away?'

'That's the plan.' So much for that, he thought.

Jennifer stood up and leant over the desk until her face was only inches from his. 'Like hell it is!' she cried. 'I have to keep the weapons with me at all times and if you're miles away how on earth am I going to be able to help you when they make their move.'

'Simple. You give me custody of the HK417 and the automatic.'

'What! That's impossible. I will be signing for them and they must stay in my possession. That means wherever you go I go.'

He could see that she was becoming very angry and he yielded. 'Okay, but I must have control of the rifle as that is going to play a major role in altering the odds against us.'

Jennifer hesitated before nodding. 'I remember that you were a good shot at the academy. I hope you still have capable hands.'

'You're the best judge of that,' he murmured as he moved closer. She backed away from him just as Miss Lightbody entered the office with a knowing smile.

'What shall I do about other callers, James?' she asked.

'Nothing at all because I want you to be as far away from any danger as you can.' Seeing his secretary's puzzled look he explained, 'It must look as though the office has been closed for a few days. That way nobody can expect my secretary to be here to take my calls.'

'I get it,' Jennifer interrupted. 'If Agnes was suspected of being here they might grab her to force you to give up the real petri dish like they did with Lin-Lin.'

'Right, but they won't try it again with the Choi family because they know there's little chance that I will be in contact with them while I'm away. I'd have no reason to.' James stood. 'I think it's time to throw a few things in a bag and get going before Rackman gets the results of his laboratory tests.'

Miss Lightbody put on her coat and after kissing Jennifer on the cheek and giving James a brave smile she left the office to go home and pack a suitcase. She had a small hotel on the Suffolk coast in mind – she hadn't used before and was planning on paying cash so that her credit cards couldn't be traced. She had learnt a great deal from her employer in the short time she had worked for him.

James and Jennifer went up to the apartment and within minutes they were packed and on their way to East Steading police station to meet Sergeant Briscoe.

'Somehow I don't think the answerphone message will be needed,' James murmured as he glanced in the rear-view mirror. 'We have a black Ford on our tail and he's still there even after our occasional back-doubling and speeding.'

Jennifer discreetly looked back and was able to recognize the driver wearing dark sunglasses. 'I believe it's the big man who was at Lydd Airport. Do you think he's just waiting to hear from Rackman about the virus before he lets us go or tries to stop us?'

'It wouldn't surprise me but it's going to surprise him more when he finds out where we're going.'

James kept an eye on the Ford as they climbed the steps of the police station. The big man had driven on for another hundred yards before parking on the opposite side of the road and James couldn't detect any movement inside the car to suggest that the driver planned to get out.

They crossed the detective's common room and Shawcross looked up from his form-filling to scowl at James as he passed. They ignored him and went into Briscoe's office after a light tap on the door. Detective Inspector Tilley was sitting opposite the sergeant in one of the visitors' chairs and he acknowledged the couple with a short mechanical nod.

'Good afternoon, Goodfellow,' Briscoe said as they shook hands. 'I have informed the inspector that you are believed to be in mortal danger from a Chinese gang who are trying to muscle in on your landlord's restaurant business: as you present a threat to them you need a discreet form of police protection.'

James nodded and Tilley turned to fix Jennifer with a penetrating look that seemed to be assessing her worthiness for the job. 'The sergeant has told me that you have the necessary qualification to be armed and to act as a bodyguard for a few days. So, until the sergeant has investigated the matter concerning the triads I will allocate adequate funds for this and I will also approve arming you.'

The inspector slid three sheets of paper across the desk. 'Sign these, Constable,' he said officiously. 'Then I'll send you to the armoury where Detective Sergeant Briscoe will select the weapons he deems suitable for the task.'

Jennifer scrawled her name at the bottom of each authorization and the trio went up one floor to the weapons vault that Briscoe unlocked with an electric keycard. 'As I stated on the form you will be taking out an HK417 plus a SIG Sauer P226.' He switched on a brilliant white light that illuminated dozens of weapons and took a semi-automatic from a pistol rack and two 15-round magazines. 'The rifle has a twenty-inch sniper barrel and I can let you have two 20-round magazines only. Just remember they'll be gone in the blink of an eye if you're on fully automatic.'

Jennifer strapped on a well-used calfskin holster beneath her arm and slipped both cartridges into an inside pocket. James guessed that it was her own weapon that was kept for official use. He reached out to take the rifle but Briscoe shook his head. 'Until you're well away from here it must remain solely in Constable Kent's care.'

They all left the armoury and when they reached the ground floor James said, 'I suggest that you leave by the back door and I'll meet you in the back alley. This will prevent Brian, if that's his name, from getting sight of the case you're carrying.'

'Won't he follow you?' Jennifer asked.

'He won't be able to enter the alley as it is too narrow for two cars and I will be reversing in. I'll pop the trunk just before you reach the back of the car so you can slip the case into the trunk, close it and get into the car beside me.'

Briscoe shook James's hand and gave Jennifer a light pat on the shoulder before they went their separate ways. 'God be with you both,' he murmured to Jennifer's surprise as she had never thought the gruff sergeant to be the slightest bit religious. James looked down at the piece of paper the sergeant had pressed into his hand and saw a telephone number scrawled in pencil.

'Use it if the water gets too deep,' Briscoe had murmured before he turned and walked away.

They were just passing Royal Tunbridge Wells and making good time on the A21 heading towards the coastal town of Hastings when James spotted the Ford. It was ten cars behind them. 'He's back,' he said briefly.

'He's going to be with us all the way to your parent's place,' she murmured as she touched the lump beneath her arm for reassurance.

'I'll pull into the next shopping centre so that we can get some fresh milk, coffee and a few things to eat for when we arrive,' he said ignoring her remark.

She took his calm attitude on board and felt herself relax a little. 'That's a good idea. I'll be able to make cheese and tomato omelettes tonight.'

James smiled and looked once more at the black Ford behind. He frowned when he saw that the car was no longer occupied by Brian but filled with a large group of men. The Illuminati were not taking any chances on losing the virus this time.

They pulled in at the next service centre and while James kept watch on the black Ford that had stopped on the other side of the car park Jennifer went into the small supermarket to purchase the basic items they would need.

21

HONG KONG

O'ROURKE WOKE THE NEXT morning to a sky that was black with storm clouds. The cyclone that had been forecast the previous evening was fast approaching and he quickly showered, dressed and went down to a hurried breakfast. The rain was lashing at the windows and the sound of the howling wind was penetrating the double-glazing by the time he had returned to his room. O'Rourke swung the disguised sword case over his shoulder and went to the car. Lightning was now regularly illuminating the clouds as he drove out into the strong wind with windscreen wipers valiantly working to clear the cascading rain.

He took the road along the seafront until he was able to enter the comparative calm of the Eastern Harbour Tunnel. As he drove far beneath the harbour waters and the car shuddered as gusts of wind were funnelled through the long concrete tube. The heavy rain beat upon the vehicle once more as he emerged in the district of Kwun Tong Tsai Wan and took the Clear Water Bay Road. The heavily populated urban sprawl soon thinned out and the road became lined with dense undergrowth and trees. The occasional houses were now for the wealthy and private drives were heavily gated for security reasons.

At the next parking area designated for tourists O'Rourke stopped the car and checked the automatic that was always kept in the hotel room safe. Taking the long case he left the vehicle and entered the saturated forest to take the path leading towards the coast. He was now leaning slightly into the wind and seeking moments of respite from the gathering storm behind the larger trees.

Twenty minutes passed before he caught a glimpse of a white building. He had arrived at his destination. He slowed down and cautiously approached the electrified chain-link fence encircling the property. The owner of the luxury villa had taken all precautions against unwanted visitors.

The trees and shrubbery ended twenty feet from the fence and the ground had been bulldozed down to the bare earth to create a no-man's land. O'Rourke stepped out of cover and looked both ways but the sheets of rain being driven into his face obscured his vision and he assumed that it would be doing the same for any patrolling guards and electronic surveillance equipment. He knelt in the mud and putting his head down he studied the muddy surface for any signs of pressure mines.

With the tip of the sword he gently probed the ground ahead for any metal objects and inch-by-inch he crossed the open space. O'Rourke had just reached the fence when he spotted the light of an app[roaching guard. The man was on the other side of the fence, his head down against the torrential rain that beat upon his sou'wester with the non-stop rhythm of a kettledrum.

Unable to reach cover in time O'Rourke flattened himself alongside the fence and took out his automatic. If he was seen he had no option but to shoot the man and pray that the raging storm masked the sound of the gun. He held the gun out in front and sighted the silhouetted figure as he drew closer. Suddenly there was an electronic hiss and a voice squawked in Cantonese from the guard's walkie-talkie. The guard stopped and listened before responding briefly and turning back to the house.

O'Rourke had made out that the guard would be relieved in fifteen minutes but because of the storm he might just as well return to the house. O'Rourke gave a mental sigh of relief and after pocketing the pistol he started off in the other direction to look for an alternative way to gain entrance.

He had only covered fifty yards when he spotted a flaw in the electrified fencing. Two of the ceramic terminals weren't connected meaning that different generators had been used to power the perimeter. The gap between the two was only two feet wide but more than enough to let him through at the top.

Slinging the sword over his back he removed his shoes and socks before climbing the chain-links with his fingers and bare toes. He forward-rolled through the gap to drop into the garden. O'Rourke moved downhill towards the white building with all his senses alert for any movement in the gardens.

The wind was increasing and progress was becoming harder. He crossed the huge lawn that stretched down and around the sprawling property. He circled a kidney-shaped swimming pool and stepped onto the huge verandah with eyes checking each lit window. Storm shutters rattled in their fastenings and he wondered why the occupants hadn't closed them in preparation for the cyclone.

There was another burst of static and O'Rourke spun round to see a different guard approaching. His head was bowed against the foul weather and he was completely unaware of the Irishman's presence until a pair of powerful hands gripped him by the throat. He tried to scream but the throttling fingers prevented all sound and he died silently in a roaring world of wind and rattling shutters. O'Rourke rolled the dead man into the pool so it would appear that he had slipped and fell in during the storm. He put the walkie-talkie into his back pocket after switching it off and then walked round the house until he reached a pair of French windows.

The curtains were half-drawn and O'Rourke was able to peer into a large room. Although the lights were on the room was empty and he worked on the locks until one of the doors clicked open. He slipped inside and closed the door as fast as possible to prevent the increased sound of the storm from alerting anybody in the house.

A large elm table with ten high-backed chairs on each side dominated the room. Shelves on three walls were elegantly arrayed with fourteenth century blue-and-white, or Qingbai vases, pots as well as bowls from the fabled Jingdezhen town in the Jiangxi province. This town was known as the Porcelain Capital for it had produced fine pottery for more than 1,700 years. O'Rourke was looking at priceless objects that surpassed those he had seen in the Museo di Doccia.

He crept round the table with its exquisite Fu Dog relief carvings and placed his ear against the dark wood of a large door. He could hear a slight murmuring of voices and after a while it was clear that he was listening to an action movie. O'Rourke depressed the handle slowly and pushed with his shoulder until the door had opened an inch. Looking through the gap he could saw a Chinese man who was lounging on a red silk settee and looking at something out of O'Rourke's eye-line. He surmised that it was the television screen and he waited until he heard the commercial break to see what the man might do. The stranger, dressed in an immaculately tailored three-piece silk suit, reached for his wine glass to find it empty. With an annoyed expression on his face he rose to his feet and walked out of sight. O'Rourke took the opportunity to push the door open and slip into what appeared to be a sitting room. An LED screen that dwarfed all else was mounted on the wall and a woman was demonstrating a carpet cleaner with unbelievable enthusiasm.

With hardly a glance at the large antique wool carpet O'Rourke started to cross the room to follow the man, who had obviously gone to refresh his glass, when he suddenly reappeared. There was a brief moment when both men froze before they were able to react.

O'Rourke reached into his pocket for the automatic while the other threw his glass of wine. The crystal glass shattered against Sèan's forehead and very expensive Château Lafite Rothschild streamed down his face. The red wine splashed indiscriminately and stained the fantastic yellow and white characters in the carpet.

Sèan reeled back, his vision impaired by the wine and blood that flowed from the cut above his eyebrow, and the first shot he fired missed its mark. His target ducked back out of the room and raced down the corridor to seek help.

Pulling the trigger had coincided with the restart of a battle sequence from *Saving Private Ryan* and the single shot had been lost in the pandemonium enhanced by the quadrophonic speakers. O'Rourke quickly followed the fleeing man and caught a glimpse of him as he disappeared through a door at the end of the passage. The door was still open when O'Rourke reached it and he looked down a short flight of stairs to see a steel door that would make the Bank of England proud. The CCTV camera mounted over the door was already moving and he watched as it turned to point directly at him. O'Rourke knew that he was being filmed and and he made a rude gesture.

Spotting the discreet microphone by the camera he shouted, 'Tell Pengfei Shing the *Mountain Master* that Sèan O'Rourke the *Red Pole* wishes to return a favour. I know he sent Xun to Britain to steal the *ding* from its rightful owner and to kill me.' He reached over his shoulder and withdrew Dragon's Breath from its scabbard. 'This I promise will kiss the *Mountain Master's* neck in a final farewell.'

O'Rourke raised the blade above his head and slashed down as though executing somebody before slipping the sword back into the leather scabbard. He then hurried back the way he had come, knowing that while he had been wasting time the person inside the 'safe' room was warning the remaining guards by phone and walkie-talkie.

The storm had reached its peak and O'Rourke battled to cross the lawn in the roaring gale that constantly snatched at his clothing like an invisible mythical beast. At the fence he turned and made his way to where the two unconnected terminals.

Something heavy smashed into the scabbard, instantly followed by a gunshot, and he was thrown forward onto his face. Stunned by the force of the impact he lay for a brief moment before rolling swiftly and saving his own life from the second bullet that ploughed soundlessly into the grass. The automatic was now in his hand and he sighted into the pouring rain at the shadowy figure that was running towards him.

One squeeze of the trigger and the .45 steel-jacketed, hollow- point cartridge stopped the running man in his tracks, throwing him back a pace before he sank to his knees. Blood flowed from his open mouth as he attempted to raise his weapon again and O'Rourke fired once more. The man was killed instantly and without any hesitation the Irishman ran to check his identity; to his dismay and disappointment it wasn't Pengfei Shing and he raced back to the fence.

The wood was now a more menacing place and Sèan took more care, checking every shrub and tree that he approached for concealed triads. The closer he came to where he had parked the car the more cautious he became until he was able to peer round the last tree to study the rain-lashed parking area.

The tropical storm had now transformed the tarmac road into a minor river and Sèan took his time in scouring the open area for Shing's men. He had guessed that they would know he had some form of transport and would have placed men at the only car park on that particular stretch of the road.

His eyes were soon drawn to a darker shadow amongst the shoulder-high shrubs on the perimeter of the white-lined area. It moved and a red glow grew and faded as the man carelessly drew on his cigarette. O'Rourke slipped back into the trees and worked his way slowly round the car park until he judged he was behind the triad before creeping forward.

The lookout had his head tilted forward so that the peaked cap could protect his cigarette from the rain. O'Rourke reached back and slowly unsheathed the sword. The man became aware of another presence when O'Rourke was only three paces behind him and he spun round to receive the fatal thrust through his throat. As he fell to his knees choking in his own blood O'Rourke withdrew the sword and stepped back. His eyes swept the area for any other movements and soon saw another triad sentinel crouching by his car with a waterproof cape pulled over his head.

O'Rourke searched the rest of the perimeter for lookouts but finding no other triads he considered the distance he would have to cover to reach the man in the open. It was too far for the sword to be effective and he decided to gamble on the sound of the automatic being lost in the storm. He moved through the trees until he was on the opposite side of the car and swiftly ran to it and then round to confront the triad who was holding an Uzi sub-machine gun across his knees. The startled man turned but his assailant was faster and he fell back with two bullets in the brain.

O'Rourke crouched down beside the body and took his time to look round. Once again he searched the perimeter of the car park and the road for more signs of life. Nothing stirred apart from the trees that were settling down in the dying wind.

The storm was beginning to pass as he drove back towards Kwun Tong Tsai Wan. He had only travelled three miles when he noticed a tiny piece of insulation tape on the passenger seat. He stopped the car and leaving the engine running he got out and walked around the vehicle looking underneath. He shone his pocket torch but could see nothing to arouse his suspicion. He looked under the car seat – again nothing but when he got in and opened the glove compartment he sucked in his breath. A brown paper package the size of a paperback had been sealed with insulation tape and wires had been spliced with a charge lead that was plugged into a cheap Nokia cellphone.

O'Rourke sat for a few moments before snatching up the sword and leaping out of the car. He knew that someone would dial the Nokia number when the killed assassins were found at the car park. He started trotting down the hill in the fine drizzle trying to put as much distance between himself and the car as possible.

The sound of a misfiring engine alerted O'Rourke and he stood to one side with his hand inside his jacket as the inadequate yellow headlamp of a Lambretta scooter approached. He held up his hand and a teenager wearing a helmet that was two sizes too big squealed to a stop beside him. A quick glance told O'Rourke that he wasn't a triad and he asked if he could get a lift to the island. A friendly grin that revealed immaculate white teeth answered his question and the big Irishman mounted the pillion and the scooter struggled to get going. Fortunately they were going downhill and they were soon moving at speed. They were passing through the village of Ha Yeung when O'Rourke heard the dull crump of an explosion. Looking over his shoulder he saw the last remnants of an orange flash illuminating the low rain clouds. With his helmet tightly buckled the young lad was oblivious to anything but the slick road ahead and the sky rapidly returned to darkness.

Conversation was impossible and they rode in silence until they had passed through the Eastern Harbour tunnel. The young man stopped at the island's first interchange and told O'Rourke he was turning left to the Lei Yue holiday village. O'Rourke thanked him and he walked the few hundred yards to Quarry Bay Station where he took a fast subway train to Causeway Bay. O'Rourke walked back to the Excelsior Hotel and after two warming brandies and a hot soak he was soon revived. Having had little success at Pengfei Shing's home he began to work out a way to locate and confront the *Mountain Master*.

The Irishman rose early and had left the hotel before most guests had even thought of leaving their beds. He had removed the petri dish from the room safe and it was now safely tucked in his jacket pocket which he patted for reassurance as he took a taxi to the Garden Road Terminus. Within seven minutes the Peak Tram had climbed 396 metres to arrive at the iconic Peak Tower. From there he took a lift to rise a further thirty-two metres to the Sky Terrace and emerged on the 360º viewing platform where he had arranged to meet the government agent called Xiang. He strolled round the wide terrace paying little attention to the panoramic views of Hong Kong and the outlying islands of Cheung Chau, Lamma and Lantau. Behind the safety of his dark glasses he studied the two people who were leaning against the rail until he was able to identify Xiang whom he had met before. O'Rourke approached the agent who was studying the beautiful scenery below through powerful Kunming binoculars. He was slim with short black hair that had begun to silver at the temples. He carried a fawn raincoat over one arm while holding the binoculars up with the other.

'Wonderful sight, isn't it?' O'Rourke said in a low voice. When the man lowered his instrument and turned he continued, 'But not when it rains.'

'You can never see much during the monsoon.'

Satisfied with the response O'Rourke started to reach into his jacket but was stopped by a warning look from Xiang. 'I believe you have acquired a tail,' he murmured and turned to move away but a gigantic man wearing a tram engineer's uniform was blocking his path. He carried a large steel wrench in one hand but kept the other hidden inside his overalls in a manner that suggested he was holding a weapon.

O'Rourke looked round and saw a second man approaching them. It was the taxi driver who had dropped him at the Garden Rose Terminus and he was holding a narrow-bladed knife against the side of his leg. It was only seven-thirty and nobody else had ventured out onto the terrace. Without hesitation he drew his automatic and shot the approaching man in the face. He spun round to confront the spanner-wielding man who had already struck Xiang with the wrench and was in the act of tipping the senseless man over the rail. On seeing the weapon in O'Rourke's hand and his partner's demise the triad dropped Xiang and reached inside his overalls. His Chinese army-issue Type 80 handgun was withdrawn as three rounds, in quick succession, punctured his lungs and heart.

O'Rourke watched the man drop and then looked round to see if there had been any witnesses to the shooting. The terrace remained empty and he strode across to the taxi driver, dragged the man to the railing and dropped him into the undergrowth far below. The same disposal method was used for the heavyweight and O'Rourke had to strain every muscle to lift him over the chest-high railing. The wiped-down steel wrench followed the triad and he hurried back inside the building and took the lift down.

There was a nervous five-minute wait for the next tram down from the Peak Tower during which he covertly eyed the other passengers. None appeared to represent any threat but he didn't relax his vigilance until he had safely returned to his hotel room.

O'Rourke put the petri dish back in the hotel safe and then flicked through his address book and dialled the number listed as a Chinese laundry in the Tsim Sha Tsui district.

'Sing Li Laundry, how can I help you,' a male voice said in perfectly enunciated English.

'My white shirt is badly stained.'

'What colour?'

'Red.'

'I cannot help you with that.'

'What about another item that seems to be a little green with mould?'

'We can certainly help you with that, sir, but as I have no messenger you will have to bring it to me.'

'What is the address?' O'Rourke said with his pen poised.

'Our laundry is in the same place, sir.' There was a sharp click followed by a hiss until a second click cut to silence and O'Rourke knew that the person listening in had also hung up.

If it's on the Kowloon side then I'll have to be careful about being followed, he thought. The Star Ferry can get very crowded and is the perfect killing ground for a triad assassination.

22

ENGLAND

JAMES WAS ON THE outskirts of Hastings when he managed to lose the car behind. He had turned into a residential area and after a dozen left and right turns he was able to double back to return to the main road. He sped through the town and passed the famous fire-gutted pier before staying on the coastal road to Rye. Jennifer spent most of the time looking through the back window until poor light and misty rain made any car identification difficult.

James was familiar with the ancient town and climbed the narrow cobbled streets like a local resident until they reached the Hope Anchor hotel at the highest point.

'As I said, James, I'm not staying in a 'safe' hotel, no matter how comfortable it is, if it's miles from you and the weapons that I was made responsible for.'

He turned to look at her, determined to convince her it would be best for them both but the resolve in her expression and determination in her tightly compressed lips convinced him to accept her decision and he restarted the car. They retraced their route through the maze of cobbled streets in silence until they reached the main road leading out of the town.

'You can come with me but only if you do exactly as I say and when I say it,' James said flatly and Jennifer nodded slowly.

'Provided it doesn't infringe any laws of the land.'

'Agreed.'

Jennifer spent the rest of the journey watching the road behind and as James took one minor road after the other. The landscape became flat and treeless and she was able to see vehicles that were a mile distant. They passed a massive wind farm with three-hundred-foot high turbines and then a well-attended golf club.

'We're approaching Camber,' James explained as the road became lined with small holiday residences. 'The bungalow is on the other side of the town and close to a very large public car park.'

Within minutes they had parked the car in the pebble drive of a white, clapboard cottage. Net curtains were drawn and a small dog began barking in the adjoining property when James unlocked the front door. They left their bags in the hall before going into the kitchen to put all the perishables in the refrigerator.

Jennifer placed the canvas bag containing the HK417 and its magazines on the kitchen table and James began checking the weapon. He became very familiar with the gun in police training college and the routine of stripping it down and reassembly came back with astonishing clarity the moment he touched the cold steel.

'I hope you never have to use that,' Jennifer murmured as she watched his fingers nimbly put each piece of the mechanism in place.

'Self-defence, Jenny, purely self-defence,' James muttered as he completed his task with a final metallic clatter of the twenty-round magazine being pushed home. 'I suggest you check your own while I take a look around outside.'

James left the bungalow and went down the narrow garden to the back gate that led onto the first of many sand dunes. Clumps of marram grass that had been planted to help stabilize the dunes and prevent coastal erosion bent before the off-shore breeze. He dug the toes of his shoes into the loose sand as he climbed to the top to survey the terrain in the rapidly fading light. A solitary gull flickered pale grey as it wheeled one way then the other while soaring over the breaking wavelets. It was the only moving life form in close proximity to the bungalow.

Rackman had received the latest report of Goodfellow's movements from the unmarked car and had also accessed the financial records of Captain

Richard Goodfellow. He trawled back five years before finding the property name *Captain's Cabin* and the address of the holiday bungalow.

'Make sure you recover the petri dish,' he instructed his agent who, having tracked their quarry by pure luck, was sitting in the bar of the Hope Anchor hotel. 'then bury him deep in the sand.' Rackman closed his mobile and slumped back in his favourite armchair. He sipped the whisky and the satisfaction of moving in for the kill made it that much more pleasurable.

Brian Chessman slipped the phone into his pocket with a predatory gleam in his eye that his two companions instantly recognized and they all stood up and left the hotel, eager to bring the hunt to a close.

'We have been instructed to do some pest control but not before we've found the dish containing the bacteria,' Chessman said when they were in the car and fitting silencers to their automatics. 'Then we take the bloody dish back to Rackman.' He started the car and taking the Lydd Road out of Rye they were soon driving through the village of Camber.

They parked in the municipal car park at the end of the road and walked slowly back towards the address Rackman had given them. The clapboard house seemed a little tired and the net curtains in the bay window betrayed nothing inside. The three men paused briefly before continuing along the road and then turned round to make another assessment. The car they had been following was parked in the drive but there was no sign of life.

Chessman opened the gate and beckoning to his companions he walked up to the front door and rang the bell with one hand tucked beneath his jacket.

The three men waited a full minute before ringing again. They could hear the bell chiming inside and there was a slight whiff of frying bacon when Chessman looked through the letter slot, yet nobody came to the door.

When the couple heard the door chime they reacted as planned and headed for the back door. James studied the back garden through the window before venturing outside and the couple raced down the path and out through the gateway.

They were running across the second dune when Chessman rang the bell for the second time and by the time the three assassins had checked the back door and found it wide open James and Jennifer had placed four more dunes between themselves and the gunmen.

'When should we stop and make a stand,' Jennifer asked when they paused to catch their breath in a small dip.

'When we are far enough away from the built-up area to ensure there are no people walking their dogs or wooing their girlfriends. I don't want any collateral damage if it comes to a shooting war.' He rose to his feet and started up the next dune. James had just reached the top when a bullet passing through the marram grass with a loud hissing noise on his left. that he recognised as. It was followed by a distant cough that was the trademark of a silencer.

He grabbed Jennifer by the arm and roughly pulled her down. 'They've caught up with us already,' James whispered as they lay side by side. He pulled the HK417 from under his coat and cocked it. Jennifer looked at him with startled eyes.

'Is there really any need to use that?'

'A bullet has just missed me by inches and you ask a question like that.'

'Sorry, I didn't know.'

'We'll also need the Sig Sauer or we'll both be in big trouble,' he whispered as he cautiously rose above the grass to peer along the darkening seashore. A single man was silhouetted against the lighter sky as he crested a dune approximately two hundred yards away. James raised the weapon and looking through the scope he fixed the crosshairs on the man's torso. Applying a slight downward pressure on top of the weapon to compensate for the recoil James lightly squeezed the trigger.

The scream of pain was whipped away by the wind and the dark figure collapsed to merge with the dark landscape.

'My God, you hit him, James,' Jennifer exclaimed in horror.

'Yes, that was the objective because he was trying to hit us.'

'Couldn't you have just warned him off?'

'When it comes to using a firearm on someone who is shooting at you there's no time for niceties such as firing across the bows or aiming to wound. However, there is the possibility that that is all I managed to achieve,' James said while keeping his eyes fixed on the same dune. 'In fact that's what I did do. Can you see? The bastard is getting up.'

Jennifer strained her eyes and saw in the gloom a man stagger away and disappear behind the dune.

'He screamed, I heard him.'

'So I nicked him. Good!' James grabbed her arm and led her over the next dune before lying down to await the next development. 'They will undoubtedly be trying to circle us on the land side, targeting the dune we had been hiding behind.'

'The reason for moving?' The perilous situation they were in prompted Jennifer to take the automatic out of its holster and check the magazine.

'Not exactly,' James whispered. 'I also noticed that we were exposed by the lack of sand grass that could, in this poor light, have camouflaged our contours.' He raised his head a little and stared into the ever-increasing darkness. 'I wish I had night glasses.'

'Do you think they are using such things?'

'The SIS are equipped with the very latest weaponry and it wouldn't surprise me at all if they started firing mortars and throwing grenades in our direction.'

'Sshhh.' Jennifer raised a finger to her lips. 'I heard something on the right.'

'And on the left,' James replied sotto voce and the couple, reading each others minds, turned so that they were back to back to await their adversaries' next move.

It was Jennifer who first saw movement and was able to identify a crouching figure slowly moving along the shoreline. He was fifty yards distant and his outstretched hand held a silenced automatic before him while the other held a mobile phone to his ear. James briefly looked where Jennifer was pointing before acknowledging with a nod and turning his attention back to the left. There was a brief clatter and a curse as someone stumbled over a discarded child's bucket and spade.

'It's okay, I bloody tripped over something,' a voice informed his partner. He sounded closer than James had anticipated and his hands tightened on the HK417. He gave thanks that he had taken his medication that morning.

'They couldn't have gone very far – ' the speaker stopped as he appeared over the dune and saw the two prone figures at the same time that James saw him. He dropped the mobile he had been using and raised his weapon. James was a millisecond faster and his bullet struck the agent's forearm.

The man's instinctive reaction pressure sent the bullet wider than intended and the 9mm passed painfully through James's side.

'Don't try it,' James shouted as the man, gritting his teeth against the excruciating pain in his arm, bent to retrieve his weapon. He ignored the command and grabbed at his weapon. As he rose James fired once more and the man fell dead. The pain was now burning up his side and James gritted his teeth as he studied the fallen man.

His colleague on the foreshore had started running as soon as he heard the gunfire and Jennifer held the Sig Sauer in police academy textbook style as the illuminati raced towards them.

'Shoot, Jenny,' James shouted but as she pulled the trigger the cartridge jammed in the magazine. 'Shoot,' he repeated as the man raised his weapon and began firing.

A familiar paralysis raced through James's body and his vision blurred. Bullets hissed through the air and *thunked* into the sand around them as James flopped back in a deep sleep.

Jennifer twisted round with tears of frustration and witnessed James's narcoleptic attack. She twisted the HK417 from his paralysed grasp and switched to fully automatic.

The short *burrrp* of a full magazine emptying in the direction of the running assassin dulled Jennifer's hearing and she was horror-struck by the sight of the man being flung back onto the wet sand as most of the twenty rounds of steel-jacketed projectiles passed through his torso and head. He lay unmoving as the incoming tide swirled and washed around his body drawing crimson ribbons out to sea.

'I'm going to have some explaining to do when I'm accused of murdering SIS officers,' Jennifer muttered to herself. She bent over James and lightly patted his cheek for a few minutes before she was able to elicit any reaction.

Dark eyelashes fluttered, both lids opened and James looked up into the green eyes he loved so much. The paralysis rapidly wore off and reaching up he pulled her head down to kiss her soft lips.

She jerked back. 'He's dead, James,' she said tearfully. 'I'll be charged with murder, possibly treason for killing an SIS officer.'

'Briscoe knows these men weren't on official SIS business when they began hunting us,' James hissed through his teeth as he gripped his side. 'That's why he armed you. You'll be okay.'

'But you're not,' Jennifer exclaimed. She had been perplexed by his speech, thinking that it was one of the after-effects of narcolepsy, but then she saw the blood seeping between his fingers. She took his hand away to inspect the wound. 'A through-and-through,' she murmured to herself as she took a clean handkerchief from her pocket and folded it to make a pad. 'Hold this against the exit wound as that seems to be the one losing most of the blood.'

'Let's get back to a phone,' James said with a grunt as he staggered to his feet. They inspected both men to confirm they were dead and headed back to where James thought he had hit the first assailant. Apart from a bloodstained patch of sand there were no signs of a body and he assumed that he had only wounded the man.

'Please remind me to take my Xyrem pill when we get back,' James said guiltily. 'I almost got you killed this time.'

'You'll take two or I'll kill you myself,' Jennifer said with a relieved laugh.

With James leaning against her they made their way back to the bungalow. Jennifer found the medicine box in the bathroom cabinet and after splashing on plenty of antiseptic, causing James to suck air between clenched teeth, she wound a whole roll of bandage until the seepage ceased.

'You need a doctor as soon as possible,' she told him as she used the old landline phone to dial the number that was written in James's father's squiggly handwriting on an emergency card pinned to the wall above the phone.

When the doctor arrived Jennifer showed him her official warrant card and he immediately set to work to effect a temporary repair, inflicting considerable pain on his patient as he worked.

'Strange that you suffered a gunshot wound on the same evening a man was admitted to Rye hospital with a bullet hole in his earlobe,' Doctor Anders murmured as he finished the last stitch and began applying surgical dressings.

'Quite a coincidence,' James said with a slight smile. 'It must be the first day of the pheasant season.'

'I don't find that amusing, Mr Goodfellow. As your colleague knows all gunshot incidents must be reported to the police.'

'I shall be doing that myself as soon as I arrive back at the police station,' Jennifer said and flashed her warrant card once more, immediately regretting saying anything when the doctor handed her his own cellular phone.

'You are very welcome to use my phone,' he said with a look that implied she couldn't ignore his offer without having East Sussex squad cars causing a traffic jam outside the bungalow.

Jennifer retired to the corner of the room and dialled East Steading. Once through to Detective Sergeant Briscoe she rapidly sped through the sequence of events and then waited for the bombshell to detonate.

There was a tense period of static hiss on the line before the sergeant responded and she was surprised to find he was a lot calmer than expected.

'I'll speak with Inspector Tilley who will undoubtedly communicate with the Sussex police to put them in the picture. Recovery of the bodies will then be their responsibility but I want you out of the area before they pick you up for questioning. I want the weapons returned to *our* armoury immediately and your statements to be taken here, in East Steading, by me at 9 a.m. Is that clear?'

'Yes, Sergeant.' The phone went dead and Jennifer relayed the orders she had been given to James. She returned the phone with a thankful smile as Doctor Anders finished packing his medical case.

'Before you go to the police station you must have this temporary repair attended to in a hospital,' the doctor said and James reluctantly nodded.

'I'll take him to East Steading where I am known,' Jennifer said as she helped James to his feet.

'And what about the man who was treated in Rye hospital?'

'Sussex police will be talking to him very soon, so it would be wise to ensure he stays put until they arrive,' Jennifer said.

'It's a little too late to tell me that. After the wound had been stitched he was taken to the waiting room to await further treatment and he disappeared.' The doctor shook his head, gave James a box of painkillers and specific instructions on their use and left.

'Whoever the third guy was will be hors de combat but he could still be a danger,' James said as he gingerly helped Jennifer pack their travel bags.

'It may have been Rackman.'

James pondered the thought before replying, 'Or someone working for Rackman because I have a distinct feeling that he doesn't like doing his own dirty work especially when he has others to order about and take all the risks for him.'

They left the bungalow in bright moonlight and began the long drive back. James held the HK417 on his lap to be prepared for any further trouble on the road.

Jennifer avoided the motorways just in case the cameras were being monitored by one of Rackman's men at SIS headquarters. Hawthorn hedgerows glistened beneath a covering of mist and yellow eyes occasionally glowed in the surrounding woods as their headlights swept round the corners of the country lanes.

James's side was beginning to ache as the anaesthetic wore off and he took one of the powerful painkillers the doctor had given him as they entered East Steading and headed for the hospital.

Not unlike a garage mechanic the admitting doctor did a considerable amount of head shaking and teeth sucking as he inspected the bullet wound. Jennifer watched as James was taken down the corridor as Sergeant Briscoe walked into the waiting room. He immediately took charge of the officious stack of forms that the hospital always produced in any case involving a knifing or shooting and the two police officers sat in total silence while he dealt with the formalities. There was no recriminating speech on completion and on completion but Briscoe sat back and stared long and hard at Jennifer.

'I gave the inspector a broad outline of the events as you told them to me and he is not a happy man,' Briscoe said finally. 'He requires the weapons to be thoroughly checked by forensics in the event that SIS decides to make a case against you.'

'I don't think they will, Sergeant,' Jennifer said. A slight tremor of uncertainty was in her voice and Briscoe patted her hand in a fatherly manner.

'If they were rogue agents acting independently under orders from this SIS man called Rackman then you are in the clear and when you produce the petri dish as evidence we can officially take action against him. The Illuminati can be listed as a terrorist organization and all the members will be rounded up and charged with conspiracy to commit genocide – '

'We don't have the dish!' Jennifer interrupted.

'What!'

'It was taken to Hong Kong by Séan O'Rourke where he plans to hand it over to the Chinese authorities. They wish to start working on developing an antidote as soon as possible.'

'Then why the hell was Rackman after Goodfellow?'

'Like yourself he thought we still had the virus and we wanted to give O'Rourke as much time as possible before the Illuminati got word and began searching for him in Hong Kong.'

'You withheld vital information, Jennifer,' Briscoe snapped. 'I trusted you to tell me the whole truth. Believing that you had I instigated a covert investigation to find someone we can trust with that deadly virus.'

Jennifer held her hand up defensively. 'I'm sorry, Sergeant, but James and I decided that we had to do it this way in case you accidentally spoke to the wrong person and became a target yourself.'

Briscoe's face softened. 'Thank you, Jenny. I appreciate the thought but you should still have kept to the rule book.'

'I remember you telling me once that there are times when the rules in the book are only meant to act as a guide.'

The sergeant frowned briefly and then burst out laughing.

23

HONG KONG

O'ROURKE LEANT AGAINST THE RAIL of the ferry and scanned the crowd of commuters thronging the same deck. He had decided against being trapped in the underground crossing of Victoria Harbour in favour of being safer, albeit slightly nauseous, on the choppy surface.

The sky had darkened and light rain has started to fall again as the ferry docked at Star Ferry Pier. A taxi took O'Rourke to the Dodol Hotel on Kimberley Road where he got out and continued on foot at a slow pace, his eyes searching for any stalkers. He paused at the small frontage of a herbal medicine shop and looked both ways before entering. The little bell above the door chimed and an elderly man, white-whiskered man appeared from a back room. He stood no higher than O'Rourke's chest and eyed the tall foreigner suspiciously until he was addressed in fluent Cantonese.

'Good evening. Do you have any special preparations for permanently removing strange bacteria?' O'Rourke asked and the man nodded and disappeared. The Irishman waited for what seemed an interminably long time before a thin European stepped into the shop. He wore dark aviator glasses and a very obvious toupee.

'We have been waiting for you, Mr O'Rourke,' he said in a precise London accent as he casually produced a Glock 17 which he pointed at the Irishman's midriff. 'You have something that rightfully belongs to the Illuminati and I insist you give it to me now.'

O'Rourke was at first stunned and then angry with himself for so foolishly falling into the trap. He nodded and held his jacket out wide to reveal that he had no weapon. 'I wasn't so foolish as to bring it with me,' he said.

'Then we will go and get it,' the man snapped. He was peeved that it wasn't a simple matter of taking the dish, shooting the man and taking a taxi to the airport. 'Do not be deluded into thinking that I am alone, O'Rourke. I have two comrades who will be with us all the time. They have been empowered to ensure that I leave the country with the petri dish.'

O'Rourke preceded the man out of the shop and into the limousine that was waiting with the rear door held open by another European. Once inside he saw that the driver was Chinese and that his hands holding the steering wheel were heavily decorated with tattoos.

'It looks like you've really betrayed your triad brothers this time,' O'Rourke said and was rewarded by seeing the colourful fists tighten their grip. He also felt a blow across his head from a pistol butt wielded by the first man who climbed in behind him.

'He knows where his loyalty lies.'

'But does he know you plan to exterminate the Chinese race?' O'Rourke asked as he used his handkerchief to wipe away the trickle of blood seeping from the cut on his temple. He saw the driver noticeably stiffen and rammed the point home in Cantonese. 'Don't you realize that the bacteria will only target Orientals? The effect will be the end of one billion people and thousands of years of culture in one single generation.'

The car braked to a violent standstill and the driver turned in his seat to address the man sitting next to O'Rourke. 'Is that true,' he demanded.

The eyes behind the dark lenses glinted dangerously when the man realized that O'Rourke planned to divide them. 'The bacteria is a weapon that can be used against all races on the planet. It is our dream to end capitalism in Europe and free the masses from the domination of the rich classes.'

'Bullshit.' O'Rourke laughed out loud and then leant far back when he saw the driver's right shoulder moving. A gun appeared over the headrest and before the man in the dark glasses could think about lifting his weapon a single shot stopped all thought and brain matter splattered the perforated back window. The European in the front passenger seat gripped the driver's wrist and plunged a knife into his side.

O'Rourke took a chance and depressed the handle. He rolled out of the car as soon as the door swung open and began running back along the road. Spotting the elderly man emerging from the herbal remedies and holding a machine pistol he left Kimberley Road and darted up a flight of outside escalators beside a Ben & Jerry's ice-cream kiosk.

After jogging through the maze-like streets lined with fruit and curio barrows for ten minutes he risked hailing a taxi and returned to the Star Ferry Pier to make the crossing back to Hong Kong Island. As he lost himself in a crowd of American tourists leaning against the rails he pondered his next move – he had lost the only legitimate contacts he had and would now have to travel to Shanghai to seek Professor Min Ch'eng himself.

Inspector Xiao Shi Huang had told him before he took his last fateful flight that he was the only senior academician capable of developing an antidote but that he had to have the virus first to begin his work.

O'Rourke retrieved his travel bag and Dragon's Breath from the hotel and using his knowledge of the city made a circuitous journey to the airport without picking up any unhealthy shadows.

SHANGHAI

The flight was uneventful and he deplaned and cleared Shanghai Pudong International Airport in record time. O'Rourke had boxed and addressed the box containing the sword for the attention of the professor at the University of Science and Technology. This combined with frequently showing his official ID card ensured that the package attracted no interest at all.

O'Rourke soon hailed a taxi and was surprised by the driver's skill in negotiating the terrifying midday traffic. He was also surprised when the driver selected a soothing interpretation of Beethoven's 'Moonlight Sonata' by Lang Lang, the country's most gifted pianist.

As they crossed the Huangpu River a dark green Lavida pulled into the traffic behind them. Two men wearing dark suits and silver reflective sunglasses seemed to be studying the taxi while a large man sitting behind them used a mobile phone.

The taxi turned off Shangda Road and entered Baoshan Campus where it headed for the Department of Biochemical Engineering. Professor Min Ch'eng and an assistant were waiting in the lobby and after formal introductions had been made O'Rourke was led to a private office. As they walked he learnt that the young woman's name was Biyu and that she was a post-graduate biochemist.

'I was very sorry to hear of Inspector Huang's death,' Yat-Sen said as they all sat at a small conference table. 'He was a very good friend and will be sorely missed.'

Biyu had removed her glasses and was polishing the lenses using a tissue she had taken from the sleeve of her cotton blouse. 'I did not have the pleasure of meeting the man but from the Professor's words I understood that he was a man of good character.' The diminutive woman's Mandarin was pleasantly attractive.

'Huang was honourable to the end as is his brother in England who has been very helpful in obtaining this foul creation.' O'Rourke took the petri dish from his pocket and slid it across the table to the professor with a distasteful wrinkling of his nose.

Yat-Sen stroked his wispy goatee as he studied the brown paper packet generously wrapped with adhesive tape. It lay innocently on the polished pine without any indication that it's a genocidal weapon. His long tapering fingers picked it up and without saying a word he unwound the tape and carefully removed the paper wrapping.

A sharp intake of breath by Biyu was the only reaction to seeing the black and red growth that now covered the bottom of the petri dish. 'Is the container safe to handle, Professor?' she asked and the elderly man nodded making the white whiskers on his chin bob.

'The last person to close it, no doubt a very cautious bio-chemist, very thoughtfully gave it an airtight seal.' He pointed at the plastic tape that ran around the edge of the petri dish.

'It's grown a lot since I last saw it,' O'Rourke observed.

'But it will soon die when it has nothing left to feed on,' Min Ch'eng said. 'I must get it to my laboratory and into the isolation chamber where I can split it amongst a number of trial petri dishes and feed it to stimulate fresh growth. I have to prevent it from dying otherwise I will be unable to develop the vital antibodies.'

'You're right, this may not be the only sample and the quicker an antidote is found the more hope there is for your countrymen.'

The professor rewrapped the dish and slipped it into the pocket of his white laboratory coat. They all stood and O'Rourke followed as they left the room and the office building.

Min Ch'eng pointed to an old Datsun that stood on the other side of the road. 'It will be quicker to take my car to the laboratory building rather than walk across the campus.'

O'Rourke hadn't dropped his guard since arriving at the university and as they descended the steps he immediately noticed the dark green saloon that had been following him since the taxi had crossed the river. It was parked directly behind the professor's car.

'We must go back into the building,' he said sharply with his eyes trying to penetrate the tinted glass for any movement within. The professor and Biyu looked at him in surprise. 'Depending on which society they represent they will want either the petri dish, Dragon's Breath or simply my death.'

Without asking any questions Min Ch'eng nodded and hurriedly ran back up the steps, his lab coat flying behind him. Bivu followed him swiftly with O'Rourke pausing long enough to check for any reaction from the parked Lavida. It was not long in coming. When they were halfway up the steps the doors burst open and the two men with flashing sunglasses left the car and began running across the road towards the college steps.

Min Ch'eng strode down one of the three corridors leading off the small lobby and ducked into one of the doors, indicating with a wave that the others should follow him. The room they entered had pull-down blackboards on two walls and was clearly meant for presentations. The professor headed towards another door at the rear of the room.

Neat lawns surrounding the building were interspersed by beds of brilliant red peonies and they hurried across the campus towards a smaller office block. The travel bag and sword case hampered O'Rourke's freedom of movement and he was tempted to discard the bag until a hand touched his and he looked down to see that Biyu was pointing at it. O'Rourke let her take the bag from him, instantly improving his balance and freeing his sword-wielding hand.

As they entered the office block O'Rourke waved the other two on waited beside the slowly closing automatic door. He could hear heavy tread approaching and he quickly withdrew Dragon's Breath from its scabbard inside the case. The door began to open and he raised the sword above his head as a hand gripping a silenced automatic appeared in the opening. He brought the blade down in a glittering arc. There was a scream outside as the gunman's hand fell to the floor. The pistol clattered onto the ceramic tiling and O'Rourke gathered it up and charged through the open doorway.

A man in a dark suit was kneeling outside and moaning while clutching at his spurting stump while his surprised partner stared down at him. Without hesitation O'Rourke shot him through the heart and then turned to point the automatic at the moaning man.

'Triad or Illuminati?' he barked and the man looked up at O'Rourke with pain and pure hatred in his eyes.

'I'm a man who failed his *Mountain Master* and you're nothing but a bloody traitor,' he managed to stutter through the excruciating pain.

'Give my regards to your ancestors,' O'Rourke whispered and the triad was wide-eyed with fear as the bullet entered his forehead.

O'Rourke leapt over the fallen men and ran back to the main building. The dark green Lavida was still parked at the kerb with its engine running but as soon as O'Rourke appeared on the steps the driver slipped it into gear and accelerated hard. The Irishman ran down, his long legs taking the steps three at a time, but he only caught a glimpse of the driver before the car raced away.

It was Pengfei Shing in the driver's seat and the few shots O'Rourke was able to fire did little to damage the car or the man inside. O'Rourke tucked the silenced weapon under his jacket before the group of students lying on the lawn and debating were aware of what had taken place. He returned to where he had last seen Bivu and the professor and found them both looking down at the two dead men in horror.

'Was that necessary,' Min Ch'eng managed to stutter with eyes unable to be drawn from the dead triad gunmen.

'They were triads and they were trying to kill me and take possession of what is in your jacket pocket, Professor. They would not only have killed me but you and Biyu as well, without the slightest hesitation.'

The young woman tentatively held out O'Rourke's travel bag with an expression of disbelief. He took the bag with a smile of thanks but she was unable to smile back at a man who could be so savage and kill without showing a single sign of remorse.

'I'll try to clear this up with the campus police before they call the district police. That should give you time to get as far away from here as possible,' Min Ch'eng said handing the sheathed sword to O'Rourke. 'As from this moment Biyu will be taking a few days holiday and as far as anybody could tell she was miles away at the time of this unfortunate incident.' He made shooing motions with his hand and with only a brief look at O'Rourke his assistant gratefully hurried back to her residence to gather up some personal belongings.

'Thank you, Professor, but will you be able to work on the virus unimpeded by the bureaucratic rules of the university and avoid possible seizure of the dish by the police as material evidence?'

The old academic smiled and stroked his beard. 'I should consider early retirement if I cannot manipulate the university system after thirty years. No, Mr O'Rourke, I'll tell nobody about the virus until I have the antidote. I will report finding these two bodies and suggest that they could have been involved in triad gang warfare that infiltrated the campus.' He pointed down at the decorative tattoos that showed above the collars of both men. 'I would imagine that the artwork covers most of their bodies. A clear indication that they were triads.'

O'Rourke laughed lightly, wished him well with the antidote and shook the man's hand before striding away towards the main gate to hail a taxi. He was twelve miles away and circling the prettily lit fountain outside the Royal International Hotel when the police started to arrive at the university. O'Rourke paid the driver and as soon as the taxi had picked up a guest and departed he walked back to the main road and hailed another taxi. He knew that his destination would be logged and he made sure the taxi that stopped for him was an illegal cab. The short ride to the Shanghai

Airlines Travel Hotel would be five times more expensive but anonymity of both taxi and fare meant the police would be unable to trace either. Their trail would end at the Royal International Hotel.

A row of obligatory fountains, illuminated bright green, greeted O'Rourke as they arrived at the main entrance of the new hotel. He paid a brief visit to the Ticket Booking Centre to reserve a morning flight to Hong Kong and then got a guestroom for one night.

He flung the travel case down and stood the sword against the bedside table before flopping down onto the huge bed. As soon as his head hit the down-filled pillow he was fast asleep and nothing could possibly wake him until his eight o'clock alarm call in the morning.

The rain was steadily falling from an even grey sky when he awoke and drew the curtains. Checking his watch he realized that it was only two hours to flight departure and he hurriedly showered and dressed.

As the lift doors opened O'Rourke checked the lobby before making his way to the checkout counter. After settling the bill he collected his air ticket and left the hotel with the long case nonchalantly slung across his back. He chose one of the few taxis ranking outside the hotel and they were soon filtering off the Yingbin Expressway to enter the airport.

There was a scattering of early travellers on the concourse when O'Rourke walked to the check-in and he scanned those nearest to him. One or two loiterers seemed a little suspicious but he dismissed them when they picked up cases and made for the departure gate. As nobody else had made a move to intercept him he proceeded with checking in both the wooden case and his travel bag. He had discarded the triad's silenced pistol in a lavatory cistern at the hotel and was now totally unarmed. As he went through the security checks he felt uncomfortably naked.

HONG KONG

The flight was uneventful even though he had a prickly feeling on the back of his neck that made him think he was being shadowed. O'Rourke collected his baggage from the carousel and hailed a taxi for the Excelsior Hotel. He went straight to his room and took a compact Smith & Wesson .45 semi-automatic from between the two mattresses. It was fully loaded with one round in the chamber and he slipped the spare 10-round magazine into his jacket pocket. Feeling less exposed O'Rourke sat in the armchair by the phone and dialled a number that was imprinted in his memory.

'Who is calling,' the voice asked in classical Mandarin. O'Rourke could sense the man's suspicion and he laughed lightly before replying in English.

'This is Séan O'Rourke and I wish to inform you that I have completed the task you set for me.'

'You use my red phone for a good reason I hope?' The voice continued speaking in Mandarin to maintain seniority.

'I wish to end my contract with your government as this will enable me to terminate the arrangement I have with unfavourable company.'

'In what manner do you plan the termination?' Suspicion had now changed to an air of curiosity.

'A permanent manner.'

'If you plan to sever your relationship I will need you to change the leadership.'

'That is my intention whether I have your permission or not.'

'It is unwise to take that arrogant tone of voice with me,' the voice said with an edge of anger. 'I am your superior and I speak for the Chinese Government.'

'My apology, sir, but I will ensure that a new leader is appointed with whom you will be able to make direct contact.' O'Rourke had adopted a contrite tone of voice and it worked.

'That is very interesting. You do realize that such an arrangement will make you redundant?'

'That is my objective. However, to facilitate this new arrangement I will need some information that only your Ministry of State Security can give me.'

'Then you have my permission to proceed and I will give you a MSS number. You may contact this person only at night as it is his private number.' O'Rourke scribbled down the digits on the hotel notepad and the line went dead. He could now go ahead with his plan and he phoned room service to order lunch and a bottle of whisky.

A leisurely meal, two poorly dubbed Chinese movies and a short nap later he pulled the curtains to find that the sun had set leaving the sky with red and orange streaks that rapidly faded as he watched. He dialled the number and after giving his name the receptionist put him on hold. The well-known sweetheart of popular music, Chang Loo, began singing *'Give me a kiss.'* O'Rourke held the phone away from his ear until she was suddenly cut mid-note and a man said in English. 'I was told you would call, Mr O'Rourke. What is it you wish?'

The Irishman didn't bother to ask for the man's name as it would have been a waste of his time. 'Thank you for taking my call, sir. Can you tell me if Pengfei Shing has another home other than the one at Clear Water Bay?' he asked deferentially.

'Who is this gentleman?'

O'Rourke knew the MSS were keeping a close eye on Shing but he kept a polite tone. 'He is the *Mountain Master* for the island of Hong Kong.'

'Ah yes. I will get back to you, Mr O'Rourke.' The line went dead and he replaced the handset. After two aggravating hours the phone rang and when O'Rourke replied he immediately recognized the voice. He picked up a pencil and prepared to write.

'The man you seek lives in Clear Water Bay –'

'That I know!'

'Patience, Mr O'Rourke. I was going to add and he also lives on Poi Toi Island.'

'I didn't think anybody lived on that piece of rock apart from a few fishermen.'

'You were misinformed. There is a temple, many multi-storeyed buildings and a number of people who have chosen a much quieter way of life – which is precisely why Pengfei Shing selected it. He likes the anonymity of living with only visiting birdwatchers and hiking tourists to be concerned about. His large villa is isolated on the southern headland in the Ngong Chong area and if you're going in that direction, good luck.' Once more the line went dead without a single word of goodbye.

O'Rourke took a tourist guide from the bedside table and found that the ferry for Poi Toi departed from Blake Pier at Stanley. He called down to reception and requested a taxi for the following morning.

The MSS officer had wished him good luck not knowing that the Irishman's real intention was to avenge the brutal killing of a restaurant owner's brother and a distant cousin.

Inspector Xiao Shi Huang had been no ordinary police officer. He and Séan had been partners and in the very brief time they had worked together had become the very best of friends.

A man of honour never forgets a friend.

24

ENGLAND

JAMES WOKE WITH A foul taste in his mouth and an ache in his side. The anaesthetic still made him feel slightly woozy but he knew that it would only be a matter of time before hospital paperwork entered the national mainframe and alerted Rackman. He slowly dressed and discharged himself despite vehement advice to stay another day to prevent tearing the new stitches.

The taxi dropped him at the end of the street and he cautiously approached his office on foot, studying the light morning traffic, all pedestrians and the windows over the shops for anything that seemed out of the ordinary. The door hadn't been tampered with and he bolted it securely behind him before climbing the stairs step by step.

As he entered the reception area the telephone rang. It was Jennifer, demanding to know why he had left the hospital so soon. 'Don't you know you could rip your side open,' she finished breathlessly which allowed him to get a word in.

'If I had stayed any longer, Jenny, the Illuminati would have done more than pull a few stitches.'

There was a long silence. 'I'm coming to you right now,' she said with a touch of defiance and hung up leaving him holding a buzzing receiver. James sighed and went into his office to find that it had been ransacked. Cabinet drawers had been emptied and all the files strewn across the floor. Desk drawers had also been searched and the contents had joined the numerous sheets of paper littering the room. He went to the safe and found that it too had been forced open and emptied.

James found a chipped cup and saucer on the floor beneath Miss Lightbody's desk and scooped up a spoonful of grains from the split packet that had been thrown into the corner of the room. He set about making coffee and the kettle had just begun to boil when the doorbell rang. He leant out of the office window to look down at the street before activating the door lock release. He then remembered that he had bolted the door and slowly descended to let the attractive detective enter.

Jennifer bounded up the stairs ahead of him but stopped dead when she saw the chaos. 'They obviously thought you had hidden the petri dish here,' she shouted down the stairs.

James grunted as he made the last few steps. 'Of course they did,' he muttered. 'Coffee?' She nodded and James poured a second cup. 'However, the bastards did neglect to look in one place.'

'Where can that be,' Jennifer asked returning from the disaster that was his office. 'They seem to have been pretty thorough in their search.'

James winked and pointed down at his feet.

'You left something in Feng's care?' she asked with a perplexed expression. 'But you gave the virus to O'Rourke to take to China so what was it you hid downstairs?'

'It's not so much what I hid but what Feng keeps hidden that's important. We will need some form of defence when Rackman and his renegade SIS officers catch up with me and that's precisely what Feng keeps secret. Even from his own family.' James put his cup down and crooking his finger invitingly he went out and down the stairs with a rather baffled Jennifer following.

After checking all cars parked in the street they entered the Forbidden City and were greeted by a shrill shriek from Lin-Lin. She and ran across the restaurant and into a big hug that made James wince. Jennifer bent down to kiss the round face that shone happily as Feng came to shake James's hand warmly. A few curious diners looked up and James casually checked each one until he was sure they didn't present any possible threat to them.

'I'm so glad to see that you are both safe,' the rotund man said as he led them through the kitchen doors and into the steamy environment. Jiao was busily stirring something aromatic in a large pot and James suddenly realized he was hungry. She embraced James and warmly kissed Jennifer without arresting the steady rhythm of her spoon.

'What's the latest, James?' Feng asked while passing glasses of chilled Pinot Grigio to the couple. 'Where's the virus now?'

'In O'Rourke's hands and hopefully six thousand miles away in a Chinese laboratory,' James said after an appreciative sip. 'We now have the problem of the local guys who still think I have that original petri dish.'

'They followed us to Camber and tried to kill James. They shot him in the side,' Jennifer said softly so that Lin-Lin, who was ladling some bean soup into a bowl, wouldn't hear.

'Aieee!' Jiao exclaimed and the spoon stopped. She went to James and took his hands. 'You poor dear, are you all right?'

James reassured her that he was recovering and looking at Feng he said that he and Jenny had seen the gunmen off. He placed emphasis on the last four words as he was loathe to say that they had shot both of them dead while Lin-Lin was standing so close.

Understanding what James meant Feng nodded gravely. 'How can I help you, James,' he asked. 'You obviously didn't come downstairs for a bit of a chit-chat.'

'Feng!' Jiao admonished but James held his hand up.

'He's right, Mrs Choi, and there *is* a favour I wish to ask of your husband confidentially.'

Feng took him by the elbow and guided him to the back of the kitchen and into a small room that acted as the Forbidden City's office. Jennifer followed after giving the small girl another hug and she closed the door behind them. The three sat round a small ink-stained desk covered in stacks of traders' bills, receipts and accounts books.

'What is this favour that Jiao can't be part of?' Feng asked.

'I want to talk about what you've always kept secret from her,' James said. He leant over the desk on both elbows and whispered three words that Jennifer was unable to hear. Feng jerked back as though stung and then his face broke into the broadest smile Jennifer had ever seen. Perfect white teeth gleamed like those in the jaws of a pit-bull terrier.

'It's the boy scouts code and creed?' he half sang, still smiling.

'That's right. Be prepared,' James added, also smiling.

Jennifer gave a frustrated snort. 'Can you tell me what on earth you're both talking about?'

'*Húdié shuāng dāo*,' Feng said with a laugh.

'Butterfly swords,' James translated. 'They have a wide razor-sharp blade that's as long as a man's forearm and can provide a perfect defence against close-up knife attacks. Without my father's old service revolver or your access to weapons in the police armoury we're powerless to defend ourselves.'

The policewoman's eyebrows lifted. 'Feng keeps illegal weapons on the premises?' she asked, disregarding what James had said.

'Not at all, Jenny. Feng is a *Yinhu–wu duan*, or Silver Tiger martial arts master and as we can no longer access the armoury at the police station I'd like to ask Feng if we can borrow a couple of his weapons,' James explained patiently. 'Namely his butterfly swords because they are easily hidden and can be carried at all times. Let's face it. They'll be better than nothing if we're confronted by armed Illuminati thugs.'

'I'd like to add that what weapons I have were registered at your own police station, Jenny. They are perfectly legal.' Feng gave the suggestion of a wink. 'I have also been teaching James a few lessons down at the dojo from time to time so he knows how to use them responsibly.'

'Mrs Choi doesn't like any kind of weapon which is why Feng keeps his hobby a secret.'

A mollified Jennifer relaxed as she looked from one man to the other. 'Where do you keep them Feng?' she asked, overcome by a natural curiosity that had taken precedence over doing things by the book and her sense of duty.

Feng grinned and without saying a word beckoned to them both to follow him. Unnoticed by Jiao they left the restaurant by the back door and went down the garden to cross the access road enter the allotments. Feng nodded towards his favourite retreat and James gave a knowing smile as his friend unlocked the shed door and went inside.

'You've been here before, haven't you?' Jennifer said to James as they entered the gloomy interior.

'A couple of times but I have to admit that I've never seen any sign of martial arts weapons.'

They watched as Feng went to some old fertilizer sacks that hung from the roof trusses and drew them aside, showing nothing more exciting than a wall of wooden planks. He ran a finger over one of the roughly planed surfaces and pressed on a knot in one of the timber boards. There was an audible 'click' and a large section of the wall swung open to reveal a glittering assortment of swords, daggers and other weapons that James was unable to recognize.

'My pride and joy, collected over twenty years and worth a small fortune,' Feng said proudly. 'That's why I can't tell Jiao. If she knew I'd spent this much on my passion she'd make me sell the lot and put the money into Lin-Lin's college fund.' Noticing the disapproving look that Jennifer gave him he added, 'This I plan to do later when the collection has increased in value.'

Jennifer tentatively felt the tip of one of the long-shafted weapons. 'You keep them in magnificent condition, Feng. Do you fight with them?'

'Of course not, they're far too dangerous. I only take them to the dojo when I give lectures on the history of Chinese martial arts. The one you are testing the sharpness of is a *qiang*, or spear, and is traditionally one of the four major battlefield weapons.' Jennifer flinched as she nicked her forefinger and drew a spot of blood.

'The fancy horsehair tassel was designed to blur an opponent's vision, making it difficult to grab hold of the shaft and also to prevent blood from flowing down the wooden shaft and making it slippery to hold,' the Silver Tiger said offhandedly.

James took Jennifer's hand to inspect the tiny cut. 'You'll live,' he said and laughed when she jerked her hand away with a look of annoyance that clouded her features.

'I think this is what you wanted, James.' Feng took a leather-bound box from a top shelf and handed it to James. 'Try to be more careful as they are also very sharp.'

Jennifer screwed her nose up at the rebuke while James tripped the catches and opened the lid. Sunlight streaming through the shed window reflected off the broad blades as he admired the fine workmanship of the two short swords. He had handled them only once before at Feng's dojo before being given lessons with wooden copies that were deliberately made for competition use. Jennifer was speechless as he lifted took one of the seventeen-inch-long weapons by the unique cross-guarded grip and weaved a pattern in the air with its tip.

'Beautiful,' he breathed.

'Highly illegal,' she whispered.

'Deadly,' Feng countered. 'You may need this,' he added as he handed Jennifer a lightweight, leather scabbard. 'It can hold both swords and can be worn under a long jacket or coat. Historically, butterfly swords were concealed within the loose sleeves and boots of our ancestors' robes but today you'd be a trifle conspicuous in an eighteenth-century costume in East Steading.'

'May I borrow them for a few days?' James asked.

'You need not ask, my friend.' Feng took the sword and slipped it into the scabbard Jenny was holding. The second blade was placed beside it and he passed the sheathed swords to James. It only took a matter of seconds for James to strap the scabbard on and close his jacket.

'Only the end is showing,' Jenny said studying the final effect.

'It'll be completely hidden when I wear my raincoat.' James shook Feng's hand with a brief word of thanks and they left the shed to return to the restaurant. The couple said their farewells to Jiao and Lin-Lin and returned to James's office and locked the door. They had just gone up to the apartment when the doorbell rang and Jennifer volunteered to answer it. James gratefully watched her go down as the wound in his side had been aggravated by the weight of the scabbard.

James unbelted the weapons and tossed them onto the bed just as Jennifer returned accompanied by Detective Sergeant Briscoe. He slipped the swords under the pillows and left the bedroom to see what the police officer wanted.

'Inspector Tilley believes there is no longer any need for you to be protected. Jennifer will have to be returned to normal duties,' Briscoe said with a long face.

'That suits me, Bertram,' James said cheerfully, feeling a weight lift off his shoulders. 'I've been concerned that she would come to some harm if she stayed with me.'

A look of hurt flickered across Jennifer's face.

'So you consider me bothersome; an albatross hanging around your neck?' The bitter remark made James flinch and his heart missed a couple of beats.

'No!' he exclaimed and would have attempted to explain what he meant if it weren't for the sergeant's quick interruption.

'Listen, James! I've been feeling guilty about leaving you defenceless and, no matter what you think, Jennifer's transfer to protection duty over the last few days has given me some peace of mind. She is very good at her job and the inspector's decision to remove her will put you at risk.'

'Thank you, Sergeant, that was –'

'I haven't finished, Constable,' Briscoe snapped. 'I returned the HK417 and the jammed Sig Sauer to the armoury but requisitioned a Glock 26 and ammunition.' He opened the satchel he was carrying and took out a holstered pistol and three magazines. 'I'm giving you the responsibility of this weapon Jennifer and I order you to stay on protection duty until this mess is sorted.'

James was amazed at Briscoe's courage for taking such a risk. 'This is a very generous gesture, Sergeant.'

'And one that could lose me my job.'

'Not if I can help it,' Jennifer murmured, the admiration for her superior officer clearly showing on her face. 'If I'm forced to use the pistol I will swear in court that I, and I alone, took it from the armoury.'

Briscoe handed her the gun. 'That won't be necessary, girl. I've already bypassed the inspector and written to the Chief Constable explaining all the circumstances and giving a full account of the Illuminati plan to commit genocide. He had already written out a requisition for the Glock and it was hand-delivered to the armourer with a credible explanation for all urgency in issuing the weapon to me.'

'Can you trust the Chief Constable?' James asked while watching Jennifer remove her jacket and putting on the holster harness. 'If senior people in the SIS are working for the Illuminati then they will have members in the police force, too.'

'He's my great uncle and like my father I would trust him with my life,' Briscoe said. 'He will also be making very discreet enquiries at a political level.' James was convinced the sergeant had made the right move. They shook hands and Briscoe left after giving them his home number and instructions to call him at any time of the day should there be new developments.

Jennifer closed the door behind him and then unclipped the Glock to remove it from the holster. She flicked the safety on and inserted one of the magazines before slipping it back beneath her jacket. 'I suggest we leave here as soon as possible; Rackman is bound to look for you here first and he could be on his way this very moment.'

James agreed and quickly put a few items of essential clothing into a small backpack and buckled the swords under his lightweight raincoat. The last thing Jennifer did before they left the apartment was to remember James's medication ands she dropped the little Xyrem pillbox into his pocket with fingers mentally crossed.

The rain started as they crossed the street to where Jennifer had parked her car and James was thankful that he had chosen to wear a raincoat.

'Where to?' Jennifer asked as James gingerly fastened his seat belt.

'Head for Soho, Jenny,' James said as he studied the road atlas he had found in the glove compartment. 'There's a place in Greek Street that O'Rourke had used and that Rackman is very familiar with; it'll make an excellent refuge.'

'If Rackman knows about this place won't it be on his list of addresses to check first?' The car accelerated away from the kerb and James settled himself down for the long drive to London.

'It's not very likely. He happens to know that a very violent death occurred there recently.'

'So won't the Met police ask *us* why we've pitched up on their crime scene.'

'They don't know about any killing because the house pimps will have got together and disposed of all evidence of a shooting.'

'Pimps?'

'It's a house of pleasure, Jenny. A bawdy house, bordello, cathouse, whorehouse –'

'I get the picture.'

James continued. 'Naturally the regular customers will be reluctant to visit a house where murder has taken place so the ladies have a strong financial reason for hushing things up. It's the perfect safe house which is also why O'Rourke, a Chinese government agent, triad enforcer and

Illuminati assassin, was able to kill the person sent to kill him and get away with it.' James chuckled to himself and Jennifer grinned despite hearing about a gruesome crime that should have come to light in a police interview room. Then she laughed out loud.

'Ah, you get the irony of the situation then?' James said and he closed his eyes for one of the short daily naps he was advised by his doctor to take.

Rackman arrived at Goodfellow Investigations ten minutes after they had left for London. The door locks presented little difficulty for the three men accompanying him and within seconds they were thundering up the staircase.

A swift kick gave them access and they swept through the office in yet another fruitless search before rushing up the last flight of stairs to do the same to the apartment above. More books were flung from shelves, framed photographs thrown down and crushed beneath uncaring boots and clothing was ripped from drawers and wardrobes. The slightest movement by a floorboard resulted in it being torn up and the cavity being searched thoroughly.

It took an hour to transform James's normally neat home and office into a major disaster area. Even the runner carpets on the stairs were wrenched up and each step studied for a secret hiding place. Finally a thoroughly frustrated Rackman called a halt and they left the building to drive to the bungalow at Camber. He touched the bandage wound round his head and the mutilated ear momentarily seemed to pain him more. Rackman was taking a gamble that Goodfellow would return to his original hiding place and he planned to have his revenge in a quiet place where no one would hear Goodfellow's screams. As he got into the car his eye was attracted to a couple leaving the Forbidden City and he instructed his men to wait while he checked out the restaurant.

Feng had heard the racket caused by the men and was in the process of phoning the East Steading police when he saw four dark-suited men crossing the road and climbing into a dark saloon.

'I'd like to report a burglary,' he said when a voice asked which emergency service he required. 'The offices of Goodfellow Investigations have been broken into by strangers.' Feng gave his name and the address as he watched one of the men leave the car and limp back towards the restaurant. 'Please hurry as one of the men is now coming into my place.' The man was short but had an air of authority as he entered and limped towards the Chinese restaurateur.

Rackman swept the room and noted the four diners in the far corner who were busy devouring Jiao's delicious gunpowder chicken with dried chillies and peanuts. He then saw Feng replace the phone and instinctively knew he had notified the police about the noise upstairs.

'Mr Feng Choi?' he inquired and Feng nodded.

'A table for one, sir?' Feng asked extending an arm to encompass the whole room. Rackman was aware of the sarcasm in the man's voice and he decided to make his point quick and hard. He grabbed Feng's arm and steered him through the door and into the kitchen where he pressed him back against a wooden trestle table. Jiao, who was preparing a lychee and ginger sorbet, was startled into immobility by the sudden intrusion.

'Tell me where James Goodfellow is or I'll come back and fumigate this rathole,' Rackman snarled between clenched teeth, his face so close to Feng's that drops of spittle fell upon his cheek.

The chef reached behind his back and picked up the eight-inch duck knife. In two coordinated movements he placed the two-inch wide blade beneath Rackman's nose and gripped his testicles. The SIS officer tried to pull back from the razor-sharp edge of the chef's knife but that only increased the agony in his crotch.

'If you so much as come within fifty yards of our home I'll remove your nose with this very knife,' Feng whispered with a menace that underlined the threat. 'Get out now or I'll set my wife upon you and she knows how to skin sheep's testicles in twenty-two seconds flat.'

Rackman glanced fearfully over Feng's shoulder to where Jiao had recovered from her initial shock and was now sharpening a fish boning knife on a pumice stone with grim determination. Feng released the man and he fled from the kitchen and staggered out of the restaurant clutching at his groin. The diners were so engrossed in the delectable dish that had been set before them that they hardly noticed Rackman's distressed departure.

He limped across the street and got into the car which pulled away just as a patrol car came to a halt outside the Forbidden City. Feng went outside to point after the dark saloon but by the time the police understood he was indicating that they should chase the car it had disappeared round the next corner and neither of the two officers had taken down the registration.

Within two minutes the break-in and damage in Goodfellow's office and apartment were discovered and a further three minutes had passed as requests were made to central control to find a 'dark saloon' with four men in 'dark suits'. It was the only description they had and was received with uproarious laughter and cutting comments about the Men in Black chasing aliens.

While the two red-faced constables continued to question Feng, his wife and four bemused diners the dark car sped south towards the little bungalow in the coastal village of Camber.

25

HONG KONG

O'ROURKE LEFT THE TAXI at Blake Pier and boarded the ferry bound for Poi Toi island. A large bag with the well-known Nikon brand-name was hanging from his left shoulder and the long leatherette case in his right hand could easily be taken for a tripod by those curious enough to wonder about it.

He had chosen to use the Blake Pier service to the island as it conveniently went directly to the sparsely populated region that aside from being famous for its seafood restaurants also provided hiking trails that passed close to Pengfei Shing's isolated villa.

The ferry offered three services on a Saturday, taking approximately one hour each way. O'Rourke paid the HK$40 return fare and took a seat on the upper deck where he could keep an eye on the passengers approaching to board.

As the crew cast off the irregular thumping of old car tyres against the jetty ceased and the vessel pulled away from the tableau of homes dotting the lush hills and the moored sampans and made headway into Stanley Bay.

When some of the passengers began moving about to help ease the feeling of nausea brought on by the larger waves O'Rourke watched them carefully with hooded eyes. Most were tourists in colourful shirts with a sprinkling of more soberly dressed fishermen. Two men appeared to be out of place amidst the cheerful, chattering crowd. Dark tailored suits and polished shoes marked them as being businessmen or, as O'Rourke suspected from the slight bulges under their left arms, triads. They had deliberately seated themselves at the stern where they could observe the whole deck and O'Rourke could feel their eyes boring into the back of his neck.

As they drew near to Poi Toi he made a point of moving down to the lower deck and positioning himself midship, close to the disembarkation point. As the ferry drew alongside the pier O'Rourke leapt ashore to startled cries from the crew who had not yet finished the safe mooring of the vessel. He sprinted along the covered pier towards what appeared to be a general store before turning right and climbing a flight of concrete steps that went towards the ridge. O'Rourke was hidden from the pier part of the way by trees that soon thinned out to become grassland. He could now look down on the cove and the last passengers still disembarking and streaming along the pier. The two men in suits were standing at the junction and looking both ways. One pointed up to where O'Rourke was and he realized that he was foolishly silhouetted against the sky.

He set off and reached the last of the steps and the crude trail took him into wild scrubland and then bare rock where there was another junction. He took the more rugged route to head towards the southern headland in the Ngong Chong region.

Pausing by a large boulder he looked back and saw the men reaching the ridge and considering the direction they should take. Gulls screeched overhead as O'Rourke deliberately showed himself and set off at a faster pace. He soon passed a small, automated lighthouse and undid the catches of the camera bag to remove the automatic pistol and load it with a ten-round magazine whilst still on the move.

The terrain was now wild and dramatic with the foaming sea pounding at the base of the rocky cliffs and the trail had become narrow and treacherous with loose stones that threatened to twist a careless ankle. There was a wide fissure in the cliff that could only be crossed by a suspended footbridge with waist-high handrails. O'Rourke ran across with the sword case thumping against his spine and hid in the first crevice he could find in the rock face.

He was close to the endgame and had chosen the small footbridge as the most advantageous spot to confront the two triads, he couldn't afford any mishaps at the end of the mission.

As he waited for the men to appear he screwed on the long silencer and had barely finished when he heard angry voices above the sound of the crashing surf. The two men appeared and approached the footbridge without caution while still arguing volubly about the direction they should have taken at the last junction.

The footbridge was so narrow that they were forced to walk in single file. When they reached the midway point O'Rourke stepped out of the crevice and into the open with the gun held behind his back.

Both men reached for weapons beneath their jackets and O'Rourke turned sideways and raised the silenced weapon. It coughed twice and the lead man was thrown back onto his partner. Two more rapid coughs silenced the scream of shock and pain. The Irishman ran onto the footbridge and fired again to finish the second assassin. He looked both ways to satisfy himself that no trail-trekking tourists had come their way before rolling both men under the bottom rail and into the sea that crashed and seethed below, the thick foam swallowing their bodies.

O'Rourke spotted the two guards patrolling Pengfei's villa long before they were able to see him; he bent double and left the well-worn trail which he knew would be watched more frequently. There were seventy-three minutes remaining before the next ferry returned to Blake Pier and he set the alarm on his watch.

The luxury villa, a sprawling complex of contemporary architecture, was built on a rocky bluff and surrounded by an eight-foot high wall. The guards he had spotted were freely walking along the top of the wall, an indication of how thick it was, and foolishly circling clockwise and counter-clockwise which meant they inevitably left the opposite side unguarded for two minutes when they met for a brief chat.

The landscape was now dotted with a few *feng shui* trees and he ducked behind these to move closer. The guards were directly above him and he flattened himself behind one of the trees before taking the automatic from the bag and putting it under his belt. The guards continued with their patrol and he allowed two minutes for them to meet on the other Leaving the bag behind he sprinted to the wall and leapt.

The courtyard was empty and O'Rourke dropped down and darted through an open door and into a small study. There were two computer screens scrolling the latest stock market reports from Shanghai and London. He listened at the door before opening it and stepping into the carpeted hallway. He moved towards the sound of Chinese music and was able to detect men's voices talking loudly in Mandarin.

'You put two men on his tail and they lost him?'

'I haven't heard from them since they left the ferry.'

O'Rourke recognized the first voice: it was Pengfei Shing's and knew that his hunt was at an end. He took the automatic from his belt and walked towards the room where the voices were coming from.

'He is obviously coming to this place.'

'I've got guards on the wall and we have six men inside the compound and the house.'

The Irishman stopped and looked round but the hallway remained empty. Ignoring the two men he began hunting the guards and found two in the billiard room smoking fine cigars. The taller of the pair was just lining up to pot the pink ball when he was shot and as the second man spun round speechless he was sent back upon the table with a bullet in the forehead. The balls were scattered about the table and O'Rourke couldn't help noticing the pink dropping into a middle pocket.

The next three were ironically playing *Bǎo Huáng*, Protect the Emperor, in the kitchen and one had just laid his cards on the worktable with a triumphant expression when he was flung from his chair by a bullet in his head. Struggling to get their weapons out of holsters the remaining two swiftly fell and as O'Rourke started to lower his weapon a cook leapt out of the pantry with a scream and a massive cleaver held high above his head.

Ducking beneath the blade O'Rourke brought the gun up and pushing it into the man's side pulled the trigger. The bullet smashed through his ribs and heart and killed him instantly. He didn't wait to see if they were all dead but strode across to the pantry door in time to see a second cook running towards him. He also held a wicked-looking blade and O'Rourke instinctively fired and slammed the door shut. He felt the body hit the insulated door as he pushed the bolt into place.

One guard plus an unknown number of domestic servants remained and O'Rourke was running out of time to catch the return ferry. He left the kitchen and checked the next room that was expensively furnished with silk-upholstered furniture. Lacquered cabinets with ivory-inlaid pictures of cranes lined all the walls except for one. A giant plasma television screen dominated that wall and the sound had been turned down. A race was being run at the Happy Valley Racecourse and as O'Rourke moved further into the room he became aware of a man sitting on one of the settees. He was hunched over a copy of the *Racing Post*, with a pencil stub clenched between his fingers as he stared hypnotically at the horses in the last furlong. Reclining beside him was a young woman in a short dress that was slit to the waist. Her eyes were glazed and O'Rourke noticed the residual lines of powder on the lacquered surface. A sheathed sword was lying on the low coffee table as well as a small pearl-handled pistol. A loose board creaked and the man looked up and into the merciless eyes of the intruder.

The guard froze and the girl struggled to sit upright. O'Rourke held a finger to his lips and the triad was shocked into obeying the instruction. However, the woman snarled and lunged for the pistol. Her fingertip had just touched the grip when he struck her on the side of the head with the butt of the automatic. As she fell back unconscious O'Rourke walked right up the petrified man and with the silencer inches from the man's forehead he pulled the trigger.

The house was still silent when he stepped back out into the hallway and he swiftly made his way back to the room where he had heard Shing's voice. He paused outside and then tested the door handle. It turned easily and he entered the room with the automatic levelled.

Pengfei Shing and his companion sat facing each other in high winged armchairs. The camel-bone chest of Cuban cigars that Pengfei took everywhere he went was in front of him. He was drawing lightly on the aromatic Gurkha Black Dragon when the door opened. The Irishman Pengfei had sent Xun to dispose of entered stealthily.

The triad facing Pengfei twisted round to see who was behind him and reached for his holstered pistol on seeing the tall man. One light cough from O'Rourke's gun and blood and brain tissue splattered the turquoise silk of Shing's kimono. He pushed himself back into the upholstery as his companion fell across the coffee table, knocking the invaluable humidor to the floor and spilling a fortune in cigars on the Persian rug. Smoke slowly leaked from between fleshy lips that were tightly compressed together.

'You know why I'm here, Pengfei,' O'Rourke stated in a matter-of-fact tone of voice. He had used Mandarin to show the *Mountain Master* that he was an equal.

'What are you after?'

'Payment.'

'How much are you asking for.'

'It's not money I seek but payment in kind for the life of a good friend and his brother.' O'Rourke sat in a chair next to the dead man and looked at Pengfei with eyes as cold as ice.

'What were their lives worth?' Shing said. He groaned softly for he already knew the answer.

'Those gentlemen were worth a lot more than your contemptible life but as that's all you have to offer I'll take it.'

O'Rourke rose to his feet and in one swift movement unsheathed Dragon's Breath. He placed the automatic on the coffee table and slid it towards the all-powerful triad leader. It stopped only inches from Shing's trembling hand on the polished table and O'Rourke waited for him to make his move.

Suddenly a door at the end of the room opened and a young man entered. He was neatly dressed in cream slacks and white open-necked shirt and was clearly unarmed. He stopped when he saw the dramatic tableau set before him and then continued walking towards the two men.

'Who is this man, Father?' he demanded to know, instantly revealing his relationship to Shing. The triad was unable to speak for he had just recognized the blade shimmering in the glow of the recessed spotlights.

'My name is O'Rourke and I am avenging the murder of my friend,' O'Rourke answered for the mute man. 'I am also avenging my own death for your father had sent Xun, his best assassin, to kill me.'

'Did you disrespect my father?' the son demanded to know.

'He disrespected our whole family,' Shing managed to croak. 'He stole an ancient *ding* that has belonged to our family for many centuries. It was filled with messages to enable our ancestors to reach heaven.'

'Did you steal this item from my father?'

'That would be impossible as the artefact already belonged to the heirs of Shu Du, one of the Three Guards appointed by King Wu. One of those heirs, a police superintendent called Xiao Shi Huang was killed on the orders of your father. This was a dishonourable act that cannot pass unpunished and that is why I am here.'

The young man looked down at Shing with a puzzled expression. 'Did you steal this *ding* and then kill the owner, Father.'

'It came into my hands and there it had to stay,' his father managed to whisper. 'I am the *Mountain Master*,' he added with the return of his normal arrogant attitude. 'That sword is also mine and I demand that it is returned to me.'

'Did you order the execution of the police inspector this man refers to?'

'Naturally, my son. He was on his way to Europe to steal our family's possessions that had been hidden in Italy.'

O'Rourke held up his left hand. 'He was in fact going to find a deadly virus that was hidden in the *ding*,' he said calmly while watching Shing's hand creep closer to the automatic.

'I knew nothing of that, Ming-húa,' Shing exclaimed.

'What was this virus for, Mr O'Rourke?'

'It affects the DNA of all Far Eastern peoples, inhibiting their ability to reproduce successfully. It was intentionally created to destroy the Chinese people by an organization called –'

'The Illuminati?'

'You know of them?'

'I am very familiar with their activities in our country and also of their efforts to prevent the Chinese from investing in other countries. However, I wasn't aware that they would go so far as to create a weapon of mass destruction.'

O'Rourke studied the young man and remembered his promise to the secret service officer to find a replacement he could trust and be able to communicate with. He had heard on the triad grapevine that Ming-húa had been sent to England when very young for his education. It was also a way to keep him ignorant of his father's affairs and the triad activities for as long as possible. The young man had been led to believe that his father was a powerful businessman whose family was at risk from kidnappers; justifying the inordinate amount of armed protection.

'Whether your father knew or didn't know of this shameful virus the fact still remains that he is guilty of unforgivable behaviour and I ask your permission to remove him from power. Furthermore, I believe you would be the perfect candidate to replace him as the *Mountain Master*.'

'Mr O'Rourke, you must do as you think fit,' the son said, switching to perfect English that had been clearly cultivated in an Oxbridge college. 'By his own words he has dishonoured the responsibility of his triad rank and the family name. He has also put his own peoples in grave danger.'

'You cannot disown me, Ming-húa, I am your father,' Shing shouted.

The young man thought long and hard. For as long as he could remember his father had controlled him. His education, his cars, where he lived, even his girlfriends were all chosen for him and he suddenly decided that this was the time to cut the apron strings and become a power unto himself. 'I can and despite being your only son I am compelled by my own sense of honour to do so.'

Shing's face mottled with rage. He grabbed the automatic and to O'Rourke's surprise he pointed the gun at his son. His finger had just started to take up the slack on the trigger when the engraved words *Dragon's Breath is the last touch felt by men judged evil* sliced through his neck. Shing's finger jerked in his moment of decapitation and the weapon coughed as his head fell to the floor amidst the Cuban cigars.

The 9mm bullet missed Ming-húa by a whisker and shattered a long mirror at the end of the room. He turned to look at the shards of glass and then slowly faced O'Rourke.

'I should thank you for saving my life. On the other hand I should kill you for taking my father's life,' he murmured as he glanced down at the last grimace of hate on Shing's features. 'What do you recommend I do?'

O'Rourke smiled, sheathed the blade and pointed to the automatic. 'You can follow the triad code and avenge your father's death now or you can forge a new understanding with a government official who'll make any legal businesses you want to start a great deal more profitable. However, he will still clamp down on any law-breaking activities you pursue. Is that a fair proposition?'

Ming-húa stood perfectly still for what seemed an age as he mulled over O'Rourke's words.

'If you can leave unnoticed I will say that my father was assassinated by a rival faction seeking to take over the Hong Kong company. I will then call a meeting and declare myself *Mountain Master*.' Ming-húa raised his hand. 'However, the legality of my businesses will be according to my own conscience.'

O'Rourke nodded. He knew that he could never hope to change the moral conduct of anybody but he had a strong feeling that the young man would do the right thing. He took a small notepad from his pocket and wrote down the number of the phone on the coffee table.

'Congratulations, Ming-húa, I wish you every success in any agreements you settle with the government official. He'll be calling you on that phone very soon.' O'Rourke swung Dragon's Breath round and onto his back, picked up the automatic and departed leaving the young successor to the triad leadership in deep thought.

O'Rourke's departure from the complex was unseen by the remaining guards on the wall and he knew that their incompetence would be overlooked. He checked his watch as he trotted back along the trail; crossing the footbridge he looked down and noticed that the bodies of the two assassins had been pulled down by the breakers and towed out to sea by the ever-present rip tide.

O'Rourke boarded the ferry on time and stretched his legs as he relaxed on the top deck. He called one of many memorized numbers and when a familiar voice answered he reported there was a new *Mountain Master* in town. 'His name is Ming-húa Shing, son of the late Pengfei Shing,' he said, before giving the telephone number and ringing off.

With his mission in Hong Kong completed he looked forward to returning to England to inform Feng Choi that his brother had been avenged and that he was entitled to keep the treasure once it had been recovered.

26

ENGLAND

THE NAMEPLATES THAT NORMALLY emitted a welcome glow to brief carnal pleasure were in darkness as James used the key that O'Rourke had given him and they entered the house in Greek Street.

'Doesn't look like they're open for business today,' he said with a cheerful grin as they started climbing the stairs.

'It's Sunday,' Jennifer admonished. 'It's *the* day of rest.'

James gave her a look that said 'you have to be joking' and then came face to face with Candy, a heavily made up woman wearing a semi-transparent negligee through which her voluptuous figure was clearly visible. She was standing outside an open door and holding a long-bladed carving knife.

'Who are you? What do you want?' she demanded to know as she waved the knife at him.

Jennifer caught up with James and cocked an eyebrow at the heavily rouged prostitute. 'Do you plan to use that, madam?' she asked, showing her warrant card. The knife speedily disappeared and the woman retreated back into the doorway of her apartment.

'I'm a friend of the Irishman who lives upstairs,' James said in a reassuring tone of voice.

Candy looked more closely into James's face. 'Sèan?'

'If anyone comes asking for him could you give me a call?' He handed her one of his business cards and she read it with lips moving.

'You must mean the nice man in the top apartment. He's called Sèan and he's the one who done for the bloke who beat Scarlet up.' The woman had warmed to James and her scarlet lips broadened into a smile that revealed nicotine-stained teeth.

'That's not something I'd like to know about,' Jennifer said as she put her warrant card away.

'That's good because I'm not saying anything to you anyway,' the woman snapped and then turned to James to resume smiling. 'If you have any problems luv, just shout down and Jimmy will give you a hand.'

'Jimmy?'

'He's my man.'

As if on cue a tall wardrobe-sized man in a white string vest and boxer shorts appeared behind her tapping a well-used metal baseball club in the palm of his left hand.

'Who's this, doll. Someone giving you grief?' he inquired in a bass voice that made the air between them vibrate. A descending spider shot back up to the safety of the ceiling.

'It's Sèan's friend.'

The man mumbled something unintelligible in the woman's ear. Candy looked over her shoulder and pouted a pretend kiss to the pimp and then turned to James.

'I don't know how long you plan to stay but Jimmy will keep an eye open until you leave. Won't you dear?'

The giant gave James a brief nod before pulling Candy back into the apartment and slamming the door. When they reached the next floor the door to the apartment that was directly above Candy's remained firmly shut. James saw a shadow move in the gap beneath the door and knew someone had been listening to the conversation below.

They continued to O'Rourke's apartment on the top floor and let themselves in. The front room was in an untidy state and Jennifer immediately spotted the dark brown stains on the carpet that had already attracted a large collection of houseflies.

'That's going to be a job to remove,' she said wrinkling her nose.

'Let's try and make the best of it.' James went into the bedroom and tossed his bag onto the bed. 'We should forget about cleaning O'Rourke's apartment for him and start looking for more weapons. A man with his lifestyle is bound to have a cache of knives and guns tucked away somewhere.'

'We've got swords and an automatic pistol, what more do we need?'

'An extra firearm would be useful should it come to another firefight.'

Jennifer entered the room and pulled a face. 'You're not thinking we're sleeping in *that* are you?'

'It's the only bed.'

'But we don't know who's been sleeping in it.'

'Only O'Rourke, I would imagine.'

'And there's a very good chance that it was with one of the women downstairs?' Jennifer said with one eyebrow raised as she tentatively pulled back the duvet to inspect the sheet and pillowcases for any signs of physical activity.

'Judging by what I know of O'Rourke those women wouldn't be to his taste and I'm quite sure he's not the kind of man who would pay for love.'

'Mmmmm.' Jennifer flipped the duvet cover back still doubtful about the cleanliness of the linen. 'No matter what you say I'm still keeping my clothes on and sleeping on top.'

'That's entirely up to you.' James went to have a quick look in the bathroom before returning to the front room where he began tapping the walls lightly with his fingertips. Jennifer opened every drawer and cupboard in the bedroom but came up with nothing that could be classified as a weapon.

After searching for an hour they had found nothing more lethal than a set of plastic knives and forks, two teaspoons, a blunt bread knife and a toilet brush.

'He must have something for emergencies,' James muttered and threw himself into one of the two threadbare armchairs.

Jennifer came into the room and wearily sat on his lap. 'It's lunchtime. Let's take a break and go out for something to eat before my navel starts touching my backbone.'

They went downstairs without any of the other apartment doors opening and within three minutes they were in the warm and friendly atmosphere of The Three Greyhounds to order the Sunday special. They avoided discussing the possible actions the Illuminati men might take against them until they had both finished the tender lamb shanks and were sipping fine Merlot.

Jennifer was the first to break their meditative silence. 'Do you think Rackman and his cronies will look for us in O'Rourke's apartment,' she asked as she surveyed the latest group of chattering friends who had arrived and gathered at the bar.

'They may pay a visit after exhausting all other possibilities. I pray that it will be a little while yet before they think of doing so as that will give O'Rourke more time to get the petri dish into the right hands.'

Jennifer pondered that thought for a while. 'Wouldn't we be a lot safer if we drove to a place that was more remote, such as the Yorkshire Dales where we could use a cosy hotel as our hideaway?'

James smiled at the pleasant notion before answering. 'The moment we hit the open road we will be exposed to traffic cameras and will most certainly be tracked by Rackman's men at SIS headquarters. Airports and coach and railway stations are also to be avoided as they will undoubtedly be monitored.'

James finished the last drop in his glass and went to the counter to pay the bill. As he took the cash from his wallet he happened to look across the bar and a familiar face snapped into focus, sounding alarm bells in his head. The man who had helped in the kidnapping of Lin-Lin and had been with Rackman at Lydd Airport was drinking with some of his mates. James tipped his head forward and mumbling his thanks to the barman he returned to Jennifer.

'Brian's here,' he said as he sat with his back to the room.

'Brian who?'

'Brian. The big bastard at Lydd Airport. So, let's get out of here before he spots us.' James slipped his jacket on and they made for the main doors. Jennifer went out first and as James followed he glanced back and immediately saw that the man was staring at him with a puzzled expression on his face.

James hurried after Jennifer. 'He saw us but I don't think he was quite sure that he had seen the right people,' he said as they crossed the road and stood outside the Prince Edward theatre. 'I suggest you hurry back to the apartment and I'll keep watch to see if he comes out.' Jennifer nodded and began striding purposefully away while James stepped into the recessed doorway and sat amongst the small group of teenagers who had congregated on the steps and were drinking cider and texting friends on their iPhones.

Fifteen seconds elapsed before Brian, still looking puzzled, came out of the public house pocketing a mobile phone. He stopped at the crossroads looking in each direction, trying to locate the couple. James hunched down and turned his collar up as though protecting himself from the chill breeze that was whipping round the corner. A youngster who wasn't more than seventeen offered him a 'swig' from his bottle and James smiled and shook his head.

The big man's head stopped turning and his chin went up as though he was sniffing the air like a retriever on a shoot. Brian had seen something of interest in Greek Street and James knew that he had spotted Jennifer. He rose to his feet to follow the man.

As it was Sunday the pavements were sparsely populated and James frequently had to drop back to keep his distance as they headed in the direction of Soho Square. He occasionally glimpsed Jennifer beyond the burly man until she suddenly stopped and turned into O'Rourke's building. Brian also hesitated and then continued walking until he drew level with the door that had been left wide open. The 'ladies of the night' were hoping for some extra post-lunch business and their nameplates glowed invitingly.

As soon as the big man had disappeared James started running. The thought that Jennifer would now be in great danger made his head reel and he rushed through the door. He was on the point of climbing the stairs when there was a deep bellow of pain followed by a crashing sound as a heavy body came falling down the stairs with arms and legs flailing. Brian came to a halt at James's feet and he could tell by the odd angle of the neck that it had been broken.

Blue eyes stared up at him and a familiar tingling began in his legs. He took the Xylem tablet box from his pocket and had managed to dry swallow one before the paralysis forced him to squat beside the dead man. He fought against the narcoleptic symptoms and managed to prevent his eyes from totally closing.

There was the sound of a heavy tread descending the stairs and Jimmy appeared in James's field of vision. He was blowing on the knuckles of his fist as he looked down at the investigator with a surprised expression.

'Did the bastard hit you coming down?' Receiving no answer he bent closer to look into James's eyes just as feeling began to return and he blinked at Jimmy. 'You're not dead like 'im then?' James shook his head and with some difficulty pushed himself upright.

'Just a touch of narcolepsy,' he explained which was greeted with a blank look and a shrug of the shoulders.

'Whatever, mate,' Jimmy grunted and then looked down at the dead man with total indifference until a flicker of irritation began crossing his face.

'Shit! Now I've got another one to get rid of,' he muttered more to himself than to James who was getting to his feet and feeling twinges of pain in his side.

'What will you do with him?' James asked as he closed the front door to prevent any idle passersby from looking in and seeing the body.

'Same as the other,' Jimmy said. 'I'll take him down to my brother's pigsties late tonight. Are you able to give me hand to get him into the backyard?'

'No problem, Jimmy.'

As the two men struggled to carry Brian along the passageway to the back door Jennifer came down the stairs with Candy following closely.

'Is he alright?' she asked James as they went into the untidy backyard and put Brian down.

'Perfect, luv,' Jimmy said and then laughed as he tossed some old potato sacks over the corpse. 'He's got to be alright 'cos he's brown bread.'

'Oh, Lord!' Jennifer was visibly shocked.

'Nah, you won't need him, luv, cos' this bastard won't be bothering you any more.'

Candy put her arm around Jimmy's waist and hugged him tightly. 'He's my Superman, y'know,' she declared proudly. The mismatched couple laughed and went back into the house while James put his arms around the trembling detective.

'I had just reached the first floor when that man caught hold of my arm and slapped my face,' she said and flinched on remembering the blow. 'He said he knew who I was and that I had to tell him where you and the petri dish were. I asked him where the cauldron was and he laughed and said it was in Rackman's favourite bus. That's when Candy opened her door and called for Jimmy.' Jennifer looked down at the mound of old sacks. 'The rest you know. Candy's fellow took him by the neck until he released me and then he drew back that sledgehammer he calls a fist and hit the man. He literally flew backwards and then down the stairs with Jimmy walking down after him.'

James held her close while she sobbed into his chest and he could feel the holstered pistol that Briscoe had given her. She had clearly been too shocked by the close encounter to use it and he kissed the top of her head before leading her up to O'Rourke's apartment. He mouthed a silent 'thank you' to Candy who was just entering her apartment and she smiled before closing her door. The red light hanging over the door came on and Candy was back in business.

The bungalow was in darkness without any signs of life as Rackman's car came to a stop opposite the wicket gate. The two SIS officers with him had both been brainwashed into believing that the Illuminati dogma was the only way for civilization to survive and they blindly followed Rackman's orders without question. They went to the door and used the knocker while their superior remained in the back of the car, a Heckler & Koch submachine gun across his lap just in case Goodfellow resisted. His ear still throbbed and the crystal-clear memory of the firefight in the sand dunes made him grip the weapon's stock even tighter.

The hollow sound of the knocker echoed away down the hallway and they waited two more minutes before explosive action destroyed the lock and shattered the door frame. As the two men went from room to room searching for James and Jennifer the mobile phone in Rackman's pocket vibrated. It was Brian calling from London.

'Then follow and make sure. Call me back if you can confirm that it's Goodfellow.' He closed his phone and relayed Brian's message when the two men returned to report that the bungalow was empty.

There is a very good chance that the bastard has played a double bluff and that they're staying at O'Rourke's apartment, he thought self-assuredly. He instructed the driver to drive to Soho Square before using his mobile again to call a number he had written in his pocketbook. It rang eleven times before it was picked up.

He listened to the hiss of static for twelve seconds before speaking himself. 'I know it's you, Goodfellow,' he snarled. 'Have the damned courtesy to answer your bloody phone when it rings.'

The line remained silent.

'All I require from you is the petri dish, the real one this time. Give me that and you'll not see me or hear from me or the Illuminati ever again.'

'I suggest we arrange a meeting where we can swap our items.' James's voice was low and steady which belied the nervousness he was feeling.

'Swap items! What items? You give me the dish and I give you your lives,' His menacing tone hardened James's attitude.

'The dish for the ding and all it contains!'

'What if I take your friend's daughter again? I may not be so gentle this time.'

'Do that, Rackman, and I promise you'll never see the virus. I won't bother to do any deals. I shall immediately incinerate it.' James started to tremble. He was gambling with other people's lives.

'Then I will kill the little Chinese girl.'

'And the Illuminati will never see Western dominance over the Far East.'

There was a long moment of static hiss before Rackman spoke. 'Very well, Goodfellow,' he said while silently thinking that he would never give up the fortune, too. 'Where and when do you suggest?'

'I'll get back to you.' James cut the connection and then recorded the telephone number in his address book. He took Jennifer's hand. 'It seems the fish has taken the bait.'

'But we have nothing to offer when he strikes.'

'That's why I must organize the meeting to be entirely in our favour.' He kissed her and then began packing the travel bag.

'Why are we leaving?'

'They know we're here. Brian was phoning as he left The Three Greyhounds and started following you. Rackman doesn't have to think too hard to know where we are. He'll have a team here within a few minutes and I need to warn Feng and then the girls and Jimmy.'

'The body – what can Jimmy do about that now?'

James knew what the pimp had planned but he wasn't sure he could do it in broad daylight. He called the Forbidden City and when Jiao answered he asked for Feng. He explained that there was an element of danger in the air and that he should close the restaurant for a couple of days so that he and his family could visit friends in the country.

'There's no way cheap thugs are going to drive me out of my own home, James,' Feng declared and James could tell by his determined voice that no amount of arguing or telling him that they weren't cheap thugs but highly experienced agents would convince him to leave.

'Then at least make sure that Lin-Lin stays at home to prevent a repeat of the last time. Will you promise me that.'

'Okay, and I'll take a few tools from my garden shed to even up the odds.'

Having received this assurance James broke the connection and went to join Jennifer who had left the apartment. He was about to close the door behind them when he noticed that the corner of the living room carpet had curled up in one corner.

'Wait a moment,' he said and went across the room to pull the carpet back. The short piece of exposed floorboard rocked beneath the pressure of his hand and he levered it up with his penknife to reveal the cavity where O'Rourke had hidden his Glock. James slipped the weapon into his trouser waistband and dropping the spare magazine in his pocket he rejoined Jennifer.

They went downstairs and knocked on Scarlet's door and a thin, weasly-faced man opened it to peer at them with suspicion in his eyes.

'Wha' y'want?' he growled, holding a sharp flick knife in a hand tattooed with a skull. 'Tell Scarlet that some heavies are going to come and break down Sèan's door. Do not try to stop them as they are violent men.' Without waiting to hear the pimp say that he too could be a violent man James hurried down to Candy's apartment and went through the same routine. When Jimmy came to the door he volunteered to help dispose of the corpse in the backyard.

'Nah, thanks a lot but Alfie and I can manage and I guess we'd better do it now before your funny mates turn up.' He jerked a thumb upward which indicated that the tattooed pimp upstairs had to be Alfie. 'The little piggies can 'ave an early treat for dinner instead of waiting for breakfast.'

Candy grinned at his roguish laugh.

'You spoil your bloody brother rotten, you do, Jimmy,' she said and pulled his face down to kiss him on the lips.

Jennifer's hand flew to her mouth when she realized how Jimmy planned to make the dead man disappear and she hurried downstairs without saying a word. James thanked Jimmy for coming to Jennifer's aid and after a brief wave to Candy he went after her. James caught up with her halfway along the street and they hurried to Soho Square where Jennifer had parked the car.

'I'll never eat bacon again,' she muttered.

'You're right. From now on it'll be "Brian and eggs",' James said and laughed as he dodged her slap.

27

FENG CHOI FELT EERILY calm after being warned by James. Like his father, Wing Choi, he was quite capable of defending his family.

Wing Choi had been a skilled baker with a thriving business in a small fishing village. As a young man Wing had survived the Sino-Japanese war that had ravaged China and culminated in the Rape of Nanjing when thousands were slaughtered.

When the Japanese were finally defeated Wing kept his wife and newborn son from any harm while the communists and nationalists fought over the village by Hung-tse Lake that had been home to his family for many generations.

The red tide eventually swept Chiang Kai-shek's forces south and the nationalist capital of Nanjing fell yet again.

With some quick-thinking and natural cunning Wing Choi used his senior position in the village to calm rioting communist soldiers and prevent another massacre. During those dark days the name Choi shone brightly and was respected by all.

Young Feng had been raised in a strict yet quaintly reverent society that tolerated other values alongside those of the 'little red book'. However, Ah-lam, Feng's mother was denounced for reading from the Book of Revelations to her beloved toddler. Branded a follower of the 'evil cult' of Christianity she was publicly flogged for the crime and Feng and his father were forced to watch this public degradation. The imposed exorbitant fine destroyed Wing's bakery and livelihood and Ah-lam never recovered from her humiliation, hiding herself away from all public contact and dying within the year.

Wing was devastated for he had loved his wife dearly and had always tolerated her personal beliefs. Her death had not only destroyed his life but also any loyalty he had for the communist party. He gathered a few belongings together and what little savings he had before setting fire to the bakery. Those who had denounced Ah-lam would not take possession of his successful business. Taking Feng he disappeared into the night to begin a totally new life in Hong Kong.

The sheer vibrancy and non-stop commerce of the city was intoxicating and the small boy thrived. He into a handsome young man and under his father's guidance he learnt the skills of cooking and eventually became a *Red Board Chef* specializing in Szechuan cuisine.

It was on his twenty-eighth birthday that Feng met and fell deeply in love with a young woman called Jiao. She had achieved a *White Board Chef* level in the southern style of cuisine which complemented his own skills perfectly. They married and moved to the Aberdeen waterfront where they opened a small restaurant with the financial support of her parents. The reputation of their combined talents soon attracted many of the island's wealthier businessmen and they gladly accepted Wing's assistance in the kitchen.

One morning as Wing Choi unlocked the restaurant to take a delivery of rice, a triad gangster knifed him to death: protection money had been demanded and denied with fatal consequences. Heartbroken and disillusioned by the get-rich-quick society Feng decided to find a more secure life in England.

As the memory of his tragic past flashed through Feng's mind the irony of their current situation was clear – security was hard to find anywhere unless you were prepared to fight for what you had.

He took Jiao to one side and quietly explained the situation. She calmly accepted what he was saying and went to look for Lin-Lin while Feng left the restaurant by the back door.

The rain had stopped but the day was still made gloomy by threatening clouds stretching from one horizon to the other. He unlocked his garden shed, removed the false wall and slipped a pair of wind and fire wheels into his apron. He then took the second pair of butterfly swords he owned and a Golden Wood dojo cane.

Feng returned to the restaurant and placed the swords on the work surface within easy reach of them both and leant the ordinary-looking cane against the wall.

'I hope you will use the cane first if Rackman comes,' Jiao said in a low voice. 'You know the laws about excess force in cases of burglary.'

'My only wish is to use nothing but the power of speech but if that doesn't stop them – ' the sentence was left hanging and Feng kissed his wife on both cheeks and went to unlock the front door for the early evening business to begin.

As he slid the bolts back he saw that it had begun to rain again and that the glass was prettily patterned with cat's-paws. Most passing pedestrians had their umbrellas opened and were hurrying to their destinations, except for two men who were standing by their car opposite the Forbidden City and staring directly at him.

Feng relocked the door, turned the sign back to *CLOSED* and returned to the kitchen where Jiao was prepping noodles and rice. 'We're not opening tonight, Jiao. I have a feeling we may have company and I cannot take any chances with customers on the premises.'

'I'll put Lin-Lin in the storeroom.' Liao seemed undisturbed by the news as she put the pan she was carrying down and went to find their daughter.

He returned to the front door and saw that the two men were no longer there. They've gone to the back, he thought as he hurried back to the kitchen.

'The storeroom. Go now,' he instructed and Jiao moved a wheeled trolley to one side revealing a trapdoor in the floor. She pulled on the iron ring and encouraged her daughter to descend into the cool subterranean pantry. Lin-Lin gave her father a quick hug and the two disappeared.

As Feng replaced the trolley and hurried into the short passage leading to the back door he heard the sound of breaking glass. A gloved hand was coming through the broken pane and reaching for the lock. Feng took one of the spiked metal discs from his apron and threw it in one well-practised move.

There was a scream outside and the hand, minus a forefinger, was rapidly withdrawn and the distorted shadow beyond the rippled glass moved away. There was an angry shout from a man outside and a thunderous crash against the doorframe. The second man was determined to enter.

Feng rushed back into the restaurant, snatched up the butterfly swords and returned to the back room just as a burly man rushed in with a large automatic held at his side. Feng Choi became *Yinhu–wu duan*, the Silver Tiger and crossed the room in a blur of movements; before the man could raise his weapon razor-sharp sword blades were crossed at his throat.

'Drop the gun or drop dead,' Feng hissed in the man's face.

Rackman's agent paled and the automatic slipped from his fingers to clatter on the tiled floor. Their faces were only inches apart and Feng could see beads of perspiration running from the man's hairline.

'What is your name?'

'Paul Osmond,' the agent stuttered

'Where's your partner, Paul, and where's Rackman?'

'Rackman didn't come with us and my partner went to the car to bandage his finger, or what's left of it.'

'Paul, I want you to give Rackman this message. If he or any of his thugs come within a mile of the Forbidden City or any member of my family I will remove their heads.' One of the crossed blades slid slightly and Osmond flinched as a small cut was made in the side of his neck. 'Do you understand me, Paul?' Using the man's first name seemed to make the threat more terrifying.

'Yes, yes,' he stammered.

'Then I will let you leave now to deliver my message,' the Silver Tiger said and the lethal cross was withdrawn from Osmond's neck. The agent took a step back, turned and fled down the passage to leave by the broken door.

Feng suddenly went cold and began shaking as the *Yinhu–wu duan* persona disappeared and the genial chef returned. He put the butterfly swords on a top shelf, put the automatic in an old ginger jar and went to open the trapdoor. Liao ran up the steps and threw her arms around him immediately followed by Lin-Lin.

'They won't be back,' he promised, crossing his fingers behind his back.

'You must give James and Jenny a call and let them know Rackman's been here,' Liao said as they went into the kitchen to make a pot of tea. Feng nodded and used the restaurant landline to make the call.

Finding the door locked and the interior in darkness James feared the worst and banged on the wood with his fist while Jennifer stood behind him looking round at the empty street with wary eyes. The lights came on suddenly and seeing that it was his friends outside Feng beamed and quickly unlocked the door.

Lin-Lin ran across the room to hug them both and a smiling Jiao emerged from the kitchen door with obvious relief.

'Is everything okay, Feng,' Jennifer asked as James shook his friend's hand.

'We're fine, Jennifer. I don't think they'll be returning here in a hurry,' Feng replied. 'What's been happening to you in London?'

James gave him a quick rundown on the events in Greek Street after Jiao had brought a pot of green tea and cups. Lin-Lin deliberately placed a plate of her mother's sesame biscuits in front of James knowing how much he loved them.

Reaching the point when Feng had called him, James unbuckled the belt and returned the butterfly swords. 'Thanks for the loan but luckily I had no need to use them.'

'It was lucky I had two pair or you would have found us in a sorrier condition on your arrival,' Feng said as he put them on the floor beside his seat.

'What's our next move, James?' Jennifer asked.

'I must call Rackman and arrange the handover,' James said with a thoughtful expression.

Jennifer gave a single *tut* of frustration. 'As I said before, we have nothing to exchange for the *ding*.'

'That's something he doesn't know.'

'But he'll find out at the exchange time and then there'll be hell to pay,' Feng said. 'And where do you plan your rendezvous will take place?'

'Definitely not where he's got the *ding*.' James gave a secret smile. 'If you recall Jenny, when Brian spoke to you outside Candy's apartment he said that the *ding* was being kept on Rackman's favourite bus.'

'That's right, but that could be anything.'

'Not anything. Senior SIS officers are constantly moving around the country and over to the continent so what's the easiest and fastest form of transport they could use?' There was a long silence until Lin-Lin put her hand up as though she was in school. James encouraged her with a smile.

'James Bond always used very fast cars, hovercrafts or airplanes when *he* was in a hurry,' she said gleefully.

'Give that clever girl an ice cream,' James said pinching her cheek affectionately.

'Lydd Airport,' Jennifer exclaimed as the answer hit her like a bolt of lightning. 'Rackman keeps a plane there which is what the late Brian referred to as his bus.'

'The *ding* is on a plane?' Feng asked with a puzzled look.

'That's right. So, first things first, I shall arrange a meeting with Rackman which I hope will take place in a remote part of East Steading Common.'

'But we'll be driving to the airport instead.' Jennifer stood up in her excitement. 'We need never meet or deal with the bloody man.'

'There will inevitably be a meeting but it won't involve pleasant deals. When he learns how we've tricked him he'll come with all guns blazing and therefore we have to lay a trap that also involves Sergeant Briscoe. That way we'll be legally within our rights to defend ourselves should it come to a violent conflict.'

'I'll call him now,' Jenny said.

'We don't want to do that until all arrangements are in place and we're already at the airport. I don't want Tilley sending armed response teams to any of the locations until we have recovered Feng's inheritance.'

'Tilley?'

'Look, we're claiming that a Secret Intelligence Service officer is an Illuminati terrorist planning an attack on a country that will engulf the whole world in a war of inestimable proportions. If Inspector Tilley learns of this from Briscoe he'll be obliged to tell his superior and then it'll travel up to Chief Constable who will take immediate action.'

Jenny nodded but Jiao still remained puzzled. 'But shouldn't Rackman be apprehended as soon as possible?' she asked.

'I agree, Jiao,' James said. 'But if we act too soon Feng may not have time to put together the provenance proving ancestral ownership of the artefacts. They would simply be classified as treasure trove and end up in a British Museum or Beijing after a big political row; we also lack tangible evidence against Rackman.'

They all sat in silence thinking about what James had said before he stood up and dialled the number he had stored in the phone's memory.

'It's about time you called, Goodfellow,' Rackman snarled. 'Where and when shall we meet?'

'I suggest by the two oak trees on the far side of East Steading Common at ten o'clock tomorrow morning.'

'Any particular reason for there and at that time?'

'None, other than it's a quiet place and nobody will be about.'

'Agreed. Just make sure you bring the petri dish!' The line went dead and James closed the phone and gave the thumbs up sign to his friends. There was a collective sigh from the adults that made Lin-Lin, who had been unable to understand the meaning of everything discussed, start laughing. With the tension broken they all started talking at once until James held his hand up.

'Nothing changes, Feng. You must still be vigilant and make sure you keep Lin-Lin at home with you both at all times. I'll drive to Lydd tonight and Jenny can go and see Briscoe as soon as I phone to confirm I've got the artefacts.'

'I'm going with you, James,' Jennifer said in an adamant tone.

'You need to be here to explain everything to –'

'I can use the phone for that and there's a chance you may need the help of a police officer to cut any red tape you face with the airport security people.'

James accepted Jennifer's logic and after bidding their friends farewell they returned to the chaos that was James's apartment to prepare for the long drive to Lydd airport.

The evening sky had cleared by the time they began driving and the rising moon was bathing the countryside in a silvery light. As they moved further into the countryside hedgerows were beginning to glisten under a light covering of night dew and occasionally a solitary bat flittered over the road. Jennifer found the peaceful, romantic scene relaxing and she leant her head against his shoulder.

They had passed through the town of Hurst Green when James calculated that the set of lights behind had been with them for the last ten miles. He made a left-hand turn to take a minor road and then took the next small lane to pass through the densely wooded area.

'They're still there,' Jennifer said grimly, having noticed James's decision to leave the main highway.

'I'll lose them near Peasmarsh,' he muttered. The road had begun to wind sharply with trees blocking the view ahead and after every turn James searched for any driveway or farm track to use as a bolt-hole.

They had driven in silence for another two miles before Jennifer suddenly spoke. 'There, there's a track.'

James braked hard and spun the wheel. As he accelerated into the cover he switched off the lights and kept his foot down. They bounced along the wheel-rutted dirt road until it turned suddenly to the right and James stopped the car. He powered his window down and listened.

'I can hear it,' Jennifer whispered as the sound of a car drew near and she slipped her hand beneath her coat to grip the holstered automatic. The flicker of halogen lights could be seen through the hedgerow and without slowing it flashed past the farm track and continued along the road to Rye.

'He thinks we're going to Rye so I think it's time we disappointed him and took a sneakier route to the airport.'

Thirty minutes later they had entered Lydd airport and were parking the car. He checked his watch and saw that it was just coming up to nine o'clock.

'I did a website search earlier and I believe that is where they park the private aircraft,' Jennifer said, pointing to a large hangar directly ahead of them. There didn't appear to be anything to stop them wandering about and they left the car and swiftly strode round the building as though they were legitimately going somewhere until they saw a side door that was standing wide open.

'That's handy,' James murmured and went in to be confronted by rows of light aircraft that sparkled beneath the brilliant fluorescent lighting. 'There must be over a million pounds parked here without any sign of security.'

'But how the hell can we ask which one is Rackman's without causing suspicion?' Jenny muttered when she spotted a blue-overalled engineer on the far side of the hangar. He had the cowling open on a Piper Saratoga and was adjusting something within a maze of piping with a torsion wrench.

'We ask,' James said as he boldly strode across the polished concrete. Jennifer trotted to keep up with him. 'Flash your warrant card and say that we need to check out a rumour that the aircraft was being used for smuggling stolen antiques.'

'That's not exactly a story, it's what we're actually doing.'

'Which makes your questioning sound more credible.'

The elderly engineer looked up as they approached. 'Do you have an official pass to enter this building?' he asked, suspicion apparent on his tanned and deeply creased features.

'Will this do, sir,' Jennifer asked holding up her warrant card.

The man peered closely while wiping his hands on an oily rag. 'You're a long way from your patch.'

'We wish to inspect a plane belonging to a Mr Rackman. I have reason to believe he stores it here.'

'Why do you want to see it?' he inquired, his curiosity peaking.

'We have reason to believe it is being used for smuggling purposes, what is your name, sir?'

'Harold Parks.'

'Would you tell us if the plane is here, Mr Parks?'

Putting his wrench down Harold crooked his finger and led them down the line of planes to where a black Cessna 172 was parked. 'I have a service contract with Mr Rackman and to be quite honest I'm not surprised he's up to something or other. He's always nipping off across the Channel at all times of the day. Sometimes he gets clearance to take off in the middle of the night.

They walked under the wing and stopped by the door. 'Do you have the key?' James asked.

'I use a duplicate he gave me to run the engine occasionally and do other mechanical checks,' Harold said.

Jennifer held her hand out and Harold frowned before taking a large ring of keys from his overall pocket and selected one to open the door. James climbed in to sit in one of the four calf-skin seats, he looked around but found nothing.

'Luggage space?' Jennifer asked and Harold selected another key and unlatched a panel further down the fuselage. Taking her torch she lent into the compartment that was empty except for a wooden crate.

'Looks like this is it,' James murmured as he joined her and reached in to slide the heavy crate towards the entrance.

'What's that?' Harold asked as he peered over Jennifer's shoulder. She could feel his warm, tobacco-perfumed breath stirring the short hairs of her neck.

'You'll have to move away, sir, this may be important evidence,' she said officiously and Harold backed away. She turned to help James lift the crate from the plane and lower it to the floor.

'Do you have a crowbar?' James asked and Harold went to his toolbox and returned with a large screwdriver.

'There's not much call for a crowbar around these expensive pieces of engineering,' he said. 'Will this do?'

A few seconds of levering and the top came free. James pulled out the straw packing to reveal the cauldron wound in bubble-wrap.

'This is the stolen antique, Constable,' James said in a calm, serious voice for the sake of listening ears even though a frisson of excitement was running through his body.

Jennifer nodded, equally grave in expression and turned to Harold. 'This is what we came for, sir, and I want you to leave and not say anything to anyone about the requisitioning of stolen property.' She had turned rather quickly, which accidentally flipped her jacket open, giving the man a glimpse of her holstered weapon. 'Do you understand what I'm saying?'

Harold agreed readily and after he had relocked the Cessna he went back to pack away his tools. James and Jennifer carried the crate between them and left the hangar followed by Harold who turned off the lights and locked the side door. He gave the couple a brief wave and hurried across the car park to an old Ford Focus.

Jennifer opened their car with the remote and they manhandled the crate into the boot. They drove out of the car park and took the road back towards the Cinque Port of Rye while James used his mobile to tell Feng that they had recovered the *ding*.

A dark car with halogen lights pulled out of the car park a few seconds later. Rackman's suspicious mind had reasoned that James Goodfellow wouldn't be meeting him on the common and had followed him from the moment he left the Forbidden City.

Rackman had lost them in the last few miles to the coast but guessed that Goodfellow had somehow stumbled on the *ding's* hiding place and was going there. He had watched from the open door as the old engineer showed them to his plane and unlocked the luggage compartment.

While the crate was being carried to their car he had followed Harold and slipped into the passenger seat beside him. The surprised man didn't have time to cry out before the vengeful stiletto slipped into his heart.

28

ENGLAND

O'ROURKE COLLECTED HIS CASE and the long package from the carousel and strode confidently through the customs green zone. Within twenty minutes the Heathrow Express had whisked him into central London where he hailed a taxi.

As he entered the familiar house on Greek Street he was confronted by Jimmy. 'Everyfing's gawn, Seán,' he said in his usual cryptic manner except this time it was accompanied by a very unusual smile.

'What's gone, Jimmy?' O'Rourke was baffled by his greeting.

'The bugger who woz slapping your friend's woman round is well gawn.'

James still looked at the man blankly and Candy's pimp went into a slightly longer explanation of the events that had taken place when James and Jennifer had visited O'Rourke's apartment.

'So, whoever he was is now down on the farm?' he asked.

'Nah. He's gawn completely. The pigs don't leave anything if they can 'elp it.'

O'Rourke went a trifle green at the mental picture he had conjured and then forced a smile onto his face as he tucked a fifty-pound note in the top of the string vest. 'Thanks for all your help, Jimmy. It's much appreciated by all of us.'

The pimp nodded. 'Pleasure, mate,' he muttered and his face returned to it's normal pugnacious appearance before he disappeared back into Candy's apartment.

As the Irishman climbed to the second floor Scarlet's door creaked open and he could see the pinched features of Alfie peering out through the narrow gap. The moment he realized he had been seen Alfie slammed the door shut.

O'Rourke shrugged and entered his apartment. He tossed his case onto the bed and switched the kettle on to make tea. As he tore away the phony museum seals and unpacked Dragon's Breath the phone on the bedside table rang.

'Welcome home, Mr O'Rourke,' a familiar voice rasped and O'Rourke knew that his troubles had not yet come to an end.

'What do you want, Rackman?' he asked.

'Your head, traitor.' The line went dead and O'Rourke closed the phone and tossed it onto the bed beside his unopened case. How did Rackman know I'd arrived back in the country, he thought, and then he recalled the expression on Alfie's face a few minutes earlier. 'Bloody weasel would sell his own mother,' he murmured to himself as he went to the corner of the living room and lifted the carpet. It was only a matter of seconds before he discovered that his beloved Glock and the spare magazines had disappeared. The only weapon he now possessed was the ancient Chinese sword.

O'Rourke wasn't the only person to fly in from Hong Kong and patiently stand by the luggage carousel as it endlessly went round. Ming-húa's bag emerged first through the opening in the wall and he waited until O'Rourke had retrieved his luggage before following him at a discreet distance through customs and out of the airport terminal. He took the third taxi in the rank and instructed the driver to follow O'Rourke's vehicle.

The chubby driver turned in his seat and gave him a strange look. 'You a secret agent, private eye or something, mate?' he asked but the man behind remained silent. Ming-húa opened his laptop and began writing an email message with elegantly long fingers that danced expertly on the keyboard.

Ming-húa had not been raised as a triad. He was brought up by wet nurses and then by an aunt in a protected environment where the harsh truth about his father's business and his associates was kept at a great distance.

Pengfei Shing had loved his son from the first day he had held him in his arms and felt his forefinger being gripped by the tiniest of hands. Although his mother died after a very difficult twenty-hour labour the baby survived. The little infant helped dull the pain of being a widower and as Ming-húa grew Pengfei Shing had visions of him being his successor and then becoming a powerful figure in Chinese politics.

Ming-húa was ten when he was sent to England and later went on to study at Cambridge. He worked hard to gain a degree in Applied Economics that his father thought would help him to gain the business acumen needed for his various interests.

When he returned to Hong Kong he partially learnt the true nature of the Shing organisation. At first he had been horrified by the hidden layers of violence and soul-destroying corruption he had been born into but, as the months passed, he grew to accept that it had been the only way his family could survive in the highly competitive markets his father had chosen to operate in. The young man decided to close his eyes and take a trading position with a legitimate company in London.

Ming-húa was unaware of O'Rourke until that fateful day when his father was killed. As promised by the Irishman he had received a call from the government agent but had reached an impasse on dissolving certain aspects of the family business. He had put down the phone regretting that he had ever let the *gweilo* leave unharmed and he was determined on a new course of action that would avenge his father.

Despite the cabbie's continuous stream of cheerful banter the handsome Chinese didn't respond to any questions and remained bolt upright with his hands resting on the laptop. He stared unseeing at the road unrolling before them while reliving the moment of his father's beheading.

His eyes narrowed and he slipped the smartphone from his pocket and tapped in a number. It rang for a full minute before the line opened and a woman's familiar voice answered.

'Who's calling, please?'

The soft, hypnotic lilt to the voice brought back a flood of memories. When he first arrived in Cambridge he had been totally unaware that his father had arranged covert protection for him; the first contact contrived took place on a pleasant summer's afternoon.

A young woman seemingly stumbled and fell on the footpath that ran beside the River Cam. Ming-húa who had been reclining on the bank with a handbook on econometrics leapt to his feet and gallantly went to her aid.

Almond-shaped honey-brown eyes that seemed to promise more than the whispered 'thank you' looked steadily into his as he helped her to get up. She was beautiful and shapely and he instantly fell in love.

He inquired if she was okay and on being assured that she was he nervously invited her to join him for a coffee; to his surprise she said yes. As they sipped their Arabica coffee he discovered that she ran a headhunting company in London and was in Cambridge to recruit graduates for a portfolio of blue-chip companies.

When he could find the time between lectures they met in the same Cambridge coffee house talking about the old country that he could only vaguely remember. It wasn't long before she found herself being attracted to the quick wit and intelligence of the good-looking young man and invited him to her apartment in London. On his third visit the undercover triad bodyguard fulfilled her four-year contract with Pengfei Shing to care for his son's body by taking him to her bed.

After his graduation and they had parted with promises to meet again that Ming-húa, on his return to Hong Kong, learnt from his father the real reason the woman had shown an interest in him. With a bitter heart he retreated to his personal suite for days before calming down enough to emerge and apologise to his father for his childish behaviour; he then applied for a junior position with a stock-brokerage in Canary Wharf.

Although the woman had hardened his heart Ming-húa's love for his father never waned. Unable to accept that his father was a criminal he made excuses to himself that Pengfei's violent actions were only to defend the honour of the Shing family.

Without any positive influences from his elders he never knew he had other options way in life and on his twenty-fifth birthday he was easily persuaded by his father to return to Hong Kong to take a sacred oath.

During a sky-shattering storm his father and twenty senior members witnessed as Ming-húa became a triad.

From that day the young man's sole aim in life was to increase the size of the organization and to uphold family 'honour'. The exposure of his own father's lack of honour and the ease with which he chose to kill his own son had shocked Ming-húa to the core and he accepted his father's assassination as being just. However, the whispers racing through the organization accusing him of patricide, the most dishonourable act of a son, changed his opinion.

'Who is that, please?' the voice repeated.

'Am I speaking to Sying?' Ming-húa asked in a low voice while watching the driver for any signs that he could overhear the conversation; the triad confirmed who she was without recognizing his voice.

'Then I will require your help. My name is Ming-húa, son of the late Pengfei Shing. I believe I have had the pleasure of your acquaintance many years ago.'

There was an audible gasp. 'Yes, sir. We met in Cambridge.' Sying had already learnt on the triad grapevine that the Mountain Master had been assassinated and knew that she was now talking to the new leader of the Hong Kong triads and not just a student she had seduced. She immediately changed the tone of her voice to one of deference. 'How can I help you, honourable sir?'

'I will come to you within two hours. Where shall we meet?'

Sying quickly gave her address but before she could add anything more Ming-húa rang off and went back to staring silently at the lines of traffic ahead.

In the inimitable manner of London cabbies the driver tried to elicit a little information from his fare but gave up after ten minutes and spent the rest of the journey listening to U2 tracks on his headphones.

The green meadows and woodlands soon changed to become sprawling suburbs that radiated out from the dense heart of London and Ming-húa leant forward to study the buildings lining the streets as though carrying out a reconnaissance operation for future use.

Ming-húa's taxi turned into Greek Street and came to a halt outside a building with an open front door. The three nameplates on the doorframe were too small for Ming-húa to be able to read as he went past but he felt sure that one would read 'O'Rourke'.

'Want me to stop, guv?' the cabbie asked as he slowed down.

Ming-húa looked back just in time to see O'Rourke disappear into the doorway and knew he had tracked the rabbit to its warren. He shook his head and gave Sying's address.

Jennifer had just entered a heavily wooded stretch of the road when she became aware that the car lights that had been with them for a number of miles were now creeping closer.

'I think we're being followed, James,' she said as she adjusted the rear-view mirror to dim the glare reflecting straight into her eyes. 'It's been with us for the last six miles and I think the driver's now making his move.'

James glanced back over his shoulder and then slipped his hand beneath her jacket and took the Glock from its holster.

'Tighten your belt, James, we're in for a bumpy ride.' Jennifer put her foot down and they began cornering at speeds far exceeding normal safety limits. The advanced driving course had raised her skill level way above average and she was intimately familiar with the car's capabilities.

Tyres screeched in protest as she raced away from the following car and in a long blind corner she suddenly hit the brakes; James was thrown against the door as the car swung to the other side of the road. Jennifer had spotted an abnormal gap in the trees and she quickly killed the lights as they accelerated up the narrow by-road and were shrouded in the darkness of the forest.

'Copycat,' James muttered with a grin as he recalled his own manoeuvre when driving to the airport.

The car instinctively followed the deep ruts in the earth that curved out of sight of the main road and after fifty metres Jennifer braked to a juddering standstill.

James pushed himself upright and expelled the breath he had been holding. 'Bloody hell,' he exclaimed. 'Who taught you to drive. Lewis Hamilton?'

Jennifer grinned as she looked back through the trees and caught a glimpse of lights flashing past the entrance to their lane. 'What's the plan now?' she asked. 'Rackman thinks we have the artefact and he'll be visiting your place, the restaurant and possibly my home, too.'

'We have to end this some time, Jenny. I would prefer that it doesn't happen anywhere near the Choi family as they've already been through enough trouble, but Rackman knows where I live. Also, if we hide too well it will protract the situation and I'd like to make it easy for him to find us.'

'I guess that means we'll be staying at your place so I'll notify Briscoe that we expect Rackman to make his move there.'

'There is the option of making a pre-emptive strike on the bastard in his own home but without any evidence it would be a waste of time. Our only chance is to have a witness when he attempts to kill me.' James sighed as he settled down for the drive back to East Steading.

It was close to midnight when Jennifer drove past the Forbidden City and parked in the next side street. Rain was gently stippling the windscreen as they got out and went to the boot to lift the small crate out. After cautiously checking the main street they dodged from one shop canopy to the next to make their way to Goodfellow Investigations.

The streets seemed deserted and they entered the building and climbed the stairs to the apartment with the crate awkwardly held between them.

They dried each other's hair with warm, fresh towels before stripping off their wet things and donning clean clothes. Jennifer prepared a light snack and James made a jardinière of Blue Mountain coffee. They settled down amidst the soft cushions that were scattered on the comfortable settee.

'What do we do now?' Jennifer mumbled through a mouthful of hot, buttered toast.

'We wait and let Rackman make the next move.'

'Dangerous?' Jennifer said as she used her phone to speed-dial.

'It's a bit late to be calling Briscoe now, isn't it?'

'He won't mind when he hears what's been happening.' There was pause before the sergeant answered and then Jennifer launched into her report of events since her last call. There was another pause as she listened and then she closed the phone. 'He said he'll be coming early tomorrow morning and he'll be bringing Constable Shawcross as extra support.'

'Will they both be armed?' James asked.

'Oh damn, of all the people he chose he had to go and pick Shawcross!' Jennifer exclaimed.

'You don't like him?'

'He doesn't like me and he certainly doesn't like you. If anyone was going to take potshots at you I'm sure he'd step to one side and let them get on with it.'

'Why do you think that?'

'He envies you and dislikes me for not liking him. Ever since I joined the force at East Steading he's been trying to get into my knickers and when I started going out with you he was furious.'

James began to laugh but immediately stopped and put a finger to his lips when he heard the front doorbell chime. He went into the front room and opened the window to see who was standing below. A dark figure was hunched against the rain and was standing too close to the door to be identified. James closed the window and shook the drops of moisture from his hair as he went downstairs.

'I'll see who it is while you stay at the top of the stairs with the gun,' he whispered before leaving. When James reached the door two flights down she was waiting at the top with the Glock chambered and ready to fire. He unlocked the door to find a thoroughly saturated O'Rourke outside.

'You took your bloody time,' he exclaimed as he pushed past James and entered the small area loosely called a lobby. 'Kittens have been drowned more humanely.'

James laughed and relocked the door. 'I was expecting somebody a bit more murderous than you, Séan.'

'I always knew you English were incapable of a warm welcome.'

'Would a whisky be warm enough?'

'Jameson?'

James laughed as he led the way upstairs. 'Don't push your luck, Séan.'

O'Rourke raised both his hands when he saw Jennifer standing at the top with the automatic in her hand. 'I surrender,' he exclaimed and she gave a laugh of relief.

When they were settled in the living room James showed him the crated ding and gave the Irishman a quick debriefing on what had happened. O'Rourke's face became grim and businesslike as he mentally ran through the options they had left.

'We have to make it a better trap than simply waiting here for him to strike,' O'Rourke said when James had finished. 'You don't know how many men Rackman can still command and your two front doors and a flight of stairs won't stop a hit squad of ex-SIS men with fully automatic military weapons.'

'What do you suggest?' Jennifer asked.

'The general who picks his ground wins the battle. That was the first lesson I learnt in South Armagh,' O'Rourke said as he held out his glass to be refilled.

'Where shall our battlefield be?'

29

THE TAXI DROPPED MING-HÚA outside the supermarket and following Sying's instructions he cut through to Lisle Street. As he approached the address a door opened and a giant stepped out, bowed and waved him inside. Ming-húa had made it clear that he was expected and he swept past with the hint of a nod and climbed the steep staircase.

The moment he had taken the last step a red lacquered door swung open on silent hinges and he entered to be faced by two heavily tattooed men. They were stripped to the waist and their muscular torsos gleamed with oil. Sword scabbards were held in the left hand and they both bowed deeply to show their respect for the Mountain Master.

'I wish to see the Two-Headed Dragon,' he snapped. The men pulled aside a crimson silk curtain that hung from ceiling to floor to reveal Sying sitting on a silk divan. She was just as beautiful as the day he had finished college and she bid him farewell at the airport, except this time she seemed much harder. Sying wore a charcoal pinstripe suit and her long jet-black hair had been rolled into a bun and held in place with ornate needles of silver. Brown eyes studied the handsome man and the tip of her tongue ran over her full lips until they glistened. For one brief moment Ming-húa was rendered speechless but the memory of her treachery brought him back to the present; she had been his father's servant, paid solely to keep his son happy.

'You are looking well, Sying,' he snapped in a businesslike tone.

'As do you, Ming-húa. I was sorry to hear of your father's unfortunate passing,' she purred. 'You have my deepest sympathy.'

'For my father or sympathy for what you did to me?'

Sying rocked back at the sudden surge of rage in his voice.

'He told me that he paid you to entertain me for the time I was at college,' Ming-húa shouted. 'You took his money to fuck me, you whore!'

'No! No! I was paid to provide you with protection but at the time I couldn't help falling in love with you.'

'Liar! If that were true you would at least have called me after I had returned home and explained why you trapped me into a false relationship.'

'I couldn't,' she protested. 'You father forbade it on pain of death.'

'How can you prove that, my father is dead,' he spat out, his eyes flashing dangerously. 'There was only one thing he told me about you, Sying, and that was that you're the triad armourer for all of this country.'

'That's true, my master,' Sying said with eyelids lowered.

'Good. I need the best sword and an effectively silenced pistol,' he demanded and Sying rose to her feet to operate the catch that opened the secret room. 'I also need to know everything about Mr Séan O'Rourke.'

Sying remained expressionless but her mind raced as she waited for the armoury door to open. He only needs information about Séan for one reason, she thought; he plans to kill him. Sying felt a sudden chill that made the hairs on her neck stir.

Ming-húa raised an eyebrow in appreciation of the walls lined with every type of weapon as the woman glided into the room in a sinuous manner that no longer had the power to arouse him.

While running her eyes over the racked guns she coldly listed all she knew about the Irishman except for the times they had had passionate, sweaty sex on the divan behind her. She even considered taking one of the weapons and killing the new Mountain Master herself but she knew that would only result in the wrath of the whole triad organization coming down on her. Instead she selected an oddly shaped pistol and a sheathed sword which she placed on a black lacquered table. As he picked up the long-barrelled handgun she told gave him the specification.

'That, sir, is a sanitized Welrod suppressed pistol. It has no markings to show who made it or its country of origin. It has a very easy bolt action and the 9mm rounds are magazine fed. Subsonic bullets produce a 73dB sound when fired and they have a range of twenty-three metres down to point blank –'

Ming-húa held his hand up to stop the flow of information. 'It'll do the job I have for it. Now, what about the sword? It has to have a pedigree as well as a quality edge as it needs to fulfil my obligation to honour my late father.'

Sying picked up the *Jian* by the onyx hilt and slid the 25" Damascus steel blade noiselessly from the delicate, ivory-inlaid sheath.

'This is an Angel sword and is made from the very best steel. It is my own and it has a value of £18,000.' She rested the blade on her arm and presented the hilt to Ming-húa. 'It has never been used.'

'A generous gift, Sying,' he said softly as he gripped the hilt and slid the razor sharp edge across her forearm, cutting through the expensive cloth. She bit her lip as the sting of the shallow cut took effect and then she forced a smile.

'You've had the honour of being the first blood and the Angel is no longer a virgin.'

'It was my pleasure, honourable sir,' she murmured and then turned away as she began weeping softly.

'What is wrong?' Ming-húa demanded to know as he swung the surprisingly light sword in a figure of eight pattern in the air.

Sying sat on the divan and wiped her eyes with a lace handkerchief. 'I was remembering the wonderful times we had in Cambridge,' she exclaimed emotionally. 'The moments we kissed and made love –'

'Love!' Ming-húa shouted. 'You call spreading your legs for money love? Hah! You're well titled, Two-Headed Dragon? Bitch! For you certainly presented only one of your two faces to me.'

'It wasn't like that. You make it sound so sordid.

'But it was, wasn't it? I believed you were my first love, someone I could spend the rest of my life with and then I am betrayed and discover I love a common whore.'

Ming-húa advanced on the woman with a levelled sword until the tip was only inches from the breast where once he rested his head. The memory of their summer idylls, lying on the riverbank and watching water boatmen skating across the mirror-calm surface could no longer be summoned and he flicked the sword to let the blade slice her cheek.

'I should kill you but I find it beneath my position as the Mountain Master to stoop so low.' Ming-húa Shing turned away, sheathed the sword and slipped the Welrod inside his jacket. 'Goodbye, Sying.' There was a sad finality to his voice and he went through the silk curtains.

The two swordsmen stood by the door with confused expressions on their faces for they had heard the whole conversation and their loyalty had become divided. Ming-húa advanced on them and they parted to let him leave

'There is no honour in working for a prostitute,' he murmured as he stood between them. 'You know what to do.'

As Ming-húa Shing left the room the triads bowed low. Then they drew their swords and went through the blood-red silk curtains to where Sying sat weeping.

At two in the morning after the third cafetièrre James came up with an idea to lay a trap for Richard Rackman. He rose to his feet and went to the window where he twitched the curtain to one side. Jennifer and O'Rourke stirred in their chairs to ease their stiffness and looked up expectantly.

'We're being watched by a man sitting in a dark blue Vauxhall that's parked across the road. I don't think it's Rackman but it is most probably one of his SIS men. Now that he knows where we are he'll be briefing the rest of his men before coming here,' he said.

'Then what?' O'Rourke asked with one raised eyebrow. 'Do we just wait for them to arrive?'

'No, I shall take the crate and leave now. I want you to wait five minutes or until you see the man in the car following me. That's when you'll also leave the apartment.'

'Do we follow him?' Jennifer asked with a worried look.

'O'Rourke will follow as my backup but I need you to stay with the Chois to act as their protection until Sergeant Briscoe and Shawcross arrive. You'll keep the Glock just in case Rackman doesn't take the bait and comes to search the Forbidden City as well as my place.'

'Where will you be going?'

'Not far; to the cemetery.'

'What!' O'Rourke exclaimed and he sat bolt upright with surprise.

'You aren't familiar with East Steading's municipal cemetery are you, Séan?' James asked and the Irishman shook his head. 'Well, it's extremely old and has hundreds of large tombstones and crypts that can conceal anyone who knows the place and wants to trap a rat.' James picked up the heavy crate. 'And this will be the bait.'

'What's to stop the man outside from just shooting you when you emerge and driving off with the crate?' O'Rourke said with a cynical expression.

'He won't kill me until he has instruction from Rackman to do so and by the time he gets permission I'll have reached the cemetery.'

James switched off the lights, went down the stairs and left the building while O'Rourke kept watch at the window. The Irishman slipped the automatic from its holster and opened the window slowly, prepared to intervene should the man in the car show any sign of attacking the private investigator.

James walked down the street with the crate cumbersomely held before him. He heard the click of a car door closing and then the heavy footfall of someone following. He briefly looked down at his wristwatch and as he had expected the streetlights were extinguished as the minute hand touched the hour.

It was only a five-minute walk to reach the huge wrought-iron gates but James continued on for another fifty yards before reaching the vandalized spot where youngsters and lovers had long ago pulled the chain-link fence to one side. He struggled through the gap with the crate and with feet crunching on the gravel pathway he hurried deep into the labyrinth of marble and granite monuments. Weeping angels with bowed heads and elaborately carved crosses closed in around him and he briefly paused to put the crate into a gap between two towering mausoleums. With mentally spoken apologies to any he may have desecrated James left the gravel path and silently circled round by jumping from one smooth gravestone to the next. In the deep silence that blanketed the dead he heard a brief musical tone and knew that his follower was close and that he was calling Rackman for instructions. James paused behind a block of marble that supported an eroded statue of Gabriel slaying the Devil.

'– I don't know why he came here,' James heard a voice whisper nearby and he froze like one of the many figures guarding those sleeping. 'Yes, he was carrying the crate. What do you want me to do?'

There was a long silence before James heard the musical tone as the phone was closed followed by the familiar sound of an automatic pistol being cocked. His death sentence had been pronounced.

James slowly moved away from the statue and his foot slipped on the lichen-covered gravestone. He stumbled and stepped onto the path with a rattle of gravel against masonry that sliced through the silence.

'Hold it there, Goodfellow,' a voice barked. James turned his head to make out a man wearing a dark trench coat and standing about ten feet behind him. He was pointing a mean-looking automatic at James's head. 'Where's the box?' he snapped. 'Tell me or I'll blow your fucking head off right now.'

'Do that and you'll be searching this cemetery for so long you'll need to reserve a plot for yourself,' James said loudly; his unspoken prayer that their voices would be heard was answered for the man's eyes suddenly widened and he fell forward. The gun he was gripping fired and the bullet ricocheted harmlessly off three gravestones before lodging in the trunk of a large yew tree.

James leapt forward, scooped up the weapon and crouched down and to look round. The fallen man was jerking in his death throes and James saw the thin handle of a throwing knife protruding over the collar of the man's coat.

'It's me, James,' O'Rourke called out softly as he stepped from behind a gothic edifice that glorified three generations of wool traders. He retrieved his knife and wiped it on the trench coat before slipping it back into its sheath beneath his jacket. 'I didn't want to use a firearm as it would have made a rather loud noise. Unfortunately his gun did so we had better get going before someone decides to investigate.'

'I doubt if anybody would have heard it at 3 am and if they did they would have thought it came from a backfiring car,' James said while giving O'Rourke a grateful nod for saving his life. 'Now we have two guns and we only have to wait for Rackman and his crew to come here and make their move.'

'How do you know he'll come into the graveyard?'

James nudged the dead man with his foot. 'I heard him phone.' He slipped the automatic into the waistband of his slacks and started to pull the man towards a newly dug grave. O'Rourke helped him until, with a final nudge of their toecaps, the dead man rolled into the black pit with a hollow, satisfying thump.

'By the way, where did you hide the *ding*?' O'Rourke asked as they made their way quietly back to the break in the fence.

'It's a very old artefact and therefore I hid it where dead things tend to gather,' James said with a mischievous wink.

'Everything that lies here is dead so it can't be too far. Can it?' O'Rourke asked with a puzzled expression.

'It's close but not here.'

James's enigmatic smile teased yet amused the Irishman.

Ming-húa alighted from the taxi in Chelsea and walked the short distance to Rackman's house. Sying had been very forthcoming with her information which included details of O'Rourke's involvement with the Illuminati. Ming-húa knew of the hate the organization felt towards triads and he hoped he could kill two birds with one stone.

Turning his collar up he strode along the poorly lit street until he was outside the attractive-looking property. All the curtains were tightly drawn and not a glimmer of light could be seen on the three floors. Ming-húa opened the gate on well-oiled hinges and went to the entrance to push the button beside the door. As he waited he took the Melrod from under his coat and chambered the first round.

The door swung open to reveal a broad-shouldered man without a jacket and wearing a shoulder holster over a blue striped cotton shirt. There was a low coughing sound and the man collapsed with a large hole in his face. Ming-húa stepped over the dead SIS agent and walked into the living room. Two men sat drinking whisky and watching a late-night movie. The Welrod coughed again and both died instantly, their glasses falling from lifeless hands to stain the pale cream carpet.

As he stepped back into the hallway a small, rat-faced man talking on a mobile phone appeared at the top of the stairs. His face suddenly registered shock on seeing the agent sprawled by the front door and an armed stranger at the foot of the stairs.

Ming-húa recognized the man by the description Sying had given him and he raised the Melrod. Rackman reacted fast and before Ming-húa could effectively aim and fire he had ducked to the left and out of sight.

The triad started to run up the stairs and then leapt back when a different man appeared with a Glock machine-gun and began firing randomly, spraying the walls and stairs with 9mm rounds.

Ming-húa waited until he heard the weapon click empty and the man changing magazines before coolly stepping out and shooting him in the stomach. The man fell forward with a crash, screaming with pain and tumbling down the stairs to where the triad was waiting. The Melrod coughed once more and the man's agony was ended.

'Come and talk to me, Rackman!' Ming-húa called out but there was no reply from above. He called again but on still receiving no answer he cautiously proceeded to the landing. A quick check of all the rooms, including those on the next floor, showed that the house was now empty. Ming-húa went to the end of the landing and found a set of servant stairs that led him down to an empty kitchen. There was a tray on the work surface that held six coffee mugs that were still steaming. Someone had been in the middle of making coffee for Rackman and his team when he was interrupted. An open door in the utility room leading out to a small garden told him that the rat-faced man and one other had flown the coop.

Ming-húa returned to the front door and after checking the street both ways he slipped the Melrod back into its holster and walked to the King's Road where he took a taxi to Victoria Station. He had a good idea where Rackman had gone and he planned to be there to greet him.

That would present another opportunity to avenge his father.

After O'Rourke had left to follow the man in the trench coat Jennifer went to the Forbidden City and repeatedly rang the doorbell until a light went on. Feng's familiar figure, wrapped in a terry-towel bathrobe stumbled towards the door rubbing sleep from his eyes. She could see that he was irritated beyond words and he glared through the glass door until his fuzzy mind cleared and he was able to recognize her. A puzzled grin appeared on his face as he held up his arm and pointed meaningfully at his wristwatch.

Do you know what time it is? he mouthed and Jennifer indicated with exaggerated hand gestures that he should unlock the door and quickly let her in. He shrugged, sprang the locks and the moment the door was opened Jennifer pushed her way in, slammed the door shut and reset all the locks.

'What's wrong, Jenny?' Feng said, startled by her nervous behaviour.

'We must lock every door and window and keep well out of sight,' she replied as she went to the wall switch and turned the lights off. 'Let's go into the kitchen and I'll explain what's happening.' They left the darkened restaurant to enter the brilliantly lit kitchen. 'And no lights please,' she added switching off the fluorescent tubes. Jennifer threw herself down into a chair and began relating the whole sequence of events and what was currently expected to happen down in the cemetery. Feng remained silent and when Jiao entered with a cavernous yawn and a question on her lips, he held his hand up to stop her from speaking until Jennifer had finished.

Having understood most of what Jennifer had been saying and why she had woken them at such a god-forsaken time in the morning Jiao became her usual practical self and lit the gas under a kettle for some tea. 'We need to stay calm and keep alert for any signs of trouble. I always find green tea is a wonderful tonic for times like this,' she said cheerfully and Feng chuckled, breaking the tension that had been hanging in the air.

'I don't think I've had times like this before, Jiao,' Jennifer said as Feng went to the kitchen door and held it ajar by placing a copper wok on the floor.

'I suggest that I take the first watch and sit here so that I can watch the street while you ladies get some rest,' Feng said. He took a ladder-back kitchen chair and positioned it at the door so that he had a clear view of the main window in the dining room that was now glinting with raindrops.

Jennifer unclipped her holster and placed the weapon in the man's lap. 'Only use it if our lives are threatened, Feng,' she whispered and he nodded solemnly. The two women went into the back room where they made themselves comfortable on the sofas. They talked softly for a little while before slipping into a weary sleep.

It was still an hour before sunrise and both James and O'Rourke, dampened by the soft rain, crouched motionless within the dark entrance to a mausoleum. Their eyes had now become accustomed to the dark as they swept the monochrome tombs, gravestones and memorial statues that had been stained and mottled by years of moss and various lichens. Nothing moved apart from an occasional flittering of bats and the silence of a white barn owl that swooped over the long-dead looking for the living.

'How long should we wait before we go and check on Jenny and the Chois?' O'Rourke asked in a low tone.

James looked at the luminous dial of his watch to see that it was almost five o'clock. 'Another thirty minutes should be enough time for Rackman and his team to get here.'

'How many do you think he'll bring?'

'I have no idea. It all depends on how much the SIS has been penetrated by the Illuminati organization.'

They both fell silent and while O'Rourke checked his automatic for the fifth time James pondered the problem that they were going to encounter an unknown number of terrorists with only two guns and a limited supply of bullets. In the end he had to say something.

'Can I use your sword,' he blurted out and then bit his tongue when the big man turned to give him a penetrating stare. He cocked the gun and thumbed the safety catch.

'Have you ever used a sword before?' he asked with the suggestion of a smile.

'Not really, but it would be better than nothing.'

'I believe it's more likely to do you more harm than your opponent,' O'Rourke whispered and he held out the automatic. 'You'd better use this; it'll give you more firepower.'

James looked up in surprise. 'Are you sure?'

'Perfectly.' The Irishman reached over his shoulder and in one fluid movement unsheathed Dragon's Breath and brought it to the *en garde* position. The wide blade gleamed in the dim light, taking James's breath with its naked beauty.

'Where did you get such a wonderful thing?'

'I took it from a thief,' he said as he lowered the weapon to shelter it from the rain. 'He does not know it yet but it really belongs to your friend. It was taken from one of Feng's ancestors three thousand years ago and has been handed down through the generations until it fell into the hands of a triad thug – '

'Three thousand years!' James exclaimed, totally fascinated by workmanship that could survive for so long without any signs of corrosion. 'That must have been during the Bronze Age.'

'Yes. It's one of the finest examples of one of the earliest steel weapons from the Zhou dynasty and most probably would be worth about £3 million today.'

James was about to speak when he heard men's voices coming from the direction of the chain link fence. O'Rourke put his finger to his lips and crouched down with Dragon's Breath resting across his lap. James also lowered himself in the dark recess and closed his mouth to stop any excess vapour rising in the cold air and betraying their presence.

Two shadows noisily emerged from the darkness and meandered along the gravel footpath amongst the tombstones. O'Rourke held up two fingers only and James felt relieved. One of the men was short and had a limp whereas the other was broad shouldered and tall. Both held weapons before them in a regulation, two-handed grip.

The scudding clouds were clearing and the sky began to lighten as the two men turned their heads from side to side, searching the gloomy environment for their target.

James watched them pass and was content to let them go but O'Rourke suddenly stood up and using the gravestones quietly followed. James felt obliged to do the same and he flicked both safety catches off as he circled to the left keeping the silhouettes of the assassins within sight against the grey sky.

Suddenly O'Rourke sprang forward with blade raised which briefly caught the dawn light before sweeping down at an angle into the neck of the bigger man. With Dragon's Breath still lodged in his breastbone he fell with a piercing shriek to his knees and O'Rourke wrested the blade free, releasing a fountain of dark blood.

Rackman, who had leapt to one side on the first strike, spun round and pointed his 9mm Beretta at O'Rourke's chest. 'You'd never make it, Séan. I can pump three rounds into your heart before you take the first step towards me.'

'And I can put one through the back of your head,' James shouted as he appeared behind the Illuminati.

The steady Beretta dropped slightly as the surprised man realized he was caught between a rock and a hard place. 'I'd still be able to kill your friend, Goodfellow,' he shouted over his shoulder, his eyes fixed on the upraised blade. A few drops of blood were trickling down the gleaming surface towards the hilt and Rackman had no wish to let his own join them. 'Just tell me where the crate is and I'll back off and we needn't ever see each other again.'

'My dear Second Lieutenant Richard Rackman, do you think I'm mad?' O'Rourke said. 'You're a disgrace to your rank and country. Why should we hand you a fortune in antiques when you deserve to be executed for high treason?'

'I'm still an SIS officer and I can still drum up a credible terrorist cell and have you both abducted and made to disappear as though you never existed. I can also make this happen to Detective Constable Jennifer Kent and the whole Choi family.'

Rackman's reference to the woman he loved triggered a wave of rage and the familiar numbing sensation to surge through James's body. Losing all control, he fell to his knees. The gun fell from his hand and he toppled over onto his side. In his haste to leave that morning he had neglected to take the Xyrem and stress had encouraged a powerful narcoleptic response. James fell into a deep sleep that shocked O'Rourke and amused the Illuminati.

'Your interfering friend seems to have put you on the spot, partner,' Rackman said, glancing down at the inert form behind him as he raised the gun. 'I don't know what's wrong with him but if he wakes up he's in for a big surprise.' His finger began to tighten on the trigger. 'Pity you won't see the sunrise, Séan, it looks like it might be rather nice this morning.'

O'Rourke looked up and saw that the clouds had cleared completely and the horizon was streaked with bright orange. He slowly lowered the blade and held it across his arm like a mother might hold her baby. Keeping calm in the face of certain death he looked down at the sleeping man with the single thought: I would have liked to have known James better.

A split second before O'Rourke could launch himself in a last-ditch attempt to use the sword Rackman's face seemed to spout tissue and blood from a large hole where his eye had been.

The reflex action of Rackman's finger on the trigger sent his 9mm hollow-point bullet through O'Rourke's left shoulder before he collapsed like a stringless marionette. The Irishman dropped his sword and clamped his right hand over the wound that was bleeding effusively. O'Rourke was stunned for a brief moment before a new voice put him on his guard and the excruciating pain was forgotten. He picked up Dragon's Breath and the hilt was made slippery with blood.

Ming-húa stepped out from behind a granite weeping angel and approached. A tiny wisp of smoke issued from the Melrod silencer and the triad raised the weapon again and aimed it at O'Rourke's forehead.

'I couldn't permit that filth to kill you, Sèan,' he said without any expression. 'My father would demand that his son should take the life that took his.'

'Nice to see you again, Ming-húa,' O'Rourke said between gritted teeth as warm blood ran down his arm and dribbled from his fingertips. 'I thought you intended to kill your father in Hong Kong and I know that a son should never offend his ancestors by committing patricide. That's why I did you a favour and took his life with this.' O'Rourke held the sword up and the first ray of sun struck the blade and dazzled the young man.

Ming-húa stepped back a pace. 'My ancestors would be more offended if I didn't avenge my father's murder. This I will do in an honourable manner.' He tossed the Melrod onto the path and unsheathed the Angel sword on his back. 'This will correct the wrong you have done me, Sèan.' Ming-húa leapt forward with the blade raised and O'Rourke stepped to one side, slipped on his own blood that had spilt on the gravestone and his opponent's blade sliced through thin air.

O'Rourke knew that he would weaken first and a protracted duel would be fatal. He had to end it as quickly as possible and as Ming-húa reversed the direction of his sword and swung upwards O'Rourke countered the strike with a clash of steel and a shower of bright sparks before lunging forward. As he moved in he had the satisfaction of seeing the tip of his sword entering the loose flesh of the young man's waist. To O'Rourke's surprise, instead of stepping back to pull himself away from Dragon's Breath he pushed himself further onto the blade until they were chest to chest. The stiletto that Ming-húa had taken from the sheath behind his back was plunged into O'Rourke's side and driven upward.

Mortally struck O'Rourke staggered back and looked down at the protruding hilt. 'Touché,' he murmured as he sank to his knees.

Ming-húa also stepped back and with teeth clenched slowly slid Dragon's Breath from his side. Despite the pain he was pleased to see how little blood came from the entry and exit wounds and knew that he would survive the strike. He took the offending weapon by the bloody hilt and approached the kneeling man.

'Make it easy on yourself, Sèan. Lift your head so that I can make it a clean death,' Ming-húa said.

Through the pain that seemed to roar in his ears, the Irishman detected an unusually compassionate tone in the triad's voice.

With eyes tightly shut against the pain in his body O'Rourke said a silent prayer. The graveyard seemed to become even quieter than usual as though the birds had delayed their morning chorus out of respect for the man about to die. The only sound that broke that silence was a light cough.

James struggled to sit upright still clutching the discarded Melrod he had managed to reach. He took aim, fired and watched as the young man with upraised sword toppled sideways and died.

O'Rourke lifted his head when he heard the sword clatter against the marble and with misting eyes saw James rise to his feet and walk towards him.

'Hold on, Sèan. I'm phoning for an ambulance,' James said as he dialled the emergency service.

'Don't bother, James,' he croaked. 'I'm on my way out and it would be less complicated for you if that gun were in my hand. You must get out of here before anyone sees you.'

'I'm not leaving you, Sèan,' James declared fervently and then spoke to the emergency operator to give the exact location and seriousness of the wound.

O'Rourke had now covered the surface of the gravestone he was kneeling on with his own blood; James removed his jacket and then tore strips off his shirt to make pads. While sitting beside the Irishman and trying to stem the flow of blood from his shoulder he realized the stiletto had inflicted a lot more damage than the bullet.

O'Rourke was bleeding internally as fast as he was externally and he knew that it was only a matter of time. He summoned up what little strength remained and spoke. 'I know the damned thing wasn't in the crate because I could see by the way you carried it that it had become a little lighter. So, where did you hide the *ding*, James? I'm dying to know.' He laughed at his own joke and then spat out a mouthful of blood.

James looked at the man who had changed from bitter enemy to close friend over the last few days and nodded. 'You're right, Sèan. I substituted the *ding* for one of Feng's terracotta flowerpots. I filled it with pebbles to approximate the weight of the discs.'

'Clever,' O'Rourke murmured before being attacked by another bout of coughing.

'The original is buried in the compost bay at the end of Feng's allotment.'

'Ah. That's why you said you put it where dead things tend to gather.' His voice was getting weaker and James had to lean closer to hear what he was saying. 'You didn't mean bodies but leaves.' O'Rourke started to lean forward and James reached out and held him upright until he could shuffle around behind the man. He took care not to touch the stiletto.

'Lean back against me, Sèan,' he whispered. 'The ambulance won't be long now and we'll get you to hospital.' There was a slight movement that James read as a nod before O'Rourke slumped back against him.

Suddenly James became aware of dark figures closing in on them from all directions. He picked up the Melrod that he had put beside O'Rourke and waited with bated breath. The figures were moving in a half crouch and they all held their weapons in front of them in a manner James associated with the Special Forces or an armed response by SIS agents. His grip tightened on the silenced weapon.

'Looks like we'll both be going together, mate,' he whispered.

A voice suddenly shattered the silence of the cemetery. 'Put down your weapon and raise your hands.' This was repeated over and over again until the sound blurred in James's head. He laid the Melrod down on the gravestone and holding the cloth pad against O'Rourke's shoulder with his left hand he raised the other in the air.

'Raise your hands,' the first voice insisted and then he swore. 'Oh my God. Don't fire. It's Goodfellow.' James immediately recognized Sergeant Briscoe's voice as an officer in full body armour and visored helmet rushed to his side and dropped to his knees.

'Christ, it's everywhere,' he exclaimed in horror when he realized he was kneeling in a puddle of blood. 'Where have you been hit?'

'Not me, Sergeant. I'm perfectly okay but O'Rourke has been hit in the shoulder and he has a knife in his side. The ambulance should be here soon.'

'It's here, James. I spoke to Jennifer on the phone and while we were keeping watch on the Forbidden City the emergency call came in. I held the paramedics back until my team could ensure the cemetery was completely safe.' As he was talking the sergeant had been feeling the side of O'Rourke's neck. 'I'm sorry, James, but it looks like they won't be needed.'

'What do you mean?'

'O'Rourke's dead.'

James sighed and shuffling back on his knees he gently lowered the big Irishman down upon the stone. Sightless eyes were unaware of the brilliant sunshine that kissed the face of the weeping angel and bathed O'Rourke in a rosy glow that belied his still heart.

Briscoe helped James to his feet as the armed response team methodically searched the cemetery for any further threat. 'There's someone here to see you,' he murmured. Shawcross was standing behind the sergeant and he gave James a look that said he would love to use his Heckler & Koch on him.

A panic-stricken Jennifer raced towards them and into James's arms. 'Are you hurt? Are you all right?' she asked and then went white when she saw his blood-saturated clothing.

'I'm okay, Jenny, it belongs to Sèan.'

'Where is he?'

'He was killed saving my life.'

There was a long silence during which the couple walked back to the main gates with arms locked about each other. Feng, Jiao and Lin-Lin were waiting with anxious faces on the other side of the yellow ribbon that cordoned off the entrance. The little girl gave a squeal of joy and ducking under the tape she ran to hug them both.

Her parents looked at the blood with deep concern until James reassured them that it wasn't his own.

'You'll have to give me a written statement on everything that's happened,' Briscoe said as he began walking back to rejoin his men.

'Right from the beginning,' Detective Inspector Tilley said as he climbed out of his squad car. 'And on my desk by tomorrow morning.' His face held a grim expression but inside he experienced a strange sense of relief that the personable young investigator hadn't been hurt.

Epilogue

LONDON

Delegates from the Shanghai Museum and the National Museum of China occupied the row of plush seats at the front of the large room lit by crystal chandeliers. They glanced at each other surreptitiously as though sizing up an opponent before a championship fight. To one side of the room sat a representative from the British Museum and facing him, having just flown in from New York, sat the director of the Metropolitan Museum of Art.

The atmosphere was awash with murmuring voices that suddenly fell silent as the auctioneer entered the room and took his place at the rostrum. He wore a formal dress coat, winged collar and tie that seemed to underline the gravity of the historical auction that was about to take place.

'Wow, this is going to be a bloodbath!' James whispered. He and Jennifer were seated at the back of the room with Feng. Jiao and Lin-Lin had remained in East Steading to keep the restaurant open with the aid of Feng's cousin.

'Do think they will all sell well?' Feng asked in a surprisingly calm voice for his hands were shaking like aspen leaves in a storm. He was referring to the artefacts that had caused more deaths in the last few days than they had over their three-thousand-year history.

The *ding* had been recovered from where James had hidden it beneath the steaming pile of rich compost on Feng's allotment. Dragon's Breath, after forensic testing by the investigating team, was also returned with the *ding* to the restaurateur after a number of weeks. The Choi family had decided to put all the items up for auction instead of keeping them in the bank and a world-renowned auction house was only too pleased to handle all the arrangements.

Detective Sergeant Briscoe had kept the friends informed through Jennifer on the final rounding up and trial of the few surviving Illuminati conspirators. Messages had been sent to Hong Kong and the local police raided and searched the villa and Ming-húa Shing's private quarters where incriminating evidence was found on his computer harddrives. This helped to solve innumerable deaths and robberies that had been sanctioned over the last ten years by Ming-Húa's father, the triad Mountain Master.

The gavel tapped impatiently and people who had begun talking excitedly again stopped mid-sentence and only the light rustling of catalogue pages being turned could be heard.

'Lot 42 is a ritual three-legged bronze ding of the Zhou dynasty. Often used as an implicit symbol of power it is heavily decorated with various flora and fauna subjects and is presented for sale by the current owner.'

The ding was suddenly shown on a giant LED screen as a porter simultaneously removed a velvet cloth to reveal the actual object on a small table beside the auctioneer.

Feng stirred in his seat and James, who was seated beside him, gave an encouraging grin.

'Can I start the bidding at two million?' the auctioneer asked in a casual voice as though he had just suggested a ridiculously low figure. He surveyed the crowded room. There was a brief pause. 'One million?' Another pause. 'Five hundred thousand?'

The man from the British Museum nodded his head.

'I have five hundred thousand. Any more on –'

The Metropolitan Museum lifted her catalogue three inches above a well-tailored lap.

'I have one million pounds. Any advance on one million?'

The auctioneer scanned the room until a movement in the front row attracted his attention. A Shanghai Museum delegate whose grey hair and bifocal glasses indicated his age and senior rank had raised a finger.

'One point five million!'

The National Museum spokesperson raised a catalogue.

'Two million!'

At this point the Metropolitan and the British Museum raised the bidding to three million pounds before the Chinese showed who had the greater interest and budget to fight a real battle. A rapid sequence of winking and raised digits took the figure to the final bid.

'Four point five million pounds. I'm calling it once – calling it twice . . .' He took a few seconds to look around the room and at the Internet screen. 'No more bids – sold!'

The gavel cracked down and the men from Shanghai grinned at their glowering opponents.

'My God, was that for real?' Feng croaked, his throat parched by the tension that crackled throughout the room.

James and Jennifer couldn't stop themselves from hugging each other and Feng. 'It's real enough, my friend. You're now officially a millionaire.'

The gavel cracked down once more and they turned to face the distant podium as the auctioneer calmly announced Lot 43 and the giant screen changed to show a single jade disc.

'Catalogue number 43 consists of one hundred and twenty-six Shang dynasty jade bi of approximately three inches in diameter. They were commonly known as the Ears of Heaven and reputed to come from the Shang dynasty period lasting from 1500 to 1050BC. This emperor had the largest collection of jade in China's history. Who will start the bidding at two hundred thousand pounds?'

Apart from the Texan oil billionaire who was the first to start the proceedings with a loud bellow the following bids came primarily from raised eyebrows, twitching fingers and fluttering catalogues in the front row.

'Sold!' The gavel finally descended and the National Museum of China took the prize at one point three million pounds and sat back in their seats triumphantly while it was the turn of the Shanghai Museum to glower.

Feng sat perfectly still in a complete state of confusion as an excess of adrenalin pumped through his body. James patted him on the back.

'Change my first estimate of millionaire to multi-millionaire, my friend,' he whispered in Feng's ear and Jennifer giggled from the bottled-up excitement that threatened to burst free.

'Lot 44,' the auctioneer announced and everybody in the room froze. This was the principal item that everyone had come to see. Heads craned as the porter entered the room through a side door holding a long white silk bag and the screen on the wall went black.

The porter stood the new lot on a small table and untied the white cord at the neck of the bag. Knowing he had the full attention of every soul in the room he slowly slid the bag down to reveal the decorated scabbard. While a cameraman focused on the sword the porter held it by the middle and raised it aloft to hold it horizontally above his head. He then gripped the hilt and breath was audibly drawn in as he teasingly slid the magnificent blade from its hiding place.

The engraving on the blade appeared on the screen and as the camera panned slowly along the legend the auctioneer read the fateful words.

'Dragon's Breath Is The Last Touch Felt By Men Judged Evil,' he said and being an experienced salesman he spoke the words as though performing in a Shakespearean tragedy.

The auctioneer achieved the reaction he wanted and the audience sighed as the final word was drawn out like the blade from its scabbard. They remained spellbound as he went on to describe the sword's origin. Then a furious bidding war started at two point five million pounds and hands began shooting towards the ornate ceiling.

'I now have seven million and seeking new bids.'

When the auctioneer reached the British Museum's top bid James gasped and felt a strange feeling in his legs. He gripped Jennifer around the waist. 'Hold me, Jenny, I forgot to do something this morning.'

Jennifer supported James around the waist and let him fall against her as he fell asleep. Feng first looked at her with a puzzled expression and then realised it was a recurrence of James's old problem.

'Didn't he take any Xyrem today?' he asked with the beginnings of a smile.

Jennifer shook her head. I didn't stay at his place last night and couldn't remind him in the morning to take one.' She began tapping lightly on James's cheek as the auction continued.

The battle was now between China and America as the figure crept past ten million. The Chinese delegate with steel-grey hair was wiping his forehead with a white cotton handkerchief as the elegant woman in the grey suit calmly crossed her legs yet again.

'Eleven point five million pounds.' The auctioneer's clear voice was the only sound in the deathly silence. The small man from the Shanghai Museum raised his hand with all five fingers spread.

'Fifteen million!'

There were a number of gasps and the woman from the Metropolitan Museum of Art remained motionless as the auctioneer looked at her in patient anticipation. There was a long moment while everyone in the room held their breath before she slowly shook her head and the auctioneer raised his gavel.

'If there are no more bids I declare Lot 44 sold,' he said pointing to the man from Shanghai. His gavel was brought down with a crash and the room burst into a roar of applause followed by pandemonium as the media took their opportunity to film and phone their news in.

A Sotheby's executive approached Feng, whispered in his ear and they both slipped from the room before the media turned their focus away from the sword and the successful bidder to the man who sold it.

Jennifer felt James stir and smiled down at him as he opened his eyes. 'For goodness sake James, do I have to sleep with you every night to make sure you take your pills?' she laughed as he sat up with an embarrassed expression.

'Now that is a very good idea. Did I miss much?'

'Dragon's Breath was sold back to the Chinese.'

'Good, that's where it truly belongs. How much did it fetch?'

Jennifer feigned adding up on her fingers. 'As far as I can work out Feng is now comfortably well off with over twenty million pounds!'

'Wow! I think he can safely say that he is ready to retire,' James said as they left the room and waited in the foyer for Feng to finish the paperwork in the manager's office.

'Uh-huh. While you were have a little nap he told me that no matter what the outcome of the auction was he and Jiao have decided to create a sizeable trust fund for Lin-Lin, smarten up the kitchens and restaurant of the Forbidden City and completely refurbish your place above. Expenses will be paid into the Goodfellow Investigations account and the remainder will be donated to cancer research.'

'That is so generous and no less than I would expect from Feng and Jiao.' James felt a lump grow in his throat and he fell silent, unable to speak when Feng emerged from the office with a broad smile to join them.

'We are also invited to dine in the Forbidden City free of charge for the rest of our lives,' Jennifer whispered.

Feng grasped James by the hand. 'Was the auction so boring that it put you to sleep, James?' he asked and laughed uproariously as he linked arms with the couple.

'Quite the contrary Feng. It was those telephone numbers the auctioneer was shouting out that did the trick.'

They walked out to the stretch limousine that the auction house had kindly arranged for their client. The vehicle occupied two parking bays and it quietly pulled away from the kerb and whisked them back to East Steading while they toasted the Choi family's good fortune with a complimentary bottle of vintage Dom Perignon.

As they pulled up outside the Forbidden City James pointed through the restaurant window at all the diners vying for Jiao's attention. 'Surely you'd like to stop waiting on others. Why not end the stress and live in your own country manor and be waited on by others?' he asked.

James's concern for his friend was evident and Feng's usually unreadable features suddenly broadened into the widest, happiest smile the couple had ever seen on the Chinaman's face. 'I could never stop cooking and not see the pleasure it brings to those who choose to eat our food. Apart from Lin-Lin it's what gives Jiao and myself the greatest joy in life.'

Jennifer went to say something but thought better of it, unlike James who immediately started to speak. Feng shook his head and held his hand up to stop him. 'James, let me ask you one thing. Could you ever give up being a private detective?'

'Of course not, Feng. It's difficult to explain but doing what I do is very special to me and . . .'

'Precisely,' Feng interrupted. 'So, let's go in and have a little of Jiao's signature dish, the Sichuan hotpot. And stop talking all this retirement nonsense.'

James eagerly agreed and they entered the Forbidden City to the usual boisterous welcome from Lin-Lin.

Lightning Source UK Ltd.
Milton Keynes UK
UKOW03f0111280417
300081UK00002B/76/P